The Fab

Edito

The aim of this series is _____
produced in the Caribbea _____ ...aspora, in
the four major languages ... the region: English, French,
Spanish and Dutch. It contains original work, including
classic texts, much of which is published for the first time in
English. It also aims to give Anglophone readers in particular
a broader and more profound sense of the literary culture
that has evolved in the area over five hundred years of history.
While the emphasis is on fiction, it is open to all literary forms.

Double Play

FRANK MARTINUS ARION

The story of an amazing world record

Translated from the Dutch by
Paul Vincent

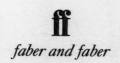

faber and faber

First published in this translation in 1998
by Faber and Faber Limited
3 Queen Square London WC1N 3AU

Photoset by Avon Dataset Ltd, Bidford on Avon
Printed in England by Mackays of Chatham plc, Chatham, Kent

Paul Vincent is hereby identified as translator
of this work in accordance with the
Copyright, Designs and Patents Act 1988

The publishers gratefully acknowledge the help
of the Foundation for the Production and
Translation of Dutch Literature, Amsterdam

A CIP record for this book
is available from the British Library

ISBN 0–571–19421–4

2 4 6 8 10 9 7 5 3 1

To women with courage

It is not in such matters, however, that the Tsar's true character appears. Politics bored him; he loved his wife and children, he liked bicycling up and down the garden paths, *and he had a passion for dominoes.* When his dear Alix had a pain in her feet he was perturbed, but when he lost an Empire he hardly noticed it. On February 23, 1917, while he was at G.H.Q. in a last attempt to escape from the Revolution, he was worried by learning that his children had measles. He telegraphed to the Tsarina: 'What a nuisance! I was hoping they would escape measles. Sincerest greetings to all. Sleep well. Nicky.' On the same day he wrote: 'I greatly miss my half-hourly game of patience every evening. *I shall take up dominoes again in my spare time!'*

Bertrand Russell, 'Freedom versus Organization'

> Wir sitzen um ein Tischchen irgendwo
> Und sagen Worte. Ineinander passen
> Die Worte, die wir vor uns liegen lassen,
> Als spielten wir zusammen Domino.
>
> Zu einem Bild bewegt sich Stein auf Stein
> Mit schwarzen Augen in dem Elfenbein.

Johannes R. Becher

Dominoes is a dangerous game: it was because of a domino tournament that in 1625 the Dutch were able to seize the fort of 'El Moro' on Puerto Rico, previously considered impregnable, from the Spaniards.

A reporter on the Antilles Broadcasting Service V

CONTENTS

PART I

Early Morning and Midday

Between Blenheim, the seventeenth-century Jewish cemetery, and Campo Alegre lies Wakota, a suburb of Willemstad. It is situated *'entre medio'*, as Curaçaoans reply when asked how they're doing. 'Oh, *entre medio*', 'in between', which usually means between the devil and the deep blue sea.

The tourist guides often mention the Jewish cemetery, but are as silent as the grave about the flourishing whores' camp on the north side of the island. This whores' camp is a lively hotel with some hundred and fifty rooms, where one can find female guests from all over the Caribbean, South and Central America.

So, pack up your troubles and visit Curaçao! The sea is beautiful, the air is pure and the women in the camp are healthy, being examined daily by a hotel doctor and given injections. And if you go, just for the hell of it look in at Wakota, that peaceful village where the houses are still a long way apart.

People there will remember that until recently four men in this neighbourhood played a game of dominoes every Sunday afternoon at the house of one of them, Bubu Fiel. They always started the game at about one o'clock, after their *sòpi di mondongo*, or tripe soup, the typical Sunday lunch dish of the inhabitants of Curaçao. They stopped at about six o'clock, when dusk, and shortly afterwards inexorable darkness, fell.

There were two hills in Wakota: Santa Gloria, named after the Catholic church sited on it, and opposite it but slightly lower, Manchi's Hill, named after Manchi from Willemstad, who had built an enormous, eight-bedroomed house there, or as some people put it a little more poetically, 'had spread it all over the hill of Wakota'.

Between the two hills ran the wide Tula road, which in the west joined the Carpata road, a four-lane highway which links the airport and the whores' camp with the capital.

To the west of Manchi's Hill, at the foot of it and closer to the Tula road than his light-red, T-shaped house, there was a quite isolated little yellow house with sloping walls. A dwelling belonging to the class of so-called slave houses, of which one can still find examples in a number of suburbs of Willemstad. Here lived Bubu Fiel. His house looked out on the road and had two rooms. The main room, measuring about twelve feet by twelve, had a pitched roof and inside was divided in two by a partition with a door in it (across which a white curtain always hung): a larger *sala* or living-room and a small bedroom into which a large double bed fitted exactly. Behind the portion with the pitched roof a smaller, wooden room with a sloping, flat roof had been tacked on. This portion was divided into three. It contained a dining-room, a little bedroom divided off with a partition into which a single bed scarcely fitted, and a small kitchen. Here Fiel and Nora lived with their seven children. Thank heavens, no longer with sixteen of them, since six had died over the years and three had already left home.

Apart from a narrow path which led from the low fence of ordinary chicken wire to the front door, the front garden was full of creeping, wild *anglo*, which with its butterfly-like yellow flowers was now in full bloom. In the left corner of the garden rose an ethereal and rusty flagpole, which may have originated from the time when Bubu Fiel had been president of the Wakota Domino Association (DSW). At the back of the plot, about fifteen yards from the house, was a wooden shack measuring six feet by six and nine feet high. It was Bubu Fiel's toilet, bath shed and spare room in one. The paint was peeling and it leaked. But behind all this wretchedness, like the promise of a Messiah, lay the excavations for the foundations of a house that equalled Manchi's in size. Except that . . . these impressive foundations must have been dug a long while ago: the sand at the edges had crumbled away, had been dissolved by the rain and found its way into the foundation sewers.

The lonely shack had been originally intended as a bathroom and toilet. So it contained a wooden chair with a hole in it; a shitting chair or 'altar toilet', as can still be found even in prosperous Europe. But it had become mainly a junk store. The acute shortage of space in the house itself meant that everything not strictly necessary in the household that couldn't be thrown away, because that simply wasn't part of the philosophy of poor people, would be 'temporarily' shoved into the junk store.

On the west side of his house Bubu Fiel had at some point built a 'temporary' garage with wooden poles and zinc sheeting. Under it he parked his 200H. 'H' for hire. He was a taxi driver by trade. On that side too there were a number of 'temporary' chicken runs.

The slope between Fiel's house and Manchi's had no houses on it. It was overgrown with numerous low succulents and *wabi* trees, but one house could be clearly seen from the other. On the east side of Bubu Fiel's house, where he played dominoes with his friends, stood a sturdy tamarind tree; it rose high above the old-fashioned house, with dense foliage that hung down to head height. In the afternoon, when the sun was fiercest, it gave copious, generous, cool shade, which according to the men had no equal, even in heaven.

It was now November and for some weeks the tree had been full of brown, delicate tamarind fruits. But Bubu Fiel's children and their friends had quickly and expertly relieved it of its burden.

3

The short walk which Manchi took this Sunday morning, as he did on all his free mornings, along the sandy path in front of his house to the Tula road, after his wife had left with the children, was not as he would have said himself, 'to stretch my legs because I am at the wheel of my car all week'. It was, as always, so that on the way back he could see his house with its eight rooms, spread out across the hill of Wakota in all its majesty.

He had built it himself and it was (together with a few other things) the reason why he was held in high regard in Wakota and all over the island. Some people had already started calling him *Shon Manchi* instead of plain Manchi.

A number of things were going through his mind at the moment: his position as bailiff of the court of Willemstad; this great house in front of him; the beauty of his wife, Solema; the fact that she had been awarded her teacher's certificate in Holland and studied all sorts of things in Belgium, France and England.

Manchi was a large Negro, nearly fifty, with powerful shoulders. He had a square head with a bump at the back. He always tried to comb his short, curly hair back with lots of grease. Mostly without success. His little curls now shone, despite the still-pleasant morning sun of Wakota, like a million tiny stars. His face with the thick, black eyebrows, the thick lips, was as usual clean-shaven. As he slowly climbed his hill, it was set in an expression of studied earnestness, such as would have befitted a severe judge. He wore grey trousers, a white, short-sleeved sports shirt and slippers.

The house towards which he was walking, because of the

6

long, arched veranda which was supported on four short columns, looked Italian. It was indeed a postcard from Capri, which he still kept jealously in his drawer-for-important-papers in his bedside cupboard, that had given him the inspiration. It had a large back patio and a wide front garden full of colourful bushes, which he now glanced at with pleasure. He also savoured the fact that his large house was still completely alone on the wide plateau of this hill. True, behind and to the left there were a number of plots, but the owners of this land must be in the same financial circumstances as Bubu Fiel: in all the years that they had leased their land they had not got beyond fencing it off. For all he cared, they could have an accident before they started building! A while ago, at a leisurely pace, as he said, he had begun building a maid's room next to the garage. He now also thought of this with pleasure.

One could characterize Manchi in all kinds of ways, both externally and internally, but his principal feature was perhaps the fact that he loved dominoes.

4

Too much perhaps, he thought, pausing for a moment in front of his house. There were two gates in the wrought-iron fence. Above the gate on the left he had placed a letter-box, which he now playfully opened, although he knew there couldn't be any letters inside. But perhaps he enjoyed playing with it as much as with his house, because it was an exact miniature replica of the latter: complete in the same colours with a veranda at the front and a patio behind. On both doors he had placed striking white boards with black lettering:

Manchi Sanantonio
Bailiff on Curaçao

7

He entered his house. In the middle of the living-room stood his wife's large, brown, grand piano. He had a sudden urge to sit at it and play.

Nonsense, he said to himself in irritation. He didn't like piano playing and of course he couldn't play the thing. He had only bought the beautiful new item of furniture because after their marriage his wife had brought a small, old piano from her parents' home, which he couldn't bear in his brand-new house.

In order to rid himself completely of the strange impulse which he suddenly felt, he walked through into the kitchen at the back to pour himself a whisky, although it was still rather early. Sipping his drink, he then began a slow tour of inspection through the rooms of his house. At the foot of the T on the south side were his *study*, his *guest room* and his *workroom*. He never had anyone to stay and he left studying, for what it was worth, to his wife. And *workroom*, well . . . Anyway, he had put a desk in his study, on which stood a telephone, a telephone directory and a typewriter. He often read the paper in there.

But there were still rooms to spare that he couldn't give a name to. Even after the eldest of his three children, his six-year-old son, had been given a room of his own and he had hit upon the bright idea of designating one of his large bedrooms as the *playroom* for his children and dubbing one room the *storage room*. This morning he again felt sorry that he had only three children.

He came back to the piano. The book of exercises which his daughter had played from the evening before was still on the music-stand, open at 'Au clair de la lune'. He again tried to suppress the strange urge to play and so surveyed his furniture contentedly. In this he followed strictly the interior of the house of a deputy-prosecutor, whom he admired because the man always demanded stiff sentences. Via a

8

catalogue which the latter gave him at his request, he had ordered his furniture from Denmark. As he stroked the shiny brown wood of the piano with satisfaction, he thought how this well-motivated taste had brought him into conflict with his wife, who when it came to furnishing the house had a preference for old Curaçaoan items that he found incomprehensible. All kinds of old things with wickerwork seats. In his brand-new house! At that time they'd only just been married and so he'd had to tackle her in the sweetest possible way. In one case he'd had to ask her fairly sharply whether for all her years of study in Europe she knew the meaning of the word *pro-gres-sive*.

Because the urge persisted, he tried to persuade himself that this piano of his wife's was no business of his. It was simply a piece of furniture which he was proud of because no one in Wakota, and certainly no black person in Wakota, and perhaps no black person in the whole island, had in his house. But apart from that . . . ?

5

Finally he gave in. He quickly closed the mahogany doors of his house and sat down on the stool at the piano. He looked for a while at the book of exercises in front of him, but the miracle which he perhaps expected did not happen. Manchi Sanantonio could not read music and it seemed that it was going to stay that way for some time. He therefore quickly closed the book, with a distant feeling of jealousy of his wife, who was a virtuoso pianist and organist, and of his children, all three of whom seemed to have inherited their mother's talent. He could, though, whistle the song 'Mon ami Pierrot', which had been played often enough by the children, and so bravely opened the lid of the piano. The impersonal keyboard confused him for a moment, but whistling the song softly, he nevertheless brought down the thumb of his right hand with some determination on one of the white keys. Sound did indeed come from the instrument and not such a bad sound, he felt. He repeated it complacently and loudly, because it gave him great pleasure to make the first music he produced resound loudly through his house. This first note was, for the simple reason that it was the first, undoubtedly the right one. That was logical. He leant back for a moment and, looking up at the ceiling, again whistled a snatch of the melody. The thing was now to find the correct *second* note which made up this song. He took a deep breath, pressed and . . . it was wrong. It was dreadfully wrong; so wrong that it hurt his own ears and he had the urge to smash the piano keys with a blow of his fist. However, the great contempt he had for Solema and everything that she stood for, caused him to control himself and continue trying. Again and again. Damn! If she and even the children could do it, surely playing the piano couldn't be that difficult? There had to be a short cut. Some cunning, secret way which would allow him to do it if he could find it?

But after a while he gave up anyway. He left the piano and opened the front door again. He observed with relief that no one had witnessed his failed attempts. He resolved to forget that he had touched that damn piano. Then he went to water his plants. At about nine o'clock he took a break and sat resting in one of his easy chairs on the porch. He surveyed the surroundings with pleasure. It was still quiet and peaceful around his house. The bells for high mass had already sounded three times. Solema, who before she went to play the organ of Santa Gloria always took their children to her parents, would not be back before the end of high mass. So he had plenty of time for his Sunday activities, which he lumped together, down to the watering of his plants, under the term 'philosophizing'. He liked to be studying some book or other at such times. For ages it had been a brown leather-bound copy of *Die Räuber* by Schiller, which he now kept carefully in his drawer-for-important-documents in his bedside cupboard. He liked simply leafing through it and using the soft, reddish silk bookmark. Taking out the book, removing the paper he had wrapped around it for safety's sake – after all, he'd been given it by a judge – and leafing through it, wondering what that *F* in the F. Schiller stood for. Because of his plans for the immediate future, however, he had had to give up this browsing in *Die Räuber* in order to occupy himself rather more seriously with another work, *The History of Freemasonry in the Netherlands Antilles*, by a certain G. Tim. The book consisted of two volumes; volume one with about five hundred pages of text in small print and volume two with photos and appendices. The language was of course difficult and there were so many references in the first volume to the second, that he doubted whether he would ever get any further than the three pages which he had struggled through in the last three weeks. This book did have one small advantage: G. Tim was spelt out in full on the title page: Gerard Tim. This 'extra' heightened his confidence in the Antillean lodge, Solidarity, which he hoped shortly to join. He now had the blue volumes on a small table beside him and decided to make a serious effort to work on them for at least half an hour. But his attention kept drifting off to what his philosophizing really consisted of: quietly surveying the whole area in order, as it were, again and again to determine his place in life, time and space. In the past, when he had only just taken up residence in his new house, he had used a telescope for this activity, which had greatly heightened his pleasure. But one of the daughters of his regular domino partner, Bubu Fiel – she was now shacked up with a welder somewhere – put an impertinent end to this one Sunday morning. More out of carelessness than curiosity (because what in heaven's name was so special about that whore of a daughter of Bubu Fiel's!), he had focused his telescope on her as she emerged from her bath shed rather scantily clad. Unfortunately she had realized this, had dropped the towel which she was carrying and, screaming abuse, which must have attracted the attention of the whole neighbourhood, turned her brown behind on him, that is, bending over and lifting up her skirt. She had hurled terrible insults at him, and in order to avoid such dents to his dignity, he had put his telescope away for ever.

He preferred letting his eyes wander, as now, beyond Bubu Fiel's house, to the far distance straight ahead, where the houses of the Prinsessendorp estate were visible almost on the horizon. This was the smart residential area – elsewhere there were also a Prinsendorp and a Koninginnedorp – which Shell had had constructed for its seconded white and privileged employees. Now that the Dutch were leaving the islands and there was even talk of independence, they were mainly occupied by an élite of Antilleans, who had often returned from Europe with Dutch wives after their studies.

Solema, with her worthless ideas, had said more than once that it would be better if they were demolished. He was against that! What would he have to compare his house with if they were no longer there? He never tired of making these comparisons, always deciding that his house was even more beautiful than those élite houses. Everything that they had – garden, gate – he had too and what those houses had and he did not – air conditioning – he didn't envy them. 'I live on a hill,' he said to himself and to anyone who was interested. 'What good is air conditioning to me? I've got wind and hence fresh air enough. For free!'

Peering at the houses of Prinsessendorp, which he had also often walked round inspecting, and his invariable conclusion, that his house was more beautiful than houses which had been built by one of the most powerful oil refineries in the world, heightened the sense of power which he had and with which he may have even been born. It proved one of his favourite theses, that a black man can get as far in life as a white man. Provided he wants to and uses his brains. The rest, and by that he meant mainly his wife's ideas, was nonsense. The notion of socialism, for example, that she often used, was for him synonymous with jealousy.

6

Unlike the majority of Wakotans, Manchi was no longer a Catholic. 'It's a typical slaves' religion,' he would sometimes observe to his listeners, 'a religion for poor, underdeveloped, oppressed and stupid people. Just look, who are Catholics in the main? Coloureds! And where do coloureds come from? From Africa. They were brought here as slaves. Ninety per cent of our population originates from slaves and ninety per cent is Catholic. There must be something *wrong* with a religion like that, mustn't there? That must mean that you're *crazy* to stay a member of such a church! The remaining ten per cent', he also said to his listeners, 'is mainly Protestant or Jewish. And they're not the descendants of slaves like we are, but of slave *owners*!'

Drawing his own conclusion from this line of reasoning, he became a Protestant, although scarcely a practising one. Despite his sound reasoning, his religious conviction may have been linked to the competition presented by the church of Wakota, which on religious grounds, although much older than Manchi's house and much less beautiful, remained (for a large portion of Wakotans) the most important building.

Now he was in the process of joining the Freemasons. So he had come full circle; because at primary school – his only formal education – the priests for whom, in the period before

John XXIII, Catholicism had consisted largely of identifying enemies, had taught him that the greatest and oldest enemies of the Catholic church were the Freemasons.

Apart from that, he didn't care much about religion and felt that the whole notion was superfluous, as was the notion of study... For the latter he had good reasons, he felt. He considered himself, to mention just one thing, more important and *better* than his wife Solema, who after all had studied in Europe and still had a head full of so-called progressive ideas, played the organ whose music occasionally reached his ear at such an annoyingly high volume this morning, and all kinds of other nonsense. If he took her studies in Europe seriously, then it had to be admitted that she had betrayed that study with her behaviour; which boiled down to the same thing; either those studies of hers were no good, or she wasn't, or neither were. In any case, someone whose studies were worth anything, didn't betray those studies through their behaviour; this was a fixed article of faith with him. He found another nice proof of the insignificance of religion in the fact that she played the organ up there. Birds of a feather flock together, he sometimes thought. And the fact that despite all her – ten or so – years in Europe, she still believed in that church nonsense, he considered the most obvious proof of the insignificance of her studies. Even he with his primary education no longer believed in that! She no longer believed one hundred per cent, although she played the organ, but up to now at any rate she had shown little interest in his Freemasonry. And shouldn't she do that if her study really meant anything? Had not Voltaire, one of the greatest minds in history – who, what's more, had always been very severe on Catholics – had not this man been the founder, co-founder, or at least a member of the Freemasons? (He consulted his thick book in order to find out exactly.) He saw his wife Solema and what she did, although she was a beautiful

14

woman, as typical of the insignificance of women in general. He felt the whole thing was nonsense. Total nonsense. When it came down to it, four years ago, he had proved far superior to the lawyer with whom she had committed adultery and with whom, if one wants to call it that, she had deceived him. Bah! He had never studied in his life, but if someone was going to call something like that study, that quaking lawyer in front of him, who hadn't clue what to do, then he, Manchi, was a professor at least. Because what is study and having studied, or being a qualified lawyer or some such thing, if it is not knowing what to do under all circumstances? And he had known, hadn't he, calmly and clearly? And he, Manchi Sanantonio, hadn't any degrees, at least no university degrees. Could you call it study, her going to bed with that young lawyer without a second thought? Too horny to find a proper place? Right there on the ground, or on the wide expanse of the beach (what's more, a dirty beach full of sharp pieces, which must have hurt her erudite back greatly), openly and nakedly in public, or at least in a place where they could bump into anyone, as indeed happened when he caught them, quite by chance, without his having been specially lying in wait for them? Study, he often thought, was also knowing under all circumstances what *not* to do.

Teacher my foot! he often thought. A teacher should be someone who could teach others what they should and should not do, as well as how to do it, and she couldn't do that. Otherwise she wouldn't have been unfaithful to him in that way! Not like a cheap native whore, who has to do it on the ground among the bushes because she hasn't got a discreet place and because, being a native, she can't get into the international whores' hotel where (as befits a hotel anyway) only foreign whoring guests are allowed. She was a whore, a cheap whore; a five-guilder whore, no more and no less, even though she was the mother of his three children and even

15

though he was forced to brag about her beauty and the fact that she'd studied in Europe!

But perhaps what he alone knew didn't matter. What mattered was that he should be held in esteem. And that things were not always as they seemed, he now knew, and perhaps there were a few other people on earth who knew, but that didn't matter, otherwise everyone would discover that wisdom: people simply believed in what they saw; that had always been the case in this island and perhaps in the world and it would probably remain so.

But he had his problems. Firstly, the unasphalted road in front of his house. Long before the house was finished, he had asked the executive council of Curaçao, which was then in the hands of the DP (Democratic Party), to asphalt the road. He had obtained the *assurance*, the *promise* that it would be done; without any problem, because in those days he was a particularly active member of this party, to which he also owed his permanent appointment as a bailiff. But by the time his house was finished, there were elections, which were won by the NVP (National People's Party), the main opponent of the DP. In revenge, especially to keep him, Manchi Sanantonio, the well-known member of the DP, in his place, the road was not asphalted! (Political vendettas in the Antilles surpass anything that the Sicilians, the – stupid – heroes of retribution, could conceive of in the area of vengeance!) Through his domino playing with Bubu Fiel, a decided supporter of the NVP, through the influence of Wakota in general; perhaps also to increase his chances of having the road asphalted, Manchi cut back his activities on behalf of the DP. To such an extent that party workers suspected him of having secretly defected to the NVP. When the DP shortly afterwards again took control of the island's government after an early election, they still refused, although not *openly*, to surface the sandy road for him.

16

Because he didn't get what he needed so much to set the seal on his status from either of the two large parties, he had subsequently (secretly) given his support to the party of which his wife was co-founder and of which her ex-lover was an ardent sympathizer. The URA. But this party, which was supported mainly by young people and intellectuals who had studied in the Netherlands, was a flop. A *screwing party*, Manchi thought angrily, looking back. The sandy road in front of his house had in any case still not been asphalted and he was now politically neutral, with an understandable resentment against all the existing parties.

Then there were the children and the goats, vying with each other in destroying his flowers and plants, and not only if the shoots stuck out through the bars of his wrought-iron fence.

He hoped to solve both problems, to which he had never completely reconciled himself, when he had sufficient power, although, now he was no longer involved in politics, he did not know precisely how he was supposed to acquire power. Perhaps through his membership of Solidarity? When he had power, the power of a minister or a judge, then he would ensure that this damn, dusty, sandy road was immediately asphalted over. Preferably the power of a *judge*! Then he could sentence the errant children who pulled up his flowers – unfortunately he could never catch them red-handed – to reformatories. And have all stray goats shot!

Manchi got up from his porch and went to water the rest of his plants. His third and perhaps most urgent problem was the fact that as a member of the Solidarity lodge he could not continue his regular Sunday afternoon game with Bubu Fiel, while he enjoyed the game so much he could not give it up suddenly or even slowly. Too much perhaps, he thought as he moved his black garden hose from a *trinitaria* bush to a *gayena*. The sound of clucking chickens, which rose from the direction of Bubu Fiel's house, caused him to look through the plants along the fence at the house in the valley. Nora was walking around the back garden with a troop of chickens behind her which she was feeding. He let the branches of the plants which he had pulled aside fall back and said gloomily to himself, I really should stop.

In order to avoid becoming depressed, while he quickly filled the hole at the foot of the bush with water from the hose, he focused his gaze on the beautiful, large red flowers from which the stamens protruded like elegant tongues. Beautiful, he said to himself. Really beautiful, he repeated. Flowers are really beautiful and I'm happy that I've got so many. He cast a satisfied glance over his whole garden, focusing particularly on the black-and-red flowers of the *trinitaria* he had just watered. He compared the flowers of the *trinitaria* with those of the *gayena*. (The flowers of the *trinitaria* grow in bunches and have very thin petals, the colour of which is such a dark red that it tends towards purple; they look like little butterflies that have huddled together in alarm.) Manchi told himself that he found the flowers of the *gayena* more beautiful. But the problem of playing dominoes as a prospective member of Solidarity, which he tried to play down by setting himself all kinds of little problems and solving them, would not let go of him.

A little further to the right and still alongside the fence of his garden was a bush the size of a man, a *kelki hil*. Manchi compared the flowers of this, which were also in bloom and which are the colour of bright sunlight and goblet-shaped, with the *gayena* flower. 'Two goblets,' he said aloud. 'A yellow one and a red one. What beautiful things nature makes! I really couldn't say which is more beautiful.' He professed humility, put himself on a par with the birds and the plants who did not toil or spin and yet had not a care in the world. He said to himself, glancing at his house, that this morning in the peaceful surroundings of his blooming plants, he should be the happiest man on earth. The smell was also wonderful. He said to himself there was nothing wrong and that he was an ungrateful wretch for feeling unhappy. Look, he said to himself, how beautifully the drops of water lie on the leaves of the plants that I water. Look how they gleam. Like morning dew. And how fresh it seemed around him; the vague and yet penetrating smell of a garden full of beautiful flowers, which at the same time intoxicates one and spurs one to action.

But, he thought, quickly picking up the hose and transferring it to the *kelki hil* after the hole around the *gayena* overflowed, what good is it my building that maid's room at the back and eventually even employing a maid, if I simply go on associating with people like Fiel, Pau and Nicolas? No, he thought, moving the hose again, I can't go on any longer. In order to reinforce that thought he added aloud: 'Chamon Nicolas is nothing but a bandit!'

The flowers of the *gayena* he was watering looked dusty. He covered the metal spout of the hose with his thumb and watered them until they looked fresh and red again. Damn sandy road, he thought, pulling the hose towards other flowers. At the same time he conjured up again the details of a fight in which Chamon Nicolas had been involved. It had cost the man a year's imprisonment and no more, because the judge had partially accepted his plea of self-defence. Stupid judge, Manchi thought now, as he moved forward, pulling the hose behind him. Crazy judge. No one who chases somebody else with a machete and then slashes his back – his buttocks, to be precise – can then plead self-defence! He had respect for the judges of the town hall but sometimes they made a mess of things. And that's because, said Manchi to himself, when it comes down to it, they can't fathom the mentality of the people here. He would do it differently!

19

He slid the garden hose further, again to a *gayena*, which was after all his favourite plant. Well, he thought again, it's a good thing they're planning to make natives judges. Natives, people like me, who speak the language of the people, completely understand their mentality. People like me wouldn't have the wool pulled over their eyes. But I really ought to stop now, he repeated in a more gloomy mood. And Janchi Pau! True, he had some respect for the man, and apart from that he was quite light-skinned, but he was still only a Shell worker, that was all. And Bubu Fiel! In himself not a bad chap. He had to have respect for the man; after all he was his own boss. But I ask you, his living habits! Manchi cast a searching glance at Bubu Fiel's house, turned round, and surveyed the arches of his veranda. *Merde*: his house was more beautiful than the one on the postcard, especially because he had made sure not to put his plants so close against the house. You could see all the arches clearly, while on the postcard the plants completely hid a large part of the front of the house. He thought scornfully of the Italian who had built such a beautiful house, only to hide it behind plants immediately afterwards. Idiots, he thought, even though they are Mafia dons!

I belong on the bay, thought Manchi, again focusing on the Prinsessendorp, and suddenly thinking of the sea, which was further on, beyond the houses, with my wife and children in a weekend cottage like all decent people on this island!

The thought cheered him up and he again enjoyed to the full the rich aroma of his wet plants. And yet ... Again he dropped the idea gloomily. He didn't like the sea! He'd never learned to swim. So that whenever he was at the seaside he always had the idea that all this water had only one purpose, to drown a person! So what? What would he have to do on Sunday afternoons if he stopped playing dominoes! As soon as they arrived here, the game at Bubu's had begun – indeed it was his initiative – and the times when he had had to forgo it because Chamon Nicolas wasn't there and they had no one to take his place he had been so bored. So what was he to do? Of course, there was the possibility of switching to another game. Bridge, for example, or canasta; games that the people at the court were constantly talking about. They talked about grand slams, small slams and Italian openings.

But he rejected the possibility of learning another game. He considered himself too old for that. And what's more, he remembered with some pleasure their game of dominoes last week. He and Bubu Fiel had won by a head: five–four.

A shame that they hadn't had ladies' shoes then! No, he wouldn't be able to play any other game except for dominoes, which he had taken up as a child. He could smell doubles a mile off. Like last week. He had simply put paid to at least three of Janchi Pau's. He smiled despite himself in the midst of his flowers. He had never played in a club, but he had nevertheless won a number of trophies in his life. Those cups and medals on the sideboard inside. No, if he changed to another game, he would probably have to lose for a long time before he learned it! And he didn't feel like that. Not at all!

Too much, he repeated to himself again. Too much. He was now really gloomy despite his flowers and felt himself threatened by this weakness, by the fact that it was so manifest that he could almost admit it to himself without feeling embarrassed. It made him very close to people like Bubu Fiel, who purely because of their lack of willpower and self-control, because they gave in to their passions, were doomed to live a life of poverty.

Producing kids, for example, he thought irreverently, craning his neck over his flowers to look at Nora (she must have finished feeding the chickens, because he no longer saw her in the back garden). Producing kids like chickens! How many do they have down there? Nine or ten? Where do they sleep? Bah! He turned his nose up at that sort of person. And then, how many *illegitimate* children did Bubu have? Seven? Eight? Nine? You know, it's an odd thing, thought Manchi without any transition, that that Nora still looks so young and appetizing. A bit plump perhaps, but still a woman you could sometimes take for a girl, with a friendly, hospitable air about her. But still . . . still not the ideal type – just as I thought. At that moment the peace of the quiet morning was shattered by the sound of Nora's harsh voice, which now seemed to be scolding someone.

Not the ideal type, he said to himself while he continued watering his flowers. If you listen to the language that's pouring out of her mouth now. He was again standing by one of his *trinitarias*: a smaller one than those close to his doorstep, of which he thoroughly wetted not only the roots but also the leaves. He wondered why he suddenly lacked the lucidity and self-control he had had when he caught Solema *red-handed*. The calm but confident way in which he had taken the necessary measures at that time still gave him pleasure. And it had been a damn difficult moment because he had had to concern himself with about four things at once. Number one: preserving his honour. Number two: putting such a fright into the chap that he would stay away from Solema from then on. Number three: not losing Solema. Number four: ensuring that the outside world didn't notice a thing.

He could also take number three and number four together. And that was not even counting the great astonishment and disillusionment that he'd felt at the time.

The wind again wafted the piping of the organ of Santa Gloria into his garden; loudly this time, so that he could no longer hear Nora, who was still cursing down below, clearly.

He looked towards the church, which he regarded with contempt, while feeling his disillusionment and astonishment anew and pushing the hose along with his feet. A woman who's been to university, he thought bitterly, a *religious* woman as well despite her strange ideas, a beautiful woman, and just like that, like a simple penniless streetwalker, having a quickie with a punter on the ground among the bushes. 'Not even *Nora*,' he sometimes said to Solema, because he didn't really like even thinking about it, and bitterly, 'not even Bubu Fiel's Nora down there would do a thing like that.'

He sniffed angrily as he looked at the brown earth at his feet. This total lack of good taste had almost driven him crazy. And if he had murdered them, it would have been basically because of that rather than for any other reason. He a lawyer, she a teacher to whom everyone said 'Miss', to whom people looked up; both of them were everything that he'd looked up to in his life. And both of them lay on the ground, *on the ground*, snorting like dogs on heat. So hot for each other, they hadn't even hidden the car. He had walked from his car to the little clump of low bushes on the beach and there they lay. Snorting. With the moonlight on their naked bodies. *On the ground*! When she has a house with a choice of bedrooms, he thought, kicking the house. Eight! Three of which are standing empty, I'll have you know! He sighed with the effort of reliving that moment, and then went on to think with more pleasure of his own reaction at the time. He had taken his decision like a wise judge. He hadn't wanted to punish them, no: he'd wanted to force their respect; show them that they, with all their schools and degrees from Europe, were no better or more intelligent than him, Manchi Sanantonio. And he succeeded. They had to admit (although no one of course said it openly), at least to themselves, that he was a shrewd fellow. An exceptional person. Someone to whom people could rightly look up. Who should be addressed as *Shon*. But why wasn't he as lucid *now*, so that he could immediately find the solution to this problem?

Learn to swim? The hole of the last *gayena* he was watering overflowed because he again focused his attention completely on the houses of the Prinsessendorp, as though the solution must come from there. He realized when his feet, which were in slippers, felt wet. He picked up the hose and screwed the metal nozzle shut so that it hummed by with a grunt.

The morning was still cool, almost mild. The wind which had risen for a moment had subsided again quickly and he couldn't hear the organ of the church further up the hill. Nora down there in the valley was also silent. The sun was still a long way from its zenith. He still had more than an hour to finish the chore that he had undertaken to complete this Sunday: the cleaning and polishing of the ladies' shoes which he had promised to take with him. He rolled up the hose and took it to the patio. Droplets of water leapt playfully from the plants he had watered when he touched them. Then with a sigh he entered his house through the back door, in order to fetch the box in which Solema had put the shoes from the lumber room. There was nothing for it: for the time being at least he hadn't found a solution and he would have to go on playing dominoes.

Perhaps, he said, consoling himself, the answer will come to me during the game.

He took the large cardboard box with the shoes in it to his porch and put it down next to the metal deck-chair in which he had sat philosophizing that morning.

The idea of using ladies' shoes was Bubu Fiel's. The week before he had suddenly said, 'We mustn't write the score on planks any longer, but use shoes, ladies' shoes, which we can hang on the branches of this tamarind tree just like the planks. What do you think?' He omitted to say that the idea came from the domino group at Caracas Bay, although the idea of using *ladies'* shoes was his.

'No!' was Janchi Pau's reaction. 'No!' And for emphasis he banged on the table with his fist and added: 'Dominoes is a game for men. Ladies' shoes have nothing to do with it.'

Manchi had kept silent. He had only one objection to the idea: that he hadn't thought of it himself. Initiatives relating to their game had up to now always originated from him. The special dominoes that they used *he* had ordered from Colombia; *he* had bought the counters; *he* had got Solema to embroider the names of each player on strips of green felt and attach them to the four sides of the table.

'What do you think, Manchi?' asked Bubu Fiel straight out. But he had still shrugged his shoulders evasively.

Chamon Nicolas, who had been having an affair with Nora for four years, perhaps saw supporting Bubu's proposal as a way of winning him over once and for all, although he had just conceived a plan to end his affair with Nora. 'It's a very logical idea,' he said in any case, with a noble look at Bubu, who was rather surprised because Chamon, when he didn't go along with his partner, usually took Manchi's side. 'If we play for shoes,' added Chamon, spreading out his arms and looking at everyone very benevolently, 'then it's only logical that the shoes should be tangibly present. We should have done it ages ago.'

'But *women's* shoes?!' repeated Janchi Pau. 'I can't see the connection and we'll easily look ridiculous in the eyes of anyone watching.'

'Precisely,' said Chamon Nicolas in a jocular tone and conveniently forgetting that that afternoon he had been on the losing side himself. 'That makes the person who loses all the more ridiculous.'

'And that's what it's about, I would have thought,' said Bubu Fiel, who was slightly disappointed that the idea had not been put into practice that very Sunday. 'We don't play for money or anything else. We play for our pleasure. It gives you more satisfaction if you can laugh at the person who loses; then at least we've got something. For that matter, Pau,' he added diplomatically, 'it's strange that you of all people should object to ladies.'

They laughed a little at this because Janchi Pau had a reputation in Wakota of being a womanizer.

'No,' said Manchi, 'no, I can't see it either. It seems to me not only womanish, as Pau here says, but also childish.' Well. A few weeks before, he had told them in veiled terms about Solema's adultery and the measures that he had taken. In his view he had thereby scored the greatest triumph that had ever been achieved at their domino table. He regarded Fiel's idea now as an attack on that triumph of his. Because why hadn't Fiel said anything to him about it before? After all, they were partners, weren't they?

Chamon Nicolas had then thought for a long time, as though it were a matter of a decisive move. When he was on trial in the chilly town hall for the slashing business, with only white faces in front of him – who spoke no Papiamento and had difficulty understanding his English – he had the idea that even the interpreter was against him; the only friendly moment had been when Manchi with his very official stentorian voice had called out, '*The State versus Chamon Nicolas.*' Because Manchi, given the fact that they'd sat at the domino table with each other for such a long time, could not pronounce his name other than with a familiar ring. And that had done him good. Such good that out of gratitude he had always taken Manchi's side when the necessary loyalty to his partner allowed it. But now the favour of Bubu Fiel weighed more heavily.

'You're jealous,' he said to Manchi. 'You don't want to support Bubu's idea because it doesn't come from you.'

'Oh, come now,' said Manchi, nevertheless surprised, 'if you don't want planks any more, I won't deny that that idea was mine, I'll arrange for a big blackboard to write the score on, so that we can nail it to Bubu's house here.'

'And what about the rain?' said Bubu abruptly. 'What about the rain?'

'But why ladies' shoes?' Manchi snapped back. 'I think it's a childish idea!'

'Exactly,' said Janchi. '*I* can't understand it either.'

So it was two against two. Bubu and Chamon for, Janchi and Manchi against. Because of the impasse in which they found themselves, the atmosphere at the table became unpleasant. In another case Chamon might have taken the opposite view with an expansive gesture and a laugh in order to defuse the situation. He didn't like this. Tensions between men on Curaçao are deadly dangerous. However trivial. Apart from that, the organizational aspects of the game left him completely cold. Now, however, he stuck to his guns and repeated his counter-arguments.

Bubu became quietly angry when they kept talking about being 'womanish' and 'childish' and suddenly said, pushing his pieces away from him with a sweeping gesture, 'If ladies' shoes don't go ahead, then this is the last time that I shall play. After all, I play for my pleasure.'

The legend surrounding Bubu Fiel was that it took a long time for him to become really angry, but that he was capable of terrible outrages (as his outbursts were dubbed) when he did get angry. He was about six feet five tall, with long, powerful arms, a large head and, moreover, had a thick, black moustache. People were afraid of his physical strength.

At any rate, Manchi was afraid that afternoon, and consequently quickly said, 'Okay, okay, let's keep the peace. We play for our pleasure.'

Janchi Pau could no longer do much except shrug his shoulders (although Bubu's outbursts made no impression on him), because now Manchi had given in it was three against one anyway. Apart from that, he was too fond of dominoes to make too much fuss about the trappings.

'I'll provide the shoes,' Manchi had then said, thinking that in this way he should really be regarded as the initiator.

Now three pairs of shoes would have undoubtedly been sufficient, because the friends usually beat each other by a small margin. Janchi Pau was definitely a good player, the best of all of them, but his partner Chamon Nicolas generally played with so little concentration that their play always descended to the level of the other two. And sometimes they even lost.

The friends said goodbye, still in an atmosphere of general satisfaction. But Manchi was afraid that his companions would think his wife was short of shoes if he were to appear with a small number the following Sunday.

He asked Solema for twelve pairs. That corresponded best with the prestige he had to maintain among his domino friends.

Solema gave him ten; reluctantly, because she would definitely have to give up three pairs that still had some wear left in them. But what could she do? Grumpily, Manchi had accepted the shortfall, which undermined his authority.

8

He wondered where his wife had got to. The church bell above had already long since tolled for the end of mass. His gold wristwatch showed half past eleven. He was working on the sixth pair of shoes. The other five pairs, which he had already blackened, stood on the low wall of the porch in front of him. With their small openings, they looked like ominous black birds, ready to fly off.

For a short while the Tula road had been full of people who were hurrying home after high mass and Solema was still not back. He missed her mainly because he now had to keep interrupting his work to pour himself a glass of whisky.

Just as he was beginning to get angry about this, she came up the hill. Holding a number of music books, she got out of the small car, which she parked in front of the front door. She was on the porch in a few quick steps. She was wearing a cream dress.

'Why don't you put it inside?' said Manchi, pointing to the car with the toe of one of her shoes into which his left hand had completely disappeared.

Perhaps she hadn't even intended to say hello to him, but now she stood looking at her shoes which he was busy ruining. Some of them might even have been less badly worn than the black shoes she was wearing. 'Why?' repeated Manchi.

'I've still got to collect the children,' said Solema, about to continue on her way. But Manchi stopped her. 'Why do you have to play that thing so loud all the time?'

'What thing?'

'What thing! That organ of yours! You know,' he said reflectively as he turned a shoe around and around in his left hand. 'I can summons that Father Dirks of yours if I want.'

She smiled in spite of herself. 'Do what you have to,' she said, continuing into the house.

'Anyway,' he said, 'there's no need to play so loud. There's no point!' he called after her. 'You're playing for the people *in* the church, not for the people outside. What kept you so long?'

She had expected the question, which she had tried to avoid by walking indoors quickly, and called back: 'Preparations for mass this evening.'

'Oh?' said Manchi to himself, and then after a while called inside: 'You spend too much time on that church. Much too much.'

Solema said nothing, she pretended not to hear him. She was busy getting undressed in order to take a shower.

9

She was a beautiful woman, Solema, one whom the men of Wakota were wont to describe again and again in lyrical terms.

'Her stomach's flat, her waist's so slender . . .'

'And her legs are just perfect.'

'Not too thick, not too fat and not too thin . . .'

'Round . . .'

'No, firm . . .'

'You could say slim . . .'

'Yes, *slim* is the word . . .'

'And her *breasts*!'

'Ah, man, they're just perfect. Just like her bottom . . .'

'And her neck?'

'Great, man. Just right . . .'

'But most of all she's got a beautiful face. Nice and round and not too square . . .'

'That's the difference between black women and white women who are beautiful. White women often have a chin that's far too pointed.'

'Something masculine about them . . .'

'But Solema's chin is round . . .'

'Solema is a beautiful woman.'

'Her lips are very thin . . .'

'And black. Very thin and black. She's one of the few women I know who doesn't use any lipstick. Not even any make-up.'

'Ah, the joys of her face, man! Have you noticed how perfect they are?'

'The joys of her face! Man!'

'I'd like to put my face against it.'

'And close to her ears she's got those delicate little hairs that you only see with Latin American women, Italian women and suchlike. *Real* white women don't have those delicate things.'

Someone once said to someone else that he was crazy about the quality of the brown of Solema's skin, to which the other replied that it was rubbish compared with the perfection of the skin itself.

Strangely enough, the men usually ended their commentaries on her beauty by assuring each other that they didn't want to go to bed with her, precisely because they admired her beauty and her chastity so much.

'I don't want to go to bed with her as such,' one said. 'I'd just like her to take me into her service . . .'

'Why?'

'So that from early in the morning until late at night I could remove each speck of dust that falls on her beautiful skin.'

'With your mouth, I expect,' said someone else, to which the man replied, 'No, even if it was only with my fingers. Really!'

She had straight hair, Solema, which, however, she had cut short and deliberately permed with little curls, to Manchi's great irritation. She had perfect white teeth and a small nose.

But all her attraction concentrated itself in her alert black eyes, whose deep-brown pupils constantly glittered in a wide and clear field of white. The thought that she was back again made Manchi happy.

Which of them, he thought at a certain moment, sipping the new glass that she had brought him, can have himself served like this on Sunday morning? By such a woman?

He was working on the eighth pair of shoes and by 'them' he meant not only his domino colleagues but perhaps the whole of mankind. He felt like a prince, a king, an emperor: Napoleon, Hitler, Bonaparte, all put together. (Like many people, he was in the habit of seeing the different names of the same historical personage as separate entities.)

He thought of Prince Bernhard and wondered with a smile whether it was possible that the Queen of the Netherlands sometimes served the prince herself, like Solema did with him, whenever he wanted. He decided not. People like that can't even sleep together, he thought happily.

10

'Are you coming?'

He had almost finished his chore when Solema appeared in the doorway again to call him for lunch. The tantalizing smell of *sòpi di mondongo* hung everywhere in the house and on the veranda. Carried on the wind, it mingled with the same smell from the house of Bubu Fiel and other houses, and particularly because of the typical smell of the maize in it was *the* Sunday afternoon smell of Curaçao.

'I'll be finished in just a moment.' He looked at her as he said this and suddenly felt powerfully attracted to her, which he was only able to hide by focusing his glance on the last shoe that he was working on. There was a gleam in her eyes which he had never seen before. In order to suppress his desire for her body, he said to himself that it was only because of the whisky. Since her adultery he had made a point of avoiding any evidence of passion in his dealings with her. He took her, when he did, as though it were an unpleasant duty which the two of them had to fulfil now and then. Particularly now he had the number of children that he wanted to have.

While she waited until he was ready, her glance fell on a lonely figure walking down the Tula road in a westerly direction. He was dressed in white and had a grey hat on. Her looking attracted Manchi's attention. 'Who is it?'

'Pedro.'

'Oh,' said Manchi, putting the last shoe on the wall in front of him.

Since his wife had died, the sexton of Santa Gloria had made a habit of having a few drinks in a bar before going back to his lonely house. He had obviously had one too many, because now and then he drifted towards the middle of the road.

'They should punish people like that,' said Manchi, who got up to look at the man. He seemed to be waiting for a bus, he kept turning round and round. He kept wiping his face with a white handkerchief.

'If I were a *judge*,' said Manchi again, while he kept staring at the sexton, who would probably not get a bus very quickly because most bus drivers at this time were naturally also getting ready to start on their *sòpi di mondongo*. 'If I were a judge, people like that wouldn't know what hit them. He's a danger to traffic.'

'You're exaggerating,' said Solema, quickly clearing up. 'Anyway, it's *not* the judges who make the laws.' Nowadays, she disagreed with him more often, sometimes surprised at how easy she found it.

'Who does, then?' said Manchi, piqued. Solema didn't

33

reply: she disappeared into the house with the bottle of polish and the whisky glass. Manchi just kept looking at the wobbling figure of the sexton, until the latter vanished from his field of vision at the junction of the Tula and Carpata roads. He hoped that the man would actually be run over so that he would be proved right in front of Solema.

11

While he washed the sticky black polish off his hands at the green wash-basin in his bedroom, he thought with something like pleasure of his triumph under the tamarind tree at Bubu Fiel's. It was not a score that could be expressed in ladies' shoes, he thought contentedly. Not ten and not twenty. As it often did, the conversation had turned to women and particularly to the adultery that they can commit. The question was, who could provide the best means of preventing this evil? And what should be the actions of a man who had become a victim of it? It had been a few weeks ago, after he had decided to apply for membership of Solidarity. Various theories had been put forward, but when Manchi had told his story, there had been a great silence around the domino table. He had made it appear as if the principal protagonist was one of the judges of the court. He regarded this as a double triumph, since his friends would be bound to think that he was on intimate terms with the court judges.

It was just that he couldn't help being amazed at Janchi Pau's reaction. Jealousy? That was plausible, because before Manchi had come up with his story, Janchi Pau had been regarded at the domino table, if not as the greatest womanizer of the four, at least as the greatest connoisseur of women. Of the four of them and of the whole island. He had to admit this despite his triumph in 'literature'. It meant that he, Manchi, would henceforth have a certain dominance over his friends in the area of sexual life. Janchi's jealousy, which in his view expressed itself in a greater reserve towards him, he would simply have to take as part of the deal. In fact, it actually pleased him: the more honour and acclaim he received in his life, the better. But he thought, as he dried his hands and admired himself in the mirror for a moment, that it might not be a bad idea if in future he took his little revolver, a .32 calibre, to dominoes. One could never be too careful: Janchi Pau was known not only as a womanizer, but also as a fierce knife man when the chips were down.

12

Janchi Pau lived in the overgrown valley behind the church of Wakota, about two miles away. It was a house with three bedrooms; the model of a so-called modern (but mainly cheap) villa of which the designs are mass-produced with all the attendant faults (such as leaky roofs) by the public works department of the island for more progressive citizens.

The house was unusual in that it was still not completely finished: he had intended it for his mother, but when she died, shortly after he had come ashore for good, he had lost all enthusiasm for it. The walls were unfinished both inside and out; the windows still had no hinges and had to be kept in their openings by cross planks. The floor was not yet completely finished either. And Janchi relieved himself outside in the wood. However, in the living-room, which he had occupied for almost three years, he had put a few planks on the ground. Apart from that, there was a single bed of fragile iron, a chair and a table, a two-ring kerosene stove and a drum in which he kept drinking-water that he got from a neighbouring well. Oddly enough, he did have electric light.

On his bare walls there hung a guitar and the heads of two large fishes which he had caught himself.

On a plank against one of the walls there were a large number of mugs, which he had collected over the years. Apart from that, everything was scattered through the unhygienic-looking house. After the death of his mother, Janchi Pau had not only stopped working on the house, but had seemed to lose all appetite for life. Even before that, his life might not have had much content, but it did follow a pattern that he had become used to over the years: he sailed all over the world and when his ship called in at Curaçao he visited his mother. But finally, her sad letters, in which she kept complaining about her loneliness, had made him give up sailing. Particularly when she suggested that he was actually abandoning her, just like his Venezuelan father – she herself was a Curaçao Negress – had done in the past.

He remembered his father only as a foul-mouthed tyrant who had made life impossible for her. As a boy, he had often resolved to have his revenge for this later. But nothing was to come of this because at a certain moment the man disappeared from his life completely. He couldn't say whether he was dead or alive.

Janchi did know how much his mother had done in order to bring him up by herself, to the age when he could fend for himself, and he decided, now that she was old, to do something in return. He would build a house for her where she could spend her old age peacefully. From the moment he had resolved to do it, he regarded this as the only obligation in his life. And at the same time, perhaps, as his only real pleasure.

Consequently he saw her death, just at the moment when he could crown a life which was useless to him with something important, as a very sick joke.

It embittered him and alienated him from God and man, even more than was already the case.

At any rate, the thought of completing the house that he had begun seemed absurd to him after he had buried his mother; all her life she had lived in a wooden hovel in the town, sometimes selling her body to survive and bring him up. Should he now finish his house so that some woman or other – because that was what it came down to: a man built a house for a woman – who had never in her life done anything for him should benefit from it? Some woman or other who, fickle as those creatures are, would suddenly up and leave him for someone else? No, he would simply go and live in his house alone, then he would at least have a roof over his head.

So he lived in an unfinished house and tried to amuse himself as much as possible so as not to become the victim of those numerous incongruities in life which people never understand. Like a lonely hunter, silent and determined, he chased women. He sometimes even took them for a few days to his unfinished house, which seemed to have a certain attraction, because he often had difficulty in getting them out again. On Saturday evenings he usually went fishing and for the rest he played dominoes, at any rate on Sunday afternoons at Bubu Fiel's. He no longer went to Campo Alegre.

Janchi's neglect of his house, however, meant that it became almost overgrown by the rampant, long-stalked *palu di lechi*, the wild sage, the *flaira* and other plants which – rain or no rain – flourished in the strikingly fertile earth behind the church of Wakota; his house could scarcely be seen from a distance.

Various vines with yellow, purple and red flowers on their tendrils climbed as though in competition up the two columns of his porch, like women of easy virtue. The porch itself was full of goat droppings because these animals had gradually made it their evening resort. Since the house still didn't have a ceiling, birds flew in under the pitched roof in order to build their nests at the top of the roof wherever they liked. 'I live in an aviary,' Janchi sighed sometimes; particularly in the mornings when the various kinds of birds which had nested at the same time in his house began flying to and fro above his head and woke him up with their chirping, screeching, cooing and singing.

But for a long time he couldn't have cared less about the noise. They made good company, became more and more brazen and never minded where they left their droppings. These days they weren't even frightened of him, appeared to regard *him* as the intruder on their domain.

In the beginning, he sometimes caught birds in his fishing net. He then roasted them and ate them, actually more in revenge for their closing him in on all sides than from necessity. Gradually, however, he began to appreciate their company so much and became so proud that even birds, usually so shy of human beings, were not frightened to fly into his house, that he stopped doing this. He said to himself that he could do it again whenever he liked, but in reality the birds had tamed him. He now regularly scattered bits of leftover bread for them on the unfinished porch when he went out and when it was very dry he even put out bowls of water for them.

Despite the rampant undergrowth, which covered both Janchi's house and the land around it, one could get quite close from the west along a road between two rows of *palu di lechis*.

That morning, Solema came from the east.

From that side there was no good road to Janchi's house. She had to leave her car open and unprotected on a sandy road which went in the direction of Campo Alegre in order to reach the house through the undergrowth of prickly cactuses and *wabi* trees. Walking was made even more difficult for her by the heavy bag of groceries which she was carrying and which she had put into the boot of her little Fiat the evening before. Her headscarf caught on a *wabi* bush and when she went back to get it she tore her stocking on a thorn, which stuck deep into her leg. Bleeding but happy, she finally reached the house. She climbed the porch on the west side with its faintly stinking goat droppings and knocked on the closed door. Because there was no immediate reply, she began calling Janchi's name softly. Despite the thick undergrowth, which meant that she could scarcely be seen by anyone here, she was still anxious to be careful. But when she still heard nothing, she called louder: 'Janchi, Janchi!' She wanted to see him and she wanted to do something about her bleeding leg. But there was no reply. All that happened when she kept on shouting was that a goldfinch flew out from under the roof, chirping just over her head.

She felt disappointed, the more so because it had taken so much planning for her to be able to come this morning. She considered just sitting on the edge of the porch, when her eye caught a specially felled trunk of a *wabi* tree which stood in the left corner of the porch.

Her heart lit up. Hadn't he promised her the Sunday before that he would make her a table of *wabi* wood? She put down the heavy plastic bag and stood looking at the trunk. She laughed, despite her vague disappointment, at the thought that he had wanted to keep his promise so quickly. The trunk looked so newly felled and still smelled so fresh that it seemed to her that Janchi could not possibly be far away. He might have even cut it this morning early. She went to the door and pulled at it: to her amazement, it opened without much effort.

'Janchi?' She was now absolutely convinced he was at home, as people in love are when they visit their loved one unexpectedly, and refused to accept he was not there. She went inside with the idea that she would see him as soon as her eyes adjusted to the darkness inside. It didn't occur to her for a moment that he could still be asleep (although it would be the only reason for him not replying when he was there), because in her eyes he wasn't the kind of man who spent the mornings in bed. But Janchi was asleep. She finally realized from the gentle snoring sound which reached her from the far corner of the room, while she stood getting used to the darkness by the door which she had half-closed behind her. She stood indecisively in the room. She now remembered that he sometimes spent all Saturday night fishing and thought it was cruel to wake him. But neither did she feel like simply going away again. She walked to the bed and leant over him.

'Janchi?'

He started awake.

'Solema! How did you get here?' He seemed to be seized by panic, throwing his legs out of bed in order to get up, but she held him back with a cautious hand on his chest.

'I've come to visit you.'

'Now? What time is it then?'

'A little after eight.'

'So late?' He was confused because until now she had always come to visit him *in the evenings* and if it was as late as all that, it would mean that something terrible had happened to him, namely that he had completely forgotten his Sunday game of dominoes at Bubu Fiel's. Moreover . . . it was possible one of his domino pals would come and have a look and see why he hadn't turned up, although people seldom visited him. Then they would find her at his place. He had got up, despite the fact that Solema kept assuring him that she'd only just come to see him, but bent down and looked under his main pillow where he normally kept his knife. It wasn't there and his panic seemed only to increase. Solema, who didn't understand his confusion at all, grabbed hold of his naked body – he was wearing only his underpants – to calm him

40

with hers. But he tore himself free almost brusquely. He had the feeling that Manchi was chasing her without her knowing and wanted to be prepared if Manchi came charging into his house in a little while. But when he saw his knife lying there in the part of his house which could be called a kitchen, he felt relieved again. He had sat cleaning the fish which he had brought home the night before for a little while before going to bed, and had left his knife here. The ray of light which shone in through the half-open door also convinced him that it wasn't yet evening. But he still found it strange that she had come to see him *during the day*. He wanted to ask her, just to be on the safe side, whether something was wrong, but couldn't ask immediately because she was busy opening the only window on the east side of the house which had hinges.

'Is Manchi after you?' he asked as he turned round.

'No, darling,' she said, coming towards him laughing, walking in the wave of light which suddenly shot through the house through the opened window. And because he continued sticking the knife in the wood of the chest without saying anything, she quickly added, 'There's nothing, really nothing. I simply wanted to bring you your breakfast. Look . . .' She remembered the bag of groceries and rushed to the porch to get it. She came back with it and began to unpack the things on a table by his bedside. As she did so, she went on talking non-stop for a long time, because she still had the impression that she had to put him at his ease.

'I couldn't let you know, darling. But I had such a wonderful opportunity to come. You see, I knew a few days ago that a priest here who is visiting today was coming to play our organ. Our priest telephoned me. Luckily he got through to me and not Manchi, and I decided immediately to come and see you this morning. Manchi thinks that I'm up there in church.' She pointed in the direction of the church. 'I'm sorry I had to wake you.'

'You're bleeding,' he said thoughtfully. 'You've got blood on your hand and on your skirt.' He spoke in a calm, almost satisfied tone. So there *was* something wrong, although she maintained the opposite.

'Oh,' she said. 'Oh, the cactuses behind your house. I pricked myself. Look.' She lifted her right leg and showed him her torn stocking. 'I forgot all about it,' she added with a laugh.

Only then did he smile. 'So Manchi thinks you're in church?'

'Mm.'

He pulled her to him with his left hand while with his right hand he rubbed his eyes. 'You're a brave woman.' She didn't reply, but kissed him on the mouth, his shoulders and the light hairs on his chest. He wanted to add one or two things to what he had said; that what she had done was dangerous, although he considered her courageous, and where had she left her car, which could so easily betray them? But for a long time she allowed him no time to do this, pressing his head against her with her right hand while she tried to take off her shoes and stockings with her left hand. He was a little confused and a little overwhelmed by her exuberance. So instead of speaking he picked her up and carried her to bed. She scarcely wanted to let go of him to undress completely, but nevertheless he raised himself off her.

'First your leg,' he said. 'And you can't go back to Manchi later with a skirt covered in blood like that.' He filled a bowl from the iron drum and washed her leg. Together they washed the small stains of blood from her cream dress, which they then hung to dry over the only chair he had in his house.

Afterwards, as he lay beside her in the narrow single bed, she suddenly remembered that she wanted to make him breakfast. She had looked forward to that particularly when she was making plans to visit him this morning. She made a faint effort to get up.

'Let me get you something to drink first, Janchi.'

But it was now as if her impulsiveness had infected him completely. He did not reply, but stretched his slim and sinewy naked body completely over hers, and instead of continuing her attempt to get up, she began exploring and feeling the grooves in his body, slowly and intimately, until she experienced the wonderful feeling she always had when she lay with him: that she fitted completely inside him. After all, their mutual understanding was so complete that his penis slipped into her without one of them having to use their hands to guide it. Then they made love calmly, as people do who know what the point of sex is: a very special way of talking, in which the smallest and most insignificant movement is a token of value, and which for that reason takes time. Moreover, they knew from experience that they had to be careful on Janchi's narrow, fragile bed. They scarcely talked. Speaking when they were lying like this would unnecessarily interrupt the conversation of their bodies.

'I'd like you to stay,' he said, when the bells rang for the end of high mass.

She had told him she could stay until then and he'd automatically followed the ringing of the bells: beginning and end of the children's mass, beginning and end of the high mass.

'Me too,' she said, making no move to get up. 'But Manchi's expecting me.'

He rolled onto his side without saying anything, but with a rather forlorn air. They remained lying there like two sardines, half covering each other in the narrow bed. He felt

43

sad because he knew for certain that he would never have enough of her. Even if he had years to spend on it, he would never know her body so completely that he would tire of it. Or rather, the reverse was true, he knew her body so completely that he knew none would suit him better, that he would never want anyone else.

'That's not what I mean. I mean *stay*, for good.'

'Janchi!' she said in alarm, feeling that he was in the process of spoiling something infinitely good.

'That's what I mean,' he said simply. On the tip of his tongue were the words 'I love you' (whose meaning he understood for the first time in his life). This formula, which he had never used before, still seemed too unreal to him and he said: 'That's how it has to be, Solema.'

They stayed clinging to each other for a little while in the narrow bed without talking.

'My children!' she said, but more to the uncovered dark roof above her and to herself than to him.

'With your children. Believe me, that's how it has to be. Didn't I tell you that you've got to leave him if you don't want to go crazy?'

'I don't care any more, now I've got you, Janchi. I'm not even frightened of him any more.'

'It's not about Manchi any longer,' he said. 'It's about me.'

Because she kept looking at him inquiringly, he said by way of explanation: 'I love you, Solema.' He was happy that he'd dared after all to use this formula; it finally gave him the liberating feeling of being like everybody else.

Resting one elbow on his body, she sat up on the bed with her feet on the ground. He remained lying on his side.

'I didn't expect this,' she said after a while.

'Neither did I,' he said. 'I mean, I've loved you for ages, really. I don't know how long. And anyway I've admired you

44

ever since I've known you, but I'd thought that it could go on like this, that I would never feel the need to have you with me for ever.'

Because she still said nothing, he sat down next to her and put an arm round her splendid brown back. 'I'm quite simply jealous,' he added by way of explanation. 'I'm not used to sharing a woman with another man. It makes me edgy.'

'But my children, Janchi. You're forgetting my *children*.'

'You care about me too, don't you?' he asked.

She nodded, while she slowly surveyed the interior of his unfinished house. He noticed this and guessed her thoughts: that it seemed impossible, even if she were to decide to leave Manchi, to move into this unfinished house with her three children.

'I know what you're thinking,' he said suddenly with a childish joy in his voice, 'but it's all very simple.'

He jumped off the bed, stroked his black pencil moustache once or twice, and began surveying the house as though for the first time. Looking at the stalk of a *palu di lechi* which was growing in from under the roof, she pulled on her panties.

A little later, as she was about to put on her dress, he prevented her by placing a hand on one of her breasts, whose nipples were as black as her lips. 'Don't worry about this mess. I know what you're thinking, but don't worry about this rubbish. It'll be finished in a couple of months if I want, everything will be different here. If you love me, it's very simple.'

This last statement was directed more at himself than at her. Then he cast inquiring glances at the roof of the house, the floor and the bare walls, and suddenly said, 'In three months if I do it alone. In two if I can find someone to help me.'

'I've got some money,' she said abruptly after she had put on her dress. But he shrugged his shoulders and quickly put his trousers on.

'Money's unimportant. Money is always unimportant! You're the most important thing. Look,' he said as he tightened his belt, 'I didn't really need to ask you. For me, the fact that you've come to see me this morning is the best proof that you love me. Up to now I hadn't even considered the possibility. But' – he thought for a bit, while he tried to look deep into her eyes and then went on – 'when a woman grows courageous because of a man, she loves him. That's true, isn't it?'

She nodded. 'I love you, Janchi,' she said slowly and emphatically, but just as slowly and emphatically she added, 'but you've taken me by surprise. If I were alone it would be a bit different.'

'Can't you bring your children here?' he asked suddenly, almost gruffly.

'No, Janchi,' she said very sadly. She thought he would get angry or would chase her away, or even *hit* her because she herself felt how much she was insulting him by her way of reacting. 'Whatever I do and whatever happens to me,' she said, when the outburst that she was expecting didn't come, 'is my affair, but my children mustn't suffer because of it.' The *palu di lechi* which was growing into the house again caught her eye: she was suddenly so absorbed in it that she stopped combing her hair. 'If your house were finished . . .' she said afterwards, staring ahead of her thoughtfully.

'I hoped you'd say that,' he said, embracing her, 'but you must believe me, it'll be finished. Really. All I need is a good bricklayer. Do you believe me?'

She nodded and he pressed her to him, long and hard. They were standing by the open window in a ray of light in which millions of microscopically small particles of dust wafted into the room from outside.

'I must go, darling,' she said. 'I really must go.' She wanted to go quickly not only because Manchi would miss her, but because Janchi's sudden proposal had thrown her into complete confusion.

He noticed her confusion and said, 'I'm just as selfish as Manchi in any case. I let myself get carried away. You must forgive me.'

She kissed him fleetingly.

'But I do want you to stay with me,' he added quickly. 'Right away or when the house is ready.'

She didn't react, but pulled him gently with her to the door. However, he seemed completely indifferent to her haste; he stopped her in the middle of the room and squeezed her against his naked chest with one arm.

'If you don't come, I'll leave.'

'I'll come, I'll come.'

'If you come, I'll finish the house.'

'Yes, but let me go now. I'll come this evening.'

'This evening?'

He looked over her for a moment to repeat in a surprised tone: 'This evening?'

'No,' she said quickly, correcting the misunderstanding that she heard in his inquiring tone. 'I mean that I'll come again this evening as usual. Idiot,' she added, laughing.

Janchi's face clouded slightly. 'I thought *this evening*,' he said pensively. 'I really thought you meant to come *for good* this evening.'

He stood in the doorway and she kissed him to get past him, but he pulled her hard to him as though he didn't intend to let her go. She kissed him with a touch of fear because she was suddenly frightened; frightened that despite the thick undergrowth they would be seen now they were in the open doorway; frightened that something would go wrong in their relationship now Janchi was asking her for the ultimate, which she couldn't give: her children.

As though this was not a man with whom she'd just slept intimately for three hours, but a stranger trying to assault her, she suddenly pulled herself free of him and ran out of the house, off the porch, around the corner of the house and through the dangerous field of cactuses. But in the middle of the cactus field she stopped and turned round in the hope that he was following her.

He was. With his upper body still bare, he stood at the corner of the house looking after her.

'Until this evening, darling,' she called to him as softly as possible. He raised his hand and waved to her, coming towards her in his bare feet, stepping over the small cactuses. She was the first to speak: 'Do you really mean it, Janchi?'

'Yes, Solema. If you don't come, I'll leave.'

She felt threatened and caught off-balance. She was also frightened because she could be seen by any person who came along the sandy road where she'd parked her car. She had no choice. She also had the feeling that if she didn't agree he wouldn't allow her to go home.

'I'll come, Janchi,' she said. 'I promise you. When the house is finished, I'll come.'

'You're a brave woman,' he said. 'Till this evening.'

'Till this evening.'

They parted without another word. He to his unfinished house and she to her car. They didn't even look round, because they both needed to beware of the troublesome cactuses. Janchi all the more so because he was barefoot.

13

Solema slowly pulled away. The sense of haste, panic even that she had felt a moment ago, left her. Now that she had promised Janchi she would move in with him, she felt as if Manchi no longer meant anything to her. She asked herself, as the little Fiat moved into fourth gear, why she didn't do it at once. She could drive straight to her parents', collect her children and move in with him right away. But the thought of the unfinished interior of his house gave her the creeps.

I'm not as brave as all that, Janchi, she thought to herself. Not as brave as you, in any case. But was it a matter of courage or was it about simplicity? That's how he saw everything, as simply as a young boy. With that same boyish simplicity he had come to her, one Sunday afternoon after church, to offer her his help against Manchi. He hadn't mentioned Manchi's name, but she'd understood everything from his direct words, which were only different from those of the schoolboys who came so often to offer their services because he spoke more slowly and more seriously. 'Miss Solema, if you need my help for any reason whatsoever, you can always count on me.'

'Well, what do you mean, Janchi?'

'You know, Miss Solema; I live in the unfinished house behind the church.' He had quickly explained to her how she could drive there and finished by saying, 'If you need help, you can come.'

She had thought that it was an invitation to go to bed with him and that he was asking her in this direct, insolent way because he knew that she already slept with other men; a form of blackmail, that is, because she wouldn't be able to say anything to Manchi if she didn't agree. For that reason she had told him that she'd bear it in mind, with the sugges-tion in her voice that she understood that he had her in his power and she would therefore have to pay the ransom. She didn't find that a difficult task: he was good-looking; he was a sinewy, slim mulatto, with a determined jaw. But above all she was attracted by the thought of deceiving Manchi with one of his domino friends!

No more than a week later she knocked on the door of his unfinished house. It was a Sunday evening after church (after the domino game at Bubu Fiel's had broken up) and she had dreamt up an excuse that enabled her to stay with him for hours if he wanted to.

Her mistake still made her laugh.

'Oh,' he said in alarm, when he saw that it was she who had knocked. 'Is Manchi chasing you?'

But he seemed to be more concerned about something else; without inviting her in, he first of all went to put the shirt that he seemed just to have taken off back on. He also quickly slipped his shoes on again.

'Excuse me,' he said, 'I've just got back from playing dominoes and I was going to take a bath . . .'

'Aren't you even going to ask me in, Janchi?' she said, deliberately being familiar to put him at his ease. At that moment she felt pleased with herself because she thought he was surprised by his rapid success. She enjoyed seeing a renowned womanizer looking awkward.

He hesitated. 'It's a terrible mess here. You know I live alone and then . . .'

But she had already come in of her own accord and stood, rather taken aback in spite of herself, on the unpaved floor.

'Is Manchi after you?' he asked again, sitting down on the bed and leaving her standing.

'No,' she said, adding suggestively, 'It's perfectly safe. My car's parked over there between the *palu di lechis*.' (This time she'd driven up from the west side.) 'And it's dark . . .' she said in a friendly voice. 'No one knows I'm here.'

'Oh.' He took a deep, relieved breath. 'Then it's okay.'

She had sat down on his only chair, rather surprised that he made so few moves to take the ransom she had come to offer. The fact that he lived in a place that was so nicely tucked away meant that she suddenly hoped he wouldn't be satisfied with just this once.

'Why have you come, then?' he asked her, turning on the light.

She found him rather mean at that point because he found it necessary to abuse his power over her, but told herself that perhaps this went with blackmail. 'You know very well.'

'No,' he said, shaking his head. 'If you have no problems with Manchi, I don't know why you've come.' As if by inspiration he added, 'Has he hit you perhaps?'

'No, Janchi,' she said. 'I've come to go to bed with you. You want to, don't you?' She got up and sat down next to him on the bed. She suddenly found him a strange person and wanted it to be over quickly. She undid her headscarf and put that on the bed next to her. 'Come on,' she said in a motherly voice, 'there's no reason to be shy. You wanted me to come and I've come. But I haven't got unlimited time.'

Instead of touching her, as she expected, he bent his head over his knees for a long time. Even when she put a hand on his shoulder he stayed sitting in the same position. But finally he carefully moved her hand away. 'It's a misunderstanding, miss, I didn't want to go to bed with you, it wasn't a trick to get you here. It's best if you leave.' He turned his face severely towards her: 'Someone like you should not be here.'

Then he smiled again and she saw his white even teeth beneath his black moustache and fell in love with him. There was something diabolically calm about him, which attracted her like a magnet and inspired confidence.

'You're playing with me,' she said thoughtfully. When he didn't reply, she said, 'Why not?'

He got up and sat down on the chair at the table. 'Because you are Miss Solema, I've always admired you, and,' he added, emphatically, 'I *respect* you.'

'If you know so much about me that you found it necessary to come to me, then you also know what you just said is not true. Surely you must know that I'm no better than all the women who come to you here?'

She had got up abruptly. 'Janchi, there's no need for so much ceremony. You know that I *have to* go to bed with you – and I find you attractive enough to enjoy doing it – because otherwise you would tell Manchi that I sleep with other men. You don't have to make a fool of me, although I can imagine that you enjoy it. Sadistically perhaps . . .'

'Me?' he said in real astonishment. 'Me, Miss Solema? I really know nothing about you. Really not. I just sat at the domino table and guessed that Manchi is treating you in a terrible way, teasing you and taunting you. That hurt me because I've always admired you and I wanted you to know that if you ever need help against him . . . You see, perhaps I shouldn't have done it, it's really not my business, but I really can't stand that smugness of Manchi's! He thinks he's God, because he's got such a big house. Anyway . . . I don't care. I don't want to go to bed with you. That's an end of it.'

Her elbow was on her knee and she was resting her chin on her hand. Though she began to see that she had made a mistake, that no longer made any difference. Now she wanted to go to bed with him! Whatever happened. Even more than before.

He kept looking at her and to console her because he seemed to assume that she would be ashamed now she saw her mistake, said, 'Perhaps you made a mistake, that's all. It certainly doesn't make me think . . .' He seemed to be looking for a suitable word.

She raised her head and looked him straight in the face.

'Go ahead and say it,' she said, finishing his sentence for him: '... "that you're a whore".'

'Exactly,' he said emphatically, 'you're *not* a whore for me. Manchi is crazy and he wants to make you crazy. That's why I came to warn you.'

He briefly told her the story that Manchi had recounted to them a little while ago at the domino table. It was indeed her story and she gave him the details that Manchi had deliberately omitted. But after a while she said, because she wanted him not to find anything wrong in sleeping with her, 'Since then I've been to bed with even more men. Lots of times.'

'That's your business!' he said quickly. 'I'm really more concerned about Manchi than about you; no one has the right to treat another person like Manchi does you.' With a slight smile he added: 'Slavery was abolished in 1863.'

'Has he ever done anything to you?' she asked, being familiar with him again.

'No. I simply don't like the fact that he thinks he's always right. He could have just let you go, which would have been easy for him, because he had the law on his side.' He suddenly spread his arms in a token of incomprehension. 'If he had beat you, or even murdered you, I would have been able to understand. It's human, although if two people can't get along together any more, the best solution seems to me for them simply to let each other go ... But this ...'

She was silent because she was ashamed; particularly because he had to admit in the face of his honest indignation that more than anything else, more than death itself perhaps, she had feared the scandal which would have enveloped her if Manchi had acted differently, if he had told everyone the whole story ... And he could still do that ...

'You're right, it might have been better.'

'Definitely,' he said emphatically, adding after some time,

'At least, I can't imagine how I could go on living with a woman for whom I've got no respect at all and whom I don't trust. A woman, forgive me, whom I would have to treat like a whore, like Manchi does you.'

'He does trust me now,' she said as a kind of defence.

'That's not trust. He thinks he's got a hold over you.' He laughed aloud to himself. 'But it seems he doesn't have that hold, does he?'

She nodded. She felt a warm attraction towards him which she didn't have to explain and wondered why he was making things so difficult for her, while she was here and wanted to give herself to him, as she had often given herself to others for whom she'd felt less and sometimes nothing. Therefore she repeated, pretending to be sad, 'Yes, I go to bed with other men.' She thought: he must understand now.

He said, as calmly as a doctor certain of his diagnosis, 'So he's already beating you. So he's making you throw yourself away, destroy yourself.' Because she said nothing, he asked, 'Do you care about those men that you go to bed with?'

'No,' she said without thinking, 'usually not.'

'Exactly!' he said aloud. 'He's turning you into a whore.' This time he didn't offer excuses for the word 'whore' and she got up, a little alarmed because suddenly she wasn't sure that he didn't see her like that. Suddenly she wanted to hide the attraction she felt for him at all costs, because she was afraid that if he noticed, he would think her more of a whore than he perhaps did already. That would make him reject her even more finally. She didn't want that to happen. 'I'm going,' she said quickly.

'Good,' he said, handing her her headscarf, 'but let me say that I still admire you.'

'Do you mean it?' she asked, just to say something to avoid him noticing her real feelings.

'Yes,' he said. 'Very much.'

'Even after this evening?'

'Yes, anyone can make mistakes. I was born out of wed-
lock myself, as they say.'

She nodded. Something became clearer to her because of
his last observation.

'Can I come and visit you now and then?' she couldn't
help asking, while he helped her off the high porch. 'Just to
talk to you a bit if I'm having a difficult time? I've got no one,'
she said almost pleading, 'and you know all my secrets
anyway.'

'Yes,' he said, 'but be careful.'

14

Manchi had not completely broken her with his sadistic
treatment since he had caught her with Feliciano, and the
meeting with Janchi gave her a push in a new direction. His
elemental humanity and understanding seemed to wipe out
everything that she might have done wrong. She believed that
it was possible for her to be clean and pure again, and now,
because of him, felt the need to be. She stopped her superficial
adventures, which she had so often kept up to take revenge
on Manchi and through a desire which she didn't fully
understand to throw herself away and finally to destroy
herself, with two doctors, a teacher and another gentleman.
With none of them had it developed into anything permanent,
of the kind that she now had with Janchi. After the first time,
which was mostly spoiled by mutual lack of familiarity, she
seldom wanted to see her partners again and in that way her
means of avenging herself on Manchi caused her more pain
than him, since he knew nothing about it. She had started to
feel lost.

Janchi, whom she went to visit again not long after the
first occasion, gave her back a feeling of self-worth, more and

more completely. He didn't consider her a whore and it was obvious that their relationship, which was quickly consummated, was taken seriously, although he didn't seem to have any need to keep her all to himself. In particular, the sometimes almost childlike awe and respect with which he continued to treat her finally convinced her that her mistake was correctable. She began, as it were, to live again, like an invalid sometimes does after a long and dangerous illness, and the whole world of idealistic thoughts which she had had before the incident with Feliciano returned. She also began to see clearly where the mistakes she had made really lay. She shouldn't have married Manchi. Although she might have done so because deep in her heart she was just as conservative as he was.

15

During her years of study in Europe, alone and with others, Solema had examined critically and studied the complexities of Antillean society, which she wanted to help renew. Everything she found there she had weighed carefully in order to ask herself whether it should be introduced into the Antilles or not. She was convinced that innovations had to come, but also wondered if there should be a limit and where it should lie. In this way she wanted, alone and with others, to develop a completely unique Antillean vision, particularly cultural, because she was convinced that social and economic relations between people everywhere were determined by cultural causes. An in-depth psychological analysis would have revealed that in reality all she wanted was to preserve the Antilles of her youth, which despite the limited economic resources of her parents had been particularly happy, against the changes that *had* to come, and the longer she stayed away from the Antilles, the more strongly she felt attached to the

Antilles of her youth – fighting for them, even, while making plans for an Antilles of the future. Touching self-deception, in love with what it wants to change! Touching pride, which refuses to accept the Europeans as gods although they may be gods – or three-quarters gods at least. She cropped her hair, which was long, black and straight and suited the dark-brown colour of her skin like a goddess's hair, and put curls in it to be able to join in the chorus of African Americans singing: *Black is beautiful*. In her studies (she deliberately studied anthropology for three years in Belgium), she looked for things that she could present to Europeans with an: '*At least we blacks, we Antilleans, have this, which is better than what you have. This at any rate we're not going to change!*' For her, this was a question of life and death because if she found nothing, then her logical and fair-minded intellect, which despite everything she kept pure, would have to acknowledge not only the technological superiority of Europe, but also its cultural superiority...

She often had intense and sharp conflicts with her comrades in the struggle, who, for example, called the hospitality of the Antilles, which she knew and loved so well, profligacy. She spoke up for the reserve of Antilleans in social intercourse – which others regarded as an expression of an inferiority complex towards whites, and hence wanted to combat. She showed, that in parts of Africa, in East as well as West Africa, the same reserve in intercourse between people exists; a greater sense of community, which she brought into focus and defended against the pronounced individuality of the European, which according to her could lead to nothing except barbarism and exploitation, as is shown, for instance, by the history of slavery.

She became acquainted with the increasingly free American–European sexual behaviour pattern, but kept her virginity because on the Antilles the custom was that the bride's bedsheet had to show a spot of blood on the morning after the wedding night. For her, it was a symbol of her self-esteem.

She met Manchi at the town hall, when she went there to protest against an interrogation that in her view a Dutch policeman had once unjustly subjected her to. She got talking to Manchi, who noticed her interest in the traditions of the Antilles, and was bold enough to invite her to come and look at the large house on the hill which he was building practically single-handed. The walls were not yet up when she visited him the first time, but the blocks that he was making himself with a crude, iron machine were piled in large heaps and in long rows all across the site. The faith of Manchi, who was indeed making his blocks all alone, with his upper body naked and a hint of dogged stubbornness, fascinated her. She went there quite often. She talked enthusiastically to her friends about it and sometimes took them with her up Manchi's hill, while he went on with his work without stopping, to make a picnic for the evening with the drink that they brought with them. A kind of romantic moonlight party under the star-studded tropical heavens!

She had seen him sweating with the effort of mixing cement and sand (when he worked, he wore a thick canvas band around his waist, the kind she had sometimes seen her father wear), and then putting it in the machine. She asked all kinds of questions which he answered patiently. Block. Block. Block. He damped down the mortar a number of times, and later opened the machine again, which then opened on four sides like a flower, with a wet, grey, square block in the middle. Each block that he made meant a personal joy for her and if she hadn't been there for a while, the first thing she did when she returned was to count all the blocks.

She wrote to her ex-fellow-students in Europe: 'He's a perfectly ordinary man, a bailiff without much education and without much money, but if you see him working there, confident and self-assured, making his own blocks – he needs several thousand of them – when you see him getting closer and closer to finishing his own house through his own efforts, and not a small one at that, then it does something to you. At any rate I think it's marvellous and perhaps I'm a little in love with him. We should have more people like that, people who can commit themselves to something as completely as he does.' And she added in a PS: '*And just think that over there you people sometimes have to wait years to be assigned a house . . .'* Sometimes she even took schoolchildren with her to Manchi's hill, to tell them about building *one's own house* . . . Apart from that, she fell in love with the starry sky, which from Manchi's hill, where the filthy smoke of the Shell refinery did not reach, was wonderful to gaze at. She couldn't remember having observed as many stars in Europe as she could see there.

One of the times she was there, Manchi told her that he had to stop work on his house for a while, until he had saved enough to continue. The fact was, he told her, he didn't want to increase his debt with the bank and the suppliers of his materials, which was already large. Impulsively she offered to lend him just under two thousand guilders.

Stagnation, which is usual with people who build their own houses, formed a threat to her idealism, of which Manchi's house had become the symbol. In a way, his house was *her* investment too.

She had been coming to the hill for two years and they got used to each other, were fond of each other even, although she knew that Manchi differed from her in more things than he had in common with her. For example, he was a conservative member of the DP (in those days) while she on the other hand was preparing with others to found the URA, which was about to expressly oppose the traditional parties.

When he asked her to marry him, she agreed almost

without thinking. It was simply the culmination of an unreal adventure that had gone too far. Perhaps she also did it because she thought that in the long run she could make him progressive; win him over to ideals that she held dear, make him young. She had some reason to believe this as well, because in their conversations on the hill, despite his fundamentally conservative attitude, he nevertheless showed himself open and susceptible to reason. He was interested in Europe, although he couldn't hide a certain irritation when she went on too long about things which he hadn't seen and probably never would.

Immediately after their marriage, however, she realized that she had been too impulsive. Manchi became authoritarian and strict. For a start, he wanted her to stop working (which she didn't agree to), and by constantly making a fuss managed to make her leave the associations and discussion groups that she belonged to. He behaved annoyingly in the company of her friends, who took the hint and gradually avoided their house; later, he placed a more or less official ban on her receiving her male friends, at home or elsewhere. She became isolated. Her ideals became watered down. The only things that were left were playing the piano and reading and playing the organ in Wakota church.

She couldn't immediately abandon him because this would have meant too great a defeat for herself too. Then the first child arrived and divorce became even more difficult . . .

At this period she bumped into Feliciano, who was to become her second great mistake after Manchi. Not because of the fact that Manchi had caught them together, but because it emerged then how little Feliciano cared about her. (He had long since returned to the Netherlands, where he had studied, saying that he couldn't stand it in the Antilles.) With hindsight, she even suspected that the socialist baggage with which he had come to her at the time when URA was being set up was no more than a way of getting her into bed. In any case, subsequently he had accepted a well-paid job in the Netherlands with the parent company of Shell, no less. Apart from that, she now also knew that even in Holland, where she had the reputation of being 'beautiful but sexually unattainable', he had wanted to go to bed with her.

16

After Solema had gone, Janchi took a quick bath to the east of his unfinished house, throwing water over his body from a large bucket which he used specially for the purpose. He then prepared himself a simple meal on his kerosene stove from the fish he had caught the night before and the things that she had brought him.

He remained full of her. It was strange how much he had grown towards her in the short time they had known each other. How many things he had adopted from her; how much he needed her. It wasn't a casual threat that he had expressed when he had said to her that if she didn't come he would leave. Otherwise he wouldn't be able to go on living; not here at least. He might go to sea again ... In any case, she had managed in a short time to make things here matter to him very much. Perhaps he had an exaggerated love for this island (otherwise, after his mother's death he would probably have gone somewhere else, where he had fared better at times), but since he'd been back on shore people had left him fairly indifferent. He had felt resentment now and then at the way in which the rich people behaved on this island, but had never really regarded it as his affair because he himself had always easily managed to earn a living: as a carpenter, a welder, a motor mechanic, whatever was needed ...

But he also belonged to the people of Bolivar, even if only on his father's side, and did worry about it occasionally.

Except that it hadn't become much more than an unfocused sense of grievance, and in the last analysis probably only related to his father and the churlish way in which he had abandoned his mother.

So she had put things in their context. She had pointed out to him the inadequate educational system, which was at the root of unemployment on the island. She brought to his attention low wages and the constantly rising price of groceries, which always had to be imported, since agriculture on the island was at a virtual standstill. She gave him the *terminology* to think about it. After he'd eaten, he went and shaved at the small mirror above a windowsill on the right in his living-room. On that windowsill lay his domino trophies, displayed there after he had taken them out of the case under his bed and given them a polish. In the middle was a large silver cup; around it, smaller ones in gold and also a large number of medals, all on a beautiful black velvet cloth which gave a chic touch to his unfinished house.

He talked about his trophies to her and she wanted to see them, and when she'd seen them she insisted that he display them.

Women are like that, he thought to himself, smiling. They make you do one thing after another.

'No one ever comes here, Solema,' he had protested. 'Why should I display those things?'

'*I* come, don't I? You've got lots more than Manchi.'

And there they stood; trophies that he'd won all over the world playing dominoes; alone and as a member of a club. They filled the whole windowsill and were really the happy centre of his living space.

In his left hand he took the large silver cup, on which was the emblem of the company for which he had sailed for so long, and weighed it, wondering how much he'd get for it if he sold it. Real silver. He needed all the money he could get to finish his house. But no, there was too nice a story attached to it for him to get rid of it. He would prefer to get rid of all the others together. The ship on which he had been sailing was leaving Le Havre and he was standing by the railings with a number of others who had got off work. He was working as a ship's carpenter at the time. On board, a domino tournament was in progress, which had lasted for quite a long time and which he was now winning. The large silver cup was the trophy. He remembered everything very well, the ship and the crew, because he had been the only black on board. The tournament would be continued once they were on the high seas, on their way to Brazil.

Ahead of his ship to starboard there was a small, open pleasure boat on which a number of people were engaged on a quite noisy tour round the harbour. Suddenly they started making double the amount of noise, calling to the ship on which he was sailing and to shore. Then, in the calm water, disturbed only by the waves that his ship was making, he saw a small blonde head. He had the impression the person was not swimming, but was drowning; also, that the motorboat was not sailing in the direction of this person, perhaps from fear of the screws of his ship. He climbed onto the railings and dived into the water just as another member of the crew threw out a life-buoy. He grabbed the young girl, who could not see the buoy because she was going under for the umpteenth time, and swam towards it with her. The motorboat then came in their direction and he and the girl were hoisted on board. He himself applied first aid to the child, who, thank God, survived.

Often, when he thought of Solema, this helpless girl came into his thoughts. He felt that it was the same kind of situation. He remembered the rest of the episode with pleasure. How the young girl's parents were reluctant to let him go in their gratitude and wanted to take him ashore with them. He might indeed have let the ship sail on without him, if there hadn't been a domino tournament going on. So he insisted on rejoining his ship, and a police launch took him out to it. But when he was back on board (and this was the surprise for him), the whole crew came to meet him with this cup. He had won it, they said. By his courage.

Janchi wanted to refuse because it was a matter of honour that he should not simply accept the cup for which they had been playing for over a year. But they persuaded him that because of the large lead he had, he would probably have won the cup anyway.

Here he stood now. Strange how a woman can change someone's life, give a meaning to it. 'Production, Janchi, production, that's what we need. I know you don't like the foreigners here and the fact that they take all the profit they make out of the country. But at least they *produce*. You look at it in too personal a way. It's no good to us if we drive them off the island. Our own people don't grow anything, they don't make anything, they don't even have shops. We have to learn that first, before we chase the foreigners away.'

He remembered that he once had a socialist idea, which had made him say to her that there should be a better distribution of total income, to which she answered, 'Distribution is all very well, Janchi, but doesn't there have to be something to distribute?'

Take a woman like that, he now thought, still busy shaving in the small mirror in front of his trophies: she was right. Nothing could be distributed if there was nothing to distribute, could it? Take a woman like that with her wonderful brown complexion and her firm breasts, which were almost pitch black at the nipples . . . Like her lips; her eyebrows; eyes. Perhaps her dark-brown colour sometimes reminded him of the tables of *wabi* wood which he used to make to sell to the tourists in town and one of which he was now making for

64

her. She knew the tables and was pleasantly surprised to hear that he made them, when he told her about it. 'That's one of the few things that we make for ourselves, Janchi. How fantastic! Will you make one for me?' He had nodded before she had even fully expressed her wish. And yesterday afternoon he had started to keep his promise. That was in fact the hardest work: felling. Now all he would have to do would be to plane, polish and varnish the wood; dark-brown like her complexion.

'But why don't you make more than one, Janchi? I mean, so that you can have a regular income and wouldn't have to work for Shell any more?'

What a woman! The things she thought of.

'You mean a whole industry?' he asked in alarm, although, knowing her, he had realized at once that that was what she meant. 'I can't do that, darling. You see, if I make such a thing for myself and I sell it for three hundred guilders, so that the shopkeeper can sell it for five hundred, or just for someone, then it's a lot different than if you wanted to make a whole lot of the things. And you'd definitely have to have an electric saw. And a proper workshop. Anyway, a lot of money. Apart from that, I'm not a very good salesman. I haven't got the patience or the knowledge for it.'

He'd made her see that things weren't as simple as all that; she thought in theoretical terms. Most things required capital, which he definitely didn't have, but because he didn't like to put a complete damper on her idealism, he had nevertheless observed hopefully, 'Perhaps when I finish this house.' In fact, even then he had begun to think realistically of the possibility of having her with him, for ever. She made him young, energetic. In particular she made him see that he wasn't an outsider with no influence on the course of events, but that he could help to make a difference, at least to the life of his country. She took away some of his isolation, which had only increased through years of solitude, and made him involve other people in his thinking. What a woman!

'Why don't you go in for politics? Janchi? You'd certainly be able to *do* something.'

'No, Solema. I know too little. Others know too little as well, but they're not aware of it. I am.'

'But I could help you, couldn't I?'

What a woman! She was admirable, because she never admitted being down or defeated. She always came bouncing back in some way, usually better and sharper. The most remarkable thing, he thought to himself, was that he never felt his masculinity threatened by her. He was not only prepared to learn from her, he wouldn't even have minded being led by her. For that matter, who else had given him the great enthusiasm he now felt for finishing his house?

Again he looked intently at his domino trophies. He had collected them in so many different parts of the world that together they formed a kind of biography of his wanderings. He had won many of them in Portuguese territories; in the romantic Bairro Alto of Lisbon and in Bahia in Brazil, both cities in which women made love with an unbridled animal passion, except that in Bahia they were darker-skinned . . . No, he needed all his money – because with the hundred guilders a week that he earned at Shell, he would definitely not make it – he would only sell his silver and gold trophies at the last moment. Or perhaps . . . About two or three thousand guilders would get him a long way: if he took his axe and felled ten *wabi* trees he could make about ten tables in about ten weeks, if he worked on them every evening. That would definitely bring in about three thousand guilders. And if he did it in half that time? He thought of Solema, and of her skin which, because of its perfection perhaps even more than its colour, reminded him of the polished tables of *wabi* wood . . . Wait a bit, he would first drop by and see Diego the gravedigger to ask how much he would charge to help him with the bricklaying for the house. Then, instead of making tables, he could start building straight away. Then perhaps within a month he would have reached a point where she could move in with him.

Contrary to his usual habit, he put on a white shirt with long sleeves, because today he felt a need to look neat and respectable; and he chose a purple tie to go with it.

When he was ready to leave, he wondered why he still went to play dominoes at Bubu Fiel's. The game would soon be wound up, he thought, once Solema and her children had moved in with him, because then there would be a public split between himself and Manchi. He smiled at the thought, because he felt no fear at all of Manchi. On the contrary, for a long time he had been thinking of giving the guy a good hiding; to pay him back for what he was doing to Solema.

Women, he thought, feeling lucky because Solema loved him and at the same time enjoying what she had confessed at the beginning of their relationship, namely that she had liked the idea of deceiving Manchi with one of his domino friends. He laughed aloud at the humour of the situation: *if ever a man was thoroughly deceived by a woman, when he thought that he had her in his power, it was Manchi.* That meant of course that the guy would get terribly angry when the news about him and Solema got out. He took his knife and sharpened it a few times on a whetstone in the kitchen on which he also sharpened his axe. He wasn't an aggressive person, although he had the unjustified reputation of being one – just as everyone who knows how to defend himself well gets that reputation in the end – but it was his habit to be prepared for what was likely to happen. A confrontation with Manchi now lay in the order of things.

He now had to be doubly on his guard, because Manchi – as everyone knew – had a revolver. However, he didn't feel that put him at a particular disadvantage with regard to Manchi, because he could also throw his knife fast and with a sure aim.

<h1 style="text-align:center">17</h1>

The sun slowly passed its zenith. The green of the vegetation between Janchi's house and the hill of the church of Wakota looked fresh and bright: that was due to a slight shower a week before. The beginning of the afternoon was still cool.

Janchi walked towards the church with loping strides that were characteristic of his long, sinewy legs. His purple tie flapped merrily up and down in the gentle wind and the long elegant stalks of the *palu di lechi* tapped his shoulders; occasionally even, as in a friendly greeting, his face.

The land across which he was walking was soft and had a dark-brown, chocolaty colour. It was fertile land, which would not disappoint anyone who had the idea of putting a spade into it. It seemed to be no accident that it was called the Good Hope.

It was the fertility of this land which led him to site his house here, because his mother had complained about the city, where she had to buy everything. Here at least they had been able to plant some vegetables: tomatoes, *promentes*, beans and lemons. He himself also loved the soil, and even if it was a joke, he had wanted to show that not only the Chinese and the Portuguese, who at present were becoming rich on it, could make it productive. He saw the land already in bloom; lots of maize and beans; this area was perhaps best suited to those. As he walked on, he pondered on the landscape, on her and on the money he needed to finish his house. What a woman!

But he couldn't agree with her about everything. For example, she believed that Curaçaoans disliked agriculture and in fact work in general because they associated it with slavery, which had been abolished just over a hundred years ago. He thought this all very fine and learned, but in his view it wasn't true. They had what he called a lack of heart. They didn't care about the land in general and they didn't care about this country. They had no contact with it. They didn't care about it, or about the sea for that matter, or about vegetables or fruit, which they didn't eat much of either; too little, as the newspapers were writing recently. Was this all connected with slavery, this sickness? At any rate he found his compatriots a careless people, who let things take their course, and this lovelessness would prove fatal one day. They were sick and stupid, he thought: the few vegetables and fruit that they ate were not even grown by themselves, but were bought in the town from the boats of the Venezuelans which the tourists always found so picturesque but which he felt were dirty, because he hated everything that came from Venezuela. Or had Shell corrupted them? With its filthy smoke in their lungs and its wages that were earned too easily? He still knew people who spent their whole time at Shell sleeping behind some tank or other. In the past when there were even fewer checks, that was much more common.

The Dutch had always said that this land was arid and dry and that it never rained on Curaçao, and Curaçaoans echoed them in everything, and meanwhile in many places the Chinese and the Portuguese were cultivating the weirdest things successfully. They were even making money out of it. Did the Dutch deliberately want to keep this land backward and stupid? Or were the Dutch, who for so long had presented themselves as gods here, in fact as stupid as the Curaçaoans? He thought they were.

Hadn't Solema told him that Israel was also an arid and dry land, a desert, and that they still made something of it? Because Solema had brought this to his attention, it had struck him how shamelessly the Jews here had got a campaign launched to forest Israel. Give a tree for Israel, they announced over the radio and television and wherever people wanted to know, because they had money, but even they, together with the Dutch and the Curaçaoans, continued to call this island arid and dry. And this was stupid, too, because earlier they were precisely the ones in control of the slave trade, and had at least two hundred plantations on this island. *Two hundred*! It wasn't necessary to plant this island with trees: one could begin with bushes. They were all sick, he thought. Heartless and sick. But even if he tried to put everything out of his mind, he wouldn't be able, certainly not alone, to cure this three-hundred-year-old sickness, although now he had Solema he felt strong and capable of a lot, and angry enough to do a lot. But he wanted to concentrate his attention on his house, because this was at least a kind of start that he could manage best. When he had his house, Solema would come and live with him; and when she was with him, everything was possible.

Passing close by the church, he went down the hill, before him a panorama of the whole cemetery. The large mausoleums were at the far end, parallel to the Tula road. Diego Manuel was working in the middle among the ordinary graves. He wondered if Diego would accept one guilder an hour, which would mean a special price for friends and family. Then he would need at least three hundred guilders for bricklaying – that is, without cement and sand. And then he still had nothing to put in the house itself. No chairs, no refrigerator, nothing. A feeling of panic came over him and he paused on the slope, wondering whether he shouldn't ask for a loan somewhere. But where?

He continued to the cemetery wall and leant over it to call the gravedigger, who only looked up when Janchi had called his name twice. He was wearing brown trousers and a shirt, which must have once been white, half open and fastened over his belly. He had a broad-brimmed straw hat on, but was barefoot. He walked up to Janchi, wiping his hands on his trousers.

'Hi, Janchi, how are you?'

'*Entre medio*, Diego.'

After the usual introduction, he explained things to Diego. Diego wanted two guilders. 'And that's a good price, Janchi,' he said. 'Other people ask two-fifty.'

Janchi said he couldn't pay that.

Diego thought for a moment and asked: 'Are you getting married, wanting to finish your house so suddenly?'

'Yes.'

'Oh, that's a different matter. I almost understand you. But are you seriously going to get married, Janchi, and who to, then?' Diego burst out laughing while he scratched his half-bare chest.

'I don't even know who yet,' said Janchi, also laughing, 'but I want to.'

'Yes,' said Diego, 'you can't stay alone for ever, although it may be nicer alone. You enjoy your life more. And that's the only thing a man has' – he pointed to the graves with a broad sweep of his hand – 'before he finishes up here.'

Janchi tried a different tack. 'Let's say I give you three hundred guilders and you do all the bricklaying in the house?'

'Inside and out?' asked Diego in astonishment. 'You want me to do all the bricklaying for your house inside and out for three hundred guilders, Janchi, that big house of yours?'

Janchi shrugged his shoulders. 'You just see where you can get that kind of money.'

'You're right.' In fact, Diego was quite inclined to accept the deal there and then, but hesitated because he had the feeling he had already been swindled that morning by Nora, to whom he had had to pay the abnormally high price of ten guilders to screw her for half an hour, there behind the vault of the first priest of the parish. Rather than be taken for a ride a second time, he made a counter-proposal: 'What do you say to one-fifty, Janchi?' he asked, considering that in time, when he got to the point of being able to build his own house, he probably wouldn't appeal to Janchi in vain.

'Okay.'

'When were you thinking of beginning?'

A feeling of resentment came over Janchi. In his enthusiasm he had negotiated with Diego as though the latter could begin the following day, but he couldn't. He would have to pay Diego by the hour in cash when the latter chose to work. For that he would first need to save for at least two weeks.

'I'll let you know,' he said quickly, 'I'm not quite ready yet.'

'Okay,' said Diego, 'but don't wait too long because prices go up every day on this damn island.'

They shook hands over the wall of the cemetery and Janchi continued on his way to Bubu Fiel's house.

18

When Manchi took his place at the dining-table in his great house to eat his *sòpi di mondongo*, he felt very tense, as he always did when he sat at table at home. At that moment he couldn't help reliving the cruel moment when he had caught Solema with Feliciano. Certainly the greatest torture was for Solema, who every time they sat down to eat had to produce a five-guilder note and put it next to Manchi's plate on the table. It was the means by which he kept her in control; he felt he had to protect himself from further adulterous behaviour on her part. But it had been going on for four years and Manchi thought it was one of the things that made him tense. When would he stop it? In principle, never! It was a punishment for life.

Nevertheless, he had been happy when a few weeks before he'd been able to reveal some of his great secret disguised in other characters. The triumph he had achieved with his story had relieved something of the tension in which he lived; so much so that it became more and more tempting for him to strip away all the masks from the story and put himself in the place where, for his domino friends, he had put a Dutch judge. This afternoon, for example. While he waited at table for Solema to bring his food, he weighed the risks attached to telling his story in full. Certainly, after that he would probably not have to do anything else in his life to enter the history of Wakota and the island as a famous man. It would give him more prestige than having the most beautiful house in Wakota. But – and that was the point – what would be the effect on Solema? Would she still stay with him if he exposed her to publicity and scandal? He didn't think so. He played thoughtfully with his cutlery. In fact, he was certain she would leave him if he did that. So in some sense he would suffer a defeat after all. The point was that he had devised a way of ensuring that she didn't commit adultery again and therefore stayed with him.

An intellectual approach was suitable for a woman who had studied as she had, and not a thorough good hiding as Fiel had suggested. If she went away, there was no longer any point to it.

Having decided after all not to tell the story openly at the domino table, he revelled in the dramatic way in which he had settled his affairs at the time. Oh, he need only change a few details and they would have the story as it had actually happened to him. Just substitute himself for the judge, whom he had invented. But he warned himself not to do this even in thought, because it might lead to his making a mistake in

73

the future. The friends might want to return to the story at some point, and it was vital that he should dish it up precisely as he had told it *then*. Come to that, with the judge in the main role he had almost slipped up once.

19

That time he'd leapt out of his chair. 'You here, Janchi Pau,' he'd said to Janchi who was sitting on his right, 'are my –' Damn, at this point, in his enthusiasm, he had almost blurted it out. He was going to say: *You here are my wife Solema*. But he managed to keep himself in check: 'You here are the judge's wife,' he'd said, patting Janchi on the shoulder. The latter had looked at him in astonishment. 'Just for a moment,' he said, slightly alarmed, because he knew that Janchi didn't like people fooling around with his masculinity. Nor did any of them, in fact. 'Can you *imagine* something for a moment?' he had added. 'You're not stupid enough to think I take you for a woman? Come now!'

Janchi had shrugged his shoulders and Manchi was able to continue the performance of his drama.

'And you, Bubu Fiel my friend, you are the man my wife is carrying on with. That is, if you don't mind me being the judge for a moment and Janchi here my wife. Okay?'

'Go on,' Bubu had growled. 'What matters is your story and not who is who.'

'But I'd rather you didn't call me a woman,' said Janchi, 'Pick someone else.'

'Okay,' said Manchi. 'You, Chamon here, are the woman. Is that okay?'

Chamon Nicolas shrugged his shoulders. 'It's the *point* interests me,' he said, 'not who's who, as Bubu here says.' He looked at the latter for agreement, which he received with a nod of the head.

'Don't forget,' said Manchi to Bubu, 'don't forget that that other man is *also* a lawyer.'

'Doesn't interest me,' said Bubu, 'I'm not a Dutchman and I'm certainly not a judge, but if it makes you happy, fine. I really ought to put one of those black dresses on for it, oughtn't I?'

'Yes,' said Chamon Nicolas – who had had dealings with the law. 'A black dress and a white thing round your neck.'

'Okay,' growled Bubu again, 'I'm the other man who is a judge and Chamon Nicolas is your wife.' Chamon Nicolas laughed out loud. He didn't mind it very much. As a Windward Islander he had been able to adjust to Curaçaoans so well that they could say anything they liked.

Manchi had continued: 'Well, one evening I'm passing a field with cows grazing in it and I find you, Bubu Fiel here, lying with my wife.'

'*Well*,' said Bubu Fiel. 'Well I never.'

'Brrh,' said Chamon Nicolas, 'it's *damn cold* in Holland. All the Dutch leave Holland because it's *damn cold* there, isn't that so, Janchi?' Janchi nodded.

'And they come here,' said Chamon Nicolas in a reflective tone, 'to the Prinsessendorp, Koninginnedorp, Julianadorp . . .'

'It was in the summer,' said Manchi imperturbably. 'Everyone except an ignorant person like you, Chamon, knows that it can be just as warm there as here in the summer and even *warmer*. The whole of Europe is just as warm in the summer as here, isn't that so, Janchi? You can confirm that because you've seen it all for yourself.'

'It's usually warm in the summer in Europe,' said Janchi, 'but it can also be cold.'

'It was a *warm* summer,' said Manchi, unmoved.

'None of this matters,' said Bubu, who already found the story too gripping to keep interrupting it. 'Let Manchi go on with his story.' But he couldn't help adding himself, 'Warm or cold summer, that woman's lying there in the field with her legs wide open under me.' He looked at everyone with a triumphant laugh on his face. 'Isn't that so, Manchi?' Manchi nodded brusquely.

'So I was busy humping her,' asked Bubu in a smug tone, though rather superfluously.

Again Manchi nodded.

'It *stands to reason* if you're lying on top of her,' said Chamon Nicolas laughing.

'Well,' said Bubu Fiel, 'just get on with your story. Otherwise I'll come before you finish.'

However, Manchi took his time to build up suspense. Finally he said: 'You, Bubu Fiel, you may be big and strong' – he looked at Bubu Fiel with a superior smile – 'But you can't do a thing to me.'

'Of course not,' said Chamon Nicolas again, who seemed to be able to picture the whole thing. 'Of course not, if he's there on the ground on his belly on top of your wife, of course not.' Manchi ignored the laughter of Bubu and Chamon and stated calmly, 'Because I've got a revolver aimed at you.'

The laughter suddenly died away completely and he said: 'Apart from that, you're taken by surprise. You're surprised because you've been caught, and because you're frightened to death that you're actually going to get a bullet through the head.' He had, in order to dramatize the story even more, bent over the domino table to pretend (with his index finger) that he was pointing a revolver at Bubu's chest.

The latter raised his hands. 'Hm, that's true. You immediately stop humping in a case like that.'

'But I don't shoot you,' said Manchi, reassuringly. So Bubu Fiel dropped his hands and Manchi sat back again. 'I'm a judge and I know better. I don't shoot anyone, because then I'll go to jail.' As he said this, he looked at them all calmly one by one, to bring out the cunning of the judge in question. 'Can you three *understand* that?'

Damn, he thought now, as he watched Solema fill a deep plate with *sòpi di mondongo* for him, I sold myself short. Those chumps now admire this *imaginary* judge too much. He wanted to think about this fact, but noticed that Solema had sat down opposite him without as usual first putting the five-guilder note, which was as necessary as his cutlery, next to him on the table. She immediately began eating her *sòpi di mondongo*. He grabbed the edge of the table with both hands and looked at her pointedly, but she went on eating as though nothing special had happened till she noticed that Manchi was staring at her.

'Your food's getting cold,' she said automatically. Her thoughts were so much with Janchi that she'd completely forgotten the usual ritual.

But it was her look of innocence that was too much for Manchi. He banged both fists hard on the table. The soup in the plate overflowed and the soup tureen toppled over; yellow pieces of fragrant maize and cubes of sticky tripe poured over the white tablecloth. The pungent smell of the splendid dish penetrated the whole house.

'Why are you doing *that*?' said Solema remarkably calmly, paying less attention to him than to the numerous stains on her frock. By way of reply he banged the flat of his hand on the table. Not hard this time, but rather the way that judges do with their little gavels when they call an accused or a lawyer or the public in the court to order. He himself was also covered in hot soup.

'Get the money!' he said sternly. 'Whore!'

'I am *not* a whore, Manchi,' she said pushing her chair back in order to avoid a stream of soup which was coming towards her over the table.

'Oh no?' he said. 'Oh no?'

77

'No!'

'If you start talking back to me, I shall make it public one of these days. Then we'll see if they think you're a whore or not.' She got up and folded up the tablecloth in order to stop any more of the spilled soup from pouring onto the floor. An almost happy smile appeared on his face when he said, 'I could do it this afternoon. I could begin this afternoon by explaining to my . . .' – he hesitated for an instant because the word had not come that naturally recently – 'domino friends, who of course all respect you as a teacher, the kind of woman you really are. The kind of adulterous woman,' he added viciously. He hoped again that one day it would be possible to tell this story openly to his friends, with himself as the main character instead of the imaginary judge. The triumph that he experienced would outweigh the fact that everyone would know that he had been deceived by his wife and perhaps even the fact that she would probably leave him. But after that he would have no more power over her, as he had now. And that mattered a lot to him. For the moment, he opted for power, and said in an almost friendly way, 'If you just go and get it, I needn't tell them anything. No one need know and these things need not happen.' He therefore pointed with feigned displeasure at the spilled soup. 'We can't have this sort of thing,' he said in a sickly sweet tone.

She was now holding the two plates, because she had to clear up in order to lay the table again. An impulse to hurl them at his head, pack her things and leave, welled up from deep inside her. But she stood there for a few moments, her eyes shut tight with rage and humiliation, and suddenly burst into tears and ran to the kitchen sobbing with the plates.

'Why are you crying?' he added spitefully as he followed her to clean up too. 'You weren't crying when you were lying under that little shit, were you? Or only with pleasure, whore that you are!'

'Say what you like, I don't care any more!' She thought he would hit her, but he did not. She went on clearing the table and relaying it. He looked at her questioningly as she again served him his *sòpi di mondongo*. 'Are you going to do it or not?'

He was now sitting exactly as before, holding the table with both hands and leaning back a little.

Then she knew that she didn't yet have the necessary courage to leave him. But perhaps that was *too* much courage, and amounted to suicide. Besides, her children would suffer because of it. In any case she went back to the bedroom with tears in her eyes, wishing she had the courage to fetch his revolver and shoot him instead of handing him the five guilders. But murder was not in her nature and she perhaps was also thinking of Janchi and her children. So she simply took the five-guilder note out of the special box in the bedroom cupboard; she came back with it and put it next to him on the table.

'Put something on top of it,' he said, 'so it doesn't blow away.' He made a deliberate habit of touching the money as little as possible.

When she put the salt cellar on top of it, he gave her a broad smile, which made the golden caps of his teeth gleam more than before. He took a spoonful of his *sòpi di mondongo* as if nothing were wrong, 'Mm, mm, excellent soup. You may be worth *ten* guilders now.'

She sat down and dished herself up a new plate too. She wanted to force herself to eat normally to deprive him of the pleasure of seeing how much he hurt her. But he seemed more fiendish than usual today. 'It's best to bear your punishment calmly and patiently, that's always the best thing,' he said.

When she did not react he lifted his head from the plate and said, 'You know, Solema, I hope you'll agree with me that you're a whore. The difference between you and the

79

women in Campo Alegre is just that everyone knows about them, and I'm the only one who knows about you. And that' – he shook his spoon in her direction as a warning – 'depends on you. The moment you no longer want it to be that way, and no longer do what I say, everyone will know. Then you'll be just an ordinary whore like the women in Campo Alegre and no longer a special whore like now . . . Yes, yes,' he said. 'Now you're a *special* whore.'

At that she could stand it no longer. She got up and left him alone. While he went on eating he glanced at the five-guilder note in amusement now and then, savouring the triumph of his wonderful story:

' "Are you married to her? Are you the lawful spouse of this woman?" I'm asking you, Bubu Fiel. You may understand that I am playing a game with you, but you don't know exactly what. So you're frightened of answering because you're frightened of giving the wrong answer. In fact, of course, you can only answer that the woman is not your wife. But you also know what that means, namely that *in that case you shouldn't be lying with her in a field*. You know what that means.'

'So I know I'll be putting myself in the shit if I say no,' said Bubu, truly sorry, because he completely identified with the role that Manchi had given him, which had such pleasant aspects to it.

'Right. So I suggest that he passes his own sentence. He doesn't want to, of course, and therefore he simply goes on staring at me without saying anything, so that I simply push a revolver against his nose. Then he really gets frightened.'

Chamon Nicolas, who was staring at him in delighted suspense, asked in a childlike voice, 'And what then, Manchi?'

'The judge of course answered no.'

'Because he was frightened that otherwise you would shoot him dead,' said Chamon, nodding understandingly.

'Exactly, that's what that judge thought.'

'You mean *I*,' said Bubu Fiel, who wanted to play the role of the judge consistently.

'Yes, I mean you, Bubu Fiel, you say no. Then I, to go on making it difficult for you a little longer, say, "Did you have my permission to be with her here?"'

'That's fantastic!' exclaimed Chamon. '*Fantastic*! Did that judge *really* do that?'

He nodded seriously and went on: ' "No," you answer, Bubu, in a squeaky little voice. Whereupon I say, "Don't you know just as well as I do, my dear colleague, that you are taking *illegal* possession of my property?" '

'What's *illegal*?' asked Chamon.

'It's a technical term,' said Manchi, 'which means that someone does something against the law.'

'Aha.'

'What do *I* say?' asked Bubu Fiel.

'You agree. What else can you do? You mustn't forget that they're both judges.'

'You and I, that is.'

'Yes, you and I are both judges, so you understand exactly what I'm getting at. So I say, "You will have to compensate me in some way or other." '

'A good idea,' said Bubu Fiel, 'an *excellent* idea. Don't you agree, friend Janchi? You've said nothing the whole time. Don't you think it's brilliant, what the judge here is doing?'

'Yes,' said Janchi, 'but . . .'

'Wait,' said Chamon Nicolas, completely fascinated, 'first let Manchi go on with the story.'

Janchi had wanted to ask what the woman in the story was doing all this time, but he couldn't ask anything and Manchi couldn't go on with the story because at that moment

Nora appeared with the four glasses of rum which she regularly brought the men.

When she had gone, he continued, 'I say to my colleague Fiel here that in the first place I'm taking back my property.' Here again he had made a slight slip, by tapping Janchi instead of Chamon. Janchi, who had been listening in silence the whole time said in annoyance, 'I told you I'm *not* a woman, Manchi.'

Chamon Nicolas said in a calming voice, 'Oh, Pau, it's just for the story.'

'I know,' said Janchi stubbornly, 'but we agreed that you would be her, not me.' He began really to dislike the gloating way Manchi was spinning out the story and also suspected him of telling all kinds of lies.

'But then you must also compensate me for the use,' Manchi continued. 'Do you three understand what I'm getting at?' He had waited until the others, Janchi included, had shaken their heads and said no. Then he had come out with his trump card: 'I say to you, Bubu Fiel here, that you've got to pay sales tax for the use of my wife!'

'So what was your wife doing the whole time?' Janchi asked.

'Oh, she was trying to get dressed a bit. And crying, of course . . .' He shot Janchi a rather piercing look as he said this, but when the latter indicated his satisfaction with a nod of the head, he continued. ' "Hire charge," I say then.' He now turned particularly to Janchi. 'My wife starts crying her eyes out because she of course doesn't know where to put herself, she's so ashamed. That's the point, of course: *I have to do something with her that ensures she is never unfaithful to me again in her life.* So in fact it's not the judge who matters, no, it's *my wife*. But wait, I'll come back to that in a moment. In any case I had a real stroke of luck, because what happens? This judge didn't have a cent on him! Not even a cheque book which

82

judges and suchlike – as you know, or perhaps you don't – normally have on them. Nothing, or *practically* nothing. I'll come back to that in a second.'

'Make it quick,' said Janchi Pau at that moment, 'make it quick. After all, we've got to continue the game.'

'Oh,' said Chamon, 'patience, friend Janchi. Manchi is telling the story beautifully. I can see it all so clearly. I expect you can too, can't you, Bubu?'

Bubu nodded, smiling. 'I can *feel* it,' he said to Chamon.

'As you like,' said Janchi, 'but this way there won't be any time left to play . . .'

'For every time you've been with her,' Manchi went on quickly, annoyed that Janchi should interrupt him now, just as he had got to the point, 'you will give me five guilders. That's the price of a whore on this island, for each time.'

'You mean in Holland,' said Chamon calmly. 'Whores cost more here these days. The other day one asked me for sixty guilders. She was a pretty thing, but *sixty* guilders!'

That was a bad mistake, thought Manchi, looking back on it, but he was relieved that the observation hadn't come from Janchi Pau. Anyway, he had of course tried to correct himself. 'That's what happens, when you try to tell a story in such a way that everyone can imagine things vividly: you automatically relate everything to yourself. This judge said, of course, that in *Holland* the price of a whore is five guilders, but this judge added that five guilders is the price of a *cheap* whore, that's the point.'

'That's what I thought,' said Chamon, 'you can sometimes get cheap whores for two-fifty.' And he went on philosophizing, completely out of character, 'If a woman's in great need she'll screw for anything.'

'Even for a lift,' laughed Bubu Fiel.

'*Do you get the point*?' asked Manchi. 'This judge wanted to make clear to his wife that she wasn't just a whore to him, but

83

a cheap whore into the bargain. That's an important difference, because an expensive whore you can still have respect for, isn't that so? But a filthy, dirty, *cheap* whore that you can have for a song, or even for a lift, as Bubu Fiel here says, that's simply someone you can no longer have the slightest respect for.'

'If that judge of yours had been a man,' said Janchi, leaning forward, 'I mean that judge of yours who was caught in the act, then he would have let himself be shot rather than subject himself to this, don't you think?' He looked at Bubu and Chamon Nicolas expectantly. '*I* would in any case,' raising his voice when the others did not immediately agree with him. '*I* would have said to you, "Either shoot or let me go. One or the other".'

'Come now,' said Bubu Fiel, defending himself or his role. 'No one wants to die just like that.'

'That's right,' said Chamon thoughtfully, 'on the contrary, everyone wants to live for as long as possible.'

'I would have done it,' said Janchi with determination. 'And if he hadn't shot, then *I* would have given him a damn good hiding. Christ,' he added, 'what a hiding I would have given that guy!'

Chamon Nicolas also began to see the humour of that possibility and shook with laughter.

Janchi Pau then said thoughtfully: 'What's more, that judge wouldn't have shot, I think. You either do something like that *at once*, or you don't do it.'

'You can't know that, friend Janchi,' said Bubu.

'Sure I can, the moment you stop to think, you don't kill another human being, unless you're a real murderer.'

Chamon Nicolas agreed and began to recall conflict situations that he had experienced or of which he'd heard in order to prove his partner's point. In the end he asked Manchi, who had been waiting expectantly, what he himself thought.

After all, the judge had told *him* the story.

'Of course I can't be *certain*,' said the latter, 'but I think he would have done it. At any rate, the judge who told me the story is a determined person. As judges usually are,' he added portentously. 'If he decides to do something, then he's likely to do it. But I'll ask him to be certain . . .'

'Good,' said Bubu, 'but we can assume in any case that he, the judge who'd been caught, believed, that you, the other judge, would shoot me, isn't that so? And in that case, of course, the situation remains the same.'

'Yes,' said Manchi, looking triumphantly at Janchi. 'As I said, when I have a chance I'll ask the judge in question for all the details, but the situation remains the same, of course, if we accept what Fiel says, isn't that so, Janchi?'

Chamon ventured to observe rather accusingly to his partner, now he was not in a very strong position, 'Besides, Janchi, how can you first take his wife away from him, and then give him a good hiding as well! That's not *right*!' He gave a thundering laugh.

Bubu Fiel also said, laughing, 'That really is just too crazy, friend Janchi. But of course, *you're* capable of anything.' He leant straight across the table and gave Janchi a friendly slap on the shoulder.

'You're right,' said Janchi. 'Perhaps that's going too far. But he mustn't start shouting his mouth off and humiliating me too much. After all' – he looked at Manchi as he said this – 'after all, the woman is lying with me, with the judge, in that field of her own free will, as you say. I mean, she wasn't assaulted or anything. So the judge doesn't have to let himself be humiliated. At least, that's how I see it.'

'You're right,' said Manchi, with surprising magnanimity. 'I'm saying already, whatever I do, whatever this judge does with the other guy, is ultimately done in order to get at the *woman*, do you understand?'

'No one wants to die just like that,' repeated Bubu, completely out of the context of the story. 'Come on, Manchi. Go on with the story.'

'I look at that judge, or rather' – he found this more dramatic at this point in his story – 'the two judges look at each other. The husband-judge says, "You can give some more if you like. I said that five guilders is the price of a *cheap* whore, but as for you she's a very *expensive* whore, from whom you've had great enjoyment, then of course you'll give a lot more. You see. I leave it entirely up to you what she is." '

Bubu laughed.

Manchi then bent forward slightly. 'The judge leant against the tree and made the other guy hunt through his pockets. He hunted and hunted but couldn't find anything.' He had scarcely been able to hide the enjoyment he had actually felt when he had made Feliciano turn out his pockets.

'I've *got* them. I've *got* them,' he said, almost shouting at his domino friends. 'You, Bubu Fiel, of course start shaking. You're not shaking from fear of my revolver now – anyway, I'm only pointing it vaguely in your direction – you're trembling because you've taken out your wallet and emptied it in front of me and haven't found anything. And you've been through almost all your pockets and turned them out for me, and you haven't found anything! And what conclusion must I draw, if you really find *nothing*? That my wife here is the cheapest whore you've ever met in your life; a whore you can screw for a lift, as Bubu here just said. Do you understand? And there's probably not one man on earth who can do that, who can say to a woman who's been to university like my wife, that he doesn't think she's worth anything, thinks she's a cheap whore, directly after he's had her – while he's still wet from her, so to speak. You see, if you don't find anything, you know, not even one cent, then it's not me who's destroying her and hence punishing her for her adultery, *but you yourself*, the one with whom she's committed the adultery! If you don't find anything, surely that must mean you think she's worthless?! That's all there is to it! *Worthless*. And a woman will never forget this; the man she's been with calls her worthless. Through no fault of his own, of course, but that doesn't matter!'

'A difficult case,' said Bubu Fiel.

'Of course!' said Manchi, slightly less excitedly. 'A difficult case, even if that judge has lots of money. Because supposing he has money, how much can he offer me? A thousand guilders? Two thousand guilders? A million? Do you see, the problem is that *a woman becomes a whore the moment you try to express her value in money terms*! Do you see? That was the shrewdness of this husband-judge: he acted as if nothing special was happening; a simple legal dispute that could be settled with money. So the judge who's been caught red-handed is in trouble, whatever happens: he has to make his mistress a whore, whatever happens. A cheap whore if he offers nothing or little, an expensive whore if he offers a great deal. But in either case, a whore! He automatically proves the proposition that a woman who commits adultery is a whore. It's not simply something that the deceived judge says in a rage, but something which is decided by the lover himself. So a woman like that knows that she's a whore if she commits adultery and won't do it in future! Certainly not if she's constantly reminded of the situation and doesn't really have a whore's nature.'

This was in fact the end of the story, or at least the point had been made that he wanted to make, because the issue was the best attitude for a man to take who is deceived by his wife. Consequently he said nothing for a while, giving the others the opportunity to think and ask questions. When none came, because his friends – particularly Bubu and

Chamon – were so full of admiration that they didn't know what to think, he stressed the point that for him was the most important one. 'So the lover himself makes his mistress a whore! In that way it's not the husband who's deceived as people think, but the other two, the man because he makes a whore of her, the wife because she's made into a whore by him.'

'And he's simply laughing at the two of them,' said Chamon Nicolas.

'Exactly!' said Manchi, completely relaxed and at his ease.

As an afterthought, Chamon Nicolas said, 'And of course the chap can't put a high value on the wife, because if he does that, he'll immediately be penniless. Suppose he were to say he thought the woman was worth a million guilders. Ow, ow, ow, then he'd really be in a fix.'

'You see exactly how the land lies, Chamon.'

'Well,' said Bubu, curious as to how his role continued, 'and what then?'

'Well, I make it easy for them,' said Manchi nonchalantly. 'And when the chap has been through all his pockets and he's completely in despair that he'll find anything, he remembers his breast pocket, puts his fingers in and finds . . . *five* guilders.'

'It was dangerous to let him feel in his pockets like that,' said Janchi, who after all was a little overwhelmed by the details of Manchi's story.

'Maybe,' said Manchi magnanimously. Because he now felt so sure of his triumph, he no longer considered it necessary to justify everything. 'Maybe . . .'

'And what next?' It was now Janchi who asked in suspense for the denouement.

'Well,' said Manchi amiably. 'Bubu here holds the crumpled note guiltily in his hand. "Is that all?" I say. "What a coincidence! Exactly the price of a cheap whore!" "Do you *really* want money?" you ask me and I say gruffly, "I thought that the matter was settled! You do know, don't you, that you owe me compensation if you use my property?" You shrug your shoulders in defeat. My wife bursts into sobs. (So she's got my meaning!) She also wants to go on getting dressed and wants me to let her and her lover go, whereupon I turn my revolver on her. "Whore!" I say. "How can you imagine that I'm going to let this chap go off without paying?" After that, I ignore her for a while. "How many times did you have her?" I ask him.'

Bubu coughed meaningfully. Chamon Nicolas was screaming with laughter. And Janchi joined in too.

'You say, Bubu Fiel, "I haven't got any more. This is all." I say, "You mean that it doesn't matter how many times you've had her because you can still only pay for one?! Do you mean that?" You say nothing. I say to you, "You really do think my wife's a damn worthless whore! You should be ashamed!" Then I tell my wife to take the five guilders from you. And believe it or not, the judge told me that that seemed to be the most difficult thing of all. His wife simply refused for a long time to take that money, and he thought he would have to wound her with a shot before she would do it.'

'Women are sometimes more courageous than men,' said Janchi, suddenly serious again.

'Well, finally she took it, because I said that if she didn't, both of them and I – I mean, the judge – would have to stay in that field all night. Both of them were practically naked, of course. That settled it. I took the money from her. "Now we can go, my property has been paid for."'

Chamon Nicolas had got up. He first walked around the table in circles laughing, bent double, and when he wasn't able to do that any more, he stood and leant against the wall of Bubu's house to laugh and finally came back to the domino

89

table to laugh, with his head on his arms, shaking as if he were crying.

Bubu Fiel also got up. He had first leant against his house with his long arms, then he had embraced Manchi from behind, laughing, then he had banged his fist on the domino table with laughter, and then he had finally gone to the bath shed, because he was pissing himself laughing.

Janchi had said he thought it was a damn good story, but his reaction wasn't overwhelming. He stayed sitting, playing thoughtfully with the domino pieces, as though he were expecting the solution to a great problem.

The overwhelming laughter of the men caused Nora to appear to the east of the house with some of the children. She did not dare ask why the men were having such a whale of a time, because she suspected that it would relate to parts of women's bodies, and that he wouldn't tell her anything anyway, but when their laughter simply didn't stop, their mirth was infectious, and she joined in. Even more when she saw Bubu coming out of the bath shed in a soaking wet pair of trousers, because then she had a concrete reason to laugh. She pounded against the wall of the house with her fist, in laughter, and held her belly with laughter and she pointed to Bubu's fly and the children laughed together in a rather embarrassed way while they ran around the table looking for the real reason for so much laughter. The youngest climbed onto Fiel's empty chair and put an arm round Nora's neck to kiss her and laugh cheek to cheek. Nora picked her up play-fully, and because there was such happy laughter and she had no special cares that day – she always had some worries – she went inside with her youngest daughter on her arm to get rum for the men and so increase the atmosphere of enjoyment and happiness which prevailed so tangibly for her there to the east of the house. When she came back she immediately regretted it, because the men stopped laughing in order to drink; in the case of Chamon and Bubu, however, the tears still ran freely into the glass of rum that they knocked back.

20

The reality that Manchi would have liked to reveal, now he had told the story after all, was this: Feliciano had wanted to go, but he had prevented him. Just with his hands, he hadn't even drawn his revolver! Then he'd sat on a stone, and while they sat in front of the car and in front of him, he had given them a thorough lecture. He had made the young lawyer ridiculous by asking him simple questions about buying and selling, the hiring of things and the *illegal* use of the property of a *third party*. He had scarcely been able to restrain his laughter when it turned out that the chap had only five guilders on him. His wife had cried and they both thought that he was going to murder them. Particularly his wife, who knew that he might have his revolver with him. But why should he really do something like that?

'And what happened afterwards?' asked Chamon Nicolas, when he had finished laughing.

'Every day,' he'd said, 'when they sit down to eat, whether it's in the morning, the afternoon or the evening, the judge's wife produces the five-guilder note. Do you understand? Just as in the Catholic church they light a little red light because they believe that Christ is in the tabernacle. That's why she has to be reminded that she has been a whore. Do you understand?'

'Every time?' Chamon Nicolas asked with some astonishment.

'Every time!'

'A woman like that will commit suicide one day, if she doesn't leave that husband,' Chamon Nicolas had observed wisely, and Bubu Fiel had nodded in agreement.

'She won't go!' said Manchi with conviction. 'Because she's frightened of the scandal. You know in those high circles they do all kinds of things, but nothing must leak out . . .'

Chamon Nicolas got up and patted him on the shoulder, and he was so happy with the success that he didn't even register this unusual behaviour towards him as overfamiliar.

'I've always thought judges were a cruel bunch,' said Chamon Nicolas, thinking of his sentence, 'but this takes the biscuit!'

It was clear that all the stories ever told at this or other domino tables paled beside this tale of the brilliant judge.

'A real judge,' Chamon Nicolas kept repeating. 'A real bastard of a judge. Ha, ha, ha!'

'Those people don't study so hard for nothing,' Bubu Fiel suddenly observed thoughtfully. 'Not for nothing. They know how to settle their affairs. Nora here,' he said, 'thinks that Ostrik should study to become a doctor, but I think that a judge would be better. There's nothing better than having someone who's in the law.'

Chamon Nicolas agreed.

Manchi had then sat watching Janchi Pau from the side for a little while, because he was astonished at his generally lukewarm reaction. 'What do you think?' he asked directly.

'In my opinion, a woman has to be very sensitive for something like that to make an impression on her. Most women will probably dismiss it, tell themselves, "I'm not a whore", and ignore something like that. And simply go on whoring.'

'Or she'll spend the money,' said Chamon Nicolas cheerfully.

'Exactly,' added Manchi, without responding to Chamon's observation.

'That's what I'm saying: the wife of the judge is a woman who's been to college, someone of the calibre of Solema.'

And then suddenly there was silence. They all respected Manchi's wife and found it rather sacrilegious simply to mention her in connection with such an affair and such a woman.

Was that when Janchi started suspecting? In any case he said, 'Exactly! *That's* what I thought.'

'Of course, of course,' Manchi had said. 'It's like I'm telling you: an educated, sensitive woman, who nobody thinks would commit adultery. A splendid woman to look at, it's true, but very reserved. Really, a woman like my wife. I know her. Yes, a *Dutch* woman, of course, very moral-looking.'

21

When Janchi came through the gates of Fiel's yard, Nora was standing in the front doorway of her house looking rather absent-mindedly at the road. He said hello to her in a friendly way, but briefly, as was his custom with people who meant nothing to him and who he did not want to mean anything to him. Nora returned his greeting, but more cursorily than usual, because she was concentrating on watching out for Chamon Nicolas, whom she must try to get hold of the moment he came through the gate. Janchi went on through to the domino table and sat on the chair against the wall. It was Bubu's place, but until the game began he wanted to sit there, because then he could look directly at Solema's house. He hoped she would come out onto the porch. Because the branches of the tamarind tree got in his way, due to the position in which Nora had placed the table, he moved the table and the chairs a little to the south, so that they were almost at the corner of the house. Then he slid open the box of dominoes and let them clatter onto the table.

22

The pack of dominoes with which the men played at Bubu Fiel's was standard for the Antilles, as was the way they played. It had twenty-eight pieces, which were divided into two halves. Both were mostly black with white eyes. On each half, or each section, the pieces had eyes, varying from none to six. Seven pieces were doubles, so there was the double blank, double one, double two, etc., up to the double six.

The game apparently consists of nothing but laying the pieces next to each other in two directions, mostly beginning with the double six. After every game the pieces are turned over and mixed together, or shuffled by one of the partners who have won the game. When he has finished, the person shuffling is supposed to wait until all the others have picked up their seven pieces before he picks up his. If one makes the first choice immediately after a shuffle, it is impolite because it suggests greediness and is also suspicious. In order to decide who is to shuffle first, each player takes an arbitrary piece turned over on the table, and the one who has the highest number shuffles.

Double pieces are always laid crossways in the Antilles, at least among men. Children and women do such strange things with dominoes (children also build castles and such like with them) that a domino player immediately goes and sits somewhere else if children or women are playing with dominoes.

Dominoes, then, is a completely 'unemancipated' game in the Antilles. Because it is a man's game, the pieces are frequently slammed down hard on the table. No, that's why it's probably a man's game. The odd thing is that everyone is usually telling someone else that he mustn't slam the dominoes down so hard. The same as in politics: one person reproaches the other with something that he himself constantly does. But that's why politics is still a man's game too.

So you open with the double six, but every domino is in principle suitable for opening. When someone has no more dominoes in his hand which fit the ends of the game, he passes. The first person to play all his pieces, or dominoes, wins.

Sometimes the game is 'blocked', which means that the dominoes which the players have in their hands can't fit what's on the table. In that case, the person with the lowest number of eyes wins. If the winner's domino fits both ends of the game, he makes *changá*, double play. When one can no longer play a double piece, the domino is said to be 'dead'. So a person left with a dead double domino always loses, unless he's lucky and the game is blocked, because then with the dead eyes of his double domino he may perhaps win anyway. Especially if that piece is the dead double blank. In that case, the loser really does take all.

Every game won counts as one point. On reaching ten points, one side gives the other, if they have not scored five points, a pair of shoes; at least if people aren't playing for something else (for example, money or drink), but purely for pleasure as they say.

Shoes occupy a special place in the social history of the Antilles. For example, slaves did not generally wear shoes; so that not having these attributes, more than not having any other item of clothing, had become the symbol of poverty on these islands; officially until shortly before the Second World War. In those days, for example, the rule still applied that the barefoot were allowed to cross the Emma Bridge, which links the two halves of Willemstad harbour, free, while those in shoes had to pay two cents.

The poor, who at that time had shoes, developed the crafty habit of taking their shoes off at the start of the bridge, and only putting them on again on the other side.

Class consciousness and even class struggle, then, clearly play a part in the game of dominoes; in the paradox that precisely those who are defeated receive something from the others. In that way, the shoe-givers fill the shoes of the great businessman-philanthropist, or of the rich widow or doctor's wife, who spend their free afternoons distributing clothes. For these people, giving is mainly a status symbol.

With five points, one can escape the fate of receiving. One of the most exciting moments in dominoes is consequently the moment when one pair is on four and the other on nine points. Because things can go one way or the other. At that moment, if they play with signs, or 'coding', which is quite normal in some of the numerous clubs, the players become human and very mobile signal boxes. For that matter, a little cheating always goes on, even in the clubs where it is strictly forbidden to play with coding, so that even when a player shifts position it can be seen as a suspicious movement.

Double pieces are widely detested in dominoes; they constantly cast the shadow of death ahead of them, as it were, and many a domino player would appreciate the game more if they were left out. The double five is particularly loathed, probably because besides being a double piece it is also ugly; because of the position of its eyes (always four in the corners and one in the middle), it is reminiscent of strange and monstrous things: frogs, Cyclopses and rhinoceroses. Children in the Antilles are wont to shout after people with protruding teeth or bulging eyes: 'Double five!'

The dead double four is creepy because in the Antilles the number four evokes unpleasant associations with the four candles which burn by the coffin, and makes a player who receives the piece often feel that death is sounding him out. The double six in turn has a hybrid character, in life perhaps the most beautiful piece: one can lead with it and thereby dominate one's surroundings, just like a parade of smartly dressed soldiers on a public holiday. But if it is dead it is very reminiscent of a pope lying in state. And a pope lying in state, in all his glittering gold and brocades, is after all mainly a *dead* pope. So the double pieces all have their own sad character. Consequently, for many players the point of the game, even more than to win, is to get rid of these monsters as quickly as possible; some people are mainly concerned with killing them off. These men played their dominoes as honestly as possible, that is, without making too much use of coding. As is fitting among friends who play purely for pleasure.

23

Janchi also opened the box of counters: two piles of ten, a green and a red one. He took the green pile, counted them and put them in the compartment where he was sitting. If he and Chamon Nicolas won, they would be paid by Bubu Fiel. He counted the ten red counters as well, and put them in the compartment to the right of where he was sitting, where his partner Chamon Nicolas would eventually sit. He in turn would have to pay Manchi if they lost. He placed the boxes for both the dominoes and the counters against the wall on the ground. He shuffled the pieces several times and then sat with his chair resting against the house. He began to long for the game because he had a feeling that this game, and in fact everything that he did in future that was not connected with Solema, was standing between him and something great. So it had to be got over with quickly.

He tipped his chair back quickly and picked up one of the dominoes that was lying face down. It was the double six. He smiled. He pushed the other pieces aside, placed the double six in the middle of the table and with the others began to make a fence around it. At that moment the thought of Solema was so powerful that he looked up towards her house; she was now wearing a white dress instead of the cream one in which she had come to him that morning. He told himself that the whole situation was crazy and he felt that he ought simply to get up and go to her and that he had done right this morning in asking her to come to him for good. He forgot all caution and waved to her. She did the same.

24

He had promised her the money for ages. So solemnly, in the middle of the week, that she had believed that the fact he was shortly to become president of the taxi drivers' union had made a different man of him. A responsible man. But up to now there had always been something else. He had the money, that wasn't the problem, he said, but he had so many other bills to settle that he couldn't afford it at the moment. The previous day, when he was at home at midday for a meal, she had asked again. He replied that it had been a bad day. The fares that he'd carried would scarcely pay for petrol. 'But this evening,' he said, 'there's a big tourist ship coming into Caracas Bay. Before midnight I'll be home with enough money to buy hundreds of shoes.'

It must have been about three o'clock when she heard him driving into the yard. A little later he came into the house and then into the bedroom and slumped down on the bed next to her like a dead weight. He stank of drink and perfume.

'The Holland plane was late, Nora,' he said in a slurred voice. 'The Holland plane was impossibly late.'

'What Holland plane, what Holland plane, for God's sake? There aren't any Holland planes on Saturdays, are there? And you were supposed to be driving tourists from *Caracas Bay*, weren't you? Bubu! You're *drunk*!' she said accusingly, but he was already snoring. It was the fact that besides smelling of drink he also reeked of perfume which made her think of the whores' camp. She was stunned and sat down in one of her two rocking-chairs. Had Bubu Fiel simply squandered the money on the whores in the camp? Like a boy of twenty? Bubu, a man of nearly fifty? She decided to wake him up after a while and ask him. If it were true, there was no telling what she would do. She felt quite capable of murdering him.

'Bubu! Bubu Fiel!' But his snoring continued. It was as though he were still making fun of her in his sleep, with his promise to provide money. She wanted to wake him up and give him a piece of her mind, but remembered it was Sunday. She would be in a terrible state if the first day of the week began with cursing. Then God would definitely not be on her side and she needed him now more than ever.

25

She hunted through his pockets but found nothing except a matchbox. Even his wallet he seemed to have lost. She threw some water over herself near the bath shed in the yard in disappointment and got dressed for early mass.

The first bell struck. It was only four o'clock and so in fact much too early for mass, which began at five. But she didn't feel like staying in the house next to Bubu Fiel's stench any longer. Outside in the fresh morning air she thought of how she had got to know him, about twenty years ago; he had stopped and offered her a lift and she accepted. At that time he was dressed in a jacket and tie, had a hat on and spoke so gallantly and charmingly to her that she began to see him as the man of her dreams. He seemed to her a reliable, solid person. Unfortunately Bubu had never belonged to this category, and that became clear not long after their marriage. In the last few months of her first pregnancy – to make matters worse, twins – he suddenly abandoned her. He came home in a tearing hurry one Saturday afternoon to collect some clothes, saying that in the Americans' refinery on Aruba there was suddenly 'money like water to be earned', provided he left at once. That was what he did. He left his car at the airport, so to speak, and went. It later turned out that he'd taken a woman with him. He was gone a year. On the few occasions that he wrote to her, he kept saying that he wasn't earning enough yet to bring her and the children, whom he hadn't even seen since their birth, across. He let a distant relative use his taxi, but the man didn't bring her a single cent, and on top of that one day smashed up the car. And Bubu sent so little money that she had to leave the house they had rented when they got married. She went back to her parents on Bandabou, who were just as poor as most of the people on Curaçao. It became a dog's life! Then she'd gone out working, for example as a servant and a washerwoman in the Prinsessendorp where the rich Dutch people still lived. Despite everything, her need was so great that she feared for the lives of her little children, and she had sought help from other men. Since then she had possibly slept with other men as often as with Bubu, although all their children passed for his. Which in a certain sense was only right and proper.

Three years ago she had appealed to the laughing Chamon Nicolas for help and their affair had begun immediately.

Her second help in emergencies was Diego Manuel, the gravedigger of Wakota. That was all, at the moment. For a long time, manageability had been a requirement in her affairs with men.

She was pinning her hopes for that day on Chamon Nicolas, although she was also thinking of Diego. Could it be half and half?

When she reached Manchi Sanantonio's house she paused

for a moment. Manchi always left the porch light on, and it shone out invitingly from the round arches. She wondered slowly and at her leisure (after all, she had plenty of time before mass began), whether a time would ever come when she could live like Solema.

Would he get a scholarship? So much depended on that! The thought that her son Ostrik might not get a scholarship when he had finished secondary school in a little while sometimes choked her with fear. She knew people who for years had not been able to get any scholarship for their sons because they were members of the defeated party. Eventually these people tried to play it clever and sometimes switched parties just before the elections because they wanted to be on the winning side. But then the winning party lost and again their sons received no scholarship. It made a person frightened and angry at the same time.

26

She formed a kind of focal point at the first mass in Wakota. With some justice. She had a genuine interest in others and sometimes quickly forgot her own worries in order to empathize with other people's. But the women who joined her this morning on the road by the corner of the cemetery found her quieter than usual and began inquiring about the reason. No one was in a hurry; people felt protected, because the church with its lights was only a hundred yards away up the hill. And only the first bell had rung.

'Did you hear a plane land at the airport here last night?' She addressed the question generally to a group of six women who had gathered at the right-hand corner of the cemetery.

'Late last night?'

'Yes,' said Nora. 'Bubu just came home, blind drunk you should know, and says that he waited for the Holland plane.'

'He was in Campo,' said Amaida with certainty. 'Mine always has the same kind of excuses.'

'I think so too,' said Nora calmly, 'but I must be certain. It may be . . .'

'Did he smell of perfume? You must always check if they smell of perfume. You have to smell their neck.'

'The terrible thing about men,' said Hermina, giving her son, who was about twelve, a push as a sign that he should wait for her a little further on, 'is not so much that they deceive us, but that they come to us with childish lies afterwards.'

'They don't just cheat on you,' said Nora, 'they try to drive you crazy.'

'Then they can take up with another woman,' said Amaida.

'Exactly!' said Serafina, joining the company with a shuffling gait.

'It doesn't matter if they tell us nonsense,' said Hermina again. 'What's terrible is that they expect us to believe it.'

'It's humiliating,' said Nora. 'Did you hear a plane land very late last night?'

The group waited tensely for the answer of Serafina, who lived closest to the airport.

'No.' Then they knew more or less for certain: Bubu Fiel had lied.

The group started moving. Half-way along the cemetery wall, Diego Manuel stuck his head over and called Nora. She separated from the others with a slight feeling of elation and went towards him.

The other women waited for her a few steps further on. It was perfectly normal for the gravedigger to speak to someone. The fact that on this occasion it was Nora wasn't anything special because after all she had children in the cemetery (which fact now contributed to her popularity among the women). Perhaps something had to be done about their graves.

'Hello, Nora. How are you?'

'Well. And you?'

'*Entre medio*. Are you coming in for a moment?'

He asked so suddenly that she was slightly alarmed. It was true that she was happy that he was there, because he wouldn't fail to help her with her difficulty if he could, but she hadn't counted on his wanting her to lie down with him immediately. They always made their dates a week in advance; in the morning or at times for after evening mass. Then she could take account of it better by not putting on a petticoat or panties. Now she had everything on. 'Can't I do it another time?' she asked, very careful not to offend him. With her nose, she pointed to the group of women who stood a little further on, buzzing with conversation and waiting for her, and added: 'They're waiting for me. After mass perhaps?'

'It's been so long,' complained Diego. 'And you know . . .' he added in a sad tone, 'Margarita is no good to me at the moment.'

'Oh yes,' said Nora, remembering: Diego's wife was expecting their ninth child.

'Are you coming?'

She wondered why she was still hesitating. God himself knew her wretchedness better than anyone else, and must have sent him at this time.

'Is there a dead body coming?' she asked, playing for time in order to review the situation. He nodded indifferently.

'Tomorrow afternoon as it happens, but I've got another job for tomorrow morning. And,' he added, full of desire, 'I was hoping to see you this morning.'

She immediately thought to herself: If he came to the cemetery specially for me, he'll probably have some money with him. She thought it, although their relationship wasn't so businesslike. She lay with him whenever he wanted to and he gave her something when it suited him or when she was in some difficulty or other, or he did something to the children's graves. But now her need was very great.

'Have you got fifteen guilders?'

'Fifteen guilders?' asked Diego aloud.

The women who were standing waiting for Nora heard and turned their heads in their direction. They thought it was about the price of the maintenance of the graves of Nora's children.

'Nora's a good mother,' they whispered to each other for the umpteenth time.

She asked him to speak more softly, for goodness' sake. 'Fifteen guilders,' he repeated to himself, still full of amazement, but now in a softer tone. 'You've become even more expensive than the . . .'

'It's not a matter of the money,' she said interrupting him quickly. And cajolingly: 'You know that I could do it just as well for nothing with you. But I need a pair of shoes for my son Ostrik. You know that the boy goes to an important school and he must look neat. At the moment he hasn't even got shoes. Because of that, he's been stuck at home for a week.'

'But fifteen guilders, Nora?' said Diego shaking his head. 'Fifteen guilders! That's a whole day's work for me. And you do know, don't you, that I've got children to bring up too? There'll be a new one shortly,' he added gloomily, as though someone else were responsible.

However, Nora went on imperturbably, 'If he doesn't have any shoes, he'll have to miss another week. Bubu was supposed to bring me the money, but he blew it all last night. And next week's the boy's test week. If he misses it, his studies will be affected and perhaps he won't even finish school. I don't want him to miss anything,' she added doggedly. 'Do you understand?'

Diego nodded.

The sexton of Wakota sounded the second bell for the early morning mass with two booming strokes.

'We'll be off,' called the women. They felt that Nora's business was taking a little too long after all. Apart from which, the fresh light from the church, where they could go and whine about their worries to their hearts' content, was more attractive than standing here, waiting aimlessly. They pulled their scarves more tightly round their heads and continued up the church slope.

'That's okay,' said Nora waving back. 'I'm dealing with some things with Diego and I'll see you later. Or tomorrow.' To Diego she said, 'You'll have to hurry if you want to have me. It's getting so light. Are you going to do it?'

As soon as Nora started talking to him about her son Ostrik, who was attending the *skol grandi*, she made him feel tender. Not only would his own three boys (who were thick as two short planks) never attend secondary school, but Ostrik was known in the whole area as a good student. Everyone was convinced that he would go far. In Wakota, which is not particularly blessed with clever people, people saw in him not only the hope of Nora, but in an almost mysterious way the hope of the whole district. And the thought that by helping Nora he was helping the boy and thereby also Wakota, made him feel almost sentimental. But fifteen guilders!

'You want to make a doctor of him,' he said with his heavy, cool voice and tried as he did so to put a friendly hand on Nora's shoulder over the church wall, which she, however, quickly pushed away.

'Yes,' she said, 'but be careful, someone can always come by.'

'And he needs shoes?' Diego went on asking.

'Yes. Otherwise I might do it for nothing with you. You know what I'm like. You help me now and again and I help you now and again. But now it's no game. He really can't go to school tomorrow if I can't get the money for shoes from somewhere tomorrow morning. As I said to you, Bubu...'

'I've got ten guilders. The priest will pay me at the end of the week for the grave that I'm working on now; and then you can have some more.' He again put his hand on her arm. 'Will you do it?'

She was so relieved that she forgot to push his arm away or warn him to be careful. She didn't have to think about the proposal for long. The other five guilders would give her no trouble... She certainly wouldn't have to wait a week for it, and Ostrik would be able to go to school again tomorrow.

'Ten guilders is okay,' she said. 'Ten guilders is fine. I'm coming.'

Diego disappeared without another word in order to wait for her at the entrance to the cemetery. She herself walked as calmly as possible along the wall of the cemetery, to where it curved eastwards. Then she turned the corner to where the main entrance was. Diego swung the iron gates open, with a soft, creaking sound like in a church portal as they turned inwards. They were no longer visible from the road past the cemetery because of the tall graves on this side. Diego, who knew this, said playfully, 'Come on, Nora darling,' grabbing her hand and leading her into the cemetery with something like pride; as though it were a palace, with a driveway and all.

At the back was a vault in which he had not made any floors for coffins; he used this as his changing room, eating place and rest room. There was a piece of cardboard on the floor. Nora knew that he also slept there with other women.

'A quarter of an hour,' she said as she walked towards it with him. 'I have to go to mass.' In fact she felt particularly calm. The affair with him was the safest one she had ever had. Because anyone who saw her here with Diego wouldn't find anything unusual in it. Because of the children who, as everyone knew, were buried in the middle of the cemetery.

The empty vault was perhaps six feet wide and a four feet six high. She stopped in front of it and began taking her clothes off. The cool morning air made her shiver slightly.

Diego hesitated between taking off his own clothes and touching her body as it was gradually revealed. He was eager.

'Did you shut the gate?' she asked calmly.

Diego nodded in the dark.

'Did you lock it?' she asked.

He lifted his head from her breasts and again said yes. 'The money,' she said. The stress of almost a week over the fifteen guilders made her behave in a less friendly way than usual.

'Always the same thing,' said Diego, exaggerating, as he gave her the ten guilders, which she put into her small, black handbag. 'Always money,' he added. She said nothing. She was about to lie down on the cardboard, but had second thoughts. She had to go to the church immediately afterwards and couldn't risk the dirt of the cemetery sticking to her dress. She said this to Diego, who took the cardboard out of the vault. She spread her dress, her headscarf and her stockings on it.

A beautiful, black figure, but almost invisible because of the darkness of the morning, she stood for a moment in front of the vault, then she dived into the small space with Diego, who pulled her eagerly towards him. Diego was so horny because of the days he'd had to abstain because of his wife's pregnancy, that he could not wait until she'd taken off her white lace panties. He destroyed them with quick, rough gestures. He was so wild and reckless that for a moment she regretted having lain down here with him. At any rate she became angry at Bubu; and when Diego with his heavy weight (he was heavy although he was short) lay on top of her, she was in agony, because of the hundreds of sharp little stones which she felt cutting deep into her whole body.

But she had a sense of humour, did Nora. Her humour was a kind of strength which sometimes made her capable of withstanding the severest pains. By way of revenge, because she had humour and because she was angry at Bubu Fiel for making her endure these hard stones in her body and the impulsiveness of Diego – because at that moment she was certain that Bubu was trying to make a fool of her – she said softly to him, 'That Holland plane of yours is coming into land in my cunt.' This was one of the few times that it gave her pleasure to deceive him, because in all the years she had been married to Bubu, that had never been her intention.

'What did you say?' said Diego frantically.

'Do calm down a bit, I've got no back left!'

She now began thinking how to get the rest of the fifteen guilders from Chamon Nicolas that afternoon. But she still tried to give Diego value for money. That was her way. After all, he was helping her a lot with the ten guilders. She pushed her pelvis laboriously up and down. She did her bit; as always.

27

Afterwards, in church, she could scarcely sit down. When she tried kneeling, she almost screamed with pain. 'God,' she muttered, 'you really let Diego work me over this time.' She hadn't even had a cup of coffee that morning. She left the church as the collection was being taken.

When she got home it was still very quiet. They were all still asleep. Bubu was snoring in the bedroom. On the west side of the bath shed she again poured some water over her body. (She hadn't been able to use the bath shed at all for some days because Bubu had put two sacks of cement in there, which must not get wet.) It provided little relief. Anyway, she put on a clean dress and then sat down in her armchair for a while. Then she ironed the clothes of the children, who had to go to the children's mass at half past seven. When she'd finished, Ostrik was angry because he still didn't have any shoes. He said that he'd never go to church again in his life. She replied that he would just have to go to the bay to amuse himself and promised him he would have the shoes the following day. Come what may.

When the children, who after mass would wander off in all directions, had gone, she cleared up the mats on which they slept on the floor, spread throughout the two rooms of the small house, and their dirty clothes. Then she fed the chickens. Then she began preparing the *sòpi di mondongo*. She went through Bubu's pockets again and again found nothing. Nor in his 200H. She tried to wake him because she knew that on Sunday mornings he fixed all kinds of things on his 200H, before eating and playing dominoes. But she could not. When she kept trying, he even kicked out at her, which made her angry and so she cursed him, despite the fact that it was Sunday. She stood over him in their little bedroom and said: 'You must try and pass your lies off with other women. That Holland plane you were talking about this morning didn't land at the airport, but here in my cunt. Do you hear that, in my cunt! No one in the whole district heard a plane landing this morning. You simply went to bed with a whore in Campo. At your age. And you were stupid enough to give her all your money.'

She had a filthy tongue when she wanted to. And she could give free rein to her rage as well, because he was so drunk that he couldn't even get up, let alone hit her. 'Here in my cunt,' she repeated through the house and to herself when she thought of what she'd had to put up with that morning. 'Here in my cunt, I expect.' The accuracy of that observation at least satisfied her somewhat.

The five guilders she still needed kept buzzing through her head so that she became excited and confused, a little drunk. If she hadn't counted on Bubu then she would have made a paper with numbers on it, a hundred numbers. Bubu didn't like it, said that she was putting him to shame all over Wakota by selling lottery tickets from house to house.

'People think I don't give you enough money,' he was bold enough to say, 'and I do give you enough, don't I?'

She sat down at the small table in the dining-room and began to make the paper anyway. She went on with it for an hour and then spent an hour going round the houses in the vicinity of the junction of the Tula and Carpata roads without selling a single lottery ticket. At a certain moment she became frightened of the risk: instead of making thirty guilders' profit if she sold everything, she would have to come up with twenty if she only got rid of half or less. Twenty guilders which she certainly didn't have. She decided to stop and again pinned her hopes on Chamon Nicolas. He would have the money on him. He always had some money on him, Chamon Nicolas, she thought with something like pride. Even if he didn't have it with him, he could make sure that she got some in the evening or something. She began to long for the game of dominoes. So at about eleven o'clock she took the domino table out of the bath shed and four chairs from the living-room, after which there was scarcely anything left to sit on. She also put out the boxes with the dominoes and the counters. Against the wall she placed the wooden bench that she had made for the first communion of one of the children, for any spectators. She liked getting things ready. She was always cheered up by the thought that people were coming. The more the merrier was her motto. And she found dominoes a sociable game because it meant that her husband was home all day long. Although she had to be on call all day if they were playing, in order to take drinks out to them the whole time. But when she went to wake Bubu up again at about eleven o'clock her mood once more changed completely. He suddenly stretched out his arms and pulled her on top of him. This made her see red. He whispered sweet nothings in her face, in broken, Campo Spanish.

At that moment Bubu made a terrible mistake!

28

About twenty-five years before, when the oil refinery was at the height of its activity, Chamon Nicolas, who had been born on Saba, had come to Curaçao with a large group of Windward Islanders. He immediately got a job with the oil company and it looked as if he would go far, although he had no formal training. It looked like that for ten years, but on a certain day, or rather night, he was caught stealing materials from the company with a number of other employees. They thought they were being crafty: they dug a tunnel under the high, barbed-wire fence of the site near the famous Jewish cemetery. The tunnel also ran under the walls of the historic cemetery and came out under some of the graves, most of which had wonderfully carved tombstones. Both during the day and at night members of their gang pushed all kinds of useful material under the two fences into the graves: pots of paint, nails, screws, planks, safety shoes, helmets, pincers, saws and many other things; in fact, everything which could be carried unobtrusively to the tunnel under the fence around the refinery site. Then at certain times they collected everything from the cemetery. When Chamon Nicolas was caught, he was living with his mother, who had followed him from Saba with his sister, in a suburb of Willemstad, not far from the cemetery. With the stolen material, and partly with the money he made from selling it, he had built himself a small house in the slum district of Valentijn, slightly north-east of the Jewish cemetery and close to Post V, which he rented out to other Windward Islanders. It wasn't much more than a small stable, but he was able to get a good rent for it, because foreigners, many of whom were working for the company, were delighted to find anything at all. Even in a district like Valentijn, where many small shacks still surround what long ago was a large pig-sty. It was dirty and stank.

The company wanted to go further than firing him. He was lucky that his sister went to plead his case with the management. Clemency was shown and they left it at dismissal.

Chamon himself did not regard what he had done as theft, firstly because he had disliked the gentleman owners and bosses for whom he worked (who always had to be white, imported from Europe) and secondly because there was always a great surplus of the things which they took from the site. For example, tons of nails often lay rusting for months, and the company often had to throw things away that it could no longer use because they'd been exposed for too long to wind and weather. Chamon also saw all the things the company did for the so-called seconded employees, the houses, clothes, cars and perhaps even free food from the company, and felt no one had the right to consider him a thief if, in order to do a job at home or even to build a small house which he could later rent out, he took a few odds and ends home with him. Moreover, in comparison with these so-called seconded employees, who often had to be taught the job when they first arrived, he earned a pittance.

After his dismissal, Chamon lived as well as he could from the proceeds of his house in Valentijn and from all kinds of odd jobs, of which there were still plenty. A second visit of entreaty from his sister, who spoke better English than the Dutch director at the time, however, led to him being re-appointed. (In the boom time of the company, so many people were required that it was sometimes cheaper to take on somebody who had stolen or was stealing from the site than not.) However, this time he was employed on field work. He had to work on houses in the Prinsessendorp, where the so-called seconded employees of the company lived their princely existence.

With the materials that, even here, he was able to remove, a few at a time, he was able to build a second shack in the same district of Valentijn. Then he was more or less secure. Both houses, in which many people lived under one roof, brought him in fifty guilders net per month. When he was dismissed the second time (on this occasion because political developments and the lay-off which the company implemented meant that not so many Europeans were being sent out), he was given an *ex gratia* payment of two thousand guilders, which he immediately deposited in the bank.

So he was now a small-scale capitalist, Chamon Nicolas, with his two hovels and two thousand guilders. Still, he preferred to present himself as very poor, because he felt this was more cautious. So for most people he remained the rather run-down Windward Islander who lived from doing odd jobs.

However, the only thing one could not doubt, when one saw this cheerful, rather thickset Negro of middling height, on the small rather than on the large side, with his square head – he had one front tooth missing – was that he ate well. Indeed, Chamon gave his full attention to this. His mother, who had now died, had taught him that a man should eat lots of eggs. Lots of eggs and fruit juice guaranteed that a man would keep his potency for a long time. Well, he did that, because he liked going to bed with women. But what he most liked doing was eating, and when it came to eating, well, he liked Libby's brand corned beef, with or without cheese and eggs mixed with it and fried.

Because he spoke and read English, he had access to an extensive world of literature, of which the uneducated Antillean, who speaks and reads only Papiamento, was completely deprived. He made use of it only occasionally, leaving his Curaçaoan friends, who could chatter away very well, speechless. (Curaçaoans in fact philosophize with the ease and and fluency of the Ancient Greeks, like Socrates, Plato, Aristotle, etc., but because of lack of information never go into things very deeply.) Only occasionally, because he had no need to outshine everybody else and make them jealous so that they would do all kinds of things to him. He wanted them to respect him a little, and for the rest he was happy to keep his mouth shut and live as peaceably as possible among them.

He didn't worry too much about his appearance; one could easily have taken him for a tramp. In the last analysis it was his shabbiness that had led him to get involved in the fight in which he'd given a chap a slash with a machete. Although the immediate reason had been the money in a dice game in which he occasionally took part. It was the custom to tease him because of his shabby appearance, particularly among those who knew that he had two houses. Sometimes it became more than teasing, and they called him a damn miser who came to make himself rich on Curaçao and then abandon the island when there was nothing more to be squeezed out of it. He was sometimes even called a rat, a Dutchman, a Portuguese or some such thing. In the fight in question, the man with whom he had the dispute had said something similar to him. Chamon had objected that he had been in Curaçao for a long time, spoke fluent Papiamento and so scarcely needed to be demoted to the rank of foreigner. In order to substantiate this, he had insulted the man's mother in his Papiamento, which had a thick English accent. What he had said was *Den conjo di bo mama*, intending the formula more as an illustration than as a real insult. However, the man had immediately drawn his knife and tried to stab him. Everything took place at about five in the afternoon. In order to defend himself, Chamon Nicolas, who at that time still walked around unarmed, broke into a run. The man began chasing him.

Everyone started screaming – the women loudest – that a murder was about to happen. Chamon could indeed remember that he'd thought his number would be up in a few minutes' time. At a certain moment he felt tired and could feel the man was gaining on him. He tried to think up some trick as he ran along, but he was so overcome with fear that he couldn't think straight. He had run about a hundred yards, when out of nowhere – he couldn't see anything at that moment – he heard a voice calling him, 'Here, you!'

One of the few men who still worked on the land in Curaçao was on his way home with a bundle of clothes on his back and a long machete in his hand. He offered Chamon Nicolas this knife. The latter was so amazed that he stood stock still: he seemed suddenly to have completely forgotten the danger that was threatening him from the rear. At first he was frightened, he told people later, that the man was playing a cruel joke on him, because Chamon did not know him and could certainly not remember having done him a favour. 'Here, you,' the man repeated imperturbably. 'You don't have to be killed just like that, whoever you are.' And he offered Chamon the machete so unambiguously that the latter grabbed it, the more so because his pursuer had got very close to him and was telling him in obscene terms that he was going to send him back to his mother's womb. Via her cunt, that was. However, when Chamon turned round with the long machete in his hand, the man didn't stop to think, but started running in turn. Chamon Nicolas caught up with him.

'I couldn't help it,' he told people later. 'I was so frightened and at the same time furious that I simply lashed out.' He'd aimed at the man's buttocks, but the machete caught him in the side, and would have probably cut him in two if it had not been so blunt. As it was, the man had only a deep wound from which, however, blood gushed copiously.

'You should never have accepted that treacherous knife,' said the judge when his case came up. 'You should have run away faster.'

Which Chamon would never in his life fully understand.

'But what if he'd caught up with me, Your Honour?'

'You had a head start, didn't you?' said the judge non-chalantly.

However, what the judge held against him most was that he had attacked the man with the machete. 'You should have stayed there with the machete in your hand: the man would then have run away of his own accord; which he in fact did, isn't that so?'

Chamon's plea of self-defence, which a government lawyer made for him because he had not deemed it necessary to dip into his money in the bank, was unsuccessful, which with the best will in the world he could not understand. In any case, it did not lead to his immediate release as the lawyer had argued it should. However, ready as he always was to adapt quickly to strange situations in order to survive, he blamed the fact that the judge probably didn't understand his Windward Island English, which has all kinds of typical features, or had become irritated. He was given one year.

What really upset him was the fact that the man who had offered him the machete was also put in jail for a spell, although he gave the man a gift of fifty guilders from his capital in the bank.

Manchi Sanantonio, who was acting as a bailiff in his case, had advised him to take a paid lawyer next time. 'Those idiots working for the government don't care about anyone's case,' he said. Chamon had definitely decided to do that. If he ever got into trouble again, he would do that, even if the man asked him for five hundred guilders, since he'd found that year in prison very hard, particularly because of the food. Apart from that, from then on he always carried a knife. Day and night. You never knew with Curaçaoans. It was all very well for the judge and the people in the probation office to talk, but of course they were never there when difficulties arose. And he, Chamon Nicolas, couldn't rely on there being somebody to offer him a knife next time. No, you never knew with Curaçaoans. They were as volatile as hell, which was probably because they didn't read very much. They never felt like a real fight, or they were too frightened. They simply stabbed you. In fact all of them, thought Chamon Nicolas, disliked each other so much that they seemed to be waiting for a good excuse to stab each other. For some reason or other they carried a kind of hatred in their bodies. Sometimes he thought they were cowards. Sometimes not. Then he decided that they were animals. Finally he decided they weren't, because it could also be fun to go around with them. And all in all, who else was he supposed to associate with for as long as he was here, except for these people, and for that matter, were Windward Islanders any better?

'It's a devastating hatred that the Negro carries round with him,' he sometimes thought rather sadly. He bought in any case a not very dangerous knife, a so-called *Kuchu hulandes*, or Dutch knife, though it actually originated from Germany, which he kept in a sheath under his shirt. Consequently he always left his shirt rather open at the belly. This was all absolutely *force majeure*. Chamon Nicolas, at forty-three years of age, was basically a friendly chap. At least, he meant well.

29

At any rate Nora had noticed Chamon Nicolas's friendliness the first time he came to play dominoes. She also sensed that he wasn't such a down-and-out as he had people believe, and so drew the conclusion that he was a man who wouldn't blab a lot. Everything suited her, when Bubu suddenly left her with problems for her daughter Erika's first communion.

It was all the more awful because Bubu had insisted that they should have a radiogram for that day. He had bought an expensive one on hire purchase (which had long since been repossessed because he hadn't been able to keep up the payments). She had everything for the party except the eighty guilders required to collect Erika's frock from the seamstress and the hundred and twenty guilders she needed for the communion cake, which had to be collected the evening before the party. Bubu had repeatedly promised to look after this money. Because it was a matter of a communion, she really believed him. But Bubu did not come home till seven o'clock on the eve of the party and he was blind drunk. He hadn't been able to do it, he said to her.

In her great panic, because she couldn't buy either the dress or the cake on hire purchase, she had finally gone to Chamon Nicolas. She did not find him at home and he was not due back till about midnight. She knew that at home, with Bubu drunk and the bustle of the preparations, there would be dreadful confusion. She waited with Chamon's mother, just hoping that he would have money when he came. She told him the whole story when he finally returned and simply asked him for help: half the amount she needed for the cake and the dress together, one hundred guilders.

'How do you think you're going to pay back the money?' said Chamon, stuttering in amazement, which he was finding difficult to control.

'I don't know, somehow. Whatever happens, Bubu mustn't find out.' Then when she noticed that this last remark made Chamon's amazement even greater, she'd added, 'Ten guilders a week. I'll try and give it to you on Sunday when you come to play dominoes at our place. I'll tell Bubu that I am getting the things on hire purchase with a repayment of ten guilders a week. The ten guilders that I get from him, I'll give to you.'

Chamon Nicolas thought her request strange and most unreasonable. So much so, that he began to believe that unfathomable fate was preparing a great disaster for him in the person of this woman. But he didn't immediately say no, because the astonishment fascinated him: why should he, Chamon Nicolas, lend the sum of one hundred guilders to a woman who was a relative stranger, with whom he had nothing in common? Without a single guarantee of ever getting it back? The only guarantee that there might have been, of being able to speak to her husband about it, she deprived him of in advance. And only for a very stupid man can the word of a woman serve as a guarantee of anything. Yes, it's a fool who relies on that: after all, a woman has complete freedom to change her mind.

He consequently said to her, 'Listen, Nora. If I lend you this money (assuming that I have it) or simply go and stand on the bridge in Willemstad and throw it in the water, it remains the same thing. Exactly the same. I'll never see a penny of it again. And you know that! Surely you can't expect me to do something so stupid?'

But Nora said no. She even assumed an attitude of offended pride and said that she would pay him back everything to the last cent. 'I'll go out to work, Chamon, I'll sell lottery numbers, I'll get rid of all the things in my house in order to give you your money back.' Nora pleaded. She pleaded with all the tears she had, because she could not bear to think of the shame that would befall her if her daughter didn't have a frock the following day.

Her helplessness moved Chamon Nicolas's heart. Damn, when *he* had been in difficulties, it had also been a total stranger who had helped him. Otherwise he, who was now thinking about his money like a miser, would have been a dead Negro. In order to put his mind at rest in the matter of his superstition, he asked Nora why she'd come to *him* of all people.

'Because you're a good person, Chamon,' she said. The answer reassured him. It was worth something to him to be called a good person. He had then taken that risk that often makes men of men who think they're men already; he had put the money he had at home in an envelope and given it to Nora, the whole amount she needed.

Perhaps Nora had done her best. On two Sundays in succession after the first communion service she actually gave him ten guilders. After that, she had given him nothing more and he hadn't asked her for any more. He regarded the money as a gift. Not long afterwards she came to him for help again. Because he'd already done it a first time, he saw no objection to doing it a second time. Eventually, because his mother now lived with his sister, they went to bed together. It became an affair. It wasn't unpleasant to Chamon Nicolas, because he didn't have to spend so much money on other women, for instance, those from Campo. His life became more manageable, he thought, because Nora was also particularly good in bed. With a high cunt. For her part she found the affair particularly pleasant and convenient, because Chamon Nicolas lived in town. It was easy to spend a few hours with him when she had to go shopping there. Besides, she was a little in love with him because he had saved her from the biggest disgrace of her life and gave him more of her femininity than was strictly necessary in return for his helping her out with money. It was a good contract for both of them. Erika had got her beautiful lace frock in time, and the white cake in the form of the Eiffel Tower had stood in state for weeks in a corner of the house. She had been able to force the makers of the dress and the cake to accept half the money in the middle of the night. With the rest she had been just about able to organize a little party, for which the radiogram provided the music. There was dancing. Then she had persuaded the priest of Santa Gloria to tell Bubu that she had borrowed the money from him.

Despite his warm heart, Chamon was not so discreet that he felt remorse about going to bed with the wife of one of his domino friends. If Nora wasn't going to bed with him, she would be with other men, he was sure. He felt that the cause of it all lay with Bubu Fiel himself. Yet he had reservations about his sexual affair, which gradually became greater because he knew that he was exposing himself to the fury and revenge of Bubu. And he was frightened of the physical strength of Bubu Fiel. In any case he had to bear in mind that if the affair with Nora came to light, it would be the end of dominoes at Bubu Fiel's for ever. And that would be a heavy price to pay. Then what would he do with his Sundays? Of course, he could play dominoes whenever he liked, although he couldn't join a club because of his prison sentence. In Steenrijk itself, where he lived, there were enough places where there was always a game on as there were in the back rooms of the various little bars in Otrabanda. Even in Campo one could find a game of dominoes. But nowhere was the same as under the tamarind to the east of Bubu Fiel's house. For a start, in those places one never played with regular partners and one couldn't play many sets, because there was always a queue of men waiting for their turn. Apart from that, it was dangerous there, because the men often played for money or drink, and because they sometimes didn't know each other, they soon lost control when arguments arose. No, he found playing dominoes casually more and more tricky and was determined to avoid it as much as possible. In Wakota it was really a kind of friendly club. Besides, Chamon Nicolas greatly valued his contact with Manchi Sanantonio. The man was a bailiff and one could get all kinds of tips from him which one could use for one's business. Hadn't he been able to get a small shed from Manchi in the city a while ago, which he rented at a good price to an Arab who used it for a warehouse? It was precisely his association with Manchi that had made him realize that putting his money in the bank was pointless, because in that way it didn't *produce* anything. What particularly impressed him was the fact that Manchi had observed at the domino table that someone who had money in the bank had to bear in mind that the prices of things rise while money remains the same.

'In that way, the value of money', added Manchi with his omniscient wisdom, 'is constantly falling.' He also mentioned numerous cases of rich traders who had gone bankrupt because they had handled their money badly. He, Chamon, was already past forty and had to ensure that he could have a carefree old age. And if things became more expensive, he knew that on this damn island that didn't produce much for itself, it would affect first and foremost foodstuffs, eggs, fruit juice, the tins of Libby's corned beef from Argentina.

Well, that Monday he had bought the small place on Scharloo which he now rented out to the Arab for two hundred guilders a month. In six months he would have made two hundred guilders' profit and then he would have earned back the money that he had given to Nora. He thought Manchi's theory was quite sound. And the cool shade to the east of the house was a good place to spend time.

30

That Sunday morning, Chamon set off early because before the game he wanted to go and collect his rents. The Arab paid on Mondays, which he thought better, because then he could take the money straight to the bank and didn't need to walk around with it on the island, which was dangerous. He planned to go to Valentijn, because he also wanted to buy a few lottery tickets, with which he was often lucky, before evening. He took a bus into town from Steenrijk. He crossed the bridge to Otrabanda. Here in the street one could find the male and female lottery ticket sellers. Although lottery-ticket selling was officially prohibited, they were nevertheless allowed to ply their trade – it was a fruitful source of employment, and the officers of law and order are often themselves passionate buyers of lottery tickets, with numerous relatives who sometimes also engage in this illegal business. Chamon Nicolas was going to go back to Brion Square again after he'd bought his tickets in various places in Otrabanda, in order to take a bus to Valentijn, but he didn't need to, because an acquaintance offered him a lift. The man waited until he'd collected his rent and then drove him to Wakota. It was still only twelve o'clock, so Chamon thought it was too early to go to Bubu's. Apart from that, he felt thirsty, and he decided to go and eat in the bar-cum-restaurant at the junction of the Carpata and Tula roads. Not having much to do, his acquaintance went with him. In the space behind the bar–restaurant, however, there was also a domino table and two men invited Chamon and his acquaintance to play a couple of sets. He really preferred not to, because he had once had words in this bar with a man who had made a remark about his missing front tooth. But it was quiet at the moment, and still too early for Bubu. Well after one, when normally he would long since have arrived at Bubu's, he was sitting in that bar–restaurant playing dominoes and drinking rum. Nora waited for him in vain.

31

Bubu Fiel had finally managed to get out of bed, but he was tired and confused. Even after he had thrown some water over his body behind the small bath shed, matters didn't improve. He had what is known as a hangover. It would be better, he thought, if he lay down for the whole of Sunday and didn't play dominoes, but he felt trapped, because he knew that Manchi would not take this. It might mean the end of their friendship if he simply went and told Manchi and the others, particularly Manchi, that he wasn't playing that afternoon, without good reason. And Manchi would not accept a night in the happy camp as a proper reason. On the other hand, if he played anyway, which he was therefore bound to do, he wouldn't be able to do much good this afternoon.

In order to get going, he decided to wash and polish his 200H himself and not leave the chore to his sons as usual. He said little to Nora, because seeing her simply increased his great feeling of guilt. After cleaning the car, he pushed himself underneath it on a mat. Ostensibly to make a small repair to the brand-new Dodge, in reality to hide. Normally he enjoyed lying under his 200H; he could lie there and think about all kinds of things. Now at least he could escape Nora, perhaps until the dominoes began, because then he wouldn't have to speak to her for the whole afternoon. He dozed off. He was so tired that the coolness under the car sent him straight off to sleep. But Nora, who was feeding the chickens near him, noticed that he was lying under the 200H and began screaming at him again.

'Can't you see that you're much too old for this kind of

dissipation?!' she shrieked in her harsh voice.

He started awake and squeezed his tall, large body out from under the car where, now that Nora had caught him snoring, he could only make himself ridiculous.

'That Holland plane of yours must have landed here in my cunt,' she said for the umpteenth time that morning, looking at him contemptuously from head to toe. She said it aloud so that everyone who wanted to could hear. 'Old whore-chaser,' she added.

'Shut your filthy mouth!' he said, throwing the mat away in irritation.

'Oh, aren't you, then?' she said. 'Old whore-chaser! How's your boy supposed to go to school tomorrow when you've frittered away the money?'

'Shut your trap!' he said. He wanted to add that otherwise he'd hit her so that she'd whine, so that they'd be able to hear her all over Wakota, but he didn't say that and he didn't do it. He had the feeling it wouldn't make much difference to the fact that she was right. In order to give effect to the vague feeling that he had to make something up to her, he went into the junk store to tidy things up a bit. Apart from that, he tried to console himself with the thought that Nora was exaggerating. The boy had stayed at home for a week already; one day longer wouldn't do him any more harm. He would earn those fifteen guilders the following day. He put the sacks of cement in a corner of the bath area, covered them with some tarpaulin and now that he could relieve himself and throw a bucket over his body in the small shed, he felt rather more sure of himself. But he had a hangover. Not because of the skinful of whisky he'd had the previous evening, but because of the Dominican girl with whom he'd spent a large part of the night. The memory of her flesh intoxicated him whenever he thought about it. He longed more than anything else for that woman, and realized that the fate that had befallen him was that in the coming days he would have to develop huge strength of will to stay away from the camp and her room.

Nora thought she was letting him off too lightly and was a little too sure of herself because she didn't really think she would be unable to get the five guilders that day. She decided to use his feeling of guilt to remind him of the other things which he also let pass. She followed him to the bath shed.

'You're not really going to finish the house with those few bags of cement,' she said, extra bitchily. 'You ought to set about it seriously.'

'Leave me alone, woman.'

'If you don't start building seriously, you'll be behind all your friends. Look at Manchi Sanantonio.' It was very un-original to use Manchi as an example, but she did it anyway. 'And it seems that shortly he's going to be adding another building on, a kind of maid's room.'

'You mustn't forget that Manchi isn't alone,' retorted Bubu. 'His wife works too. If you went out and did something . . .' It was a kind of defence that Bubu never used and that suddenly hurt her very deeply. All over her back she again felt the pain she had endured on the hard ground, lying under Diego Manuel. She became so furious that she blurted out too much.

'You can say that, but Chamon Nicolas, who hasn't got a wife, is better off than you are. He's got houses!' She immediately regretted it.

Bubu dropped the spare tyre he was holding onto the canvas with which he'd covered the sacks of cement. There was distrust in his voice when he asked her, 'So, has he got houses? How do *you* know that?'

She tried to distract him by affecting indifference. 'I don't know, people say.'

'I thought you were sure; that he told you or something.'

'Damn,' she said. 'I've told you that people *say* so! And if

126

people say so, then some of it is probably true, isn't it!' She hoped he wouldn't pursue the matter. She was actually so angry that she had been indiscreet in her fury that she was quite capable of telling him openly about her affair with Chamon Nicolas. Come what may. After all, she did not do what she did for her own pleasure. Sometimes she herself suffered because of it. Like this morning.

Bubu said nothing.

'I simply mean that you should do something about our house,' she said more calmly. 'Everyone in the area is getting on, but you stay where you started.' She then turned round and went back inside, this time to prepare his meal.

Bubu didn't think much about the remark that Chamon had houses. He was simply aware that he had indeed done nothing to his new house for years and wondered for the umpteenth time in his life why it was that he never got beyond good intentions. And as always he told himself that it was because he hadn't had the sort of breaks in life that his son Ostrik, who was at an important school, now had. He came from a large family, the kind he now had himself, except that they were even worse off than he was. But that wasn't true, or at least wasn't the whole story. He had rather been the victim of the great prosperity which prevailed on the island during the Second World War. Money circulated fast and in large quantities in those days, not least because of the Puerto Ricans and Americans who were stationed there. When he was twenty he bought a second-hand taxi and started up in business for himself, like many others. It was a pleasurable life, full of money, women and drink. Damn, he'd never thought it would come to an end! Sometimes he was convinced that he had made a great mistake by marrying Nora when he was only twenty-three. He'd taken up with her with the intention of ditching her one day, but she had taken him to her house, introduced him to her parents and married him. As a result, his marvellous, carefree existence had come to an abrupt end. It wasn't long after their wedding before he disappeared with a woman to Aruba, out of a sort of nostalgia.

Bubu Fiel knew that he was a tough, powerful Negro. When he shaved himself properly, put a brush through his short hair, donned a white shirt and tie and sometimes even a jacket, and topped it off with his grey felt hat – he sometimes preferred the Italian borsalino from his bachelor years – he knew that he was an impressive figure of a man. (In fact, that was what had proved his undoing last night in that camp!) Perhaps because of his height and his slow, calm way of speaking? He wasn't sure. Whenever a problem needed solving, they came to him. Quite naturally people had come to him when the National People's Party, Wakota Section, was looking for a district head and he had filled the post for a while, until he thought it was better to resign because people were about to accuse him of irregularities with party funds. Later, he was made President of DSW and then chairman of the newly established Wakota Community Centre. In the end, after a period of enthusiasm, he soon lost interest in such things. He got stuck somewhere, without knowing precisely where or why. And yet he kept beginning afresh: again and again there was huge enthusiasm, which inspired everyone around him and made them see him immediately as their leader. Take last Monday. They were sitting there under a *wabi* tree on the Caracas Bay road – a harbour on the east side of the island where large passenger ships moor – and were playing dominoes. They were waiting for fares, especially from a ship which was due to put in to the island for a few days with a large group of American tourists. And then, at the very moment the *Bounty* came into harbour, two of those great buses which could carry at least a hundred passengers drove up. The buses of the largest travel agency in the town which for years had been in the habit of collecting its passengers from the ships and taking them to their hotels in the town. The taxi drivers' union had protested about this often enough. But the politicians did nothing. They hid behind the arguments of the travel agency that transport by taxi wasn't fast enough, or was too expensive, or whatever. And so every day they took the bread out of the mouths of Bubu and his colleagues. He did not know what got into him that Monday, but he told his friends that they couldn't stand for this any longer. Most of them shrugged their shoulders and said – as usual – that they preferred to keep out of trouble. But Bubu said that sometimes one could not avoid trouble. 'If the authorities on the island won't do anything to help the taxi drivers, then we've got to help ourselves.'

When they asked what exactly he had in mind, he replied that they must simply stop the two large buses from taking a single passenger from the liner into town.

The men, having been irritated by the situation for long enough, quite quickly agreed with him. First, they very sportingly went over to the two bus drivers and told them what they were planning and said it would be best if they simply took their buses back. However, the latter were not very willing, since their livelihood depended on the same thing. Then the ten taxi drivers who were there became so heated that they told the bus drivers in no uncertain terms that if they did not leave with a good grace, they would be treated roughly. The two made the best of a bad job and drove off without even phoning their bosses first. By the time they returned later with their bosses and a police escort, the group of taxi drivers had already driven half the passengers from the *Bounty* into town, some of them having made three trips.

Looking back on it, Bubu Fiel was appalled that he had involved himself in the whole business. Because what was happening now? The news of the initiative he'd taken spread among all the local taxi drivers – in fact, the incident got into the papers – and there was such enthusiasm in the union that people went on meeting fervently all week to discuss further ways of getting the better of those impudent travel agencies for good. People even discussed the co-operative buying and running of a number of buses themselves, in order to serve large loads of tourists and excursions, such as the drivers on the Windward Islands and Aruba had already done. As a result, Bubu wasted a lot of time. All the money he had earned that Monday went into the meetings, which of course required lots of drink. And what he found even worse, a large group of taxi drivers came to him with a request that he stand as a candidate for the new executive of the union. They wanted to depose the chairman and put Bubu in his place, because last Monday this important matter had finally been set in motion through his initiative. The union chief had already managed to ensure that when a large group of tourists landed at the same time the travel agencies could not send more than one large bus – for all the travel agencies put together – to the quay. That was certainly a step forward. 'And we owe that to you, Bubu Fiel,' said everyone.

His refusal was not accepted. They were so insistent, always saying that he after all was the person who took the initiative, that he gave in. The meeting at which the old executive was to be voted down and he was to be elected, undoubtedly by acclamation, was to take place that evening in the union headquarters in town. And that was why he felt such a dislike for himself this morning. Because of what had happened to him the night before. Because of the domino game that he was more or less obliged to play in a while, though he knew he would do better to prepare for the meeting that evening. No. That wasn't true either. He was also apprehensive about the meeting and disliked himself because he wasn't able to stick to his original position that he wasn't going to do it. If he took on the business, his personal affairs would be certain to get into a complete mess. His debts, his family, to say nothing of his house. Perhaps what had happened yesterday was no coincidence, perhaps he'd simply wanted to give himself to that woman from Campo Alegre to escape the prospect of what awaited him if he accepted the chairmanship. After all, wasn't it good that he could still play dominoes this afternoon and so enjoy a last carefree afternoon with his friends? But he had a hangover like he'd never had in his life before, and was uneasy about the game mainly for physical reasons.

So what had happened yesterday shouldn't have happened . . .? So was it another of his great mistakes . . .?

He felt physically ill and mentally confused and didn't blame himself, as he usually did, but his line of work. Damn, in one respect it was the nicest job imaginable, and that's why he had always held on to it, despite these bad times. Because you could be completely free and be yourself if you wanted to. You could work wherever and whenever you felt like it. He, for example, didn't do as certain taxi drivers did, parking at the same place every day, nor did he hire himself out as a courier for some company or other. He worked wherever he wanted to. When he had waited for a long time at the airport, he drove to Campo Alegre, and if there was nothing doing there either, he drove back to the hotels in town. If it was empty there, too, he drove to Caracas Bay. You might cross the bridge or you might not. You did what you wanted to do. There was never enough work anyway. Just enough to live on. Particularly since the travel agencies and hotels had got into the stupid habit of driving their guests themselves – to the town and from the town – in large buses, and rich owners ran tour buses with which they drove tourists all over the island. A terrible situation, about which the government did nothing. Oh, after 30 May this island would perhaps become even more miserable, because there might be new political parties, but everything would continue in the same old way. You had to swallow it when you saw the people who had made a mess of things come crawling out of their holes one by one like rats to create another disaster. People paid their taxes and what did they get in return? The more they paid, the less they got! Sometimes he was really sorry that he had chosen this occupation and stayed with it. This wonderful, freelance occupation. One sometimes became intoxicated by this complete freedom. Undoubtedly that was partly the source of the disasters which could befall him so often and so unexpectedly. How else could he suddenly have taken off with that whore to Aruba? But what a wonderful body, and such soft skin that you stuck to it if you weren't careful! Just like that skin of last night. Looking back on it – looking back on it, he regretted all this, because to start with he'd turned Nora into an adulterous woman. She thought, of course, that he didn't know, that he would murder her if he ever found out, but that was nonsense. He knew all about it, but what could he do? He'd gone away, dammit, hadn't he?

He couldn't shake off the mood. It was all because of this damn occupation of his. Sometimes he got so angry that he decided to sell 200H and take a permanent job. A job as a bricklayer, the occupation he'd started out on as a young man. And then look after his home and children like normal people – even including other taxi drivers, who seemed to be able to put up with this occupation. But he could never, *never* do that! He didn't do it because when he raced across the smooth roads of his island in his large 200H, life was as carefree as it could be. And none of his problems could make any difference to that. The shimmering asphalt in the afternoon with the sun on it – the long road which seemed to stretch into infinity. The quiet along the road, in which, driving carefully, you could think about nothing or about a woman you'd just had or were going to have. And under your borsalino, the gently wafting wind, and your radio on softly under your dashboard. Now and again a cigar. That kept you young. It gave you an appetite for this life, which the moment you got out of your 200H became a wretched existence. With your 200H you suddenly found adventure. A woman stopped you in the middle of the day and asked you if you could take her to her remote house, because she'd been waiting for a bus for a long time. And you took off your borsalino and said that she could get in, and she didn't have to pay, and you were going that way anyway. And then you let the music wash over her gently and you scattered a few compliments in her direction and asked her why she was sitting so far away from you. And when she, with an embarrassed smile, moved a little closer to you, you turned off to the deep caves on the north side, or sought another discreet spot. Or a beautiful white woman waved you down and you took her to her remote country house and she gave you a cool drink because of the heat of the day and you stayed on . . . Weird, he sometimes thought, that there were men who couldn't have children. He, in a manner of speaking, had only to touch a woman's thighs to make her pregnant. If he could summon up the courage, he thought, he'd have an injection, and sometimes if he got very angry and seemed to realize the cause of his misery, he even resolved to have himself castrated.

32

'*How* did you actually get through the money?'

After clearing up the bath shed he'd sat down on the altar toilet to think about his life, trying at least to get his mind relatively clear. Nora had called from the house a few times that his food was on the table.

Because he hadn't reacted, she'd come to the bath shed herself. She thought that he'd fallen asleep again there, as he had done just now under 200H. Because he did not answer immediately, she repeated her question and opened the door of the bath shed, which he'd not put on the hook.

'Playing poker,' he said.

'At poker? Where do you play poker, then?'

'At the airport. I'm telling you that I was at the airport last night.' He decided it was better not to say anything more about the Holland plane.

'Well,' said Nora, who was now so certain that he had been in the camp that she was actually embarrassed for him. 'Your food's on the table.'

But Bubu Fiel wasn't lying entirely, although, as Nora thought, he had been in the camp last night. At least, he had lost the money at poker and hadn't given it away to a whore as she wrongly assumed; the whore had been free.

33

Micha, who had been living in the camp for two months in room 102, had woken up on Saturday after a relatively good Friday with a need to throw a party; she had a daughter of twelve in her homeland of the Dominican Republic whose birthday it was. She'd already sent the child presents and that morning at about nine o'clock she also rang her. She loved her daughter and knew that she would be sad if she let her birthday pass 'quietly'. And if there was one thing you couldn't afford to be in this camp, that was it. One moment of sadness or homesickness could lead one to pack one's things, disappear from the camp and go home . . . to slip back into the poverty from which one had come, or to resume the whore's life in the capital, where one earned less than here in Curaçao, where the competition was practically

134

non-existent, certainly from the native women. Apart from that, if you treated Curaçaoans in at least a friendly way, they were cordial and pleasant to you. She herself already had a brand-new portable television; a combination radio and record player, a pile of clothes and many more things, all given to her by them, and not so much in return for services rendered, but out of affection. (Or if one likes, love, because Curaçaoans fall in love relatively easily.) To say nothing of money . . .

No, at all costs she had to avoid sadness; it had happened in this camp more than once that a woman had been driven mad by sadness and unpleasant thoughts. Micha wanted to keep in control of such terrible things. She decided to celebrate her daughter's birthday by going to bed that day with all the guys that she liked. By screwing for her pleasure, which otherwise she didn't do at all. Early in the morning she met a young man who was playing truant from school for his visit to the camp and she stayed with him until one o'clock in the afternoon. She'd spoiled him, told him a lot of things, and to his complete astonishment had even bought food for him. When she sent him away because she wanted to rest for the evening, he was so grateful that he left behind a number of joints. Under her bed she even had a few bottles of whisky.

34

That Saturday afternoon at about six o'clock, Bubu Fiel had been intending to drive home and give Nora the money he'd promised her, because he was having no luck in town. He was just about to drive away from the entrance of Hotel Curaçao International when an American with short, straight hair came out of the hotel, panting, and leapt into his cab. Only as Bubu was driving past the hotel did he say that he wanted to go to Campo Alegre. This suited Bubu very well, because then he could be home immediately after he dropped this passenger off in the whores' camp. So he drove by way of Wakota, past his house, and took the man to Campo.

But when the latter got out, he said: 'Wait for me, driver. I have to take the plane to New York tonight.' He gave Bubu Fiel a ten-dollar note, which was a very good price, and when he saw that Bubu was hesitating, he leant through of the window roguishly to confide to him: 'I've heard so much about your Campo Alegre that I want to experience it for myself, but unfortunately I've got to go straight back. My wife's waiting for me at the hotel.' Bubu said that he would wait faithfully although he had intended to go straight home.

While the American quickly went into the camp and began sizing up various women who were walking around or sitting at the doors of their houses, Bubu got out of his 200H to sit down on a stone block which was positioned up against the office where the women registered and came to pay their rent every day. He didn't like waiting in the cab itself, because he knew his weakness.

The taxi drivers who were waiting for passengers to the town came up to him immediately. Again he spread it around that he would rather not become chairman of the union, hoping that at the very last moment there would be some kind of salvation for him. Again, most of the drivers there felt that he, as the person who'd taken the initiative in the struggle, should also become chairman of the Association. After a while, women from the camp also joined the group. But Bubu Fiel broke away from them, because the women in the camp also said that he should accept the chairmanship of the Association. It even became a matter of prestige for them when they realized that the present chairman of the union was a driver who kept exclusively to the south-west side of the island, in front of the large Hilton Hotel, in contrast to 'their' Bubu. With their loud, shrill, Spanish voices, they immediately made it a matter of Hilton *versus* Campo Alegre, and later even the United States *versus* the Dominican Republic. From then on, it of course became an issue between socialism and capitalism. They began reminding him of the numerous times America had simply violated their sovereignty without much ceremony – as is usual for America – by occupying the Dominican Republic.

'*Abajo los yanquis!*' they cried. '*Nixon go home!*'

At any rate it was the prospect of earning another ten dollars that evening that kept him there in the camp. Then he would have at least sixty guilders in all. The thought gave him a pleasant feeling, because then he would be able to surprise Nora in a way which didn't happen very often.

'Here,' he'd call to her, 'here's your damn money. Go on, buy shoes for everyone and let us starve. Here's sixty guilders . . .' That's how he talked whenever he was able to give her a lot of money at once. He was now anticipating the delightful way she would let him come to her that night, because in his experience she – and women in general – always behaved nicely towards a man when they had just received money from him. And she was a good woman in bed, Nora, with relatively soft skin and a high cunt.

Because waiting made him thirsty, he went into the camp to buy a beer at the bar in the middle of it. He took it away with him in a cup – it was busy in there too – and now sat down in the camp on a wooden crate in front of the office. It seemed that nothing would happen to him if he sat there like a good taxi driver calmly drinking his beer – waiting for a high-paying customer. The women who knew him and were free just waved at him because they preferred to join the large group who were standing talking about him outside the camp.

35

Suddenly Micha was standing in front of him. He recognized her immediately because she was beautiful and he had driven her here when she'd arrived. She had stood with the group outside for a while and now she was on the way back to her room. She still wanted to have a party.

He had brought her here and at the time had treated her like a lady, and sitting there alone, he looked like a nice, dutiful paterfamilias, reminding her of the happy marriage she'd never had. She decided he was exactly the man she needed for a day like this. And wasn't he soon going to be chairman of the taxi drivers' union, which would certainly mean that she would have a particular aura about her in this camp if she became his girlfriend? The boy hadn't been bad, but this was something else . . . She told him it was her birthday and invited him to come and have a drink with her. She said it was *her* birthday because she thought that that would make more impression than the birthday of her daughter. He refused and told her about the American. She thought it was a nuisance, but said that she could understand. 'Shall I bring the whisky out here, then? Then we can drink to my health here?' Bubu shrugged his shoulders and she hurried off and reappeared a little later with a bottle of whisky and two cups with ice in them. She sat next to him on the wooden box and they started drinking her health together. She said it was a shame that he had to wait for the American, otherwise they could continue drinking in her room. She winked at him as she did so. He understood and smiled, and said that it was definitely a pity because he simply had to wait for the American. She observed that it was a shame that things didn't always work out in life the way one wanted. He nodded and she took out a letter that her daughter had written to her from the front of her dress and read him a few lines from it.

'A nice girl,' he observed. She liked the way he said it so much that she offered to go and see where the American was. 'Perhaps he'll be a long time yet,' she said to him. 'And then in the meantime you can come to my room to see a big photo of my daughter that I've got in my box.' She didn't like going around the camp with that photograph, otherwise she'd go and get it. 'What's more,' she said, 'I can tell the American if I find him that the driver of 200H is in number 102 when he's ready.' He thought it was a good idea.

She came back a little later. She told him that the American was with a friend of hers and that he was going to take his time; 200H could still count on another two hours or so. She gave him a ten-dollar note which the American had sent him, in order, as he had said to her through the window of her friend's room, to drink a few drinks to his health if it took too long.

However, once he was in her room, she didn't even take the trouble to continue the game with the photo, but said openly to him that she thought he was a marvellous man and wanted to have a party with him. So she showed him the four large bottles of whisky which were under her low and rather dirty bed. He said that was okay, provided that the party only took two hours, but he had to take the American into town. She said okay and then called to everyone standing on her doorstep that they were going to have a party.

In a trice her little room was chock-full. Some young people began dancing as well as they could in the tiny space. Another group started a poker game on Micha's bed. When Bubu saw that they were playing for high stakes, he thought he understood in a moment of lucidity why God had sent Micha today of all days, on her birthday, on the eve of his election to chairman of the taxi drivers' union, namely to ensure that he would become rich or at least well off, and make such a killing that he could become a good chairman of the taxi drivers' union without financial problems. Micha put a new record on her radiogram and took off her blouse so as to be able to dance with him with just her bra on. He put his hands around her delicate waist and was so carried away for a moment that he felt marvellous. He considered breaking up the poker game on her bed in the bedroom and starting screwing Micha, but controlled himself because he thought she hadn't been sent for that, but to get money for him, at least in the first instance. So, still holding her with one hand, with the other hand he joined the poker game with the almost one hundred guilders that he had.

A quarter of an hour later, he'd lost everything. He was really upset, but felt it was his own bloody stupid fault. God hadn't wanted to give him any money, but a good free screwing session and that's why he'd lost. For a while he drank with Micha, while she kept clinging to him. He'd thought about turning it into a great orgy, in which anyone could screw any woman or the women could perform lesbian acts with each other in order to amuse the men, but decided not to because he felt that God would again interpret that wrongly. He had to make it intimate; just himself and Micha alone. So, after less than an hour had passed, he said that that was the end of the poker game and that everyone must go. He embraced Micha demonstratively and the people realized with a laugh what he meant and quickly dispersed.

He thought of the American, who would be waiting for him, or would even come and call for him, but he had the feeling that he would never leave this room, because he would immediately die from the feeling of guilt which was already starting to take hold of him. He also told himself that he disliked Americans. He wanted to get drunk as quickly as possible and be with Micha in order to forget. What else was left?

Afterwards the whore and he had undressed completely.

They had closed the doors and windows and put on a slow record to which they danced. He now wondered if the cigarette which she had got him to pull on frequently was marijuana and so had given him an extra hangover. But he couldn't say, because he'd never tried marijuana before. Anyway, as they danced they said that it was great dancing like that together and having a party. Then they embarked on their private orgy. He made her damn well crow with pleasure in and over her whole body, and she made him feel something that was a mixture of pleasure and melancholy. She had sucked him so completely dry that he waddled out of her room late at night like a squeezed lemon. And she had no breath left either, even though she groaned softly as he went that he should come back. As often as he liked.

That afternoon, as he listlessly downed his *sòpi di mondongo*, he tried not to think of her. 'Damn whore,' he kept saying to himself, because he felt sick with her: a sickness which seemed to be a kind of memory of her skin, which concentrated itself in his lower abdomen. That was where the softness of her skin had touched him most, and that was where, though he tried not to think of her, he had to keep gently rubbing himself. It was so wonderful it almost hurt.

When he'd finished his meal he put on a clean, white, long-sleeved shirt that he did not button up but fastened in front of his belly. From the boot of 200H he took a gallon of rum, which he'd bought as usual with the money that Manchi had given him, and brought it inside. He still felt so bad at that moment that he decided not only never to go to Micha again, but never to take a passenger to the whores' camp again. Even if I'm offered a hundred dollars, he said to himself. Consequently he hoped that the afternoon's domino game would help him forget her wonderful body for good.

PART II

Afternoon and Evening

Finally Manchi said (so he could at least savour the taste of saying it) that he intended to build a weekend cottage. At West Point. It tasted very good.

Solema was startled at the news because she immediately connected his plan with her affair with Janchi. The weekend cottages were sited there because of the wonderful view. And mostly on the edge of the steep, rocky coast: it wouldn't be difficult to give somebody a push there!

'Why so suddenly?'

'It isn't *suddenly*, I've had the plan for a long time, but I wanted to wait until we'd paid off our mortgage on the house.'

So what she was thinking made good sense. It might even mean that he had known about her affair with Janchi for ages; that he'd only waited this long to get rid of her out of *business* considerations. Rather confused, she lay down in the bedroom to ponder this new turn of events.

'Can you play bridge?'

She had another fright when he suddenly stood there full length in front of her. And his voice sounded threatening, as though at that moment her life depended on whether or not she could play bridge.

'Why?'

'I want to learn.'

She felt somewhat relieved and sat up on the bed. 'Yes, I can play bridge.'

'Is it difficult?'

She was actually going to lie to put him in a good mood, but decided not to. 'Yes, very difficult. And besides, I can't play very well myself.'

'You women can't do anything!'

Apart from that, he ignored her completely while he began to get dressed for dominoes. Although he did not show it, he was quite excited about his decision: a weekend cottage. Although the problem of a new game remained, of course: most owners of weekend cottages there on the bay didn't play dominoes. They played bridge, for example.

He put on a pair of well-ironed grey trousers and a long-sleeved white shirt; also crisply starched and ironed. He rubbed some more grease on his hair and brushed it back. The little stars shone brightly. Then he put on a plain black tie. In contrast to most people, who consider black a mourning colour, he decided that it was very distinguished. He *liked* black. Black reminded him of judges' gowns. Afterwards he decided it was a shame that because of the heat he couldn't put on a jacket: then he could have taken a revolver along with him unobtrusively. Now the thing protruded rather annoyingly out of his right trouser pocket, the more so because to be on the safe side he had first wrapped it in a handkerchief.

The shoes weren't completely dry yet, but Solema, who had been entrusted with packing them, decided that that wasn't her concern. A large cardboard box was too clumsy for him to take with him and so she put them in a nice brown case. She didn't consider it her business either how the men were supposed to write the score in chalk on the wet shoes. As Manchi had asked her, she simply put lots of pieces of white chalk from her school in with the shoes. As she was closing the case, she saw Janchi Pau sitting at the domino table. A spontaneous feeling of safety caused her, without thinking, to wave at him immediately. He waved back. They abandoned all caution, because when Manchi came to see how far she'd got, they were still waving to each other. She was so frightened that she put her hand to her face when she

146

heard him behind her, so that he did not notice her waving. He did see Janchi waving, though.

'Look,' he said to her, 'that Pau's got a tie on today... That's why he's waving to me, I'm sure.' He waved back rather nonchalantly.

He was surprised. Janchi's behaviour was certainly unusual.

'Perhaps it's his birthday,' she said nervously.

She wondered why he did not mention the fact that she had waved, thinking that he must have seen her. When he made no comment, her suspicion grew that he knew all about her and Janchi, and that his plan for the weekend cottage was nothing but a ruse to get rid of her. As a result, she began to consider Janchi's proposal that she should move in with him quickly more seriously.

He tugged at the case a number of times and said, 'You'll have to drive me, this thing is much too big to lug along the road.'

'Too *heavy* for you, I expect you mean,' she said spitefully in order to wound his male pride.

'You'll have to drive me,' he repeated imperturbably.

2

A little later, when they were already on the Tula road, he asked her to drive back again. When the car drew up outside the door of their house, he got out, went in and put his revolver back in its place in the bedroom. He had thought about it, and decided that with a weapon in his pocket he was lowering himself to the level of the three men he was about to play with. A danger that had become more concrete now that Janchi Pau had appeared at the domino table in a *tie*. Come to that, Janchi had waved to him anyway, hadn't he?

3

The domino table was out of bounds to Solema. She was glad of that now as she dropped Manchi off. Even at this distance, without approaching him closely, the presence of Janchi made her excited. Without saying goodbye, and without closing the door, Manchi got out with the case in his hand and went over to the domino table where Janchi was sitting. He said hello to Nora, who was so tense watching out for Chamon that she answered his greeting much less spontaneously than usual. Nor did Nora see that Solema was waving to her from the car, until Solema pressed the horn. Then she waved back rather laboriously. On this Sunday afternoon of all days Chamon was keeping her waiting.

4

The two men shook hands and said '*Entre medio*'. Had both of them suddenly forgotten the waving incident? Neither of them mentioned it.

Manchi put the case on the bench against the wall of the house and when he'd opened it said, 'Here they are, then. I could have brought more, but you know what women are like: they've got a hundred pairs of shoes that they never wear, but as soon as you need a few of them, they start protesting.'

'That's true enough,' said Janchi, 'but what are you actually going to do with them? Are we going to write the score on the shoes or something? I mean, we have to know who gives who what kind of shoes.'

He studied the shoes, which looked like a consignment of dead ravens, with amusement. Manchi, who had sat down opposite, said that he didn't understand what Janchi meant.

'They're all black,' said Janchi with a boyish laugh.

'Of course. Of course. The idea is that the score is written on them in chalk each time. Look, my Solema has put a whole lot in with them.'

Janchi looked at the shoes more closely.

'We can't do that, they're still wet. Besides, I don't think you can write that well with chalk on leather and polish.' He picked up one of the shoes and turned it over thoughtfully in his hands, noting with pleasure that it must certainly be Solema's. 'It would have been better to have them in different colours,' he said, putting the shoe back with the other. 'For example, black and white.'

'We didn't discuss that,' said Manchi, irritated.

Janchi raised a hand to calm him down.

'No, but it would have been better.'

Fastening his shirt under his belly with a new and better knot, Bubu Fiel appeared to the east of his house. He was in slippers and his trousers were hanging far below his bulging belly because he'd forgotten his belt. His large navel was visible. His short, curly hair, which was rather longer than Manchi's, was uncombed.

'Hello, chairman,' said Janchi, who liked Bubu Fiel best among his domino friends, '*Are* you chairman already or do you still have to be elected?'

'Tonight,' said Bubu, sitting down for the time being on the south side of the table between the two men, and shaking hands with each of them in turn.

'You don't seem too pleased about it,' said Manchi.

'I'm not. It's a heavy responsibility. It'll take up so much of my time that soon I won't be able to do anything for myself.'

'But you're the brains behind it all,' said Janchi almost proudly. 'If you hadn't stopped the tour buses taking the passengers, everything would have gone on in the same old way.'

'Well, that's what everyone says,' said Bubu, 'but I didn't stop those drivers taking the passengers from the *Bounty* single-handed. All of us did it.'

'Of course,' said Janchi, 'but I heard that you fired the others into action.'

'I may have. But I don't see why just because of that the whole weight of responsibility should fall on my shoulders.'

'You'll see,' said Janchi, a little disappointed, 'that it'll be better than you think.'

Manchi, who considered the aspirations of the taxi drivers scarcely worthy of attention, thought they were in the process of breaking with an old habit which prevailed at the domino table, namely not to bring the conversation round to their professional fields, and said, 'You're right, Fiel, you'd be better off using all the time it's going to cost you for yourself. I assume, for example, that you intend to finish your house one day . . . ?' But Bubu shrugged his shoulders and said nothing, because that alternative wasn't very pleasant either: shattered as he felt at that moment, he doubted whether he would *ever* finish his house.

Manchi saw no point in letting a chance of scoring a new point for his prestige pass. He looked from one to the other (everyone knew that Janchi lived in an unfinished house, although people said that he'd got further than Bubu Fiel) and said with taunting slowness, 'Building a house costs a damn lot of effort. And money of course,' he added with an amused smile.

'Yes,' said Bubu Fiel and Janchi Pau together, nodding at each other in mutual understanding.

'Marvellous, Manchi,' said Bubu, to steer the conversation in a different direction, 'I think you brought shoes for all of us.'

'I could have brought more. I was just telling Janchi here: my wife has got a *cupboard* full of shoes that she no longer wears, but the moment I touched them she started going on about me wanting to steal *all* of her shoes.'

'Yes, women,' said Bubu, 'women . . .'

'How many are there exactly, Manchi?' asked Janchi.

'Only ten pairs.'

'That's a lot,' said Bubu pensively. 'I don't think Nora has had that many shoes in her whole life.'

'And I really wanted twelve,' Manchi went on inexorably.

'But we've still got the problem of the score,' said Janchi quite sharply. 'We won't be able to write in chalk on the shoes, and apart from that they're still wet.'

'We'll leave them in the sun, and they'll dry while we play,' said Manchi.

'Maybe,' said Janchi, 'maybe.' He had to admit that Manchi was right.

'We don't have to *write* anything on them,' said Bubu suddenly in a flash of lucidity, which made him feel optimistic. 'We'll divide the tree here into two, one half for Chamon Nicolas and Janchi here, the other half for you and me.' He had the feeling that he was shaking off the after-effects of Micha and explained enthusiastically, 'What do you say to that? On one side we'll write *Pau and Nicolas* and on the other side *Fiel and Sanantonio*.'

'Excellent,' said Janchi, shaking Bubu's hand, 'excellent!'

Manchi nodded a number of times in silence. Then he said, 'That really is a good idea. But we'll have to divide the tree exactly in two, otherwise we'll get into trouble shortly.'

'We'll do it right now,' said Bubu.

He got up and stood in front of the tamarind tree, looking at it first from the left and then from the right to find the exact centre. When he believed he had done it, he took a piece of chalk, went straight to the tree, bent down close to it and, walking backwards in that position, constantly looking up at the tree (so as not to lose sight of the imaginary centre that he had found), drew a line on the ground which ended when he hit the wall of his house with a *bump* with his backside.

'Right,' he said, looking at his friends triumphantly, 'we can't go wrong.' While he indicated the directions, he said, 'The shoes we give to Janchi Pau and Chamon Nicolas will be put on this side. Any shoes we get, on this side. *If* we get any,' he stressed with a laugh.

Manchi got up and stood with his back to the trunk of the tamarind tree in order to inspect the line. 'It's completely crooked, Bubu, *completely*.' So he rubbed it out with his foot and drew a new line.

Janchi, who could not judge the line from a distance (it was a long way from the tamarind tree to the table, since he himself had shifted the table even further to the south), got up and joined his friends with a piece of chalk in his hand.

'Your line isn't bad,' he said to Manchi, who stood demonstratively wiping his hands with his handkerchief. 'It's just that it would be better to divide the tree itself in two, wouldn't it?' No sooner said than done, and he drew a vertical line from the top to the bottom along the tree trunk. 'Which side do you want?'

Manchi pointed to the north and Janchi wrote $N+P$ in chalk on the north side of the trunk, and $F+S$ on the other side. It wasn't easy on the rough bark of the tamarind, but he managed it. While he was wiping his hands, Manchi said that it was better to write the names in full. Bubu Fiel agreed with him.

'No problem at all,' said Janchi, 'but you could have said so before.'

'I've only just realized,' said Manchi.

'But the names Nicolas and Sanantonio are too long to write in full on this tree. You yourself can see how difficult it is on this rough surface.'

Bubu agreed and Manchi gave way. 'Well, at least put the initials with them,' he said, to have the last word.

Janchi shrugged his shoulders and corrected it to: $CN+JP$

and *BF+MS*. Now they had only one problem: string to tie the shoes together so that they would be able to hang them up on the branches of the tamarind tree. Bubu went to his bath shed to look for some and came back with an old dress which he started tearing into strips, throwing the rest on the ground. He took the shoes out of the box and put them on the bench in the sun to dry a little more. Then he sat down again in the seat of Chamon Nicolas, who was still not there.

'I think I'm going to have terrible problems with the sun in a while,' Manchi said suddenly. 'This table is too far south.'

Janchi cursed inwardly. But it was true, he had moved the table so far to the south that shortly, when the sun reached its zenith, they would be outside the shade of the tamarind tree.

However, when Manchi and Bubu had pushed the table so far to the left that it was more or less in its usual place, Janchi protested that he would be right in front of the thick trunk (and hence not be able to see Solema, when she came onto the porch of her house). So he insisted on pushing the table a little more to the right, but Manchi objected. He said that in that case Chamon Nicolas, who wasn't there yet, would be troubled by the sun later in the afternoon.

'Then we'll have to move the table *during* the game,' he said, 'and that's just a lot of fuss. This way, *no one* will be bothered by the sun.'

Janchi had no answer to this argument and the table finally stayed on the line which Bubu had drawn and Manchi had improved, against Bubu Fiel's house. The latter now sat down and leant against the wall. Janchi also took up his usual place on Manchi's right.

Then, after all these preparations, there was nothing for them to do but what Nora had been doing for at least an hour at the front door of her house: wait for Chamon Nicolas, whose absence was all the more striking because he was normally one of the first.

'It's long after one,' said Manchi, with an irritated look at his gold watch. 'If he had a *telephone*, I could go up to my place and ring him . . .'

'Perhaps he won't come at all today,' said Janchi, who still blamed himself for being prepared to *play* all afternoon, when he ought to be spending his time on other, more important things.

'Chamon always comes,' said Bubu. 'Let's have a drink for now. Nora!'

5

He had to call at least three times, only getting a reaction when he used the strongest curse in Papiamento, *conjo*, in front of her name. At that she screamed back loudly: 'I'm coming!', and left the front door to pour three drinks. When he called her while he was at the east of the house with his friends, it was scarcely ever for anything except rum. Pouring the drinks took her some time, since because of her nervousness (she was worried that Chamon would arrive just when she was in the kitchen), she was not able to get the gallon bottle open that quickly. She also had to get the glasses out of her best sideboard and wash them, and find the tray (and wipe it). As she did so, she tried to keep an eye on the gate in front of her house, but unfortunately for her Chamon Nicolas came running into the yard, panting, just as she was pouring out the rum on the little kitchen table.

When she arrived with the drinks to the east of the house and found him sitting there, still panting and in his usual place – that is, with his back to her – she felt like bursting into tears. All in all, she'd been waiting in the doorway for him for at least an hour. Now he was sitting there she probably wouldn't be able to exchange a word with him for the whole afternoon: not one five-guilder word.

'Bring us another rum, Nora,' said Bubu, downing his drink in one gulp. 'Friend Chamon has arrived.'

Chamon, who already felt rather embarrassed because of his lateness, said as he wiped his brow with his white handkerchief, which was no longer very clean, 'Hello, Nora ... Don't worry ... don't bother.'

But Bubu said fiercely, wanting obedience from his wife in the presence of his friends, 'Out of the question! I've told Nora to bring another drink and she'll do that.'

When Nora brought Chamon his lonely drink on the large tray, she was hoping to be able to give him a sign. Any kind of sign. Chamon, feeling that he had to catch up with the others, downed his drink fast, without paying any attention to her. Immediately afterwards, in order to play down his lateness, he put both hands on the domino pieces face down in front of him, and said, 'Right then, let's begin.'

At that moment Nora felt great contempt for him, because he had noticed nothing of her plight.

6

So they were all seated in their places: Chamon Nicolas and Janchi Pau, south–north; Bubu Fiel – with his back to his own house – and Manchi Sanantonio west–east.

Manchi shuffled. 'You're late this afternoon,' he said to Chamon Nicolas, lifting his hands off the table after taking quite a while over it.

Chamon Nicolas took out his pieces and said, 'A damn friend of mine. I simply couldn't get rid of him.'

'Can happen to anyone,' said Manchi, with a hint of reproach.

'Anyway, I'm always one of the first.'

'Yes,' said Janchi, 'but I'm actually angry with you, because

155

I wanted to give these two twelve pairs of shoes today, but since you're late, we can only make it ten.'

'Ten's quite a lot!' said Chamon, feeling at home again.

'Right,' said Janchi, still joking, as he shook Chamon Nicolas's hand across the table. 'So we'll make it ten pairs.'

7

The first two games of the first set went quickly, like the finger exercises of a good pianist. The odd fact that they were both won by Janchi Pau and Chamon Nicolas the men regarded as pure chance.

The third game went slightly more slowly.

Chamon Nicolas led with double six. Manchi placed the six–three next to it, and Janchi set down his double three. At the other end Bubu 'broke' the six with six–two, and Chamon replied to this with two–blank. In turn Manchi put the blank–four on this. At this point the pace slackened. Chamon Nicolas was talking about the expensiveness of foodstuffs. Janchi extended this to all other items and various explanations were put forward. In a long tirade, Janchi inveighed against the 'foreigners', blaming them for everything that was wrong on the island. Now he sat there, while the others thought he was mulling over the game, admittedly with his eyes focused on the table, thinking about Solema and feeling that his tirade wasn't entirely true.

'We must produce for ourselves,' she had said to him. 'It's not only the foreigners, we're to blame ourselves, too. Why can't we do what others can do?'

Perhaps, he thought slightly bitterly, she's not quite right? With a loud bang, he played the four–three to the blank–four, which Manchi placed with a measured gesture, and left threes at both ends. *Four* was pointless for him as he had no fours left. 'The others can do everything that we natives can't do because they have *capital*,' he then said. 'They lend each other money and support each other and oppose us.' He thought of his conversations with her about the serious manufacture of *wabi* tables and again said, 'Until we do something about the foreigners, we haven't got a chance.' Chamon Nicolas, who was emboldened by the two easily won games, said, 'You're right.' He even ventured a joke in the direction of Bubu Fiel. 'You taxi drivers are the only black capitalists on this damn island. You do whatever you like.'

'As long as the tour buses allow them,' said Janchi teasingly.

Bubu, who preferred not to be reminded too much of the impending chairmanship, made a defensive gesture in Janchi's direction. Suddenly he felt tired and listless again, now, right at the *start* of this game. True, he had found himself with four twos in his hand, which under normal circumstances certainly gave him a chance of winning, but he felt gloomy about things. No, he simply couldn't *see* the game, the relatively short wait for Janchi's move just now had made his thoughts wander again to the joys of the previous evening. I must make sure that I don't lean against this wall too much today, he said to himself as he stretched his back lazily against it, otherwise I'll fall asleep. He began slowly playing with his navel with his right hand while he thought about how wonderful a sleep would be: over there on a piece of cardboard, under 200H, or in a hammock here, in this rich, cool shade, where now, because he couldn't give in to sleep, it was such an ordeal.

'Your turn, Bubu,' said Manchi.

Bubu dropped the three–two casually from his hand and went on rubbing his belly. At that moment it was the only piece he could play anyway.

'Don't be so careless, friend Bubu,' said Manchi again,

putting the piece back neatly with the rest of the game.

'Okay,' said the latter absent-mindedly.

Now it was Chamon's turn. Besides three other pieces he had the three–blank and the three–one; he had no twos. At one end of the game there was a two and at the other a three. So he didn't have to think for very long, all the more so because he had played a blank previously, which Manchi had promptly 'covered': he should now play blank again and that had to be the three–blank on the open three. However, he decided to take his time over his move and pretend he was thinking very hard. As a result Bubu and Manchi might assume that he had plenty of threes and twos – which he did not have at all – and might no longer lead these to him, reducing his chances of passing.

His unnecessary reflection bothered Bubu Fiel most, of course. At a certain moment, in order not to drift off completely, he leant his broad torso across the table in order to be able to stare at it for a long time with his eyes wide open. He pretended to be thinking ahead and perhaps he was sincerely trying to. But he was troubled by the sun, which was now being reflected fiercely off the red roof of Manchi's house. His eyes began watering and the eyes of the dominoes suddenly started dancing across the table like little stars; little stars in a dark night. Fortunately he realized the eyes of the pieces were subtly hypnotizing him.

He sat up and rubbed his eyes as unobtrusively as possible. He was still troubled by the sunbeams which were being reflected from Manchi's house, which he normally never noticed. He thought it was a shame that because of Manchi he couldn't tell everyone where he'd spent the night: in Micha's arms. That would perk him up, he believed. Although he might also have to mention those eighty guilders. It really was stupid to risk everything on one bet. Of course he could also tell them that *lying in bed all night with that whore hadn't cost him a cent*! No, he'd definitely do it because that was undoubtedly an achievement of the highest order, and Christ, what a lovely wet cunt! And she wasn't a woman, he thought, experiencing the ecstasy anew, who waited for things, but one who came to get them for herself. A damn *greedy* woman! Who kept asking for more, daddy, daddy, *daddy*! *Give everything you've got! Haven't you got any more . . .?!* Oh, *Bubu*! No one had wept over his prick like that for a long time. Not for a *long* time! For that reason, this game of dominoes was cruel, too cruel. When a man had been to bed with a woman like he had with Micha, he could do two things: tell his friends about it in vivid terms, or lie there thinking about it the whole day, pondering and enjoying the afterglow. But not talking about it and not being allowed to talk about it, because of having to put it out of your mind because something else is demanding your attention: oh dear! And the way in which he'd pulled her! Damn, it surely meant something when a woman like that comes to you and chooses you to help celebrate her birthday? *For nothing?!* There were *other* men in that camp, weren't there? The itch increased and he began laughing visibly as he rubbed his abdomen. Damn good trick to lure him to her room with that photo of her child. What a woman!

'You mustn't scratch like that, friend Bubu,' said Manchi suddenly, 'it's not very nice. And you, Chamon, it's about time you played.'

Bubu started out of his daydreaming and said, 'Sorry.' In order to rehabilitate himself a little he turned to Chamon, 'Why don't you play, so that something *happens* at this domino table this afternoon? You know it's your turn, don't you? Or are you sitting daydreaming?'

'I'm just having a quiet think,' said Chamon, leading them up the garden path. 'I'm entitled to do that, aren't I?'

'Hmm,' said Bubu. He told himself that he must do

something. He must make sure that something happened quickly at this domino table, otherwise it would get too much for him and he'd simply be calling out her name, Micha, Micha, *Micha*. 'Nora,' he called suddenly: 'Nora, Nora, Nor*aa*!' He had to *do* something!

'I suppose you'd like another drink?'

Everyone said yes, thank God, although it was their custom only to drink after a game, never during it. Instead of making his move, Chamon put his pieces on the table while he pushed his chair back slightly, in that way suggesting a break, which would have to last until Nora arrived with the drinks. Convinced that he had caused confusion both in Bubu and Manchi because of his thinking for an unnecessary period of time and with the prospect of an extra drink, he then said genially, 'It will put an end to all our difficulties, if our friend Manchi here becomes a judge.'

'For God's sake, stop that nonsense, Chamon,' said Janchi.

'Nonsense? Why? Manchi's been with the court for ages, hasn't he? How long exactly, Manchi?'

'Over thirty years.'

'Nonsense,' said Janchi, unimpressed. 'A bailiff can't become a judge just like that.' Glancing fleetingly at Manchi, he added, 'Not *normally* at least.' He put extra emphasis on the word *normal* because he wanted to be unpleasant, but Manchi ignored the insinuation with all the appearance of dignity.

'It doesn't matter to me,' said Chamon. He believed that he could express his opinion freely to his partner because he had led and because he was the one who in the first instance could win this game for them. 'Besides, they're all there simply to give us citizens grief.'

The playful new turn that the conversation had taken grabbed Bubu's attention. It reminded him of Manchi's story, weeks before.

'How long would you have to study, friend Manchi, before you were promoted to judge?' he asked with interest.

'Oh,' said Manchi, unperturbed, 'three years, I think.'

'Is that all?' said Bubu.

'I've got experience.'

'You've really got a chance, Manchi,' said Chamon chuckling. 'They take black people today too.'

'But not just *anyone*,' said Manchi. 'They're starting to do it now, it's true, but they don't take just anyone.'

'It wouldn't be *right*, anyway,' said Bubu with a shrug of his shoulders. 'After all, certain standards have to be applied to a judge.'

Nora appeared with the drinks, which the men downed quickly. Chamon squeezed his eyes tight shut because of the sharpness of the alcohol in his stomach. Janchi drank his down nonchalantly. Manchi said 'Thanks very much' to Nora and then wiped his mouth with a handkerchief. Still smacking his lips, and rubbing his stomach, which was now also on fire, Bubu said with a laugh, 'Just imagine. Our friend Manchi here, a *judge*!'

'That will make life very easy,' said Chamon.

'Then you must make sure,' said Bubu, after he'd sat relishing the humour of this thought, 'that another judge doesn't pinch your wife, as happened to that judge of yours.' He roared with laughter; the rum was doing him good. Chamon's paunch, of which the navel was showing, also shook with laughter. 'That's a good one!' he said.

Manchi looked at him with a good-natured smile. The memory of his triumph was flattering. Because Bubu had come out with this, he forgave him his careless play and filthy scratching. But he did think that Janchi was a little too cocky, and decided to give him something to reflect on.

'All things considered, it's ridiculous to talk about foreigners on this island. After all, we're *all* foreigners here.

Chamon here even comes from Saba, don't you?'

That remark hurt Chamon.

'Come on, Manchi, I'm a Curaçaoan all in all, because I *feel* like one. What in heaven's name would I do on Saba? I've been here for over twenty-five years.'

'I know,' said Manchi spitefully. 'I know.' He paused for a moment and then went on, 'But in the eyes of the *law*, friend Chamon, in the eyes of the *law* you're a Saban. And the law is the law. You can't do anything about that. Neither can I. You can live in a country for a hundred years, but the law remains the law.'

'But in any case I'm an Antillean,' said Chamon with relief, 'and as such not a foreigner.'

'That's not the same,' said Bubu, reacting as the typical member of his party that he was.

'All that matters is *Curaçao*, the rest is just paper.'

Chamon said nothing.

'So if Manchi becomes a judge,' said Janchi to Chamon with some *Schadenfreude*, 'do you know what's in store for you? He'll deport you from the island, isn't that so, Manchi?'

'Of course not. Who would we play dominoes with, then? No, I simply want to keep sight of the fact that we're in fact all foreigners on this island. A lot of us came from Africa in the past, a proportion of us came from the Netherlands, then there are the Jews, the Arabs, Chinese, Portuguese and many people from the surrounding countries. I once read that there are more than fifty nationalities on this island. Yes, I read that in one of my reports. So it's an island without natives.'

'That means a *nobody's* island?' said Bubu sceptically.

'Or *everyone's*,' said Manchi triumphantly. 'That's why it's nonsense to stress race or origin. The island simply has to become *democratic*.'

'You mean DP,' said Chamon Nicolas, who as a Windward Islander nevertheless voted NVP, since his mother had considered it the party with more 'learning' because of its founder, a doctor of law.

'But we coloureds are in the majority,' said Janchi. 'The others have money, but we are the majority; whichever way you look at it. *We* should really have the power in our hands.'

He had the feeling that Solema would have agreed completely with this, if she had been present. Even more than himself, she was for 'all power to the people'.

'Let's continue,' said Manchi rather too quickly.

'Right,' said Chamon Nicolas, 'the majority is black. So blacks should have the power, whichever way you look at it.' And, slamming his piece down hard, he finally posed the three–blank. The pieces bobbed slowly up and down on the table and just above it, like seagulls on the water.

'Exactly,' said Janchi putting the pieces in order again here and there, 'I'm completely in agreement with that Black Power of yours, Chamon.'

'Oh,' said Manchi in irritation, 'you and your Black Power... Negroes can't govern. It's been proven often enough. They're lazy. They've no sense of responsibility.'

And with a gesture of obvious disdain, he played the six–blank on the three–blank of Chamon. It was the only move he could make, but he hoped that in so doing he was going to make Janchi pass.

'The coloureds don't get a chance,' observed Janchi Pau, without indicating whether he could play or not. 'They haven't had any chance at all since the time of slavery!'

Manchi said nothing. He had no desire to go further into this political point, because he knew that these kinds of conversations could easily turn into arguments. And he didn't feel like that at the moment, especially without his revolver. Apart from that, he was curious to know whether Janchi would pass or not. The latter suddenly leant over the pieces in deep concentration.

8

They were familiar with Janchi's occasional habit, four or five moves before the end of a game, of studying all the pieces with intense concentration as if with a searchlight. From what was on the table and what he had in his hand he would conclude what the others must have according to their positions and build the rest of his game on that. And they had no little admiration for the flawless conclusions to which he usually came on those occasions.

Consequently, Bubu Fiel put his heavy hands involuntarily over the four pieces in front of him on the table as an extra cover. Manchi moved his pieces, which he also had on top of the table, unobtrusively below it. Chamon Nicolas put his four dominoes flat on the table and rubbed his hands with a triumphant smile on his face. He was in such a happy mood that he forgot his fear of Bubu and the knife at his side. Suddenly he also felt that he should look smart and buttoned up his shirt.

Once Pau had realised that the blanks were in Chamon's hands, no one could touch them. But wasn't he even safer than that? He didn't even need Janchi's help. He was bound to win. He felt it was a bit of a shame that his partner didn't play at once so that he could quickly put an end to this game.

But Pau was thinking. It was a damn good move that Manchi had made and he admired it. It was also a challenge for him to go further than he had originally intended, because the pieces that he held hadn't inspired him to do so before. Could he do it? *Did this game, which up to now had proceeded so calmly, contain a chance of a double play?*

The point was to collect information about the blanks, sixes, fives and ones. The point was to have an overview of *everything*. Because Chamon had played nothing but blanks, he assumed that the latter, who now had four pieces, had at least the five–blank and the one–blank. The last remaining blank piece was the double blank, and he had that. Bubu Fiel and Manchi had the twos, that was obvious. He himself had three fives: the double five, the five–three and the five–one. Where were the remaining two, the five–four and the six–five? For a start, they could of course both be with his partner. But . . . Chamon had thought for an especially long time before playing the three–blank a while ago. That meant that he had still more threes. One in any case. *But suppose Chamon had been faking?* It was a damn nuisance if you played half-honest and half-dishonest. You never knew where you were. In this case, he decided intuitively to discount the possibility of Chamon's faking. So he *had* to assume that Chamon had threes: that made five threes on the table and he himself had the five–three. He quickly calculated: so Chamon must have the three–one. Nice. So his partner had the five–blank, the one–blank, the three–one and one other piece. That meant they had *two* direct chances to win, via blank and via three. Experience had taught him that if there were two chances of winning, there was always also the possibility of winning the game *double*. The thing was to be very self-disciplined and choose the right way. He discarded the possibility of the three–one, because apart from the one which he was now going to play, he had no other ones. What was Chamon's *fourth* piece? For psychological reasons, he suddenly opted for six–four (since he had the feeling that Chamon wasn't worried about his double five). This meant that besides the five–blank which because of his run of blanks he had to hang on to, Chamon had no other fives, and so couldn't do anything about his double five. It was also probable that

165

Chamon, who had led with double six, had one more *six*. Otherwise, and according to the custom of good dominoes, he would have led with another piece. *So that if Chamon had no other fives apart from five–blank, but did have one six, then that six could only be the six–four, because only this six and the six–five had not been played yet!* The double play was complete: it had to come through Chamon's six–four, to which Manchi or Bubu Fiel had to play the six–five, so that Chamon Nicolas could make a double play with the five–blank. Like clockwork. The ironic thing about all this, he thought, is that if Manchi simply lets me play my double five, or at least plays a five himself in a moment, they may well win the game (if the six–five really is with Bubu Fiel), by closing out the game with the four–one! He smiled over the pieces, glancing almost scornfully at Manchi. Because he was sure *Manchi would never do that*! On the contrary, Manchi would try as hard as possible to prevent him from playing his double five! With a crash that was so hard that it could have felled a fully grown man, but so controlled that the pieces scarcely moved as a result, he finally played the six–one in reply to Manchi's six–blank. Then he put his hand in his pocket to get out his handkerchief and remembered his stiletto, which increased his feeling of certainty. He wiped his forehead. What he had done was damn hard work. To give himself a breather, he was going to say something else. However, he had to wait, because Bubu, who had been very bored by Janchi's long reflection, played his double two with a mighty crash. The impact was so fierce that the domino pieces flew off the table in all directions, like frightened frogs, into the men's laps and onto the ground. Manchi, Pau, Chamon Nicolas and Bubu rose to pick up the pieces. When they had put the domino snake with all its white eyes back together, Janchi Pau said, turning emphatically to Manchi, 'You can call it fair if you like, that foreigners take the chances that the natives neglect, but it's damn well not as it should be, that for money they can buy all kinds of privileges here over our people. Just look at tourism: the hotels are coming and that's good because our boys and girls are given work. But who's in charge? Foreigners! Do you think that a Curaçaoan or even an Antillean can ever become manager of the Hilton? Do you really think so?'

'If he's got the abilities,' said Manchi stubbornly.

'Oh come on,' said Janchi slightly angrily, despite the good chance of double game that they had, 'if that were true then there would have to be Antilleans in high positions already. And there aren't! Try and find them anywhere. Not just in the hotels. Just take Shell, where I work. Do you think that an Antillean can ever become a director of Shell?'

'Maybe, maybe,' said Manchi, now really cornered.

'Oh, come on, Manchi. Either you don't want to see, or you're really stupid. It'll only happen when we natives have got power. When we can simply say that there won't be a branch here without natives being in charge.'

'Calm down, Janchi,' said Bubu, who felt this afternoon that both the game itself and their conversations were much too serious. 'Calm down. None of us earn our living from politics, and besides, this is a game among friends.'

'It's nothing,' said Manchi, who didn't want to be a spoilsport. 'But Pau will surely want to be prepared to admit that we don't yet have the people for these high positions.'

'But they're not even being trained,' said Janchi violently. 'And that's the worst thing. In fifty years' time the situation will be exactly as it is now: foreigners in the top positions and Antillean slaves underneath them. And the profits leaving the country!'

Manchi said nothing, while Chamon Nicolas nodded in agreement. Bubu Fiel stared quite emphatically at the church of Wakota, to show them that in that case they would have to fight it out among themselves. But he felt that Chamon Nicolas was again taking too long over his move.

More calmly, now his argument seemed to have hit home, Janchi said, 'Besides, as far as I'm concerned, we're an exception. In every country they've got laws to protect their own people against foreigners. Take Venezuela: the fuss it takes to get in there. Not for me, because I've got a Venezuelan father. But the ordinary foreigner. Since time immemorial Venezuela has levied thirty-per-cent import duties on all products coming from the Antilles. And a Venezuelan who leaves Venezuela, even if it's a holiday trip of a few days, has to pay a huge sum. It's the same everywhere. In all the countries where I've been, you find the same protection. Just take America. The leader of democracy that everyone goes on about so: you need a visa to get in there. There's an Iron Curtain there, just the same as there is in Russia. And they have high import duties in America . . .'

'American tourists can only import about a hundred dollars' worth or something of goods duty free,' said Bubu, who thought there was something in Janchi's arguments.

'And you, Manchi, were talking about laws just now,' Janchi continued. 'Of course, you're right, we have to have them. And normal countries do have them. I'd go along with you when you say that natives shouldn't have *special* protection; a kind of democracy, a kind of "free for all". But don't you think it's going a bit far when the foreigners are privileged *above* the natives? In a normal country, when you need a foreigner, then he's allowed to come, then he's welcome, provided on the day of his arrival he starts training a native to replace him later. Venezuela has that law in any case. And so does England.'

'And Guyana,' said Chamon Nicolas, to everyone's amazement.

'Really?' said Janchi surprised.

'Yes,' said Chamon in a neutral voice, 'I read it in the *Trinidad News* the other day.'

'I'm not a narrow nationalist,' said Janchi, 'like many people on this island who can't even think for themselves. One of those followers of Doctor, Doctor, Doctor. I've seen far too much of the world for that. And I won't take away anything from people who've built up their own businesses, at least if they behave reasonably, but there have to be certain laws.'

'The Communists want to take everything away from people,' said Manchi in an insinuating tone. 'They'd certainly take away my house that I built for myself. That's what the Communists are like.'

'I'm not a Communist,' said Janchi abruptly, wondering if Solema might be, although that didn't matter very much to him. He himself at least was certain that he didn't want to give up *that much* of his individuality in order to live under a dictatorial regime.

Bubu Fiel, who considered that now they were talking about politics he had to say something in favour of his party and its late founder, said:

'The Doctor did a lot for this island. And if he were still alive we certainly wouldn't have had a 30th of May.'

'Then we'd have been even worse off,' said Janchi again fiercely. He disapproved of the fact that on 30 May 1969 a large part of the town had been destroyed and in addition considered that the whole popular riot didn't mean very much, because in the elections that followed, the Democratic Party still emerged as the winner. He had kept at a safe distance from the whole movement. Its only value, he considered, was that the foreigners had seen that the Curaçaoans would not take everything lying down. Only in that respect, in his opinion, had they made any progress on 30 May.

'The Doctor simply kept people well-behaved. Just as

the Catholic church had done before. *Order, decency and discipline*, that was the Doctor's motto, wasn't it? And if you just change that motto a little, you get the slogans the fathers used to hold up to the slaves, which mainly boiled down to their duty to stay obedient to their masters, so that the latter could go on calmly exploiting them. Do you understand? Without worrying about unrest and revolts among their Negroes. The Doctor may have done a lot for people, but he didn't make them aware of their rights. And that's wrong. He didn't make them politically aware, he didn't *politicize* them,' he said, expressly using a term that he had learned from Solema.

In order to prevent Janchi saying even more unpleasant things about the Doctor, whom Bubu Fiel had driven around often enough in 200H, and with whom he had also often drunk, Bubu put in, 'The Doctor liked a drink and in those days 200H was green, the party colours of the NVP.' He made a defensive gesture in the direction of Janchi.

'You are all being too *serious* today. There's no point in discussing the Doctor,' he said, forgetting that he himself had brought up the Doctor, 'because the man is dead. I certainly respected him,' he added with complete honesty.

'So did I,' said Chamon while he played three–one with an unnecessarily hard slam and quickly accepted the cigarette that Janchi offered him across the table. On the table there were now again a three and a two.

'I've nothing against the man,' said Janchi, giving Bubu a cigarette too, 'but it's certainly true that he didn't politicize people here, who idolized him.'

Manchi didn't smoke and was annoyed when others did so during the game. Usually they took account of this. However, Janchi no longer felt like doing so.

While Chamon Nicolas put together the pieces that he had dislodged he said, as if in a final summing-up:

'The Antilles is a *corrupt* country.'

'Politics', said Chamon Nicolas, 'is always corrupt.'

Manchi cast a confident glance at Janchi and Chamon Nicolas. He'd already had to keep quiet at Janchi's arguments twice. Now he thought he'd found something, which if it did not put an end to this political conversation, would certainly make them respect him more in this area than they obviously did now.

'You can say what you like,' he said with studied slowness, looking at his two opponents in turn. 'About Black Power, foreigners and corruption . . .' He paused and then went on to say in an almost sweet tone, 'But . . . the . . . people . . . vote . . . *for themselves*! Isn't that true, Bubu?' He looked at Bubu Fiel with an expression which said that he was the only one who stood out above the atmosphere of stupidity to the left and right of him. After all, he was his partner.

Bubu nodded in agreement and out of solidarity threw away the cigarette on which he'd only taken a couple of drags. Apart from that, it tasted bitter and the smoke irritated his still tired eyes. Chamon looked at his partner with questioning sympathy.

It was clear to him too that Manchi had scored a point over everyone at the table.

'The smoke,' said the latter, immediately exploiting his gain in prestige. Putting down his domino pieces, he began waving away the smoke that Chamon and Janchi were blowing out.

'Ah,' said Chamon, 'I'd forgotten that you couldn't stand it.' He quickly threw away his cigarette and began helping Manchi to combat the pollution of the atmosphere. He was mainly impressed by Manchi's remark that 'the people vote for themselves', because Janchi seemed to have no answer to this. Janchi was thinking deeply. Not about the game now.

171

He was focusing his concentration on Solema. On their conversations about these kinds of matters.

Manchi, who knew how to exploit a situation to his advantage, made no move to play although it was his turn. He did not even *pretend* that he was thinking about the game. He put his pieces calmly on the table and crossed his hands in front of his chest. He leant back slightly and said, 'That's democracy! That's what we've got here.'

He looked at Janchi as a teacher looks at a child who is making a mistake when it should know better:

'*De-mo-cra-cy*. The best system there is. A democracy means' – he went on pedantically – 'means, means, means *simply* that the people elect their own people. For themselves. That's the most important aspect of the whole matter: that people do it for themselves. And when you now say, as you do,' he went on, leaning forward to pick up his pieces again (a gesture designed to show that he didn't think the rest was so important), 'that they put themselves at the mercy of *foreigners*, then no one can do anything about it! I can't, Chamon Nicolas can't, and you can't either. You see, that's quite simply the *people*'s right. But the people are free just as *everyone* is free.' He turned his gaze calmly from the pieces to Janchi, raising his eyebrows. 'For example, can I prevent you committing suicide?'

He thought that Janchi, who after all was known for his sense of independence, would take the bait and immediately agree, but the latter still said nothing, his lips tightly shut under his pencil moustache, while he kept his eyes neutral.

'Or you?' Manchi went on, now pointing to Chamon with his mouth. 'Or you?' He now indicated Bubu Fiel with pursed lips. 'No,' he said, answering himself. 'No, I *can't* intervene between you and your freedom. No one can. And that's why *no one* can come between the people and its right to elect the government that it wants for itself. And no one *has the right*,

172

either,' he added finally, playing a two–one to the double two in a calm and dignified way.

Then he said, laying down his pieces on the table one by one. 'There's a French saying, that each people gets the government it deserves. That's a very correct and just saying. It means that if a people has a bad government, that's because the people themselves are bad or stupid.' Again he hoped that the two–one that he had played would make Janchi pass and waited intently to see if the pass sign would in fact come. He would kill two birds with one stone.

'You're right,' said Janchi, without immediately reacting to Manchi's move. 'At least . . . on the surface. Or perhaps I should say: in general. It would be even better if I said that what you just said is subject to two conditions. That is,' he said, slowly moving the index finger of his right hand up and down, 'that the people must be completely free to vote. That's number one. And in addition the people who vote have to be politically informed. To know what they are voting for. And there's one more thing. The elections have to be secret. And we don't have any of those things on this island,' he said, again banging the table so that the pieces flew apart. He put them back together again himself.

'The parties, and I mean mainly the DP, put pressure on people; people are threatened with the loss of their jobs if they don't vote for this or that party. And why is that possible? It's possible because the people are backward. They're stupid in fact. And because they're stupid, they allow themselves to be bribed. But whose fault is it that the people are stupid? It's the fault of those who govern, because it's their duty to look after the education of the people. So they're exploiting the ignorance of the people.' He looked straight at Manchi. But the latter kept his eyes fixed firmly on the pieces in his hands.

'What it comes down to,' said Janchi, 'is that a doctor screws a girl who's brought to him unconscious, after sending

173

everyone away. Yes, lifts up her skirt and unconscious as she is, instead of reviving her, which is his duty as a doctor, fucks her! You see, that's what the politicians we now have do to this people. They win their confidence in all kinds of underhand ways; or they simply steal their votes or they force them to give their votes, and afterwards they *screw* them. That would be all very well, *but they also allow foreigners to join in the gang-bang!*'

Chamon Nicolas looked at his partner encouragingly. Bubu Fiel, who thought that Janchi's argument was difficult and far-fetched, and not as clear as Manchi's, and hence *boring*, turned his face to the north, perhaps also because Janchi used the word 'screwing' so much and sat staring in that direction for quite a time, as though he were trying to see the women's camp over the hill on which the church of Wakota stood.

Because Manchi said nothing, Janchi went on: 'The people have to be educated politically, before there can really be any question of your *de-mo-cra-cy*.

'Do you understand?' he asked Manchi, who now he had put his political cards on the table had nothing left to say, in an insistent tone. 'Education,' said Janchi, thinking of Solema, 'education, our people have to have education! And do you know what happens,' he said, raising his voice so loud that Bubu Fiel looked at him instead of looking past him, 'if you go on exploiting people's ignorance, instead of educating them; if you go on buying them with promises and little favours; as is the case with our old-age pension and for which everyone is grateful to the DP, while we all pay for that pension anyway, things like that . . .? Then one fine day we'll have a *revolution* on this island! Not a fire, no, but a real, violent, damn *revolution*. Perhaps like on Cuba. After which the corrupt gentlemen will be sentenced to death by the people in the big new football stadium and shot one by one. *You can't go on making fools of the people for ever*! One day someone will come along who isn't a villain (like most people are who get up here and say they want to do something for the people, because if they really wanted to do something for the people then that would have happened in the last twenty years) who passes the insight on to others. Look around you. Is there *really* any effort being made to take over things for ourselves? Don't you still see Dutchmen in top positions everywhere? And don't you see Americans in the top positions in the hotels? Is there any thought about tomorrow? Is there any *planning*? Why is everyone *against* independence? Because things are going so nicely, isn't that so, nicely for all those foreigners. Independence would mean that we'd have to do it *ourselves*. Everything. From top to bottom. Then we'd be obliged to train our own teachers, instead of going cap in hand to Holland every year for them to come out. Why do our students prefer to stay in Holland when they finish their studies? Because it's a clean, flat, well-ordered country, as everyone says? But why don't they come back and make their own country clean, flat and well-ordered? *Because they've been taught that other people must always do it for us*! Others, foreigners, they themselves have only been born to enjoy. To profit.'

He looked straight at Manchi and put his face directly in front of his, so that the latter leant back. 'Do you know what will happen here if there's suddenly an unexpected war and nothing can be imported into this island any more? We'll die. We'll die because we haven't got any animals here and we don't grow anything.'

'Exactly,' said Chamon, a little worried. 'Exactly! We'll die!'

'These days they don't even plant any *beans*,' said Janchi, without paying any attention to Chamon.

'Are the people in our government capable?' he said, spreading his hands in despair before concluding for himself, 'No!'

175

'The Doctor was,' said Bubu Fiel. 'He liked agriculture too and sent our boys and girls to Holland to study.'

'The Doctor's dead,' said Janchi, 'and besides that the Doctor *didn't* like agriculture. He liked *saying* that he did, to make himself popular with people out of town who still did a bit of agriculture. If the Doctor had really liked agriculture, we'd have our own agriculture now. It's certainly true. He started sending boys and girls to Holland, but he didn't teach them how to come back. And so the mistakes pile one on top of the other,' he said after a pause, 'while our ministers drink whisky and chase women and votes. That's what they are: *woman-chasers and vote-chasers* . . . But a day will come, when something goes wrong, perhaps when *too many* mistakes are made. Then the people won't take it any more and it'll erupt. Then there'll be a revolution, a real one. Not a wild drinking and burning spree like on the 30th May, which didn't change anything at all, since the same party is in power, the same people in the government.'

'We'll have to see about that revolution,' said Manchi. 'We'll have to see.'

'It'll come. And when it does, I shall be at the forefront.'

'You, Janchi?' asked Bubu Fiel, a little alarmed by the seriousness of his domino companion. 'You? You're an individualist who enjoys life. You,' he said, thinking of Micha, 'are a woman-chaser.'

'I used to be,' said Janchi Pau quickly, 'but I've changed. Yes,' he repeated – and had to control himself not to tell them why – '*I've changed*!'

9

A cool breeze suddenly blew over the hills of Wakota and over the valley in which the men sat playing. It made Bubu Fiel even more dreamy, but it gave Janchi Pau a gratifying feeling of peace and clarity. For a moment he forgot Manchi, the conversation, and the whole domino table in fact, and thought just about himself and Solema. It was true. He'd changed, and she'd done it. There was something new in him. A desire for action, which he'd never had before. In the space of a few weeks he felt a different man. But *had* he changed? No. He was thirty-five and at that age a man doesn't change any more, he felt. No, he was the same man he'd always been. But with something extra: Solema. So, because he loved her, did he suddenly care more about this country, did the course of events leave him less cold than before? Then the analysis he'd just given was wrong. Then, from a logical point of view, there was no other way of seeing it. It wasn't education that this country needed, but *love*! This feeling that he had. Because with this feeling you could do things. You could keep animals with it and you could make plants grow with it. *You could finish a house with it*. Because you could do that, you could also build *several* houses with it. Lots of *wabi*-wood tables. And then you should also be able to train teachers with it and heaven knows what else. He formulated it slowly to himself: We need love. We've got to start loving this country more and our women too. Yes, that last point was so sensible that he almost said it aloud.

But he said nothing. A remark like that – that we had to love our women more – would just sound banal here. Hadn't he just denied that he was still a woman-chaser? What was the difference between being a woman-chaser and loving a woman, or even loving women? There was a difference, but he wouldn't be able to explain it to them. Because he felt unsure of himself in this area of love and tenderness, which was still so new to him, he quickly returned to an area that he could cope with better. 'Just look at Cuba,' he said in a somewhat calmer tone, 'just look at Castro. There too they thought that the people would take it for ever, but you can't neglect and exploit people for ever and ever. Just look at the blacks in America. One day you'll get what's coming to you. All it needs is for one person to stand up . . .'

But he had the feeling that he couldn't formulate what he felt to be the truth. And consequently he was glad that Bubu Fiel interrupted him.

The latter was still looking for the atmosphere of friendly jokes; the atmosphere of a good story, the atmosphere of small talk, of games which usually prevailed at their domino table, while they slammed down their pieces as hard as they could; the atmosphere which made a person realize that Sunday is such a wonderful, uncomplicated day, a day without the problems of the other six days. With the rum, cool and everything. Goddamn, he played this game for his pleasure. And so: the serious tone in which Janchi was talking about the revolution in Cuba and Castro, for heaven's sake! This wasn't the tone for a game of dominoes between friends, on the east side of your house on a Sunday afternoon – the only day which you really had off, which you *took* off (because you worked for yourself, after all). Perhaps this wasn't even a subject for Curaçao, where things always went according to a different pattern than elsewhere, more *orderly* than elsewhere, more *disciplined* and more *decent*, wasn't that so? None of that blood and violence, all those revolutions and such like . . . They might be normal in Cuba and other countries, but here . . . What's more, why should they bring up that word Communism on *this afternoon* of all afternoons? He couldn't have a capitalist mentality for the simple reason that he didn't know exactly what it meant, but he abhorred that word Communism because every association with it suggested there might be a regime in power which would forbid him to drive around this godless, arid island in his brand-new 200H, large and light blue, well polished and wide-winged, in the direction that he wanted, with an incalculable number of possibilities for the most varied, unexpected adventures. *Like yesterday's!* When he went to the camp over there and found that woman . . . What was her name again? Oh yes. Micha. Of course. Her name was Micha. So when he came across Micha who was having a birthday. Just like that. Can anyone under a Communist regime, or even a Socialist one, if there's any difference between the two, have such a stroke of luck? No, no! Impossible! In Cuba they'd even officially abolished prostitution. They made whores drive buses. Buses! Just imagine: whores on great big tour coaches! For that reason, he said, 'Communism will never come here. We Curaçaoans don't want that. We're individualists. We like doing as we please. Under Communism everyone has to do the same, no one has a life of his own any more.' Sanantonio nodded at his partner in complete agreement.

'That's not the point,' said Janchi fiercely. 'We simply don't want to *see* things. Because if we see things, then we have to fight them. And we don't want to do that. Not because we're afraid, but because fighting takes effort. We let them mess around with us because we like our pleasure too much. Not me,' he corrected himself hastily.

'We *don't* like our pleasure,' said Bubu. 'We *don't* like our pleasure.' He repeated his sentence in order to suppress a feeling of shame about his venture in the camp which suddenly came over him. 'We like our *freedom*,' he said triumphantly. 'Better one good day and one bad day. Better "*entre medio*" but in the meantime to be free to do what you like, than something like Communism. At least for me.'

Without saying anything, Janchi played the five–three. He decided it was better to devote his attention entirely to the game again, because he was getting angry, not so much at Bubu but at Manchi. But that was mainly of course because he had been angry with Manchi for a long time.

Pleased that Janchi's move didn't prevent him from

playing his double one, Bubu said, 'But I agree with you, friend Janchi. I too have the feeling that a few things will have to change on this island. Life is getting too expensive like this. Perhaps a new party should be created, perhaps there should be *two* new parties, perhaps we should' – and it was an odd, desperate position for a nationalist, or at least a member of the NVP like him to adopt – 'become part of Venezuela or something. Venezuela, America, the Dominican Republic, for all I care. Perhaps these islands really are too *small* to do anything with.' The thought gave him hope and he went on, 'Yes, part of America. Like Puerto Rico. They themselves opt to stay part of America . . .'

But when this provoked not the reaction he expected, but an obviously sarcastic look from Janchi Pau, he suddenly said, 'Or the *young people* must rebel! Better education or something.' He paused. Casting an appraising eye at the veranda of Manchi's house, he said, 'We lack *the spirit of enterprise*!' He smiled at the others, but with a hint of 'I'm a fine one to talk' in his attitude. He knew at least that he lacked the spirit of enterprise, especially at this table this afternoon. 'The spirit of enterprise,' he repeated pensively. 'We're dreamers,' he added in a melancholy tone. 'We *enjoy* life too much . . .' He put out his left hand and gave Janchi Pau a friendly pat on the shoulder. 'Perhaps too much. We like a good conversation, a drink, a woman. And the sun and the shade both tire us out.' He thought for a moment. 'The sun robs us of the energy to do anything, and a wonderful wind and cool shade make us nod off to sleep. Ah, this is a beautiful damn island! Like a beautiful whore, who stops us keeping to our good intentions.' He quickly took hold of himself so as not to show his listlessness and said, summing up, 'We're dreamers, we're dreamers on this damn island!'

'Oh,' said Manchi dismissively, 'you're right, as long as you leave out that nonsense about dreamers. People here have nothing because they've got no *ambition*! They simply live from day to day.'

'But they don't have any opportunities,' retorted Janchi. 'They've got nothing to start with, and if they're on their way up there's always a foreigner at the top.'

Chamon suddenly had the idea that his own lifestyle was being indirectly attacked. Very indirectly, but still attacked. So he said, 'It's like Bubu here says. We're dreamers, but there's more to it . . . We see' – he paused because he had difficulty finding the right word – 'the *relativity* of this damn life. We see that there's no point in working yourself to death to get rich like the Dutch and the foreigners in general want to. We see that you have to die one day anyway. And what then . . .? Then you have to leave everything behind. *They'* – he meant the Dutch and the whites in general – 'really are pricks! I think the people here realize that. I mean the people on Curaçao. More than the people on the surrounding islands. The people on Curaçao and the French islands realize that. The people on the English islands don't. There they're a bit like the whites. Just as materialistic.' He thought hard for a moment. Then he said with a broad smile, 'We're like the hippies! We don't care all that much about anything. And,' he added, 'we're right to be hippies, aren't we? Because the hippies are usually *rich* boys and girls who kick out at their *rich* fathers and mothers and say "you won't get happy like that", and scatter the money of their rich fathers and mothers around or use it to fund a journey to a distant country where they find happiness. Because the characteristic thing about hippies is that they travel a lot. You see them everywhere. They let their hair grow long and they don't give a damn what they look like. Because in life it's not a matter of how you look, but how you *feel*. And that's why the hippies smoke marijuana and things like that. To feel good. *High*,' he added in English, which was after all his mother tongue.

'Exactly,' said Bubu Fiel. 'I agree with those hippies, although I don't agree with that long hair of theirs. Sometimes I also think that what matters is to get as much pleasure as possible out of this life. Well, they try to do that by smoking marijuana and travelling. By getting *high*. They burn down the university and their parents' houses. You can see it all on television. And we –? They're randy as hell,' he said interrupting himself. He wanted to explain this last statement and say that he'd seen them at it often enough in 200H; American men and women, who were so horny that they got down to it on the seat behind him. When they were simply being driven from one hotel to the other. But he suddenly fell silent because the memory of Micha hit him painfully again. Again he turned his face gloomily northwards.

'I think the people here are very wise,' said Chamon aloud, without looking at any of the others in particular. He felt rather embarrassed because he'd given himself away so much and he was surprised, now that he said things like that, how attached he was to the lifestyle of the Curaçaoans, which he had adopted through the game of dominoes. Perhaps he'd come to like them. Perhaps their *language*, which wasn't spoken anywhere else in the world except on the three Leeward Islands, and with which they had developed a way of saying things and also of *thinking* about things which in his view was so unique because their language consists of practically all the languages in the world. He didn't feel like saying any more, but for himself he tried to work out how many languages Papiamento was made up of: African, Portuguese, Spanish, French . . . While he was thinking about these linguistic questions, he was also thinking about the play, and he certainly saw the chance of winning a double game, which Janchi must have just set up for him. He began arranging the pieces rapidly and nervously and started counting, for his pleasure now, the languages in Papiamento.

Then he leant over the table humming: like a beetle flying into a light source.

'English, French, Dutch, Jewish, Arabic. Is there German in Papiamento too?' he suddenly asked his comrades, looking at them one by one. Janchi and Bubu shrugged their shoulders.

Manchi, thinking of his *Die Räuber*, said, 'Yes.'

Chamon said, 'Then there are more or less all the languages of the world in it. Just listen: African, Portuguese, Spanish, French, English, Dutch, Jewish, Arabic, German . . .' It excited him to think about two things that interested him at once. And he was making fun of them for a moment.

'I don't know if there's any German in Papiamento,' said Pau, looking at Manchi suspiciously. 'There have always been very few Germans here, but you're forgetting Indian. There are Hindi words in Papiamento too. From the Indians that used to live on Aruba.'

Chamon laughed, but now his attention was mainly on the game, because he didn't want to make any mistakes.

'That's why you are such a crazy bunch,' he said airily, 'such a uniquely crazy bunch.'

Suddenly Bubu had to laugh aloud, 'And then of course you haven't included the dialects of all those languages and as you all know, every language has one or more dialects. Languages,' he said, calming down, 'are like human beings and animals. They breed and reproduce.'

He didn't tell them the real reason for his pleasure. It was the memory of the language that he'd spoken again last night, which had been emerging in the 'happy camp' for some years: a dialect of Spanish and Papiamento. A *screwing language*, he thought to himself, while he slapped his knees with laughter, but when the others focused on him, he made a dismissive gesture and said that he *couldn't* tell them, that it was something terribly funny. *A screwing language*! A language especially for screwing in!

Chamon Nicolas had played a one–blank while he'd been laughing and had six–four and five–blank left in his hand. Because Bubu refused to tell his story, Manchi slammed down the five–four on the open five very flamboyantly, although he had no other choice but to cover the five. Thereupon Janchi played his double blank with a smile. Bubu Fiel dropped the double four with a clatter and pushed it into the centre of the table with his little finger. Chamon Nicolas picked it up, arranged it more neatly with the rest and at the same time put down the six–four next to it. Manchi banged his fist on the table as a sign that he was passing. Janchi passed much too excitedly. Bubu Fiel dropped the six–four as he'd just done with the double four. Chamon picked it up and squeezed it with his fist. '*Changá*!' he cried, while he kept banging the five–blank so hard on the table that the pieces flew off it one after the other.

'Well, well,' said Janchi.

'Put the pieces on the table,' said Manchi icily.

'Oh, I'm sorry,' said Chamon, 'I'll show you.' And with teasing obligingness he put the pieces back in the right order and now placed the six–five which Bubu Fiel had set on the table too. 'Do you see now?' he said teasingly to Manchi. 'Two bullets. Two *Kugeln*, or what do you call them in German?'

But Manchi paid no attention to him. He started straight into a complicated post-mortem with Bubu, telling him that they'd lost this game double because Bubu had played his double four, so that Chamon had had the chance to play the six–four in reply, which in turn had forced him, Bubu Fiel, to play the six–five. He reconstructed the game, speaking quickly, in various ways. At first Bubu looked on, rather amused at how excited Manchi was getting. When Manchi persisted, however, he got angry and laid the blame at Manchi's door, by saying that they'd lost the game double because Manchi had been out to get to Janchi Pau's double five, which was also an exaggeration because when Manchi made such a fuss about covering the five, he couldn't have done anything else. Certainly it would have been better to play the five–one rather than the five–four as he had done. Chamon, who during all this squabbling had kept his left hand open in front of Bubu Fiel, occasionally making a V-sign or sign for two, finally made a grab for the counters in Bubu's corner.

'Next thing, you two will be saying you won,' he teased. Bubu Fiel grabbed his hand roughly, 'I'll pay myself,' he said, taking two green tokens out of the box and giving them to Chamon.

Because Bubu was losing his temper, Chamon had the chance of throwing the words that he used so often at the domino table back in his face: 'You mustn't get angry. After all, we're just playing for pleasure.' Bubu Fiel was angry with Manchi, and still tried to prove that Manchi, not he, had thrown the game away. To prevent them from continuing to reconstruct the game piece by piece, Janchi said that he was right, that Bubu and Manchi would have won if Manchi had played a five first himself, although as a result of this Janchi would have been able to play his double five. At that point Manchi gave himself away by exploding at Pau, 'Yes, and just allow you to play your double five, I suppose! Oh, come on . . . !'

'Well, you shouldn't blame me, friend Sanantonio, if all you do at this table is hunt for double pieces, instead of playing dominoes.'

Bubu said this. Manchi was about to add something else. Something bad-tempered to Janchi, who in fact had no business sticking his nose in. But Nora made temporary peace. When Bubu did not call her, she sometimes came of her own accord if she could tell from arguments or squabbling among the men that they needed a drink.

185

'I'm back,' she said unnecessarily and as always pretending to be cheerful. And now she was perhaps really rather more cheerful than she had just been because she'd concocted a plan for attracting Chamon's attention, to make it clear to him that she had something to discuss with him. Mulling over the plan in the kitchen, she had become so frightened and nervous that she had even dropped the tray with the glasses on it. Two of them had broken, and some rum had been spilled for nothing. As she refilled the glasses, she thought how much simpler everything would have been if Manchi had given *her* the money for the rum. How much easier everything might have been if she had had an affair with *Manchi*, however close by he lived, instead of with Chamon. In any case, glad that no one had noticed her little mishap, and determined to execute her desperate plan – something could easily go wrong – she went out to the men.

She did not go round the table with the tray as usual but squeezed her way between Chamon and her husband, and, bending over the table, handed Manchi the tray first with her left hand. What she had to do next she had also rehearsed a couple of times in the kitchen: as Manchi brought the glass to his lips, she turned her body from right to left, bending forward in order to move the tray towards Janchi. As she did so, she gave Chamon Nicolas a push with her right elbow – which she'd intended for his shoulder, but which actually landed on his chin. She pushed too hard, so that she went too far to the right with the right side of her body, and the tray started to sway dangerously. To regain her balance, she had to rest her right hand against Chamon as hard and as quickly as possible, almost pushing him off his chair. It was all terribly clumsy. Bubu Fiel, who had noticed how she leant against Chamon so as not to fall, although he'd missed the first blow which she gave to Chamon's chin, nevertheless lost his temper:

'Woman, what's wrong with you! You can't just push Chamon Nicolas off his chair like that!'

'I lost my balance,' said Nora truthfully.

'But why do you hand us the drinks suddenly? Why didn't you simply go round with them?'

'It's quicker like that!'

'Really? Quicker? You almost knocked Chamon here off his chair! What kind of nonsense is that! Eh?'

Nora said nothing else.

Chamon Nicolas had had quite a fright. Like a driver who has almost run over a child. (He thinks less of the possible death of a child than of the difficulties which it would have caused him.) What gave her the right suddenly to come and give him a thump with her elbow while he was quietly sitting playing dominoes? At that moment he was moving forwards a little. *Luckily*, because what a disaster it would have been if he'd been downing his rum! Then he wouldn't have just lost one tooth but *all* his teeth. Perhaps he would have choked on his drink and have suffocated then and there. Perhaps if she'd smashed the glass against his teeth he would have swallowed the pieces, which then would have cut his innards into little pieces, into little cubes like for *sòpi di mondongo* . . . then he would have *died*! Thank God, Bubu didn't seem to have noticed, to have realized that she'd tried to give him a sign. Because that was it: of course she wanted to give him a sign, that she needed him. And she always needed him for one thing: money. She never dropped in to see him to see how he was getting on, or check whether he was still alive (after all, he lived alone): she came for money. And then, because she was there anyway, he took her . . . but what kind of screwing was it, all things considered, with a woman who kept saying that he must hurry because she had to go? Because she *wanted* to go, he now thought to himself. And of course she wanted to go, because she didn't give a damn about him. She just wanted his money; she'd have taken it from him without ever going to bed with him, if she could have, if that were possible . . . He thought this over and quickly decided that he ought to break off with Nora. Right. More than anything else, at the moment it was necessary to allay any suspicion on Bubu's side.

'It's nothing, Fiel,' he said. 'I scarcely noticed.'

At that very moment Bubu was putting his empty glass on the tray held by Nora, who was still standing next to him. He held on to it in bewilderment and said slowly, with maximum amazement in every word: 'That's crazy. That's crazy. That is *totally* crazy.'

He looked at Chamon in an almost friendly way, with the kind of friendliness with which one looks at a lunatic. 'My wife here almost knocks you off your chair, on purpose, for no reason, at least anyone who saw it happen would think that, and you, Chamon, say that it's *nothing? That you scarcely noticed?*' The last part of this sentence he spoke in with a terrific crescendo. The word '*noticed*' resounded right across Wakota.

He brought his face very close to Chamon's: 'Are you *drunk*, Nicolas?'

'Oh, I mean I don't mind it that much, but of course I *noticed* it. Yes, I noticed. It still hurts.' He took out his handkerchief, dabbed his chin, while Bubu kept looking at him, shaking his head as though he were a very strange creature. 'But Nora didn't hit you there,' he said, 'not in your *face*. I thought it was more against your *shoulder*?!'

'No,' said Chamon, firmly. 'My chin. Of course she can't help it.'

'Maybe you think I'm drunk? *Nora hit your shoulder, man!*'

'Perhaps I did,' said Nora, who thought the best thing she could do would be to avert the danger that she had herself caused. 'Perhaps you *are* drunk.'

188

'Why?' said Bubu, innocence itself, because he didn't think that his wife would dare go any further in the presence of his friends.

She didn't react at once. First she said to Chamon, 'I'm sorry if I gave you a bang with my elbow somewhere, it was an accident.'

Chamon shrugged his shoulders, 'Of course. That's what I'm saying to Bubu here, that it was an accident.'

Next she said to Bubu Fiel, *'You didn't come home very early last night!'*

He was more hurt than angry and looked at her in disbelief. But when she gave him that very defiant look which said 'Isn't it true, then?', he quickly decided to let the matter rest, glad that the meaning of her words did not seem to have dawned on the others. At least not on Manchi. Nora, who thought that she had saved the day pretty well in that way, turned to go. In order to normalize things from his point of view – that is, to show them that he was still master in his own house – he called her back and said, 'In future, wait till I call you.'

'Just as you like,' she said, 'I'm close by, anyway.'

The others began turning the pieces over. He watched his wife as she slouched off with the glasses in her left hand and waving the tray by the side of her body.

At the corner of the house she stopped, turned round and called out, 'Does anyone want any water?'

In doing this she was waiting for one more opportunity to give Chamon Nicolas a wink, so that he would realize that she really had something urgent to say to him.

However, she looked straight into the eyes of her husband, and so couldn't execute this new plan, although Chamon did actually turn to look at her. While she stood there waving the tray gently, almost a little embarrassed by her standards, they said 'no' one by one.

'No,' said Bubu too.

'If anyone wants water, then just come along and get it,' she said, turning the corner.

'How thoughtful Nora is,' said Manchi.

Chamon held his tongue nervously.

'Yes,' said Janchi.

'Very thoughtful,' repeated Manchi.

She still acted oddly, thought Bubu, who was so used to Nora never letting anything of his dissipations out of the bag, that he really couldn't take it in that she'd just threatened to reveal his late arrival home, and his adventure, as far as she suspected it, to his friends. Had he hurt her so deeply that she was out for revenge? For Christ's sake, it wasn't the first time that something like this had happened. She went droning on, talked drivel, swore at him, even, when he went too far, as he had yesterday evening, to be honest, but she'd always hidden it from his friends.

Would she really go that far and actually make a *scene* in front of his friends as she had done this morning, and blurt out that he'd been in the *camp*? Oh no! It must be something else! While he kept his hands resting on the pieces in order to be able to concentrate, he wondered if she were simply *angry* with him for remarking on the fact that she'd almost knocked Chamon off his chair.

'Nora nearly knocked you *over* just now,' he suddenly said, more calmly, to Chamon.

'Oh no,' he said, keeping his eyes firmly fixed on his pieces and nevertheless with a slight feeling of apprehension in his abdomen. 'She just *leant* on me for a moment, because she nearly fell over. She lost her balance, I think. As she said herself.'

'Really?' said Bubu, looking from Chamon to Manchi and Janchi, registering the fact that Chamon didn't look at him. 'Really? I thought my wife had something against Chamon here. It looked to me as though she were trying to knock you over on purpose. I'm telling you! And I was suddenly so surprised that I had to mention it. Why would she do something like that? Has she got something against you?'

'Oh, come on,' said Chamon.

Manchi said nothing and studied his pieces. He considered the whole matter unimportant, and apart from that he felt that Bubu was behaving rather strangely this afternoon, a little befuddled or something.

'It's nothing,' said Janchi, who although they were partners didn't have the slightest suspicion that there was anything between Chamon and Nora. 'Nora couldn't help it, if you ask me. She simply bent too far forward when she handed me the drink, so that she lost her balance and had to lean on Chamon so as not to fall. Or in any case to make sure that the glasses didn't slide off the tray. She couldn't lean on you, because she had the tray in her *left* hand.'

Bubu nodded gratefully a couple of times. Janchi had a direct, quick way of explaining things, so that you were bound to understand properly. Like just now when he showed Manchi that it was Manchi's fault they'd lost the game and not Bubu's.

'When you put it like that,' he said reflectively.

'No,' said Chamon, again taking more courage now his partner was getting involved with the matter. 'It really wasn't anything.'

But if it wasn't *anything*, why did she get so angry suddenly? thought Bubu. And why hadn't she simply gone round with the glasses as usual? Why?

Under normal circumstances, that is, if he'd been completely involved in the game, he probably would have dismissed the whole incident, particularly after Janchi's clear explanation. But that was precisely it: he had the feeling that because of his absent-mindedness he was missing far too much, as the game that had just finished had shown. And he involuntarily seized on all the details that he thought he'd registered for certain: for example, that his wife Nora had *deliberately* pushed his domino companion. A shove that had been meant as a little nudge and perhaps turned out rather too hard, so that she had to lean heavily on Chamon so as not to fall face-down on the table. She'd had her big backside almost in his face, so that he couldn't see exactly what was going on between her and Chamon, but he'd been able to observe her all the better from this side. And she didn't for a moment lose her balance on the left-hand side, as Janchi here was suggesting to him. With the intention of calming him down, of course.

It's well meant by Janchi, he thought to himself, but it's not true: Nora didn't lose her balance on my side, otherwise in order to restore her balance she'd have pulled Chamon with her in this direction or leant on me. That was it.

It was actually his turn to play, because Janchi Pau had led, but he was still drumming on the table with his left hand, while he pointed with the index finger of his right hand to a spot on the table and kept repeating to himself: Here! Here! Here! She would have landed here on the left and she'd have probably tipped the table-top over, the tray over, if she'd really lost her balance on this side, as Janchi maintains. He now saw the incident very clearly: her left hand with the tray and the drinks on it had just gone *upwards* when she leant on Chamon, which of course wouldn't have happened if she'd really lost her balance in this direction. Then this side would on the contrary have gone *down*! So she *shoved* Chamon? She was pushing Chamon away from her? And because she did it much too hard, she lost her balance on the right. That was it!

He glanced at his dominoes, but their white eyes were dancing about so much in front of him that he did not feel like concentrating on them. When he carelessly played the first six piece that caught his attention, in reply to Janchi's double six, Manchi, who'd been looking at him with a fixed stare all that time, said, 'Bubu, let's do our best to catch these two up.' And reconstructing the game they'd lost again anyway, he said, 'Perhaps just now you ought not to have paid so much attention to the twos that you had, but to the blanks of Chamon Nicolas here.'

'Perhaps,' said Bubu, irritated because Manchi was disturbing his reconstruction of the incident and the image of it was no longer so clear in his mind. Only his surprise that Nora seemed to want to take revenge on him remained; and with it a vague feeling that in some way or other he was being *threatened* because of this game that he was actually being forced to play. By Chamon Nicolas, who just now had had the nerve to take two counters out of his box. By Nora. By the chairmanship of the union. His self-protection mechanism started working.

He allowed his attention to the game (almost deliberately) to flag even more. Manchi, who noticed this, now began banging the domino pieces harder, in order to wake his partner up. Bang! Bang! Bang! He was going to remind Bubu again, when the latter passed towards the middle of the fourth game, that they must definitely not be the *first* to get a pair of ladies' shoes, because the idea had actually been theirs, but he thought better of it. Instead he told a joke, 'My wife tells me that the sexton of Wakota is in the habit of hanging around the church as long as possible until the priest has gone. And *then* he drinks his wine. Ha, ha!'

But it wasn't a success, while Janchi Pau gave him one of those odd, severe looks, which made him feel more and more uneasy.

It seemed to him that Janchi could see right through him; could see, for example, that in this case he was lying.

When Manchi went on attacking the Catholic church in

general, by expressing his support for the supposed fact that the sexton kept drinking the priest's communion wine, Janchi indeed remarked that he found the story rather strange, because the sexton wasn't known as a thief. 'He's started drinking recently,' he said, 'but that's because his wife died not long ago. He's grieving, everyone knows that.'

When Manchi insisted, saying that he himself and Solema had seen the sexton from their veranda, coming out of the church drunk, Janchi found it difficult to control himself and not remark that this was scarcely possible, because Solema had been with *him* the whole morning. 'The sexton doesn't drink in the church,' was all he said, 'but in a restaurant near the refinery. I often see him sitting there,' which his partner agreed with as he had been agreeing with everything he said this afternoon.

Janchi Pau and Chamon Nicolas won the fourth game double too, and escaped. The score was six–love, and they were clearly threatening the others with the first shoes.

In the fifth game Chamon achieved a splendid coup: following up well-calculated moves by Janchi, he finally succeeded (with a huge crash) in eliminating Manchi's double five and winning double at the same time. The blow was so hard that a large number of pieces fell off the table.

'I've asked you not to slam your pieces down so hard,' said Manchi, although the the pieces couldn't do any harm by jumping off at that moment since the game was over.

'You don't have to break them,' said Bubu Fiel, dreamily helping to pick up the pieces.

'They're *expensive* dominoes,' said Manchi.

'Exactly, you always say yourself that they're so expensive that they can't break,' said Chamon.

'Oh,' said Manchi, 'that's true. But you don't have to slam them so hard.' In order to show that he wasn't becoming disheartened because of the continuing success of his opponents, he pushed his eliminated double five at Chamon with a laboured joke, 'Here's your victim, Mr Murderer.' Chamon pushed it back without realizing the insinuation and smiling. 'Bury your own dead, my dear sir.'

He pushed the V-sign under Bubu Fiel's nose and said imperiously, 'Pay up!'

Bubu put one green counter in his hand with an absent-minded gesture.

'No, sir!' exclaimed Chamon, while he showed the one counter to the other two. 'Again it's two *Kugeln*!' He enjoyed collecting these, just as he'd enjoyed collecting the rent for his houses.

Chamon's triumph, and his teasing way of demanding payment, however, irritated Bubu Fiel and made him think of the incident with Nora again. He began looking for a way of compromising the man next to him and so bringing him down a peg or two.

He mainly wondered if Chamon had perhaps got fresh with Nora, in order to see if this aspect of the matter produced more than the other, where he had come up with no answers. Nora hadn't pushed Chamon. So had Chamon pulled Nora or *touched* her? Had Nora pushed him away because of that? He threw his head back in order to think deeply. Certainly, Chamon's right hand, with which he had taken his drink, had been above the table; high above the table, in fact, and easily visible to him and hence also to Manchi and Janchi. Right. *But where was Chamon's left hand at that moment?* He could picture it very clearly! It was actually so natural, so plausible and at the same time so obvious, so *easy* for Chamon to do, that it was scarcely possible that anything else had taken place. So he now simply had to prove it quickly. He suddenly felt completely lucid again. Impatient as a dog that has smelt its prey, he shook his head from left to right a couple of times.

10

He had done it himself so often, and it had quite often been the prelude to one of his many illegitimate children. He did it even when he was young. He and his friends made a kind of game of it! *Feeling up girls* – that is, in passing, and preferably in a street where it was busy, so that it wasn't very obvious, quickly touching the breast of a girl chosen at random. Not to hurt her, no, but just to have a momentary contact with the nice shape and that soft, womanly flesh. Ah, even in the dark . . . feeling those breasts. Yes, because when, after a time, one became expert in feeling up, one could actually work on them quickly with *both* hands. Come to that, the more furious the girl got, the greater the sport. And although they kept getting very angry, after which they sometimes said the rudest words (which in fact only described parts of their own bodies), they were still surprised every time. Sometimes the girls reported what had happened. And if their parents knew someone's parents, they came to see that person's parents and someone got a good hiding, which gave the sport a rather bitter aftertaste.

But feeling could be done in a different way: for example, when one was sitting next to a woman in a bus or wherever, by carefully putting a hand on her *thigh*, so that what was intentional seemed to be accidental. And then holding one's breath and waiting for her reaction. If she moved away from under someone's hand, it was better to leave her alone. But sometimes she smiled, letting the hand lie there or even moving so that someone could get where he wanted more easily and with less chance of other people noticing. And then a new possibility in life had been opened up: a new door.

He remembered how one of his grandfathers had felt up a newly wed young neighbour. This incident had made a particularly great impression on him, when he'd seen his neighbour and his grandfather through a chink in her wooden shack, because – *whoops!* – she suddenly pulled out one of her little breasts to let him fondle it. He'd waited until his grandfather had gone, in order to try something on with his neighbour too. However, she refused, saying that she didn't mess around with *children* – he must have been at least sixteen by then – and that if he went on pestering her, she'd tell his parents. Only when he told her that he'd seen her through the chinks in her shack did she agree. He had to laugh about it now. Unfortunately, probably because in the long run she couldn't stand carrying on both with the grandfather and the grandson, she had moved shortly afterwards. He put his pieces on the table. It was Manchi's turn and he was thinking hard. Bubu Fiel studied Chamon from the side and concluded after a while that he was far too involved in the game to be completely innocent. Or did Chamon realize that he suspected him? In any case it was what he himself would also have done if he'd felt a woman's thigh and she had given him a push: act the innocent. Poor Nora, he thought with tenderness: Chamon had tried to feel her up – and *she had defended her honour by giving him a hard push*. He'd seen that; that move. And of course she hadn't wanted to say anything. She had wanted to cover up the affair, because she knew what the result would be otherwise. He would murder Chamon! Mm. Still, he hesitated about his conclusion, because he couldn't imagine that Chamon, whom he'd known for so long and who was characterized by great caution, would have such a nerve, to start feeling up his own wife right under his nose.

Unless they were already carrying on together! Hmm. His heart started beating faster: I wonder if they've had a fling . . . ? He quickly dismissed this thought. It was simply impossible that Nora would want to have an affair with Chamon, who as everyone knew didn't have two pennies to rub together.

But how else was he to explain the violent push that Nora had given Chamon?

An accident? He shrugged his shoulders and picked up his pieces again. If he was certain that Chamon had felt Nora up, he would get up now and punch the man on the chin immediately. Yes. And more because of the man's nerve in doing it *right in front of him* than because of the fact itself. Because Nora wasn't a *virgin*, after all. If it had been one of his *daughters* . . . At any rate, he couldn't be certain. He would have to talk to Nora about it after this game of dominoes. But it could do no harm if he went ahead and sounded out Chamon more thoroughly.

'Did you guys ever feel girls when you were young?' he asked, without looking at Chamon.

'What do you mean?' said Janchi.

'Yes, what do you mean, Fiel?' Chamon asked too. 'Do you mean feel girls' flesh – because we've all done that at times! – or feel them up?'

'I mean something special,' said Fiel calmly. 'I mean grabbing a girl's breasts right in the middle of the street. Like that.' As he said this, he opened the fingers of both hands wide and closed them with a plucking movement.

'No,' said Janchi.

'Girls didn't always wear bras like nowadays,' said Bubu laughing, 'and some of those breasts were as soft and yielding as velvet. Some of those girls also loved being felt up, sometimes they let you carry on for quite a while although they pretended to be angry. Oh, oh, oh!' he said with his voice rising. 'They knocked your hand away, while at the same time pushing it harder against their breasts. They only got angry when you squeezed too hard, so that it hurt.'

He forgot Chamon completely in order to revel in the memory.

Chamon said proudly, 'Of course! The girls swore, cursed

198

you, saying you should put your hand in your mother's cunt. *But they couldn't do a thing about it!'*

'Yes,' said Bubu, who thought his memories were more important than those of Chamon. 'There were some of those proud white or half-white dollies who felt sick if you so much as looked at them because of your colour. It was a great sport to single them out. They'd say afterwards that you were a *stinking nigger*, but you laughed at them, because you'd felt them up anyway. And with breasts, race doesn't make any difference! It's all just as soft and sweet. A white girl could call you a stinking nigger if she liked, but it didn't matter, you enjoyed her breasts just as much as when you felt up one of your own girls, who called you a stinking nigger too, for that matter.' He laughed, relishing the memory. 'But feeling up seems to have gone right out of fashion these days,' he concluded with regret in his voice.

'Thank God,' said Manchi. 'Because of course it's not a fair practice, although I did it in my youth too. Just imagine my two daughters coming and telling me in a little while – when they're a bit older, of course – that they've been *felt up*! Goddamn it, my daughters, my daughters aren't *chickens*, are they?'

'It's part of nature,' said Bubu. 'The simple fact is that boys are looking for girls and they do it in all kinds of ways. You can't stop it. Besides, who's to say that my daughters don't like it too? I'm telling you, there used to be lots of girls who loved it! Oh God, with some of them you didn't even have to do it furtively and quickly. You could sometimes ask them nicely and they took out their breasts if you were in a discreet place with them, and you could play with them as much as you liked, until they got bored and put their breasts away again. You did all that if you couldn't lay her, because you preferred to do that if you could, of course. I believe that when I had my first communion, I did nothing except feel breasts. I was still so young, you know, about nine or so. But I wanted to do it so badly and the girls didn't dare to refuse me, not even the older ones, because it was *my* party.' But now the memory of Micha intervened between that distant past and himself. He luxuriated in the memory of her breasts, which had the attractiveness of being small. Small and neat, he thought. Yes, *neat*, with perfect skin and black nipples. Firm too. And no bigger than two lovely oranges. Not bursting, overripe breasts, but two beautiful, brown medlars. And with those two shiny black medlar stones at their tips. Good enough to eat, to eat right up! As he had consequently done at length!

He now wanted to abandon himself to his memory, but suddenly it occurred to him why he had started thinking about feeling breasts. 'Did you do it too?' he asked Chamon directly. 'You? Are you quite sure?'

There was a hint of a warning in his question, but Chamon interpreted his tone as a possible contempt of his person and said fervently, 'Of course, man, I'm telling you! What do you think of me, that I didn't feel up any girls? Oh man, come on, I've felt them and I've stroked them. And I've sucked them, like you can suck an orange. I've squeezed them and I've fucked them. Yes, literally, by putting my penis in the hollow between the two breasts.' He said all this panting and laughing, like a creed, but as he talked he suddenly had a feeling in the pit of his stomach that he must be careful. Bubu looked at him without saying anything, moving his head up and down in understanding. But because of that, Chamon suddenly had the vague, mounting feeling that he was talking himself into a trap, although he had more or less forgotten the incident with Nora. Nor did he see any link between this feeling of breasts and his affair with Nora, because feeling up was a general male characteristic, or at least dealing with women's breasts and handling them was. What else were they for? Besides, as regards his affair with Nora, he felt safer than ever because he'd decided to stop it. More than that: as far as he was concerned, at this moment there was no longer any question of an affair.

In order to be sure and also since he was cheekier than usual because of their winning streak today, he said: 'But why are you asking *me* especially, Bubu?'

'To find out whether you lot on the Windward Islands are as dirty-minded as here.'

'Oh,' said Chamon with relief, 'yes, completely! And *I* still am,' he added philosophically. 'We blacks are all the same the world over.'

'This feeling up of women,' said Manchi, 'can't be approved of. I repeat, although I did it a few times when I was young too.'

So, thought Bubu Fiel, so it is perfectly possible that the bastard felt up my wife, that he put his left hand up her skirt to feel her thigh! While he looked at Chamon's left hand holding the dominoes, full of suspicion, he said, still with that undertone of warning: 'But of course one has to know *who* one's feeling up. One can't feel up *anyone*. Imagine that I put out my hand and the woman that I'm feeling up turns out to be the daughter of some high-up or other! Then I'll get into *difficulties*, won't I?!' As though he wanted to stress the difference between the custom of feeling up on the Leeward Islands and on the Windward Islands, he looked at Chamon deliberately as he continued, 'For example, as children, we never felt up our friends' sisters. And I myself think it's not on to feel up each other's wives. I simply mean that there's a limit to everything. Even to feeling up!' Again he looked over Manchi's head: 'I can't simply go rushing up to the wife of one of you and squeeze her breasts or thighs or something. Of course you won't stand for that. And certainly not – he added, raising his voice – *'definitely not if one of you is sitting close by!'*

Chamon Nicolas agreed without suspecting a thing. He even went a step further and said very generally: 'Friends leave each other's wives alone. That's the way it should be.'

Paying no attention to Chamon, Janchi Pau said, 'You should never touch women, in my opinion. Women who are worthwhile write you off completely if you start by touching them, or *feeling them up* as you call it. I think it's a mild form of assault, a form of abusing your strength as a man.' He reflected, 'Just like when you persuade a woman to go to bed with you with money. It's too easy like that. I think you've simply got to do it with *words*.'

Manchi nodded with approval at Janchi a few times.

'But when you're dancing,' asked Chamon, 'you touch her then, don't you?'

'Of course,' said Janchi, 'that's obvious.'

'Haven't you got a hard-on between her legs?' he asked in a tone which implied that he was in the habit of doing this. Bubu Fiel now shot him an almost open look of distrust.

'No,' said Janchi, 'I don't like leaving things unfinished. And if I am not sure in advance that I can get a woman, I control myself. It's just frustrating otherwise,' he added laughing.

'Oh,' said Chamon, bursting with laughter, 'you jerk off, don't you?'

Janchi shrugged his shoulders: 'I put that behind me long ago!'

Chamon was about to say something else, but Manchi said, 'Sshh!' and added, 'You're really lowering the tone, Chamon.'

'Right,' said the latter, 'I won't talk about jerking off, although I think it's perfectly normal. In any case you must admit that it's wonderful to be on a dance floor with a hard-on between a woman's legs and carefully working her thighs with your thing. In a slow bolero, for example.' Making dancing movements with his upper body over the table, he said, 'Carefully sliding your thing along her velvet thighs which you can feel in the distance under her dress. And then suddenly stopping at the right place under the mound of her cunt and then planting your thing there and holding her up from behind with both hands so that afterwards she rests completely on the tip of your thing. Heaven!'

He became so excited by his own story that, feeling a powerful need for a woman, he thought of the times when he'd been with Nora. He could, if he wanted to, pretend to be thirsty and go to the kitchen and push his thing against her and cuddle her! He'd done things like that frequently. But he controlled himself. Because of the incident a little while ago, he felt he shouldn't push his luck. Apart from that, he wanted to stick to his decision to break off with her. Look at how she had put him in a difficult corner just now. Great lack of caution, *dangerous* lack of caution. And why? Surely nothing on earth could justify such a great risk? If Bubu had seen the blow she'd given him on the chin, what then? He moved his hand carefully to his side and felt his knife.

Bubu said, speaking slowly, 'Standing between a woman's legs is just the same as feeling her up, there are women who love it, and there are women who don't like it at all. And there are women,' he went on, without being able to help himself, 'who look for your thing with their cunts themselves as you dance; and if they find it, they start rubbing against it so that your thing wakes up. Sometimes it's terrible because you're in the middle of dancing with a woman with whom you don't want to have an erection, because you're embarrassed about it or because it can become compromising. And then on the contrary *she* sometimes looks for you. You evade her the first time because you think it's a chance touch, but she comes again, you evade her again, but her thing comes after your thing again. You want to almost shout that your thing is rising, that you can't help it, that she's bound to feel it if she goes on like this. And then you suddenly sense that it's deliberate on her part . . . and then you think again of the end of the record, when you have to go back to your seat in front of other people: *terrible*.' Under the table, he pushed down his penis, which kept trying to rise, firmly with his left hand.

'The most terrible thing about all this,' said Janchi understandingly, 'is sometimes those women's *faces*. They can look at you with those very innocent angel's eyes while they're unleashing a terrible war against your penis down below. Women can be so sanctimonious sometimes.'

Bubu Fiel wanted to develop his distrust of Chamon further, but for the time being he wasn't able to. He drifted off. Thanks to the subject, he found himself again in Micha's room, dancing with her again. *Naked*. An experience he'd had that night for the first time. He had danced with Nora of course – at their wedding, for example – although he couldn't remember very well. But in any case, never *naked*! When she'd completely undressed he wanted to lay her directly on the bed and finish things off, partly because he thought that that was what she wanted from him. But Micha knew that women got no pleasure from men in a hurry: that a sexually free woman has to organize her pleasure calmly, like a murder with malice aforethought. And that's what mattered to her now with this big man: pleasure. A maximum of pleasure that drives you wild, pleasure that hurts, forgetting her absence from the birthday of her daughter, for whose future she shut herself up for months in this camp, worked, slaved, toiled; like a mechanic spending all his life under cars. She had plenty of chance for screwing here. What she wanted was a desperate child's party.

'Calm down, calm down, Bubu.' With sweet words and with her small, narrow hands pushing against his broad chest, she'd made him be patient. 'I'll look after you and that terrible hurry of yours. *Like a mother*,' she had added softly, whispering in his ear.

'Do we have to?' he'd asked her jokingly.

'A mother gives herself *completely*, Bubu.'

'Then I'm your child,' he said, lifting her up with a strong movement. She giggled, grabbed his neck, threw her head back and told him teasingly that it wasn't her birthday, but her daughter's. She simply couldn't keep the truth to herself.

'Mm,' he said, 'then I'll have to show you how we here on Curaçao treat a mother who's got a daughter with a birthday on the Dominican Republic.' And then they'd started dancing, to those slow boleros of hers. That's why he could remember her breasts against his body so well now. Small, elusive things for his big hands, they brushed lightly against his chest like two . . . like two *what* . . .? The fact that he didn't manage to quickly find a new image (he'd thought of medlars just now) made him feel sorry for himself. Was the memory already fading? He put his pieces down and began rubbing his belly. Very gradually, very carefully. Like a divining rod, he felt out the area of his feeling, hoping that for the moment he would feel the pang or the pain of the memory very well. Then he'd also be able to make a new image, a liberating simile for that mighty feeling. He had to go to that woman again! There was nothing for it. He had to see her again, before she went back to the Dominican Republic. At least *one* more night with her. For Christ's sake, it would all be a lot easier then and he certainly would not feel so tired and listless and shattered if he could describe his adventure vividly. He needed to free himself from the adventure by telling it. Then he would be able to devote his attention completely to this game. Making an attempt in that direction he said, still rubbing his belly: 'You three are so *serious* today. It's as though we're not playing for our pleasure.'

'But, Bubu . . .' It was Manchi who reacted and was

amazed. 'But Bubu, don't you realize that these two guys have already won? Just check your counters! They must already have six with their two *changá's*.'

'Their two *Kugeln*,' said Chamon teasingly.

'Of course I know,' said Bubu Fiel. '*I'm* paying them, aren't I? But . . .'

'No *buts*, friend Bubu. No buts! On the contrary, we must play as seriously as possible from now on!'

11

At the end of the fifth game of the first set, Janchi Pau got very angry with Chamon Nicolas because he closed out the game which they had a chance of winning double again. They also nearly lost, because Manchi, who'd been left with double four, had almost the same total as Janchi, who had the five–two.

'You play bad dominoes, Chamon,' said Janchi.

Chamon, whose ego was pretty large that afternoon, protested. But when Janchi had explained to him piece by piece how they could have really won the game double, and without much trouble, he said rather shamefacedly: 'Well, whatever happens, we're free. Nothing more can happen to us.' But Janchi reacted even more fiercely to this: 'We're not playing just to free ourselves. Watch your pieces. We've got them seven–love: we *have* to give them this shoe.'

'You won't be able to,' said Bubu, slowly choosing pieces.

'Exactly,' said Manchi, 'if you watch what you're doing, Bubu, we'll make them stick on that seven.'

'We'll see,' said Janchi. 'We'll see. But you be careful too.' With a certain threat in his voice, he repeated to Chamon, 'Be very careful!'

12

The difference between Janchi and Chamon was particularly evident in this game.

At a certain moment Janchi had the five–three, the double four and three other fours. In that case Chamon Nicolas would have waited anxiously until a four piece had been played before playing a four himself. The life of his double four would thus have been guaranteed.

Not Janchi. He played a four, which Bubu covered with a huge crash.

When it was Janchi's turn again, he calmly played four again! Bubu left it open and played a five on the other side. Chamon now knew for certain that the double four had to be either with Manchi or with Janchi. He *suspected* it was with Janchi. The fact that he himself had double five, which he now quickly played, meant, however, that he couldn't do anything at all for his partner at this moment. Manchi gave a broad leer and banged on the open four so hard that the pieces flew off the table and a large number of them landed in Chamon Nicolas's lap. Then everyone suddenly knew two things for certain: *Janchi Pau had the double four and it was in mortal danger*!

What now made Chamon sit dumbstruck on his chair was the fact that a little later, with icy calm, Janchi Pau posed another four. On the other hand, it sowed the seeds of doubt in Manchi and Bubu: Janchi might have *five* four pieces, in which case his double four was *not* in danger. But he, Chamon, knew that his partner couldn't have five four pieces, because there were now five fours on the table: three from Janchi and two from Bubu and Manchi. With Janchi's double four, that made six in all and with the six–four that he had himself had, seven. So it was an open attempt at suicide, because, as he saw it, Janchi couldn't possibly know that the last four piece, which could be the killer or the saviour, was with him and not with Bubu Fiel or Manchi. *There was no reason at all, he felt, for Janchi to suspect that he had fours*! Because he hadn't played any. So it was a big risk. Too big a risk, since for want of pieces, he might well have been forced to kill his partner's double piece himself. So he waited tensely for Bubu's move, which was some time in coming because Bubu was daydreaming again. He prepared himself mentally for having to kill the double four. It would be asking too much of his luck for Bubu Fiel not to force him to. Passing with a six–four in his hands if Bubu played something he didn't have, was of course impossible. Anyway, they'd all find out soon enough, and then everyone would be very angry, Janchi possibly most of all. But strangely enough, Bubu played a six on the other side. Chamon had the six–four in his hand already and immediately played a four, breathing a sigh of relief: his partner's double piece was now definitely safe. Manchi passed.

Chamon lifted his head to receive the sign of gratitude which he felt he was entitled to from his partner, but saw that Janchi's eyes were sparkling with a secret, mischievous smile. Then he, Chamon, suddenly realized too and felt an idiot. Because he had been so tense about his partner's double four, mainly from fear that he would have to kill it, he had completely forgotten to count how many pieces people had left. He now quickly checked this, moving his nose over the table like a bloodhound, and sensed a happiness wanting to break out of his chest like a wave: Manchi and Bubu had both passed in this game, Janchi not at all. Watching the pieces which Janchi had played before he'd introduced the fours, he, Chamon, could finally only come to one conclusion: the double four was Janchi's last piece!

'Damnation, Janchi,' he cried leaping up from his chair. 'That's devilish play, devilish good play! I've never seen anything like that before!' He dropped the pieces he still had left on the table, and put both hands to his mouth like a loudspeaker and bellowed over the whole of Wakota, '*Changaaaaaaaaaaaaaaaaaaa*!'

It was a formality for Janchi to play, but he did so anyway: slamming it down hard, he kept moving his double four back and forth from one end of the game to the other – left, right, left, right – and only stopped when as a result almost all the pieces had flown off the table.

13

'Nine–love,' said Manchi flatly to his partner.

'Nine–love. And on top of that they keep winning *double* plays.'

'Yes, yes,' said Bubu reflectively, 'but nine–love still doesn't mean any shoes yet. You know as well as I do that they could get stuck on nine; it's happened before. Even here at this table,' he added emphatically.

'Yes, yes,' said Manchi, 'but then we really must *do* something!'

'And we *will* do something,' said Bubu, slamming the palm of his hand down hard on the table to give his words more conviction. Turning to Janchi he said, almost a little condescendingly, 'Damn risky game you just played, my friend.'

Then he said to Manchi, pointing to Pau with his lips, 'Keep this one here in check and everything will be all right.'

'I'll do my best,' said Manchi, who was nevertheless a bit disheartened: the thought of ten–love shoes didn't appeal to him at all. It would be an irreparable blow to his position here at this domino table. And on this island. Things like this simply didn't happen. Had never happened before at this domino table. Only beginners were given shoes to *love*. And it would be even more ridiculous, since he had not only provided the shoes himself, but had sat patiently painting them black. What was happening to them this afternoon?

'I assume,' he said to Bubu Fiel, 'that you, as the person whose initiative it was to have these women's shoes, have something to defend.'

'Of course,' said Bubu generously, 'of course. What do you think? You'll see how they get stuck on that nine while we get out of jail in one game after the other. Do your best,' he said to Manchi, 'and I'll do the rest.'

Manchi didn't react because he was absorbed in watching the shoes, which were arranged like birds of misfortune on the bench against Bubu's house.

'Yes,' said Bubu as cheerfully as possible. '*You* do your best and I'll do the rest,' whereupon he called Nora loudly.

But he wasn't optimistic and he was distracted. The cheerfulness he had put into his voice sounded to him like the biggest lie of that afternoon. That great lie exhausted him even more. To tell the truth, he was shattered. Simply shattered. Nine–*love*. Terrible! That woman had first taken him in her mouth and sucked him dry. Then she'd taken him between her legs and pumped him dry. Christ, he would celebrate a great triumph at this table if, now they thought that he was occupied with this damn game, he could tell them that *he'd come in her mouth*. He still carried the distinct memory of it here in his penis. A round bud of pleasure had burst open in it when she said 'Ah', and he knew that he had come in her mouth. And that had never happened to him in his life! Probably not to any of these pricks here, sitting playing dominoes with him. Not even Janchi. Wasn't that the epitome of masculinity, coming in a woman's mouth? And you had to be a special man, not just anyone, for a woman to want to do that with you. For a woman to single you out for that. He grabbed his crotch with one hand and gave it a firm push.

Colombian women often did it. They seemed to like it. And in the past, when they still came over, the Cubans. The Dominicans didn't: not for the hell of it, in any case. And as the Cubans had become bus drivers since Castro, it was only the Colombians who did it here (took your penis in their mouth). Ah. But not so that you could actually come in their mouths. Scarcely any of them did it like that. But oh yes, you were left with an empty penis. A penis which the soul had gone out of, for the time being.

Manchi would think (if he told them the story) that he was really lowering the tone, that he was going into *details* and they actually never did that at this table. But wasn't this a very different kind of detail? Then afterwards she'd ground him between her legs like only she could. Ah, ah, ah, ah! He now stroked his back with his hand. There was an emptiness there too now. He could simply point to the place in his backbone where the life juices were made that she had taken from him. They called them sperm, and you were pretty careless with them as a man. But they were your soul. You ought to be more careful with them, really. Because really, once you'd given it to a woman like he had done last night, what was left of you but a hollow mass of bone and flesh? Without a soul?! And what he was now thinking was not nonsense, as was shown by the fact that just before competitions racing cyclists, footballers, boxers and all those men who find it particularly easy to pull lots of women, are obliged to abstain completely from sex. *They take your soul away*, he almost shouted.

Nevertheless, he made an effort to concentrate on the game of dominoes. He reminded Manchi reassuringly of cases in which one side had led the other by nine, while the underdogs had still been able to free themselves subsequently.

'There's no problem,' he said. 'You mark my words: Two *changás* and we'll be there.'

'No,' said Manchi, 'we definitely won't be there. We're on *love*, Bubu!'

'Right, two *changás* and a single game then. If they can score *changás* one after the other, so can we. Or,' he said, laughing aloud at his own wit, 'are theirs the only names written on these dominoes?'

He shifted on his chair quite energetically for a moment.

But when Janchi raised his hands from the pieces he'd shuffled and invited the others to choose theirs, he said, 'Let's wait for Nora first. I need some *gas*.' In fact, what he mainly wanted to do was to slow down the fast pace that Janchi had set in the last few games. He decided for himself that this speed was the reason why he was losing, because it meant that he had too little time to think. Besides which, the high tempo automatically made the game more serious, he felt.

Nora again shuffled round the east of the house with the drinks on a tray.

This time she went round the table as Bubu wanted and as was also her custom. She couldn't look Chamon in the face when she handed him the tray because she was standing next to him, and he made no effort to look at her. However, she thought it was better like that, because she saw that Bubu was watching her closely.

The men downed their rum in one gulp as usual and then put down the glasses with a soft tap on the wooden tray. Only Manchi said 'Thanks very much' to Nora.

When they'd finished, she shuffled off, watched by Bubu, who kept having the feeling that there had been a short circuit between her and him. And he vaguely wondered whether Chamon Nicolas had anything to do with that, and if so, what. He thought it was a pity that he'd made such a fuss about the incident just now, because Chamon, if he had really felt up Nora, would as a result be even more careful. He should have kept his mouth shut and have caught the man, or perhaps

Nora, at another moment. At a moment when neither of them could deny anything! Like in the story of Manchi's judge, which now also occurred to him.

However, he could no longer concern himself with his private affairs, because Janchi, who had shuffled again, gave the signal for everyone to choose their pieces. And he had promised to do his best. Well, in a certain sense one could now say that he kept his word, because the first piece he picked up was a double six and now he had a head start over everyone. In addition he had three threes and felt that they could easily lead to a quick clean sweep in his hand.

But it was no good because Manchi did not have a single three. Most of them were with Chamon Nicolas. Besides that, Bubu held on to his three for too long and Chamon was able to make good use of that by finally luring out the two–three in order to win yet another double play! They weren't just given the first pair of shoes, they were not only losing to love, they were losing eleven–love. Something that happened very rarely at a domino table, anywhere. With what was probably an international record of *four* double games out of the five which were theoretically possible in one set. Chamon was beside himself. He gesticulated and crowed, but what he would have most liked would have been to run his hands teasingly through Manchi and Bubu's hair.

'Well,' he said when Bubu gave him his last counter, 'and what about the rest?'

'I haven't got any more,' said Bubu naïvely.

'What?!' laughed Chamon. 'Don't you know that you have to *pay* in dominoes when you lose?'

'Well, just give us a button off your shirt, Bubu,' Janchi added.

Chamon made all the more fuss about putting the first pair of shoes on a branch which was exactly on the right-hand side of the tamarind tree. He first walked round the table, swinging them like priests do with incense around the altar.

'Eleven–love,' he kept muttering to the shoes. *'Eleven–love.'*

Enduring Chamon's taunts with wry patience, Manchi and Bubu Fiel were absorbed in reflections on the past games which were as lengthy as they were pointless.

14

The clearheadedness of the Chamon Nicolas and Janchi Pau partnership increased with the amazing score. Chamon's mistakes became fewer, though they needed less and less time to think. (As a result they stepped up the tempo in a catastrophic way.) The pieces played by one partner seemed automatically to prompt the correct move from the other. Chamon Nicolas became more and more confident and Janchi more and more grimly determined. He wanted not only to win, but most of all to completely annihilate the others. Which came down to the same thing. At any rate, it meant that more and more passes rained down on Bubu Fiel's head. He, Janchi, began visibly to enjoy himself each time they won and the disgruntled Manchi threw down his last piece, with which he'd *almost* won, on the table. All the while he thought of Solema, and began imagining he was giving Manchi the hiding that he had long deserved. *Eleven–love. This was a moment he deserved*! And then there were other things which made him angry. The high price of everything; his lack of money, which meant that it would be a long time before he finished his house and could have his woman (that was how he thought of her) with him. And the high prices were also the fault of politics and politicians! And there was the fact that his view of Manchi's house was almost completely blocked by this damn tamarind tree, so he could no longer see Solema when she appeared on her porch.

15

When they also won the first two games of the second set, Janchi took a long look at the nine pairs of shoes which were still on the bench, then at the pair above his head. All Solema's shoes, he thought, finding it slightly sacrilegious that her shoes should be hanging on this tree. And after that he knew exactly what he wanted. He wanted the nine pairs which were there on the bench to be hanging on the tree too, all on one side, on Manchi and Bubu's side! Then no one would look up to Manchi Sanantonio any more as a domino player, and perhaps not at all: he would have murdered the man!

As he picked up his pieces for the new game, he gave Chamon a long, serious look.

He wasn't making any signal. They were coding less and less in this match. It was simply a look asking Chamon to play dominoes as he'd never played before and not to make any stupid mistakes. And Chamon Nicolas seemed to understand him; exactly as he wanted to be understood.

'We'll beat them to love again, Janchi,' he said. Janchi just nodded.

From the next game on, Chamon began to adopt elements of Janchi's play and hence maybe also of his personality. He adopted the broad, far-sighted game of his partner. He lost his fear of double pieces and began to regard them simply like other dominoes. He noticed that he felt more and more calm as a result and could think much more efficiently. He took risks. They were successful because Janchi was always there to support him. Just as an experienced trapeze artist is ready to catch his partner just in time.

And Janchi extended the risks that he took to new possibilities. Which again and again ended in victories. Indeed, Chamon often had the feeling that he was floating, not only as a domino player, but also as a man. *That he was changing*. Now he could concentrate so clearly on the pieces in his hand, he could not only see the *game* clearly, but also reality. Take his affair with Nora. How could he have dragged it out for so long when it had been completely forced on him? When he had always found it a *dangerous* business? True, he imagined it was easy: Nora came to him for money and so he had a fairly permanent partner and didn't have to waste his energies on a variety of women, with all the attendant dangers. Among other things, disease. But how could he have been so blind all these years? To the great danger it involved? With which he was in fact flirting, because he came to play dominoes here every Sunday afternoon?! He felt like a fool, when he thought that *he'd simply allowed himself to be used by Nora*; that he had allowed himself to be drawn like an idiot into a situation which could explode at any moment. He decided to play very good dominoes and to break off with her once and for all.

Over the years Manchi Sanantonio had come to know exactly what he could expect from Chamon Nicolas's game. Normally he could build up certain games in his timid way in the certain knowledge that Chamon would make precisely the moves that he, Manchi, needed when he had the pieces. For example, he could usually assume that Chamon in his best moments would follow the pieces of his partner Janchi. Deliberately follow them, even. But even this principle of dominoes (that Chamon would leave all responsibility for planning to Janchi) was now abandoned by the Windward Islander. The man played independently and thoughtfully; did strange things, which in fact were not part of dominoes at all (such as covering a piece of his partner's and then quite deliberately following it). Sometimes he took the initiative from Janchi and, just as the latter could, continued playing the pieces of a complete set, even if this implied danger for his double piece.

Manchi was gradually making less and less impression on the game. Chamon began doing with him precisely what Janchi had been doing the whole time with Bubu, who was sitting opposite him. It was sometimes reckless play, play that in Manchi's view made no sense, but which was characterized by the inescapable fact that Chamon usually finished precisely one move ahead of him.

Bubu Fiel fared no better: he felt himself pushed up against the wall of his house like a boxer who has been manoeuvred into the corner of the ring and is being pounded with straight punches. He passed so often that on one occasion he couldn't help saying aloud, '*Merde*, it's as though you've put me here just to *pass*!'

And yet he managed to win a game for a change, and through his own initiative too! In the second set, for example, when Janchi and Chamon were again five–love up. He sat fretting with four fives in his hand, when Manchi, departing completely from his usual custom, set down the first five piece. Janchi avoided it. Instead of playing his double five, as he normally did in such a case, he played another five. Chamon passed. Manchi put down his dominoes, bent forwards and counted on his fingers for minutes before playing: he was looking for a way to make Janchi pass, although it wasn't that important, because Chamon had led. Janchi didn't pass. He, Bubu, now played a five again with a thunderous crash on the table. *Everyone* then passed and they won this one game. Then a second game. And that was it. They couldn't reach the total of five games they needed to free themselves. And so, scarcely half an hour after their first, they received their second pair of shoes of the afternoon by ten to two.

Chamon Nicolas was much less exuberant this time. He scarcely teased Bubu when he asked him to pay. He hung this second pair of shoes next to the first pair in a very businesslike way. And he behaved as if he didn't even regard the shoes as separate milestones, but simply as parts of the great plan that his partner Janchi Pau had devised: *Because Janchi Pau, damn it, wanted to give these two married guys all ten of those pairs of shoes*! When this thought occurred to him for the first time it alarmed him. Like someone who suddenly stumbles upon a fortune. Now his heart was overflowing. The thought made him almost explode with excitement: he would collaborate in this great plan! He realized that this was a unique opportunity that he would probably never have again after this afternoon: the chance of accomplishing a heroic feat! He couldn't see it in any other way. He scarcely dared think about the moment when he had achieved it.

What would he do? Would he still be the same Chamon Nicolas afterwards? He had to control himself and keep doing his best. He felt that ascetic purity, that willingness to abstain from everything which was not strictly necessary for the immediate goal; that discipline which is the characteristic of heroes. But also the slight doubt which accompanies it. So he psyched himself up:

Why should he, Chamon Nicolas, not be capable of giving ten pairs of shoes?! Hadn't he already given *two*?! Two to *love*!

He suddenly felt very important because someone needed him: after all, Janchi Pau couldn't do it alone. He suddenly felt smarter than Manchi Sanantonio and Bubu Fiel, because, as he saw it, those two hadn't yet realized what was hanging over their heads. He had the feeling they wouldn't realize before it was too late! He went very quiet for a moment, reflecting on how Manchi, whom he had always looked up to so much, was suddenly starting to fall in his estimation. As was Bubu Fiel.

These suckers, he thought to himself cheerfully, think this
is a game of dominoes like any Sunday afternoon. A *friendly*
game. But it *isn't*! It's sad for them, they don't realize. But that
isn't the point; they're being slaughtered!

16

There's too much seriousness in this game, thought Bubu Fiel
for the umpteenth time at the beginning of the third set (they
were again two–love down). He looked at the women's shoes
on the bench and at the two pairs hanging over their heads.
True, they represented a new element in their game, but he
couldn't accept that they were really the reason for this
completely different atmosphere. Or were they? Perhaps
Manchi had brought too many shoes with him. In any case,
they wouldn't need them all; perhaps seven or eight in total,
because three–four was their average score at this table. Was
it perhaps to do with the fact that all the shoes were *black*?

'It really would have been much better, Manchi, if you'd
given the shoes at least two colours, five black, five white, for
example,' he said aloud. 'It would have been easier than
dividing the tree like this.'

'That was pointed out at the beginning of the game,' said
Manchi stubbornly.

'Black is such a *mournful* colour,' Bubu went on thoughtfully.

'It's also a *distinguished* colour,' said Manchi.

No one said anything else. No one made any remark that
could give rise to a story. And that had been the case since
that odd first set which they had lost eleven–love. *Eleven–
love*, damn it, that really was a remarkable score. Bubu looked
inquiringly at Chamon, who was becoming more and more
silent:

'You're very quiet today.'

'Yes,' said Chamon, now looking at him too with that

strange smile that he'd had on his face since the second set. But then he hid his eyes in his dominoes again.

They wanted to play dominoes! That was it. But that was wrong; that was unfriendly, *that was a betrayal*. Life didn't consist of playing dominoes as they seemed to want to make out this afternoon. It also consisted of other, more important things, precisely the things he felt a need to talk about at length this afternoon. Talk, talk, talk. Stretch himself out lazily, pat his belly a few times and talk about his adventures of the previous evening. Tell them that she had given him a blow-job and that he'd come in her mouth. And tell them about that dancing *naked*, for example. Or tell about how lucky he'd been to arrive on the very day when this woman – what was her name again? – had her birthday. Or her daughter had. You see, because he had to be quiet about her, he forgot her name. And what would happen if he couldn't remember her name? That was the advantage of telling people about an adventure, of communication. If a person later forgot all the details, they could retrieve them again, as it were; they could reconstruct the original experience completely and relive it. But if one said nothing, one ran the risk of losing the name and the experience for good. Hopeless! Look, now he'd forgotten her name and he couldn't ask one of the others. Tell me, what was the name of that woman I was just talking about? Damn, he wouldn't always faithfully buy rum with the money that Janchi gave him if he didn't play this game for his pleasure! At that moment he saw Solema standing there in one of the arches of her porch and made another great effort to remember the name of his whore (or mother). Because he was unable to, he began fancying Solema herself. She was probably about the same age as the woman of yesterday, and might also have those small, young breasts. He kept looking at her rather absent-mindedly with his head raised, as she bent over the wall of her porch and looked in their direction. As she did so, he tried to undress her in his imagination and find out whether she really did look like the woman from yesterday, whose name he couldn't remember. For a moment he'd concentrated *too hard* on the game. Damn game, he thought, damn game. But in any case she was the same colour as Solema up there. Should he? To be on the safe side, he glanced at his partner, Manchi (just as a child looks around before secretly opening the door of the refrigerator). The latter was busy studying his pieces. Should he? How could he work it out best? He suddenly became so curious about the quality of Solema's skin, about the way it would feel just above her *mons Veneris*, on which, while holding her from behind, he'd rested his hands last night with . . . *He'd forgotten her name*! He wanted to shout this out, like a drowning man cries for help, *that he couldn't remember her name*, and that with her name one of the most beautiful experiences of his life was threatening to become lost. He wondered, with another look at Manchi, whether Solema's thighs would also feel as soft. Just imagine, he thought, that you make a pass at her and get lucky, and have an affair with her . . . A young, beautiful woman, and apart from that so close to home!

He stretched out his right hand and waved. Cautiously at first, as a result of which she didn't see it from that distance. And with a look at Manchi. The latter seemed to realize that something was going on and looked at his partner.

He immediately felt he'd been caught in the act and so extended his arm fully and waved openly.

'Bubu!'

He didn't react immediately, because Solema returned his waves.

'Bubu,' came Manchi's voice again, 'your turn!'

'It's Solema,' he said. 'I can wave at her for a moment, can't I?'

'As much as you like,' said Manchi, 'but you're holding up play.'

He dropped his hand again heavily. Chamon Nicolas waved too as he said to Manchi, 'Perhaps she can sense that there's something happening to you this afternoon. Anyway, she's already got two pairs of her shoes back.'

Because Bubu Fiel kept looking at Manchi's house, Janchi, who was annoyed that everyone could see Solema and wave at her except for him, said, 'It's about time you played, friend Bubu.'

The seriousness in his voice made Bubu, as he played, pick up his original train of thought: *They're too serious today*.

Because Janchi Pau was annoyed at the fact that Bubu had a clear view of Manchi's house, he began to involve him more consciously in his dislike of Manchi, which would sharpen his senses even more for the games to come.

The seriousness of the table became more and more oppressive to Bubu. What's more, Solema disappeared from the porch again, and because he simply couldn't remember the name of his woman from the happy camp, he began to feel an urgent need for distraction.

'Did you go fishing yesterday?' he asked Janchi.

'Yes.'

'Where?'

'Daaibooi Bay.'

'Catch anything?'

'Yes.'

He abandoned the attempt and tried Manchi, but with no better results. He said nothing for a while and tried to concentrate on the game again. He didn't ask Chamon anything! A sudden cool wind descended from the hills again; it blew sweetly over the yellow *anglos* growing on the slope of Manchi's hill, irresistibly sweetly, like a young woman, still a young girl really, putting both hands round one's neck.

He had just played again, and decided that that gave him the right, for a moment, just for a moment, to let himself be carried along by this wind. Then the memory of all those men with their game of poker and their drinks returned. Go away! He didn't want to think about that. He wanted them to go away. Go away, all of you! To be alone with her. How did an angel like her find her way to this camp? But that was none of his business. His business was to get undressed, and she was doing the same. She came and stood in front of him naked, with her child's photo in her hand. What did he care about the photo! Anyway, it wasn't light enough to look at it properly. Then he felt her body against him. She deep in him, he deep in her. Her little arms, which were almost too small to go round his neck. And yet, what *comradeship*! Jesus, what a whore! What was her name again? Aha: *Micha*! Damn. *Micha*. He'd got it. Aahaa. *Micha*. *Micha*. Aha.

'Bubu.'

He was almost asleep, but managed to wake up without their realizing that he'd drifted off. It was child's play, actually, because you so frequently took a nap in your cab when there were no passengers. But you had to be able to wake up quickly too, the moment the tourist said 'Taxi' or 'Free' or something at your window. So as not to make a bad impression.

'Were you asleep?' asked Manchi.

'Of course I wasn't! I was thinking.'

'About this game?' said Manchi. 'With your eyes shut?'

In fact, if one doesn't think, dominoes isn't a difficult game. One puts one piece next to the other. And that was what he quickly did now, because he didn't have the remotest idea what was going on, and, what's more, slammed the piece down hard.

'About this game, and about something else. How long is it since you guys danced?'

Because even Janchi raised his head to look at him in astonishment, he explained: 'Yes, I was thinking about dancing just then. I closed my eyes tight' – he directed this at Manchi in particular – 'to try to remember how long it is since I was at a party. Strange,' he went on, 'when I was young I danced almost every day. And it's not that long ago' – he gave a short laugh – 'but nowadays . . .' He hoped that this would interest them, take the seriousness out of this game. It was as though they were playing for money this afternoon!

For a moment it looked as though he would actually succeed. Janchi put down his pieces and thought long and hard. 'I don't know exactly,' he finally said, 'but a long time. I don't think I've danced since my mother's death. Six or seven years or so.'

Manchi said nothing. He thought the subject, considering the beating they were taking, completely out of place. Chamon said with a laugh that he'd taken a few steps not so long ago, but showed no inclination – which was strange for him – to go any further into the subject. However, Bubu didn't give up immediately. 'In our music, in South American music in general, there's a kind of *well*.'

'What do you mean?' asked Janchi, whose turn it was, but who was too interested by the comparison not to pay any attention.

'A well of *truth*.'

Janchi, with the piece he was about to play in his hand, looked at him questioningly.

'A *well* of truth, which at the same time is also a *point* of truth,' he repeated, enjoying his mysterious paradox. But then he thought he'd really found the answer. 'I mean, something that you have to go into further and further to persuade yourself whether it's true or not. That you want to *reach* . . . or . . . simply *get there*,' he said quickly.

'You're speaking in riddles, man,' said Manchi.

'Oh no,' he said. And turning to Janchi: 'Perhaps *you* understand me. You've been with a lot of women in your life, even though you don't dance much these days. I mean something that you want to get *into* and at the same time want to get to the *bottom* of.'

'Tut, tut,' said Manchi, mainly irritated that Bubu still regarded Janchi as the specialist in matters concerning women. 'Tut, tut. It would be better if you got on with the game.' By saying 'tut tut' in this way, he always showed his irritation at or contempt for something.

Janchi deliberately took his time.

'That's why we Negroes like dancing close-up so much,' said Bubu. He was happy that he at least had Janchi's attention.

'You're talking about a *point*. Do you mean of *recognition* or something . . .?' said the latter.

'*I* don't need recognition at all,' said Manchi. 'I've got plenty of that with my work at the court. In fact they can't do without me there. That's why *I* never go dancing. For that matter, people who are concerned with the law, like us, don't dance that much.'

'That's not what I mean,' said Bubu. He wanted to go in a completely different direction from the serious one Manchi was taking with his comments about his work. 'Not recognition, but confirmation, that's what I mean. I believe that in dancing we're looking for *confirmation*.'

'Recognition and confirmation are the same thing,' said Manchi.

'No. I mean confirmation as in *screwing*,' he said suddenly. He gave them a shrewd look through his half-open eyes: this might lead to a nice, entertaining discussion.

'We're not looking for *recognition* when we screw,' said Chamon decisively, 'or for a confirmation.' He saw that Bubu was selecting a piece to play and kept his ready. He *knew* what Bubu was going to play. And when Bubu had made his move, he said, slamming down his piece hard: 'We're looking for *relaxation* when we screw. Anyway, dancing and screwing are not the same thing!'

'I agree,' said Janchi.

'But there *is* a connection,' said Bubu. He suddenly felt they were too stupid to grasp his deepest thoughts. It was even on the tip of his tongue to say, 'The connection between dancing *naked* and screwing,' but he managed to control himself in time.

'Tut, tut,' said Manchi, 'connection my foot! If you want, you can make a connection between anything.'

At other moments his theory might have led to lengthy discussions. On the sensitivity of the female thigh bone compared with the female abdomen or suchlike. With the chance of a discussion on the positions in coitus. Or at least the connection between dancing and pulling women. But the other three obviously had no appetite for such conversations today. Apart from that, he and Manchi lost *again*, so he thought it was best to keep quiet for the time being. Everyone wanted to play dominoes today, as though that was the most important thing a man could do on earth. A little later he suddenly said: 'Some of the tourists on this island are dirty swine.'

Janchi again showed interest and he told them about the American that he'd driven to the camp the night before. As he did so, he wondered what had become of the man.

'Though he had his wife with him,' he said disapprovingly. 'And then they have the nerve to say all kinds of things about us blacks.'

'He was curious,' said Manchi. 'You mustn't forget that Campo Alegre is something unique. From a *legal* point of view at least: only Germany has places like that. I mean, camps.'

'But it's not the same,' said Janchi. 'Campo Alegre is something different.'

'Hasn't it got barbed wire round it, then?' said Manchi sharply.

'But it's *not* the same, because the women go there of their own free will.'

'What do you mean, of their own free will?' said Manchi. 'They're paid to go there! Apart from that, they're forced to spend the night there. It's a *concentration camp*.'

Janchi said nothing. He didn't want to give the impression that he was defending the institution. He was particularly opposed to the fact that the women took all the money that they earned there with them when they went back to their own countries and didn't invest it in his island.

'Did he stay long?' asked Chamon.

'Me?'

'No, him, the American.'

'I don't know. He did ask me to wait for him, but I left. It was already late when I took him there. And Campo isn't that wonderful. Oh yes,' he added sarcastically, 'I'm going to wait there all night in Campo for an American.'

Manchi shifted position on his chair with something like relief. 'Right,' he said. 'But we're waiting for you to play, Bubu.'

Damn, the latter thought again, things are going so fast here today. They'd scarcely lost one game when the next one began. 'So when did you shuffle?' he asked, putting a counter into Chamon's open hand, without looking at it.

'Ages ago,' said Chamon Nicolas.

He now saw there really were only seven pieces on the table. He picked them up and happily played double six, which he'd finally got for a change. But that soon turned out to be an error. Janchi and Chamon had all the rest of the sixes and he didn't get a look in for the rest of the game.

Damn dominoes, he said to himself, as they lost their umpteenth game.

17

Chamon Nicolas was so absorbed in these damn dominoes this afternoon that when, in response to Bubu's call, Nora again came shuffling along with the rum glasses around the east of the house, he was the first to raise his hand and refuse. Bubu Fiel insisted, saying that there was *nothing* to dominoes if they didn't drink while they played, but Chamon stuck to his guns, and continued to smile mysteriously at Bubu. Bubu stopped insisting, because Chamon's smile irritated him. However, Chamon's action was such an inspiration that Janchi refused too, when Nora came to him after serving her husband and Manchi.

'What's this?' said Bubu. 'What are you planning, or what's happening to you?'

But he didn't dare insist as much with Janchi and said, 'Okay then, there's more left for Manchi and me.' When he met Chamon's mocking gaze again he said to himself, One of these days I'm going to smash that fool of a Windward Islander to a pulp.

After that, Manchi excused himself and went to the bath shed. While he disliked this degrading place, and seldom made use of it, he simply had to go. Afterwards he went into Nora's kitchen to wash his hands. Then Nora began hoping that Chamon would come too. It would have been so damn *easy*, but Chamon didn't do it. Chamon and his partner had the others five–love down again.

When Manchi came out of the toilet, he and Bubu won three games in succession, which drew the observation from Bubu that Manchi had got lucky from the bath shed. And Manchi laughed almost cheerfully. 'It's because

228

they refused their drink,' he said cautiously.

But he and his partner couldn't get beyond three after that. Chamon and Janchi steamed ahead to ten and gave them their third pair of shoes. They didn't even shake hands this time. Chamon tied a new pair of shoes next to the other two pairs.

18

At a certain moment Manchi also decided not to drink any more. Bubu insisted, but he felt that he couldn't be outdone by Chamon Nicolas and stuck to his decision. After that, Bubu simply called Nora for himself for a while, but eventually could no longer see any point. Drinking was no longer fun.

Then he began imagining he was losing because he was hot. To make matters worse, a car drove much too fast along the sandy road in front of Manchi's house, so that a cloud of dust spread over the slope, clouding his thinking even more. The rum, which normally made him cheerful and enterprising, now made him feel melancholy. His head was muzzy and was starting to spin. What he would have most liked to do would be to get up and pour some water over his body. Perhaps he would then feel fresh and cheerful again. But of course he couldn't. He was chained to this domino table until dusk. He was *doomed*.

'*Nora*!'

'Are you going to drink some more, friend Bubu?' observed Manchi, who liked the new routine, although it made no difference to the way they played.

'No, man, but I'm damn hot.'

'*Hot?*' said Chamon, now looking at him with open mockery.

'Yes, I don't know what's wrong, but I don't feel good.'

Nora arrived with the glasses of rum which she'd filled

just to be on the safe side, although Bubu hadn't called her for a long time.

'I didn't ask for any of that,' said Bubu, snapping at her without any justification.

'But you called me, didn't you?'

'Do you always have to bring *rum* when I call you? Can't I call you for some other reason?'

Nora controlled herself so as not to swear and looked at the other men questioningly.

Manchi decided to have a drink after all out of politeness towards her.

'Then I'll have another too,' said Bubu.

Janchi and Chamon refused again.

'I don't understand you,' said Nora.

'Why not?'

'You call me as usual and when I come and bring the glasses as usual, you snap at me and say you want something else. And then you take a drink after all. What's wrong with you?'

'Hot,' he said. 'I'm hot. Bring me some alcohol on a towel!'

Nora again tried to attract Chamon's attention, but Chamon was still not co-operating.

'This is alcohol, isn't it?' she teased.

'Cool alcohol!'

'You're sitting here in the cool shadow playing dominoes and you're hot, Bubu. Why is that? Look how coolly the wind is wafting through this tamarind tree. It's making me feel quite cold.'

'Do as I tell you!' said Bubu gruffly.

'Go snap at your dog!'

Whore-chaser, she was about to add. But she held her tongue and walked off angrily.

Now he had the nerve to tell her he was hot! He was ill, for Christ's sake! Now that was the last thing she wanted. A sick husband. Doctor's fees and a hospital. He had his own car and was his own boss, but precisely because of that he had no one to turn to when there was something wrong. He must have caught cold in that whores' camp. When he came out of one of those whores' houses this morning, sweaty and tired from screwing, of course. What a man! What a *whore-chaser*! Or was it all because of marijuana or whatever that stuff was called they smoked the whole time there. Perhaps he'd caught a venereal disease. That gave you a temperature too, she'd heard. The thought alarmed her so much that she simply dropped the tray with the drinks glasses on it. She gave it an angry kick. She went into the house cursing and moistened a large towel with a green type of alcohol which is made on the island and is found in every house. She also took two aspirins and a glass of water. Despite the resentment she felt because he'd frittered away the money that he'd promised her and made a fool of her with his Holland plane and despite his outburst when she tried to make contact with Chamon, she still felt sorry for him. As one does with any child that can't look after itself. Apart from that, she'd also noticed that he was losing, which also mattered to her, although dominoes was a man's game. After all, she was his wife. He had taken off his shirt and was scratching his chest and back. He refused the aspirin because he didn't think he was ill. He rubbed his neck, face, arms and chest with the damp towel and wrapped it round his neck. He sat there stripped to the waist, looking more like a boxer than a domino player.

Normally Manchi would have protested vehemently at this lack of decorum, but now he felt that if there was any way of giving Bubu a lift, it must be used. Besides, he thought his partner's example wasn't such a bad one, and decided to make himself a little more comfortable. He undid his tie, draped it neatly over both knees and unbuttoned his shirt to just above his navel. When he ran his fingers through his hair,

Nora, who had stayed looking at Bubu, asked if he was hot too and wanted some alcohol.

'No, thanks.' But Bubu insisted, glad of the distraction. 'Come on, Manchi, have some too.'

Manchi said yes. She sprinkled some into his hands and he rubbed his face and head with the quickly evaporating, cool liquid.

'Would you like some too?' she then asked Chamon. She thought it was inhospitable to offer some to Manchi and not to the others.

Chamon accepted and she poured some alcohol into his hands too. She looked at him but he did not react. Janchi refused.

Nora disappeared again round the corner of the house, offended by Chamon's indifferent attitude and by Janchi, who seemed to consider her alcohol beneath him.

But even the alcohol for external use didn't help, although it spread a pleasantly fresh and enlivening smell to the east of the house: Manchi and Bubu lost the fourth set. Bubu Fiel scratched his neck, his back and his belly. He scratched his buttocks and his groin without any embarrassment.

There were now four pairs of shoes dangling from the tamarind tree. Bubu began getting angry because he'd forgotten Micha's name again. He also began to be seriously worried about his two opponents, who were dragging him down to a dark defeat like horses that had run wild. After all, four–love was no joke. He was all the more upset because in this set they had almost escaped. They had even won three games.

The shirt which he'd taken off and hung on the back of his chair had fallen on the ground and was now blowing away in the direction of the toilet. He got up abruptly to chase it; once he was going in that direction, he decided to pop into the bath shed.

'I'll be right back,' he said to the other players.

He did not need to relieve himself, but thought it would do him good if he withdrew briefly from the domino table and was alone for a moment.

In the shed he got angry, because he couldn't find the lid of the brown hole in the shitting chair anywhere. So he just sat down on it anyway: it was the only place. If he sat down in the house for a moment Nora would start fussing over him and annoying him with all kinds of questions.

There was a dreadful stench in the small space.

Damn, he thought, burying his face in his hands, I've been playing dominoes for more than thirty years! And now I've lost four sets in a row! In a row! Without escaping even once. Was this it? The final situation that one couldn't wriggle one's way out of, as he was usually able to do successfully? If that was it, then of course he couldn't do anything about it. If the God of Santa Gloria up there had decided that he was to lose today, lose *dreadfully*, then it was completely pointless fighting against it. Everyone had a day like that. His day to live and his day to die. If it was someone's day to die, there was nothing to be done about it. Death wouldn't come a moment sooner, not a moment sooner. *But not a moment later either!*

A long time ago, at great speed and dead drunk, he'd run off the road to Bandabou and turned over several times. Why hadn't he died then?

And he had even been able to repair 200H, which at that time was a red Ford, comparatively cheaply. So he agreed with everyone who said: Bubu, it was not your day, then. If it had been your day, you'd be stone dead now. Was *this* his day then? It looked as if it was with that four–love; and with that chairmanship this evening that he also disliked the thought of. In any case, fate was against him today; the same fate which had so far prevented him from finishing his house and caused him to lose eighty guilders last night instead of getting back his stake double.

Nevertheless, he couldn't believe that fate was entirely against him. Because what was the money, compared with the happiness he'd just stumbled upon?

Oh, terrible fate, he thought, moving his head from left to right with his hands. Oh, terribly *kind* fate!

He was just driving home when that American professor, who said that he'd come to make a study of Curaçao, hailed him.

A *study* of Curaçao, he now thought sarcastically. And he was sitting waiting for him when what's-her-name came up to him and said he reminded her of her first husband, who'd been murdered by Trujillo. And that she'd like to celebrate her birthday with him.

'Me?'

What a stupid woman. Did she think that he'd believed her? How many men had she said the same thing to before? But however much she was lying to him, it meant that she was choosing *him* from all those bastards walking around the camp there. And he went with her. Of course he went with her. It's a damn stupid guy who doesn't let a sentimental whore have her own way. Well, she'd given him everything she had to give. Even though he'd forgotten her name, and the number of her room. 120? 201? 212? 221? 122? 210? 200? 202?

In his mind he wandered through the camp, which now, without her name and the number of her room, seemed unreal to him. At any rate it was something with a two and a nought, but that wasn't much good to him. He wanted to remember it exactly!

'Bubu! Bubu! We're *four–love down!*'

'I'm coming,' he shouted back, thinking: Damn dominoes. If I had the courage I'd go out there now and say to Manchi

234

that I'm *shattered*, that I've been *shattered* all afternoon and that it would be better for him too if I were to stop playing now. But then he'd have to tell Manchi *why* he was shattered. And Manchi would never forgive him. Certainly not *now*, now they were four–love down. And he was also frightened of this because he would lose Manchi's friendship. Which he couldn't risk because very occasionally, when things were really bad, he'd called on Manchi and had been able to call on him, although he preferred not to because it detracted from the equality of the domino table.

He put his shirt back on. And then his eye fell on the jack, which stood leaning against the wall of the shed in front of him. He'd changed one of the tyres on 200H and in his haste had put the iron thing into the shed, instead of into his car. He must remember to put it back in the boot of 200H. 200H, *his 200H*! *She* was the only one who knew him as he really was. When he couldn't stand it here at home because the children were pestering or Nora was ranting at him, he got into it, reversed, turned eastwards so that he was facing Manchi's house, and then drove past the east side of his house onto the Tula road, with the sun at his back, or to the right into the sun. It didn't matter. If the sun was in his eyes, he could lower the wide sunshields. And then he'd just go on driving until he'd calmed down.

Only 200H knew how everything was against him! This house of his back here, which he simply couldn't get off the ground! What he had dug out with every ounce of his strength was now being drenched with rain and again covered with earth. It might not rain a lot, but when there was a good downpour, all the water from the hill came down here from Manchi's beautiful house with all kinds of sand and gravel. The rain and the wind swept the foundations away with them. It didn't help if you covered them. The children started playing on them. The goats pushed the covers off. Nora threw rubbish into your foundations. Oh, Nora was such a *dirty* woman! You came home and all your work was for nothing. And when you were home, one of them asked for a dress, the other for a pair of trousers. Another was worrying about school fees and another one wanted shoes. Everything was on your shoulders. And you were alone and by yourself. And what did you have for yourself? Trousers which were so worn out with sitting that you felt inferior when you walked past a queue of people. So he gave in to temptation now and then. Spent everything. Threw the money away. Well, it was never enough anyway. If you had nothing, then at least you knew you had nothing. You didn't have to worry your head about it. But if you had a *little*, then they went on moaning at you about sharing that little, so that everyone got something. Oh, how good it was to think entirely of yourself occasionally and let all those cares blow away. Like he'd done last night. What was the point of worrying when he'd lost all his money?

But afterwards you felt ashamed anyway, felt guilty. Because as soon as you let yourself go there were disasters. There was Nora, who swore at him and treated him like an enemy.

And 200H. 200H, that together with him was known all over the island and which he would dishonour immeasurably if he kept losing at this domino table.

He sighed. Ha. Was what happened last night not happiness at all then, but a trick of fate? Had she been specially sent to suck him dry in this way, so that he was bound to feel languid, dreamy and absent-minded all afternoon? And couldn't think straight? So that his opponents could destroy him all the better?

He gave another sigh and resolved to turn over a new leaf. He'd soon raise the walls of his new house. He also wanted a toilet with a proper toilet bowl, with a nice enamel seat and a chain for flushing, because it hurt him when one of his friends

236

came to this place, like Manchi had just done. Manchi of all people. And a shower with tiled walls, like you saw every-where these days. In the toilets at the airport, which made them a pleasure to use. And at Manchi's. He wanted some-thing different. He wanted a kind of revolution such as Janchi had preached at the beginning of this game. A revolution in himself. At any rate, he wanted to *win*.

He came out of the shed more cheerful than he had gone in. However, he did not return directly to the domino table, but went into the house. On the table in the back room stood the gallon bottle of rum, almost three-quarters full, with the glasses which had survived Nora's accident and her rage. Nora was sitting in the *sala* with her chin in her hands and staring outside and didn't even notice that he'd come in. He poured himself a drink and downed it quickly. The rum caused a wonderful tickling sensation in his stomach and made him feel even more optimistic. Then he hurried out again, wiping his mouth with his hands.

The pieces had already been shuffled again for the first game of the fifth set. The three men had already taken all their seven pieces.

'Shuffle them again,' he said. He had the feeling that in order to win he had to do everything differently. Manchi, who had a poor hand, immediately put his pieces on the table. Chamon protested.

'What's this, Bubu? We won and we shuffled. All you have to do is pick up your pieces.'

'No,' said Bubu Fiel. 'I want to *change* my luck. I don't just want the pieces to be reshuffled. I want to do it myself.'

'You can't,' said Chamon, holding his pieces tightly to his chest. 'It's against the rules. Isn't that so, Janchi?'

'Yes, it is,' said the latter to Bubu Fiel. 'If we win, we have to shuffle. And we've already done that, as Manchi here can tell you.'

'Yes,' said Bubu. 'I accept all that from you, but as I say, *I want to change my luck*. And *this*,' he added emphatically, 'is still a *friendly* match. I can't see what you've got against my having a shuffle for once.'

'I can,' said Chamon. 'I've got damn good dominoes.'

'Yes, it's true, it's a *friendly* match,' said Manchi, pushing his pieces further into the middle.

'You two have had good pieces all afternoon,' said Bubu. '*All afternoon*.'

'There's no need to make insinuations,' said Janchi fiercely. 'You two have been able to see all the time how I've shuffled, completely fairly.'

'I don't mean to say that you two are dishonest, certainly not you, Janchi, but I'm wondering *why* you keep winning one game after another.'

'Magic,' said Chamon, looking at him disparagingly.

'For all I know,' he said rather more playfully, 'but perhaps you're sneaking a look at my pieces the whole time.' Because of the mysterious smile that Chamon was giving him so often, he thought this might be not such a bad assumption.

'That's pretty low,' said Chamon. 'How can you, Bubu Fiel, think I'm capable of something like that?'

'People are capable of anything!'

'Go ahead and shuffle,' said Janchi, 'if you feel like it.'

'How can you allow that?' said Chamon. 'It's against all the rules.'

'Let him shuffle. We'll win anyway.'

Chamon protested again but still threw his pieces onto the table.

As he shuffled the pieces with expansive swimming movements, Bubu dreamed of a wonderful hand. A hand with six sixes and the double six so that everyone would pass, from the moment he led. Or a hand with five pieces of the same suit, as had happened to him quite often on other Sundays.

He dreamed of a double play, where he kept making everyone pass and at the end exclaimed: two bullets! and then kept slamming the winning piece down on the table, so that everything flew off it. And so on and on, until they reached ten. And then again and again and again.

He dreamed of winning games, just as on his island people dream of a winning number in the legal state lottery, or the illegal lottery of Venezuela, of the Dominican Republic and all the other surrounding countries; the illegal horse-racing of Venezuela; or a great win from the daily, equally illegal numbers games. Unfortunately, in order to win those capricious lottery prizes they spent their last penny!

Bubu Fiel and Manchi lost. Again and again. Now Chamon started teasing Bubu Fiel openly, by repeatedly asking him in a seemingly friendly way before shuffling, 'Would you like to?' Janchi, too, only shuffled after giving the other two a questioning look.

Bubu accepted now and then, and so did Manchi, but because even this humiliating favour of their opponents did no good, they increasingly looked simply ridiculous. Finally Bubu snapped at Chamon when Chamon again asked him teasingly, 'Would you like to?'

'Would you like to what? You two damn well won, didn't you?'

'*Not* damn!' said Chamon at that point. 'Watch what you're saying. I'm not your wife and not your child either. You can't just bite my head off like that! You were dying to shuffle just now, although we had won and had already shuffled and apart from that I had already a wonderful hand!'

At this Bubu could do nothing except hold his tongue and look crestfallen, whereupon the good old rule of dominoes, that whoever wins shuffles, was reintroduced at this domino table.

Because of the harmonious interplay between Chamon and

Janchi, the pace of the game remained too fast for Bubu. Occasionally, by trying with all his might, he succeeded in working out what Manchi had in his hand, but once the picture was complete, it was usually too late to do anything about it. The pace of the game took him by surprise. He continually felt short of time, the more so because Chamon gradually developed the habit of waiting for his move with a piece in his hand and that cheeky smile on his face. Which rattled him even more. Because it happened more and more often that Chamon actually did know what he, Bubu, was about to play. In addition, his opponents were now playing without slamming the domino pieces. They weren't slamming and they weren't drinking. They were pushing. They were posing their dominoes like virgins or long-nosed chess players. Delicately and with self-control. They seemed to spend scarcely any time or effort any more on coding their pieces to each other, as he and Manchi did occasionally, which didn't alter the fact that they couldn't achieve any kind of harmony today. He, Bubu, suddenly missed the slamming, which gives one such a taste for the domino table; which can startle one for a moment and make one think quickly if one has drifted off for a moment. The breaks in the game, when one of the men took longer to think, were also fatal for him. He was desperately bored, and simply drifted off. And found himself in the cheerful camp with that same woman, whose name and room number he could no longer remember. Which annoyed him. And now because of his annoyance he made the wrong move.

Both the pace of the game and the long pauses tortured him. This damn game of dominoes! The passes rained down on his head. Sometimes for whole games. Then, despite his good intentions, he became apathetic, he began to feel the time spent at this table was wasted time. Who had invented this damn torture? Oh, this game of dominoes! They lost the fifth set too.

19

Bubu's son Ostrik appeared to the east of the house to remind his father again that he needed new shoes. He was wearing the sort of open sandals that are worn a lot in South America: a leather sole with straps of cheap material. These *pargatas* occupy a lowly place in the footwear hierarchy of the Antilles. He couldn't even go to church in them, let alone to the De Ruyter College, which accommodates a large proportion, if not the majority, of children from the highest echelons in this society. Even in plimsolls, which are more highly valued (and hence are worn by famous sportsmen), he wouldn't be able to show himself there. At least not on a regular basis.

Consequently the numerous financial pricks which this school gave him (books, sports kit, school parties, school trips, school fees, library fees and so on and so on) made Bubu wonder in general whether he'd been right to take Manchi's advice and send Ostrik to the state secondary school and not one of the two Catholic ones where things were probably more *moral* because of the greater *order, decency and discipline* so characteristic not only of the late Doctor but also of the Catholic Church. But Manchi's advice – which he himself had asked for – was of course compelling. Moving the boy to a new school now would anyway probably entail new expenses. Moreover, people might start thinking that he'd made Ostrik change schools because the boy wasn't good at his lessons, which was far from being the case.

When Ostrik arrived, Chamon, in the businesslike manner he had assumed this afternoon, was just tying the fifth pair of shoes to a branch of the tamarind tree. Bubu felt morally supported by the arrival of Ostrik: because of the expensive school and the fact that he was such a good pupil, the boy represented his best side. His arrival also meant diversion, *distraction.* Consequently he greeted his son with a jovial 'Oh, are you there?'

'Yes. Who's winning?'

'We are,' said Chamon with a laugh, 'can't you see?' Indeed, Janchi was shuffling for the next game.

'You two are winning *for the time being*,' said Bubu bravely. 'What's the score?'

'What's hanging over there,' said Chamon, with far too studied indifference. 'Five–love.'

'Whose idea was it for those shoes? It's nice.'

'Mine,' said Manchi.

'Well?' said Bubu.

'They provide ideas, we provide shoes,' said Janchi.

'Five–*love*?' said Ostrik. The one-sided score had only now sunk in, because in fact he'd been concerned the whole time with finding a proper way of bringing up his own business: 'So you're getting a good hiding, Dad. That's unheard of, isn't it?'

'It's nothing,' said Bubu, 'we'll soon catch up with them.'

'But five–love!' He scarcely dared bring up the question of his shoes any more, and for that reason found it particularly annoying, because actually he wasn't at all interested in dominoes. He was more of a footballer. Hence the large quantity of shoes which he wore out, one pair after another.

'We're having a bit of bad luck,' said Manchi, 'that's all.'

'A *bit*?!' said Ostrik. 'I'll be off, then.'

Bubu was very happy that he left again. He was making too much fuss about how far behind they were. In order to focus attention on something else, he said, 'I expect my son's still got to do his homework, hasn't he?'

'No,' said Ostrik quickly. 'I haven't got any *shoes*, have I . . . ?'

'Come on,' said Bubu, laughing heartily in front of his friends.

'But you know, don't you? How can I have homework if for a week I haven't . . . ?'

'Come on, come on, I'm not talking about shoes, I'm talking about your homework. Have you finished it?'

'I haven't been to school for a week,' said Ostrik in a matter-of-fact way.

'For a week?' said Bubu, acting indignant.

'Mummy says she told you I haven't got any shoes and that you promised . . .'

'Told you what! Promised what! I gave her the money for your shoes long ago. Of course she's blown it on her numbers. Off you go and make sure you do your homework for tomorrow. Those women!' he said sarcastically to his friends.

Ostrik wasn't angry. Perhaps because he was the most educated person in the house, he was aware how difficult it was for his parents to keep him at that De Ruyter College. Just as he himself found it difficult to concentrate on his lessons surrounded by poverty, cursing and swearing, by the noisiness of his father, mother, brothers and sisters, without a room of his own, without sufficient books, without anyone whom he could turn to when he was stuck. All the resources which the majority of the other pupils had. So he again told himself, as he often did, that the miracle which had helped him to get into that college would have to ensure in some way or other that he stayed there.

When he got past the junction of the Tula and Carpata roads he decided to visit a friend. Perhaps they could go and kick a ball around somewhere. Thank God he didn't need any shoes for that.

'Is Ostrik still doing his best?' asked Manchi before he chose his pieces.

'What do you mean?'

'You were talking about his homework.'

243

'Oh, yes . . . No, no. The boy is *very* good. I wish *I* had his brains.'

'If there are any problems, just you go ahead and send him to Solema. She'll bring him up to scratch.'

So Manchi scored again and that was all that mattered to him. Janchi Pau, however, asked himself if there was any end to his sanctimoniousness.

'No, no,' repeated Bubu Fiel very emphatically, finding it a great shame that he had frittered away the money for the boy's shoes, and even more so in such a stupid way. But he'd had such good intentions: Ostrik was the one thing which helped him to retain a little prestige in the face of Manchi. The thought that he would ever have to have extra lessons from Solema was very unwelcome to him.

'No,' he said again, 'there's *nothing* wrong with the boy. All I have to do is to get his mother to be a little more thrifty with the money I give her, so that the boy can always have what he needs: you guys don't know how much that high school costs. *Every month.*' No, that was one thing that they certainly couldn't know, because none of the three had children at a secondary school! 'And I'm just a poor taxi driver,' he said with feigned melancholy.

'Soon you'll be chairman of the union,' said Janchi.

'That'll make a difference,' said Chamon.

'Ah,' said Bubu in irritation, 'some difference! It'll just cost me loads of money.'

He felt the pressure of his financial situation so clearly – which was normally not the case when he relaxed with his domino friends here on Sunday afternoon – that he suddenly said to Janchi, 'You're right.'

'About what?'

'About those foreigners. What you said at the beginning of the afternoon: they've got this country in their power. They take *everything* away from us.'

Janchi agreed, but because he was vaguely aware what the real point was, added, 'But we have to produce for ourselves.'

'I don't understand what you're saying,' said Bubu Fiel, hurt that Janchi didn't agree with him immediately and unreservedly. Apart from that, he sensed a reproach in Janchi's answer. 'I don't understand you. First you say it's the foreigners. And now you're saying that it's us? You keep changing your ground!'

'I'm saying that we must *produce*,' said Janchi emphatically as he played. 'We must rise up and compete with the foreigners,' he added with renewed insight. The resentment with which he'd started this domino game had subsided somewhat. And for that reason he thought rather less excitedly about politics.

Bubu quickly tried a different tack. 'That story of yours is mighty interesting, Manchi, it really ought to be written down and sold as a book. Like the stories of *Nita*,' he added.

'Definitely,' said Manchi, finally with some trace of pleasure in his voice. 'Perhaps I'll actually do that some time.'

'Do you see that judge often?'

'What?'

'The judge. Do you see him often?'

At that moment Manchi was concentrating hard on the game and said automatically: 'I'm the judge.'

Bubu laughed out loud.

'Is it you, Manchi? Did it really happen to *you*?' he asked, finding difficulty in suppressing his imminent outburst of joy. 'So why did you lie to us?'

Janchi, frightened that Manchi would talk publicly about Solema, said quickly, 'You can see that he's thinking, can't you?'

It was just the pause that Manchi needed to recover himself. 'No,' he said. 'More's the pity!'

245

'But you said yes, when I asked you just now,' Bubu insisted. 'You said yes.'

'I'm telling you Manchi was *thinking*,' said Janchi sternly.

'Yes,' said Manchi, looking at Janchi suspiciously, 'I really was thinking.'

'Oh,' said Bubu, deeply disappointed. But it was of course *impossible*, he corrected himself. If the story had happened to Manchi himself, then the unfaithful woman in question would be none other than Solema, and he could scarcely imagine that she'd committed adultery in the way that Manchi had described. Even though for fun and because he was drifting off, he had toyed with the idea of seducing her. No, she was a respectable woman, a very respectable woman. And yet . . .

'What did you think I meant just now?'

'If I could become a judge or something. Something like what Chamon asked me at the beginning of the afternoon.'

'But you said: *I'm the judge*. That's exactly what you said. I – am – the – judge. That's what you said.'

'In a certain sense I *am*,' said Manchi, 'when I as a bailiff say to you that you have to pay, then you *have to*. Let's get on with the game. Or don't you care about these five pairs of shoes? We're losing dreadfully! Let's *play*, man!' And that was that. *For now*. Because the thought that he could really become a judge relatively easily intrigued him more and more.

As far as Chamon was concerned, Manchi already held such a low place in his estimation, that he didn't even consider it worth his while to follow this short dialogue. (Consequently he made use of the break in the game to think a long way ahead.) When Manchi drew attention to the five pairs of shoes, he began to suspect that maybe *everything* that Manchi had ever brought up at the domino table consisted mainly of lies. And that he, Chamon, because he had been such a sucker until this afternoon, had allowed himself to be impressed by Manchi.

Because he was getting nowhere with Manchi, Bubu let his attention wander off to other successful stories from the past which had often provided marvellous entertainment at this table. For example, there was that wonderful story of his own about a lady to whom he gave a lift on his way from West Point into town, and with whom he found himself spending three days in a weekend cottage – *her* weekend cottage. And for those three days the whole island was in uproar because Nora had reported him missing to the police. And when he took his leave of that lady, who was a rich white woman, he told her that she still owed him three hundred guilders: because 200H had been standing waiting outside her door for three days! And now he savoured the memory of how he had said to her by way of explanation, 'After all, I *am* a taxi driver, madam!' He had also made it clear that he would be able to hold his tongue about where he'd been for those three days – if she gave him the money. Otherwise perhaps not. She was angry, cursed a lot, but finally gave him a hundred guilders, all of which he then gave to Nora. She wasn't angry at all, but he smiled inwardly at the memory of the naïvety with which she kept repeating, 'I was so frantic with worry about you, Bubu. Why didn't you just come and tell me that you had to stay with that lady for three days *for your work*?' For that reason it was more a story about *Nora*, all things considered. There was also that story of Chamon Nicolas's: a Dutch woman had wanted to take him with her to Europe. Chamon didn't want to go, because, as he said, there was nothing for him in that *damn cold Holland*, where apart from that he'd have to speak Dutch for the rest of his life, which for him was the most difficult language in the world. He'd been in hiding for weeks because she drove all over the island looking for him like a crazy woman – crazy with love. With a plane ticket and all!

20

Three men on their way to a friendly football match, which was due to take place a few miles beyond the church of Wakota, came into Bubu Fiel's yard. They were fond of dominoes too and liked watching Janchi Pau in action.

One of them was a committee member of the Dominoes Association of Wakota, of which Bubu Fiel had been chairman. As soon as the men heard about the unusual score of six–love, with the imminent possibility of *seven*–love, they were keen to continue on their way immediately. Manchi guessed their intentions and, when they made as if to leave, said to them, 'It isn't four o'clock yet. Before it's dark we'll have caught up with them. Stay a bit longer.' And to Bubu, 'Why don't you offer our friends a glass of something?'

Glad of this diversion, Bubu called Nora and a little later she brought four glasses of rum. Chamon, Manchi and Janchi didn't drink, but Bubu drank with the three men. Nora, who knew nothing about the three spectators, nevertheless had the right number of drinks.

But it was no good. They lost: the eighth, the ninth and the tenth game. They did not win even one game to support their assertion in front of the three spectators, now more or less forced to watch, that they would catch the others in the course of the afternoon.

Nevertheless, after this set Bubu Fiel said bravely, 'These are our seven lean years. Now the fat ones are bound to come, otherwise the Bible is wrong. Stay a bit.'

But the men took their leave. The protests of Manchi and Bubu did no good. 'We've got to go to the football match,' they lied.

'We're really losing,' said Manchi to Bubu, almost groaning.

'It looks like it,' said Bubu airily, watching the men as they walked far too hurriedly in the direction of Wakota cemetery.

'We must do something about it, man,' said Manchi. 'You haven't realized yet, but we haven't got that much *time* left. About two hours at most. Less.'

'If fate is against you, you can't do a thing. We're just having bad luck today, Manchi. You said so yourself just now.'

'I expect so, but we must still do our best. You must pay more attention to what I play, Bubu, and respond better.'

'Of course, but when I respond to your pieces, it turns out I'm playing for Chamon. That's happened to me a couple of times already. You can see for yourself, can't you?'

Manchi confirmed this. Perhaps Bubu had occasional lapses in concentration. Perhaps he actually did make mistakes, but it was clear that it wasn't just because of that that they were losing. It was clear that their opponents' play was superior and he couldn't do anything about *that*. For that matter, it was all his own fault. He shouldn't be sitting at this domino table! He should have said weeks ago when he had his triumph with the story in question, 'Ah, friends, this is the last time that I shall be playing. I'm going to build a cottage to spend the weekends in with Solema and the children. What do you say to that?' That's what he should have said.

Bubu Fiel returned to the idea of a hammock. Lying down on it. With a bottle of rum within reach. The shadow of a tamarind tree is as good as the porch of a modern house. He didn't need a house and a porch like Manchi here, who had *no* great tamarind tree in his garden. The thought made him happy in a melancholy way. He told himself that the real reason why he didn't finish his house, or even start on it, was perhaps that he was actually *content* to leave things as they were, just here to the east of the house where he could sit in the evenings and occasionally do nothing except watch the traffic on the road.

He cast a lazy glance at the sunny, sloping landscape in front of him, at the *anglos* and the cactuses he was so used to. Janchi here might talk about 'producing', but for God's sake what were they supposed to produce on this island? Cactuses? *Anglos*? Once, on a piece of land belonging to Nora's parents on Bandabou, he had tried cultivating a small plot. But because of several periods of extreme drought, it hadn't yielded much.

'Janchi,' he asked, 'you talk about *producing*. But *what*?'

'I don't know myself exactly,' said Janchi. 'But that's precisely our mistake. That we don't seriously *think* about it.'

'But *what*?' repeated Bubu, looking absent-mindedly at the slope full of shrubby cactuses.

'What the Chinese and Portuguese produce, for example,' replied Janchi, 'if we're talking about agriculture. But we can also make lots of things for ourselves, if we put our minds to it. There used to be hats made here. And lace and cigars and God knows what else. Sugar,' he added, thinking of Cuba.

'They still make lace on Saba,' said Chamon neutrally.

'All kinds of things,' said Janchi. 'We can do anything. Provided we commit ourselves.'

'Yes,' said Bubu. 'Perhaps we're too easily satisfied, that's the rotten thing. We're content with too little.'

'We lack stimulus,' said Janchi.

Bubu wondered. He wondered if he was lacking stimulus and came to the conclusion that he wasn't. If he was really convinced that he had to build a house like Manchi's, then he'd do it. But he wasn't convinced! How would he ever get that conviction? If he wanted to be an unimpeachable and respected man like Manchi, who considered what people thought of him important, he could certainly achieve that too. But what people thought about him left him cold. That's why he lived life *his* way. If he thought it was important to sit on a porch with Nora like Manchi could with Solema, then he'd make a house with a porch like that or he'd build one in front of his own house here. But if he and Nora really wanted to sit in the cool, then couldn't they just simply sit under this wide tamarind tree to the east of the house?

He was slightly shocked himself when he won the first game of the eighth set, because of a minor mistake by Janchi.

'Didn't I tell you, Manchi,' he suddenly exclaimed happily, 'didn't I *tell* you? The seven fat years have begun! Let's have a drink. *Nora*! I don't know if you want to join me,' he added in an almost teasing tone of apology, 'but I'm having one. 200H can't go any further without petrol.' He began exuberantly turning the pieces over, happy that he could now shuffle legitimately for a change.

'These people here,' he said when Nora appeared with the tray and the glasses, 'have got something wrong with them today. They're ill, they're not drinking.'

Manchi and Janchi indeed refused. Chamon also, in fact, but Nora kept standing next to him insistently with the tray so that he finally looked at her.

'Come on, Chamon,' she said, 'you've drunk scarcely anything today.' As she said this, she looked at him with a pained look which she thought he couldn't possibly refuse.

'Okay then, Nora,' he said, 'to please you,' and downed the drink in one.

But when he looked at her again as he put his glass down, he saw that the pained look was still there. So he quickly turned his eyes back to the table, where Bubu was just finishing shuffling.

Nora's pained expression was indeed a new attempt to make it clear to Chamon that she had something to say to him. She assumed he hadn't understood her and was trying to be clearer.

Before going, she said, 'I wonder how you men can sit here playing non-stop all afternoon, without once getting up. Don't you have to go to the toilet now and again? I couldn't do it.' Then she shuffled off around the corner of the house, without looking back.

Chamon understood. Nora wanted to talk to him. But he didn't react because he wanted to break off with her. And he wouldn't be able to make that clear to her in the few minutes he would have with her in the kitchen. With the clarity of vision he had this afternoon, he realized that his arrangement with her had not really been very smart. True, it enabled him to have sex without the worry of a household and possibly children. But the fact remained – and there was no getting round it – that he couldn't have a woman all to himself like this! In the evenings, on dreary Sunday evenings, when other men sat cosily on the porches of their houses with their wives, or watched television with them, he was alone. Then he felt cheated, because he suddenly realized that he didn't have anything of his own; something on which one could always rely: a woman of his own!

It wasn't just out of fear of Bubu Fiel, who for that matter he didn't feel at all afraid of this afternoon, that Chamon Nicolas wanted to break with Nora. It was also out of fear of loneliness.

21

However, Nora assumed that Chamon would go to the toilet. So she positioned herself at the back door of her house, in order to go over there when he was in the toilet and to make a soft hissing sound to him. When he turned round she would gesture to him that he mustn't come out of the shed too quickly. That was her plan. She had made a kitchen cloth wet and placed it ready on the kitchen table next to the tray with

252

the rum glasses on it: when Chamon went to the toilet, then with the cloth in her hand she would go over to the washing line that ran diagonally behind the shed and above the foundations of the new house. Through one of the numerous chinks in the shed she would whisper to Chamon that she needed five guilders from him. If he said that he would give it to her, there was no more need to worry. He would make sure he found a way of handing it over to her before he went home after the game.

She picked up the soaking-wet cloth, which she forgot to wring out, ready to follow Chamon the moment she saw him appear.

Chamon didn't appear. The water from the cloth dripped onto her dress and drenched her feet and slippers. She cursed a few times, then walked out of the house slowly, wringing out the cloth in her hands.

She stopped outside the bath shed. She could see Chamon sitting there clearly, with his back to her. She began singing 'Cu-cu-ru-cu Paloma', so that he would know where she was. She hoped he would turn round. Then she would toss her head back violently and at the same time gesture to him. All he had to do was look around. She was running the risk, though, that Bubu would see her, but it was a risk she had to take.

Chamon did not look round. So she didn't go all the way to the washing line. She grabbed the door of the shed with one hand and half opened it. She remained peering inside for a few moments as though she were looking for something. Then she glanced at Manchi's house and saw that Solema was standing on the porch. She was startled at first, but then realized that the fact that she was standing here by her bath shed was just as permissible and normal as the fact that Solema was on *her* porch. Then she looked cautiously at the men, who at that moment were playing in silence, but no one was looking in her direction. She went into the junk store and a little later came out again. Humming, with the towel in her hand, she strolled towards the back door of her house.

Solema was no longer standing on her porch. If Chamon decided to get up *now* and head for the bath shed, she could still turn round and go to her washing line in order to be able to speak to him through the wall of the shed. She wanted to go there straight away, but thought that she couldn't be sure that the person in the shed was Chamon. For that she had first at least to see him get up. But Chamon didn't get up and didn't even look round.

She didn't give up. She dampened the towel again and again walked slowly to the bath shed with it, again singing 'Cu-cu-ru-cu Paloma'. Again she stood with her hand on the door of the bath shed openly looking at the men. The clarity with which she could see him was awful. Why did the wretch not look round? Not once!

When she returned to her back door, she again looked at Manchi's house. Solema, who was again standing there, now looked in her direction and waved. Nora waved back. Then she went back into her house. She was going to give up. It looked as though Chamon wasn't going to the toilet and wasn't going to turn that big head of his even if the sky fell in.

She went to the bedroom to see if the ten-guilder note that she'd earned that morning was still there, under the statue of Our Lord of the Sorrows. It was still there. In the hollow under the statue. Then she decided to try again. You never knew! Then she kept walking back and forth between the house and the bath shed, for a long time.

'Nora, will you stop that singing, for God's sake! What are you *doing* there the whole time?' It was Bubu.

'I'm hanging clothes up,' she called back.

'Clothes? Do you have to walk back and forth the whole

time to do that? Why don't you take everything to the washing line in one go? And stop that singing. It's distracting us. Such a *stupid* woman,' he said to his friends.

'Mind your own business,' she shouted.

'You're *distracting* us!'

'It's not *my* fault you're losing,' retorted Nora angrily. 'Mind your own business.'

Bubu put his pieces down in order to explain the extent of Nora's stupidity at length to his domino friends. 'The creature takes each item of clothing one by one to the washing line,' he said, 'when she could carry everything in one big basin and stand and hang it out. *Women!*' he said scornfully. However, he again felt that premonition that something weird was going on today.

Nora went sulkily back into the house. She didn't even bother to take the towel, which after all she had made wet for nothing, to the washing line once and for all. She simply hurled it onto the kitchen table next to the bottle of rum with the glasses.

'For goodness' sake, let's see what we can *do* with these people, Bubu,' groaned Manchi.

The score was five–one in the eighth set. To Janchi Pau and Chamon Nicolas, that is.

22

Nora had no idea what to do next to get her five guilders, now she wasn't going to get them from Chamon. She did know that she wouldn't get them if she stayed at home. She must get out and about.

Moreover, when she had waved to Solema just now, something of a plan of campaign had occurred to her. Anyway it was necessary that she got *out* of the house.

Sometimes, she thought, again putting on the cream dress

255

that she'd worn that morning and her low-heeled black shoes, it looks as if you're a *streetwalker*. But she still bravely got dressed. She knew what she was. She powdered her black face until it looked rosy. She put a yellow scarf on, the corner of which tapped playfully against her neck. With a completely empty, black purse in her hand she was about to leave, when she remembered her duty as a housewife. In the back room she filled a glass carafe with rum from the gallon bottle, which normally was almost empty by this time, but was now more than half full. She would take the carafe and the glasses outside: then the men could serve themselves when she had gone.

'I'm off out,' she said to Bubu Fiel, putting the carafe and the glasses on the bench. 'You can pour your own drinks.' She tried not to attract Chamon's attention again, because she felt that this would once more fail, which would make her even gloomier.

'If you want more rum,' she added to what she'd said, 'the bottle's on the table in the kitchen. I'm going to pay my respects to someone who's just had a bereavement.'

At first Bubu said nothing. Putting down the glasses and leaving! It was simple. But it was wrong! She had no right just to go off like that, especially now he was losing. It wasn't what a *good* woman should do. It was the same as deserting a man on his deathbed. He felt panic.

When Nora began walking away in the direction of their garden gate, he said, 'Will you be coming back soon, Nory?'

'I hope so,' she said without turning round.

His attention was caught by her yellow scarf which blew cheerfully after her with the wind.

'Oh?' he asked loudly.

'What do you mean?' asked Nora, turning round in annoyance.

'Are you going to give someone your condolences with a

yellow scarf on? What's wrong with you today, woman?'

'It's a while ago,' she protested. But she realized that in her haste to get out of the house she had made a mistake.

'Come on back and put another scarf on,' he said, happy that he could delay her for a moment, because he really hated it when she wasn't home when he was there. 'You can't go and give people your condolences like that,' he said, as he played, 'even if it was *years* ago.'

Nora went back into her house and put on the white scarf that she'd worn in church that morning. She returned to where the men were playing via the front door.

'Is this all right?' she asked almost coyly.

'Yes,' he grunted, 'but don't stay too long.'

She gave him a look that said, 'You're a fine one to talk!' and walked off.

'Who in heaven's name do you suppose she's going to give her condolences to?' said Bubu aloud to himself. And then to the other men: 'Do any of you know of a death here in Wakota?' For a moment he felt as disorientated as Nora had that morning when she tried to get to the bottom of the fate of his Holland plane.

Chamon and Janchi shrugged their shoulders.

Manchi said, 'You'd do better to concentrate on this game here, Bubu. We're losing *again*.'

23

That very afternoon Solema decided to go to Janchi's for good. A mixture of love and courage was decisive. Even more than the fear of Manchi, which she'd begun to feel that afternoon when he brought up the subject of his weekend cottage. She took out the two cases which she still had from Europe, put them in the front room and began packing.

Her biggest problem was her children, but she might be

able to leave them with her parents for the time being, until Janchi's house was finished. Her mother adored them and in fact often complained that Solema seldom let them spend the night with her. So it would be easy, she realized. Too easy in fact for this to be the real reason for her hesitating when Janchi asked her to come to move in with him that morning. Consequently a feeling of shame overcame her and she thought (in order to justify it to herself) of the money that she had saved. She could help him finish the house with it. She could even, she said to herself with mounting optimism, pawn her jewels if things got really bad. At any rate, she began to feel so brave that she no longer feared poverty, which though she hadn't experienced it personally, she knew well enough, since it was visible like open sores all over the island. To cheer herself up, she finally reflected that she would be able to combat it better if she'd experienced it herself for a change.

She packed her own and her children's things, and also lots of stuff to put Janchi's house temporarily in order; for example, to be able to cook a little better there. As far as the rest was concerned, she would see later. At a certain moment, to avoid the risk of being spotted in her preparations by the domino players, she drove the car into the garage. In that way she could fill the boot without anyone seeing her. It was about four o'clock.

Now and then she stopped work and went onto the porch. She didn't want to run the risk of suddenly being surprised by Manchi, even though he was in the habit of playing dominoes until dusk. On one of those occasions she saw Nora between her bath shed and house, and waved. A sort of farewell wave. She recalled the circumstances in which people like Nora lived and then thought even more courageously: 'If *they* can do it, so can I.'

24

Nora had no definite plan as she walked eastwards along the Tula road. One and a half miles further in that direction lived her daughter, shacked up with a welder who worked for Shell. If nothing occurred on the way to provide the necessary cash, she might try there. She could also go to a married son of hers, but he lived up by the airport. That was too far. She'd have to take a bus and she couldn't do that because she didn't have the money. She didn't have a cent in her black purse. She'd only brought the thing with her to have something in her hands and because it reminded her of the times when she did have something in it. Because it made her feel optimistic. She also had a son who was a bus driver, but she couldn't pin any hopes on him. His route was way over on the eastern side of the island. In order to reach him, she would have to go into town and for that she needed a bus too. With a feeling of complete abandonment she suddenly realized that she didn't even have money to buy bread and sandwich fillings for the children to take to school in the morning. To say nothing about her and Bubu Fiel. So even if she was lucky and managed to get those five guilders, she would have to find a way of getting at least one guilder more. She now started worrying about that one guilder. Who in God's name would be prepared to lend it to her? Imagine: finding six guilders just like that on a Sunday afternoon, when the new week began tomorrow. She also thought sadly that it wasn't really a pay-day yesterday, neither for the Shell people who were paid every two weeks nor for those on monthly salaries. It was the third week in the month. In the month of November, come to that. This wasn't her month, this month of sadness and mourning.

She had the feeling that all the rotten things that had happened in her life had always happened to her in the month of November: the illness of Bubu and the children, the death of six of her children. No, it wasn't her month. She was a *December* person. That month, with its parties, always brought her luck. So she couldn't count on six guilders. She must manage to get hold of five guilders and then hope that she would be able to find shoes for Ostrik for *fourteen* guilders tomorrow.

25

A pirate bus came down the Tula road. The driver, who saw Nora looking round a lot, sounded his horn and stopped. He hadn't earned much yet. Nora, however, waved, almost anxiously, to indicate that she didn't want to get on.

What's she looking for, then? thought the driver, continuing to drive alongside her in first gear. He was quite a smartly dressed man, still young, keen on a passenger or on an adventure.

Nora quickly considered the latter possibility, but decided that it was too dangerous. It was still broad daylight and, apart from that, close to her home.

'What are you waiting for, then?' the man called to her.

'It's none of your business!' she retorted sharply. 'Drive on!'

The man pulled away but kept looking at her in his rear-view mirror for a long time.

A second car passed her, driven by a Dutchman who swivelled round a long way to look at her. But Nora turned her nose up demonstratively. She hated everything white because she blamed her own wretchedness and that of people like her on whites.

She took the sandy road towards Manchi's house. As she did this, she also began thinking up an excuse for Bubu Fiel, who was bound to ask her later what she'd gone to visit

Solema for, when she'd said that she was going to give someone her condolences on a bereavement.

The plan of dropping in at Solema's had occurred to her vaguely just now when Solema – *Miss* Solema as she called Manchi's wife – had waved to her and she had returned the wave, as they often did when they saw each other from a distance. She had never been in Solema's home. Up to now she'd never had a reason to be there. But they knew each other from the church and the Santa Gloria school. Solema had taken one of her daughters, Vera, home with her a few times. The child had eaten and had a bath and since then had never stopped talking about 'Miss Solema's wonderful bathrooms, with those wonderful tiled walls'.

The closer she got to Solema's house, the more she began to lose courage. How was she to go about it? And wouldn't Solema refuse, even if she had the money? Of course, thought Nora. If I'd come here from a long way away to borrow five guilders or even twenty-five, she would do it. But because I live so close by, she won't! She'll refuse because she'll think that if she helps me once, I'll go on pestering her. But she kept going.

The splendid trees in Manchi's garden, which poked out through the bars of the fence, seemed to beg for admiration. Almost casually, she picked two of those beautiful, large *gayenas*, which she held in her hand in a bunch, a bunch of two. When she was back home, she might put them in a glass of water in front of the picture of the Sacred Heart, because that morning, in some way, she had been helped by God. Via Diego Manuel of course. Then she suddenly thought that she couldn't possibly appear at Solema's house with the flowers in her hand: She'll be angry because I've picked her flowers without permission and then she'll refuse to lend me the money. She'll refuse anyway, she thought, throwing the flowers away in irritation. She was now outside the small gate, peered inside without calling out, but saw no one.

The thought that Solema would refuse her the money for fear that she would keep pestering her afterwards, now obsessed her. Miss Solema won't want to do that, she thought. Rich people may be good and help others now and again, but if there's one thing they don't like it's for someone to keep pestering them. Rich people like their *peace of mind*.

She turned round. She suddenly lost heart. She was a brave woman, but she couldn't bear telling a woman like that about her plight and then being sent away empty-handed. Even though the woman was rich! She was proud. She suddenly found her worries too trivial to bother Miss Solema, who was so kind to her daughter Vera and to other people's children, someone whom she, Nora, also loved from afar.

Her eye was caught by the church of Santa Gloria and she thought: I'll go there. But at that moment she saw the priest emerge from his house, get into a small car and drive off. There can't be any baptisms or funerals this afternoon, she thought, and the priest is off out. Parasite – just when some-one needs him, he goes off.

The wind raised the tip of her scarf high and horizontal, as she began walking down Manchi's hill again. Damn, she said to herself, I give up: Ostrik will just have to go and work on the roads. She was tired. She'd done her best. She wasn't going to go miles further, even though the sun was no longer as fierce, to appeal to her daughter who was as badly off as she was. It would only turn into an argument.

'Mother, are you *crazy*? Five guilders, for shoes for Ostrik? And what about *me* then? And my children? No, let Ostrik go out to work! If he hasn't got any shoes to go to school in, then he just won't be able to go to school! I couldn't go to school either, could I?'

'Oh,' she would say. 'Don't you understand? He's so good

at school. He's got a good chance of turning into a great man. A doctor or something.'

'If he's so good at school,' her daughter would reply, 'he can easily take a week or two off!'

Perhaps that was true too. Perhaps Ostrik really could miss two weeks without having to leave school. Without having to go straight out and work on the roads. Besides, she remembered proudly, she already had *ten* guilders.

'Nora!'

She was just busily weaving all kinds of new thoughts which were intended both to console her and lead to new ways of succeeding, when Solema called out to her. She turned round so quickly that the tip of her scarf almost wound its way round her neck.

Solema stood waving on the porch of her beautiful house. 'Come on in, Nora,' she called again.

She began walking back up the hill while Solema came down the steps of her porch to open the gate for her. In fact she came all the way out onto the sandy road: 'Come on, Nora, come on.' She hurried. Although she felt tired, she didn't want the lady to stand holding the gate open for her longer than necessary, as if Miss Solema was some maid or other.

26

He had been observing Nora for a long time. The moment that he saw her peer into the house just in front of Manchi's gate for a moment and then turn round again, he shook his head in disbelief. And when he saw her climbing back up the hill a little while later in order to go into the house with Solema, he slammed down his domino pieces on the table.

'Your turn, Bubu,' said Janchi.

But he didn't react. 'Damn,' he said. 'Damn! You all heard my wife just say that she was going to give someone her condolences on a bereavement! Look, she's going into Manchi's house. She never does that!' He felt in a panic and gave the men an inquiring look one by one, as though the explanation for this completely strange behaviour of Nora's must come from one of them.

He abandoned the game of dominoes for a moment and positioned himself between his house and the bath shed to stare at Manchi's house, expecting that Nora would now quickly come out again.

Chamon Nicolas felt relieved. He thought he knew why Nora had gone to Solema: for money. And because of that he thought hopefully that for the time being she would stop approaching him.

Manchi didn't react openly. He would ask later what Nora had wanted and clamp down on things. Bubu Fiel came and sat down again.

'I don't understand,' he said, looking at Janchi as though help must now come from him.

'Perhaps they're going together,' said Janchi, excited by the thought of Solema.

'That's possible,' said Bubu. 'But then you, Manchi, must *know* about it? Did Solema say anything to you?'

'No, I know nothing about it.'

27

He remembered how he'd almost lost Nora years ago. It was after an accident with 200H which he survived because it wasn't his day, but which had still cost him a couple of months in the hospital, with a broken leg and slight concussion.

Nora became a cleaner at the airport and their family, which now consisted of nine children, got by. He, Bubu Fiel, had everything he needed in the hospital, but after a while he got to hear that Nora had taken up with a customs official at the airport. So the money she had didn't come just from her work as cleaner. So he knew, but what was he to do about it? After all, his children had to eat, didn't they?

He'd thought that Nora would stop when he had left hospital and he was back at work. But no; and it went on so long that he finally brought it up.

She gave him back as good as she got, saying that it was his fault that she'd taken up with this customs official. Because he'd had the crash when he was drunk. 'How else did you think I was supposed to look after myself and the children, with you flat on your back in the hospital for months?'

When he gave her a couple of slaps in reply, she walked out, saying that he was ungrateful and that she'd never come back to him. She took all the children with her, except for one daughter, who stayed of her own accord to look after him. He missed her terribly, but he was damned if he was going to go back with his tail between his legs to ask her. Finally he did so anyway. He drove out to Nora's parents' old-fashioned house on Bandabou. He drew up outside in 200H and sounded his horn.

Eventually he had to get out anyway, because Nora wouldn't come out to 200H. He was received by Nora's father, because Nora and her mother both said that they wanted nothing to do with him. Nora's mother, who had never forgiven him for abandoning his daughter for a whole year for a whore, said she'd be crazy if she went back to him.

Then Nora decided to talk to him herself and told him, with her parents and some of the children present, that she'd made a mistake in marrying him. 'You're a bastard,' she said, 'a whore-chaser. I don't need you to bring up my children.' She radiated such courage when she said this that it fascinated him. He redoubled his entreaties. Still she refused.

He began to love her because she was so brave and

independent. And sweet too, as he well remembered. She was a lamb and a tigress at the same time; a combination that he could no longer do without. Besides, everyone – his family, friends, *everyone* – was on Nora's side, because they knew she had visited him faithfully in the hospital on two days a week, washed his clothes and apart from that looked after their children. And people had seen her as a brave woman, because, for his sake, she had even gone to bed with another man. Well!

'You're ungrateful,' people said to him.

It got through to him. He didn't want to go through life as an ungrateful dog. So he began to see it as a matter of life and death to win her back. Every day, sometimes twice, he roared down the road to Bandabou in 200H, so that the wheels sung and whined along the narrow roads. First he did it through the children, to whom he took food and money every day. He behaved like a model father. He was so persistent that he completely eliminated the customs official, with some help from Nora's father, who felt that she should be with her lawful husband, the more so since he openly showed that he loved and needed her. All this lasted for perhaps a year.

He pleaded with Nora. He courted her again. Finally, she seemed to have exacted enough revenge on him. Apart from that, his persistence finally softened her mother's heart to such an extent that she was eventually prepared to accept him as her son-in-law again.

One day Nora got into 200H and he drove her back to Wakota with her cases and their children. Like a queen! They never again talked about the customs official, who disappeared from her life for good. But his fear of losing her again had remained.

She had everything. She was wonderful in bed, although her skin wasn't as fine and young as when he'd taken her from Bandabou from her parents, and her hands had grown rough in the course of time. But that wasn't the point for him any more. He could satisfy his sexual needs with lots of other women. Young, beautiful women; like that one yesterday, whose name he'd forgotten because of this damn game of dominoes. The name and the room number. Which was perhaps just as well. Because after all she was the reason that he'd sat here losing this game of dominoes, because he'd been thinking about her the whole time . . .

No, what he and Nora had was something else. Perhaps it was the fact that she'd always managed in an almost mysterious way to solve the problems of their poverty. Whether he had earned any money or not, they'd always had food on the table; the children went to school. At least *often* and always with decent clothes on. Even when he frittered away a lot of money in a fit of madness. So she was his rescuing angel. That was why he missed her now.

Merde, he began to realize the enormity of his defeat. This seven–love which was now almost eight–love, and which would soon become ten–love or perhaps even more. Because luck was against him today. And the shame: his name would spread all over the island when he got up from this domino table with this disgraceful score. Manchi and he would be finished for ever as domino players. And 200H. *Poor* 200H! People would point to her along the road and say: there he goes, 200H, who one Sunday afternoon was given eight shoes, no, perhaps even ten shoes by Janchi Pau and Chamon Nicolas. With Manchi Sanantonio.

It was a *disaster*. A disaster which began when he was driving home yesterday and that American asked him to drive him to Campo, and that continued when that woman whose name he couldn't even remember came up to him.

He stroked his belly in fury a few times, now to scratch the memory of her out of his skin for good, because he saw nothing more in her except an emissary of fate, or the devil.

Someone who'd come especially to plunge him into misfortune. *And he missed Nora!* Nora would be able to cover up the dreadful consequences of this defeat which would be absolutely impossible for him to bear alone, in some way or other: she covered up everything.

Why wasn't one of his damn children around now? Then he could send him or her up to Manchi's house to ask Nora exactly what she was planning to do and how long she was going to stay away.

He made his excuses and again got up from the table. He looked round the whole house to see if anyone were there, but no, they were neither at the front nor at the back of the house. He came and sat down again. Again he tried to reconcile himself to the thought of such a defeat by trying to interpret it as a whim of fate. After all, he thought, fate wouldn't have sent that American to him, just as he'd been about to drive off, if fate didn't have something particular in mind with this loss. Perhaps because of that he ought to stop this game of dominoes and make better use of his Sundays. 'Produce,' Janchi had said just now. *Produce*. What else did they do here on Sunday afternoon except waste their time? Yes, they produced *shoes*. Of course. And now he was getting a whole pile of them. But he could make far better use of his Sunday afternoons. Finishing his house, for example, or at least getting started. After all, he already had several bags of cement in his bath shed. And Manchi had done it the same way, bit by bit. In the evenings; on Saturdays and Sundays. And there was his wonderful house now, with beautiful arches, columns and flowers in front. A unique house! That Nora had just gone into.

Instead of playing here, they could come and help him. Janchi would certainly do that because he was a nice guy. And Manchi would also be obliged to come with him, because after all, he, Bubu, had helped Manchi. They would work

268

and Nora would provide food and drink. Just as cosy as it was now. But Nora had to be there! He suddenly said to himself that it wasn't *right* of her to go off suddenly on this afternoon of all afternoons. Nor was it *kind*. And she was a kind person, Nora, although she sometimes scolded him. But in those cases he deserved it. Like this morning. Like the whole day. Nothing worked out! How many times had he tried to make Chamon here pass? But he couldn't, while Janchi here did succeed in eliminating him. Damn! He began waiting anxiously for every piece that Janchi played. Not one piece that he played himself seemed to be right. Not one! And suddenly he felt so *cold* that he had to button his shirt up completely. That was probably because the sun was setting. Or because he'd used too much alcohol just now. If Nora were here, he'd ask her for his hat. Or perhaps even a warm towel that he could put on his neck. But she'd abandoned him! Like a dog, alone with his loss. But why did she *lie* to him like that? Why did she say that she was going to give her condolences to someone on a bereavement? And she had even put another more appropriate scarf on when he'd pointed out to her that she couldn't give her condolences in a *yellow* scarf. *Why?*

But hadn't all her behaviour been strange today?

That walking to and fro just now, when she could easily have taken everything to the washing line in one go! That incident with her and Chamon here, right at the beginning of their game! And . . . A certain pattern began to form in his head, which made him look suspiciously at Chamon. But the latter seemed to have eyes only for his dominoes.

Bubu Fiel waited until Manchi, who was ready to play, had made his move and then said to Chamon, 'Tell me, have you got *houses?*'

As he did so, he looked closely at Chamon and noted that the man was startled.

'Me? Houses? Why?'

'Nora told me this morning.'

'Oh yes? Did she tell you that? No, I've got *no* houses.'

Neither Manchi nor Janchi were interested in their conversation.

'But she did tell me. Why should she *lie* about something like that?'

'I don't know,' said Chamon. He added with a nervous laugh, 'I wouldn't call your wife Nora a liar, but you yourself can see that she just said that she was going to give her condolences to someone and . . . well . . .' He felt it was unnecessary to finish this sentence. As he shrugged his shoulders meaningfully, he held a piece confidently in his right hand to play when Bubu (whom he kept looking at defiantly) had made his move.

'Yes,' said the other in bewilderment. 'Yes.' He played.

What he'd just asked about the houses had been meant as a final attempt to incriminate Chamon. Then he would have had a subject to concentrate on in a little while when this damn game of dominoes had been so disastrously lost. Perhaps he would also have a good excuse to wipe away the mocking smile that the guy had had on his face all afternoon. That was why he felt disappointed now this plan had misfired.

28

Although he maintained the confident attitude he had had all afternoon, Chamon Nicolas suddenly had the feeling that he'd acted wrongly with Nora. Perhaps he should have listened to what she had to say to him because it might have been about Bubu Fiel as well as money. It was plain: the man suspected him of something. And why had Nora told Bubu about his houses? Had it slipped out and was she trying to warn him to be careful if Bubu asked about it? He had said no, because he preferred to keep the ownership of his houses to himself. But if the matter really interested him, Bubu could get to the bottom of it easily enough. And then Bubu would wonder why he'd denied here at the domino table that he had houses, when Nora had told him. He would put two and two together and wonder why it was that Nora knew something that he wanted to keep secret. Because Nora wouldn't be able to give a satisfactory explanation of why she knew, for the simple reason that there were very few people who could have told her, except Chamon himself. So Bubu would draw the conclusion that there was a secret between him and Nora!

'Chamon!' It was Janchi urging him on to play. Once he had analysed the predicament in which he found himself, he sat there holding the piece which he'd chosen to play after Bubu Fiel's turn as if he were frozen: *Bubu Fiel would realize that he was having an affair with Nora!* And then the fat would be in the fire. He played. Then he told himself he was a stupid idiot for not going to the bath shed though Nora had clearly indicated that she wanted to speak to him. He felt panic rising, but controlled himself; it was plain that Bubu would only find out about it when he'd been round and made inquiries. He wouldn't be able to do that this afternoon at any rate. At any rate, not while he was here at this domino table! He only need expect problems in the course of the week. Certainly next Sunday afternoon if he came to play dominoes again. So he quickly resolved not only to break off with Nora, but never to come to play dominoes here again! Starting with next Sunday. He had money. Quite a lot of money, in fact. So perhaps he'd take a plane to Saba in the course of next week. He had to get away from here. Although he no longer felt like a Windward Islander at all, it was a very comforting thought anyway. There were women enough there.

For the time being, he kept the mocking smile that irritated Bubu so much.

29

The tingling feeling of happiness that filled Janchi when Bubu suddenly mentioned Solema's name was almost too much for him. What he would have most liked to do was to push his chair back, or at any rate get out from behind this thick tree trunk, to try and catch a glimpse of her when she appeared on the porch, like Bubu Fiel here could do to his heart's content. But he controlled himself. He wouldn't have got so far this afternoon if he hadn't controlled himself the whole time; hadn't forced himself not to think of her too much, not to be distracted from this game of dominoes that after all he was only playing for her this afternoon. In order to give her shoes back, he thought with pleasure. 'Produce,' she said so often. Well then . . . He glanced upwards, at the seven pairs of black shoes which Chamon had hung over their heads. It would soon be eight pairs. Then nine, then ten.

With restraint, with almost religious devotion, he had continuously summoned up that great patience which the correct analysis of a game of dominoes requires. But he'd also been lucky this afternoon: Chamon Nicolas had co-operated in an exemplary way, after a few mistakes at the beginning. However, he felt so sure of himself now, so determined, that he had the feeling that he would have won even if he'd had to play on his own against the *three* men in front of him. As he had actually done occasionally, and gone on to win four games in succession on his own.

He realized with pleasure that the revenge he had wanted to take on Manchi had succeeded. It would now be ten–love because the guy to the left of him here seemed so tired that he could scarcely put down his domino pieces any more. A big difference from his partner Chamon, who played piece after piece for him as though to order with a cheerful smile round his mouth. And Bubu here on his right seemed to be more preoccupied with Nora than with the game of dominoes. All the better. So he was punishing Manchi for what he'd done to Solema. He had the feeling that with the power of concentration that he felt this afternoon, he could just as well have *murdered* the guy. But it was better like this. Much better.

The greatest dislike he felt for the guy related perhaps not to the remedy that he'd dreamt up for her unfaithfulness, but the fact that through his actions he'd almost turned her into a whore. She'd gone to bed with any Tom, Dick or Harry. And if he, Janchi, hadn't crossed her path, she would have gone much, much further; until she'd really become a whore or had wound up in the madhouse. And all because of one slip. One slip, that any woman can make and which women actually make every day. He shot Manchi a scornful glance, which Manchi, however, did not seem to pick up on because he was sitting looking rather dozily at the pieces in his hand (which he was now holding in both hands). It was as though he was reading through them, instead of playing dominoes. He's like a beginner, thought Janchi contemptuously.

But there were other things that he had to do for her. First of all, finish the house, of course. Something else too. The little *wabi* table that he had started for her!

He interrupted his stream of thoughts in order to play. He mustn't be too distracted by her, because then he wouldn't see his self-imposed mission through to a successful conclusion: dominoes is such a treacherous game. If you allow your attention to stray from the game for even a moment, you sometimes need several games to get back into it. But the thought that he was making the table for her excited him so much that he couldn't help dreaming on about it: he would plane, sand, polish and varnish the trunk. Then he'd be

273

finished. The table would have her colour, which wasn't the colour of medlar, not a dark *chocolate* colour, but the colour of beautiful brown *wood*. And she was right. Why should he just make one? If the fact that he could make them gave her so much pleasure and made her so enthusiastic? He could do things on a bigger scale, couldn't he? One after the other, one, two, three. In the same way as I'm sitting here making shoes one after the other, he thought, joking to himself. Strange that he hadn't thought about it, when he'd been talking just now about *production* with Bubu, who had asked mockingly, 'Cactus, I suppose!' No, not cactus! Or perhaps cactuses as well, as far as he was concerned, but in any case also *wabi* wood tables, shoes and tables. *Shoes* for Manchi and *tables* for Solema. A whole lot. A factory for *wabi* wood tables: a furniture factory. The thought excited him so much that he was on the point of talking about it. To Bubu, for example. But he controlled himself. This was too weighty, too serious, too real just to bring up at the domino table. This was something that he was really going to do. At the domino table you just joked, you told them a bit about what you'd done and all the things that you'd probably never do; you made *shoes*!

He was overcome by a feeling of haste. Haste first of all to see the plan that he wanted to carry out against Manchi through to a successful conclusion: he wanted to reach ten–love. Or more. He didn't care. But in any case he was longing for the end of this game. He was longing for the freedom to think of his new plan, which was in the process of emerging in him as if under its own momentum; and for Solema, whose enthusiasm he would need to see it through. First to finish his house, and then to start up a furniture factory. A *furniture factory!*

His enthusiasm made him want to get off his chair, apart from the fact that his backside was burning from having sat down for so long. His legs under the table, which he had to keep bent because of the others, were hurting him. Manchi and Bubu had both got up from the table and stretched their legs. And now Chamon Nicolas was going to the toilet too. But Janchi braced himself: he would not get up before the score was ten–love. Ten–love *at least*.

When Chamon Nicolas came back from the toilet, he and Janchi continued their triumphal progress to the end of the eighth set unhindered.

30

Public telephones are free on Curaçao.

The three men did not go straight to the football field, where there was a fairly large crowd and where they could have easily spread their news about the trouncing at Bubu Fiel's: their excitement made them more inventive. When they reached that point on the Tula road, the man who was on the board of DSW turned left up the long sandy road past Manchi's house. He wanted to tell the news to his parents first. Then he wanted to telephone all his fellow committee members to tell them about the great event: besides mismanaging the affairs of the club, Bubu Fiel had once behaved really shittily to him during a match. Had said something like 'Shut your *trap*' and so on. It was a long time ago, but he hadn't forgotten.

The other two walked on until they reached the cemetery. Here, one of them turned left to ring from the public telephone on the church square. The other went on to the football field. The latter had intended to walk, but he felt so alone with this great feeling of excitement that he hurriedly waved down a passing pirate bus to be able to cover the short distance more quickly.

The man who went up the church hill had no particular

people in mind to pass the news on to. So when he was in the telephone box he decided to begin with those who would naturally be interested in the news: the papers. Then he rang up the radio stations and television. Next, he was about to go off and spread the news further by word of mouth, but remembered that it would also be nice to pass the news on to all the taxi ranks on the island. He started telephoning again: after all, telephoning didn't cost him a cent!

31

Manchi began to feel his defeat well and truly when the score was seven–love and Chamon Nicolas, with his businesslike indifference of this afternoon and laughing silently to himself, hung up the seventh pair of shoes. To be precise, when the three spectators said that they had to go. He started to panic, although he put on a calm front. He could imagine exactly how they would trumpet his defeat around when they reached the football field (which of course would be full of people).

'Manchi Sanantonio.'

'Which Manchi?'

'The one with the nicest house in Wakota.'

'*Which* Manchi?'

'The one who's married to Solema, the most beautiful teacher in Wakota.'

'Oh yes, of course, that Manchi. *Shon* Manchi. Why didn't you say so at once? What's wrong with him?'

'He's *losing*, man.'

'Losing what?'

'He's losing hopelessly at dominoes down there to the east of Bubu Fiel's house.'

'What's the score, then?'

'Seven–love, man. And it will soon be *eight*–love.'

'*Seven–love*?'

'Yes.'

'Terrible. What's *happened* to them?!'

'I wish I knew.'

In a trice there would be nothing left of his reputation. Bubu might talk about the seven lean years which were now over and the seven fat ones that were beginning, but he of course didn't believe in that. That was religious nonsense that he had nothing to do with. Certainly not now. Besides which, a little later they were already four–one down in the eighth set.

At the beginning, when he lost game after game, he'd wondered whether it was because Bubu was in cahoots with the others. They were jealous of him and so capable of anything. Then he thought he was losing, not because Bubu had thrown the game but because Janchi Pau and Chamon Nicolas had practised specially beforehand in order to thrash them; which one might indeed think in view of the way in which the two partners were co-ordinating their game today. But he still hoped that eventually there would be a turning-point. Quite rightly. Because anything can happen in dominoes if the partners are equally matched.

He'd also harboured the suspicion Janchi Pau and Chamon Nicolas were 'doctoring' the pieces and he had been happy when Bubu insisted on shuffling them himself even if they hadn't won. Indeed, he would have preferred this suspicion partly because in this way he was clearing his partner automatically of complicity in underhand practices. But, damn, when he thought of how often they'd lost this afternoon, though he had wonderful pieces, he couldn't say that it was the fault of the dominoes! Well, what was it the fault of then?

He did up the buttons of his shirt one by one and put his tie on again with expansive gestures: he looked smart like that. Whatever the reason for this defeat . . . he had to arm himself against it in advance. He must stay looking smart; particularly, he mustn't let them see that he cared about anything at all. Like a judge! Oh, he thought it was a shame that he'd left his coat at home. His *black* coat. Now it was getting on for evening, it was getting cool enough anyway to have it on. And he also thought it a pity that he had not brought his revolver with him after all. It was quite obvious that they were not favourably disposed to him this afternoon here at this domino table.

From the beginning of the eighth set, he began thinking very seriously about a future as a judge and his attention centred with particular intensity on the weekend cottage, which he had decided to start building tomorrow.

It turned into a wonderful flight from reality; as wonderful as that of Bubu Fiel perhaps. He bravely dismissed the fact that he couldn't swim and didn't *like* water. Hadn't he given his children permission to learn swimming at school? Wasn't that a sign that he could do the same if he wanted to?

When people asked him later how it had come about that he'd lost by such a great margin, he would observe airily that he had more important things on his mind. 'I've just begun a weekend cottage on West Point,' he would add calmly. Yes, that's what he would say. And that would give them something to think about. That was different from this piddling little game of dominoes. What was dominoes when it came down to it? They would tell from the very way in which he announced the news that it was a completely nonsensical activity to get worked up over the result of a game of friendly dominoes. Even if it was an exceptional score! And then people on this island would finally start getting interested in things which really mattered and say to each other, 'Manchi. Yes, that guy with the big, beautiful house in Wakota. Yes, man, of course you know him: he works for the court.'

'Oh yes, *him*. The husband of that beautiful teacher?'

'That's the one. He's building a *weekend cottage*.'

'*Yes?* Ah, so that's why he had such a gruesome defeat that Sunday!'

'Exactly. He couldn't keep his mind on the game, of course.'

'Oh well, well, I can imagine. It makes that strange defeat perfectly understandable, yes. For me at least, I don't know about you, but as far as I'm . . .'

'Of course, that's how I see it too. Perhaps he'll buy a boat as well. One of those pleasure yachts, you know, with those big glass screens in front.'

'He's getting on in the world.'

'You can't deny it. He's a guy you have to respect.'

'Isn't there a rumour that he's going to join Solidarity?'

'Really? Well, even *I* haven't heard that . . . It wouldn't surprise me at all. That man can do *anything*.'

'That's how I see it too.'

He armed himself further: of course he'd go on *playing* in the future, because he recognized a hard-working person's – a hard-working *judge's* – need for diversion. But never dominoes, of course. Bowling, tennis, chess. Bridge, perhaps? Or surfing, once he'd overcome his fear of water? Damn, he suddenly said to himself, because Chamon again made him pass very emphatically. Let's put this whole game of dominoes completely out of my mind and think seriously about my study of law. Nostalgically, he reviewed the fairly small number of books on law which he'd had to work his way through several times for his bailiffs' examination. If I give up this game of dominoes for good and enrol at the College of Law tomorrow, then it's by no means impossible for me to qualify in law in a short while. A person is never too old to learn. Even stupid Chamon here can sense that. I'll be a judge in no time if I want to. So will Bubu for that matter. Mm. Perhaps it's because of that role of judge I just played in that story, but in any case it means they don't think it such a strange idea here, Manchi the judge!

He lost with a blissful smile on his face.

When Janchi had shuffled and he had taken his pieces for the following game, his happiness became even greater, because now he had the double six for the first time for ages. Besides, they had already won two games. If he won this game too they would be well on their way to an escape, which hadn't happened once this afternoon.

He led dramatically and matters indeed moved in the direction of a win, especially because Janchi, who didn't have a single six, immediately had to pass. Until he, Manchi, had only two pieces left. Then Chamon played three–blank and he had to pass. So his dream of winning was cruelly shattered and he thought, because of the pain that this caused him, After I've graduated from the College of Law I'm going to become a *prosecutor*. Then I'll teach you. Then I'll call for such sentences against you that there'll be nothing left of you. You're a bandit who chases people with machetes and should be locked up. No, he corrected himself in a determined fashion, I shall punish him severely mainly because he has made me waste my time here Sunday after Sunday. Otherwise I would have hit upon the idea of a weekend cottage long ago. He looked at Chamon with a sly smile as Bubu took his turn. Then Chamon played a three again and Manchi almost screamed with pain as he passed. This way we'll never get to five and never get free! Oh, if they could at least win one set, they could at least save *a little* face.

Janchi played and Bubu passed absent-mindedly. Chamon turned over his last piece with a matter-of-fact gesture.

Oh, thought Manchi as he pushed the two pieces that he had left back into the pack with a stoical gesture, why should I do anything to these two here? If you examine the case seriously, it doesn't matter if I get eight shoes! Or nine. Or ten. Does it? Every day you see diagrams in the paper which are reconstructions of some famous *chess* game, in some metropolis or other. Indeed, such a famous game had even taken place here. In Hotel Curaçao, just behind the court. And when you actually saw those competitors of whom the papers and television are always so full . . . Fischer, Spasski, Tal – what a skinny lot! All small and with pointed noses, it's true – that's because of all the thinking they do. And how loaded they are! Chess is a game with a classy following! With nice clocks that you press when you've made your move. You don't get any of that in dominoes. Although you think, of course. You certainly *think*. A lot. You sure do. But you can't do anything about the pieces that you get! So you're always more or less in the hands of fate. Losing and winning are *no thanks to you*. So it's not a good game: your will and your abilities don't get a look in. And you don't have one opponent as in chess, but three enemies, don't you? That's how you must see it. Three enemies, because Bubu Fiel's game is worthless this afternoon, isn't it? It's not a good game either because with all the little eyes looking at you there on the table, you can't make head or tail of it if your concentration flags even for a moment. Oh, draughts, for example, is – how shall I put it? – a much more *honest* game than dominoes. Again, a game where everyone has equal chances, in which winning or losing depends not on fate or your partner, but purely and simply on your own abilities. And yet oddly enough that isn't even a game that you can say important people concern themselves with. It seems on the contrary to be played a lot in Africa. And in the interior of Surinam. It's a poor people's game, he thought quickly, and yet, make no mistake: all things considered, dominoes has at most only twenty-five moves while draughts has got several hundred. Make no mistake: you had to think much further ahead in draughts than in dominoes! Oh, dominoes is a game for animals! For uneducated animals! Damn it, what am I doing here? Of course. I'm losing because I don't belong here. That guy on my left is a murderer, isn't he? And I'm sitting down at the same table playing with a guy like that. I must be crazy, I think. Out of my mind. And for ages too. Fancy only realizing it now . . . Yes, he's a murderer. No doubt about it. You can tell that clearly from the smile he keeps giving you when he looks at you from the side. Something like: if I ever meet you on a lonely path, I'll cut your head off. Yes, the thing is to get into a position to stop him doing that as quickly as possible.

Prosecutor. No, no, *judge*. Because as a prosecutor you can only *ask* the court for a particular sentence. Once those stupid lawyers get involved, you're never sure what the man's going to get. No, in order to sentence him you've got to be a judge yourself!

Oh, the satisfaction with which he kept making me pass just now. Once, twice, he played a three, though he must know that I can't have a three the second time either, if I passed on three the first time. He's doing it deliberately, of course. He's like that. Damn it, it wasn't self-defence as that lawyer of his protested. It was *deliberate*! Just look at him! Look at that murderer! Murder, that was it. No bull-shitting about 'secondary manslaughter', or 'assault', or 'grievous bodily harm', but simply attempted *murder*. Punishable under article . . . ? At any rate *punishable*! If *I* had been the judge in that case, what sentence would I have given him? Just let me think about it at my leisure. But one thing is certain: I'm a judge. That's one thing that's certain. It's the only way to deal with this rabble here. As I dealt with Solema and that other judge.

His endeavours, the possibility that Chamon had suggested, the role of shrewd judge that he'd played in the disguised account of Solema's adultery . . . Under the necessity of arming against himself against his defeat, all merged into one.

32

He cleared his throat to call attention to himself and thought, the first thing I'm going to do now I'm sitting at this green bench, is turn off the air conditioning. I'm sick of the thing and that's why I'm never going to get any for my own house. It gives me a rotten cold. Partly because the sessions take so long nowadays. No, my dear colleagues, I like the open air, the cool wind on the hill where I live. Come and see for yourselves. You can stay over if you like. I've got a study, a guest room, in short, everything. Yes, drop by some time. And besides, those things are far too expensive! They use far too much electricity. Oh, I'm going to have this whole court refurbished. I won't just get rid of the air conditioning but I'll get better loudspeakers, so that the journalists can hear everything better. (Didn't you know that? They complain constantly that they can scarcely follow us.) And a higher chair for myself. So I've got a better view of what's happening right in front of me and what the unruly public is getting up to. Then iron cages for these bandits here. Oh yes, and that Solema, I'll throw her in the whores' camp once and for all. It's true we'll have to make a new law for that, or an exception. Because in fact only non-natives are allowed in that camp. Although on the other hand I must admit that it may be better to close the whole camp. It's a moral outrage.

Now I'm losing again. If one can talk about losing at dominoes, of course. In that case, it's the fault of that idiot in front of me here. That irresponsible man who doesn't even buy shoes for his children.

'Tell me, as an official of the Guardianship Board.'

'Yes, Your Honour.'

'What shall we do with this irresponsible fellow?'

'Lock him up, Your Honour. He'll never learn!'

'We shall. We shall. But I've another surprise for you.'

'Yes, Your Honour . . .'

'I'm going to deprive him of his parental rights. As simple as that! Both him and that Solema. They're neither of them any good. Anything further, any other matters, Mr Prosecutor . . . ?'

'No, Your Honour, not for the moment.'

'Then I declare this court adjourned.'

33

The remorseless thing about games is that when one's losing, one can't leave. At least if, as every boy is taught, one wants to be considered a *man* afterwards. But dominoes is harder than most men's games. Take boxing, for example. However rough it gets, there's always a referee to separate the fighters if they threaten to do too much damage to each other. There is the technical knock-out; there is a trainer and a doctor present. That's why boxing matches don't usually have a fatal outcome.

There is none of this in dominoes. The only option here is *mental* flight, but unfortunately that's also a dangerous method. Manchi continued to feel more like a judge in a courtroom than a domino player in Wakota. Indeed, so intensely that his inner feelings burst into the open. But the others did not realize this because it is part and parcel of dominoes that comments which are nonsense or cause annoyance if they are related to reality, create almost unlimited jollity and hilarity when connected with the pieces. Otherwise (although Manchi beyond a certain point simply regarded all three of them as his enemies), they would have stopped the game when his madness became apparent . . . although of course nothing can be said for certain about Janchi Pau.

At a certain moment, when it was Janchi's turn, Manchi unexpectedly put his elbows right in the middle of the domino table, which he now mistook fitfully for the green justices' bench of the court in Willemstad. As he did so, he held some of his pieces in both hands and stared straight at Bubu Fiel. (It's true that some judges do something similar. Usually when the proceedings have reached a decisive point and they want to give the impression of taking careful account of the interests of the accused.) Bubu thought it was a sign concerning the game and quickly leant forward. Up to now they'd made little use of this and he thought it might be the means of giving a decisive turn to this game of dominoes. However, because no sign came and Janchi sat looking at them both mockingly with his piece in his hand, Bubu felt a little cornered. So he said extra forcefully, 'Friend Manchi, take your arms off the table. It's Janchi's turn to play.'

Chamon, who only now noticed the unusual occurrence, because he had been deeply involved in the game, said, full of bravura, 'What's this? Are you trying to stop us playing, Manchi? Are the shoes pinching? Yes. Of course they're *women's* shoes. I expect they're much too small for your big feet.'

'Tut, tut,' said Manchi.

'They really should have been men's shoes,' said Janchi. 'I warned you. But I can see your pieces like that, Manchi. What's all this?'

'Take your arms off the table, Manchi,' said Bubu again.

'It doesn't matter if you can see my book,' said Manchi.

'Well, well,' said Bubu, 'just now it was so urgent for me to play seriously and now *you* are making jokes.'

'What book do you mean?' said Chamon. 'Even the Bible can't help you now. Neither the lean one, nor the fat one.'

'Book of statutes,' said Manchi, 'book of statutes.'

'Well, well,' said Bubu, *'book of statutes.'* He had the impression that Manchi was building up to some wonderful joke that he couldn't follow because he was so preoccupied with Nora.

'I get it,' said Chamon, suddenly in high spirits. 'The book of statutes with which that judge caught out his wife and the other judge. The law of contract,' he said solemnly, imitating Manchi himself:

'Is this your wife? No? Then you made unlawful use of her!'

'Exactly,' said Manchi, 'with this book I shall defeat you all.' He looked at them all very meaningfully one by one, without taking his arms off the table.

Because Chamon thought that Manchi wanted a break for a moment, he continued in the same vein:

'Tell us, then. How are you going to do it? Of course, there's lots of wisdom in that book of statutes of yours, but I didn't know there was a chapter about dominoes in it.'

'Of course there is, idiot,' said Manchi. 'Everything's in the book of statutes, isn't it? You surely don't think that the law can allow people to play just as they like!'

'You see,' said Janchi, also putting down his pieces with a laugh, 'if Manchi becomes a judge he's going to do strange things. Deport you, Chamon, or regulate dominoes or something. And especially now we're giving him this hiding, isn't that so, Manchi? Eh? This is a terrible hiding for you two, isn't it?'

'Definitely, definitely. I'm going to lock you up too.'

'That's not very sporting,' said Chamon, 'having us locked up because we give you a lot of shoes. On the contrary, you should be grateful, man, even though you can't wear them yourself. At any rate, Solema will get her shoes back in good condition. Most of them,' he quickly corrected himself, so as not to betray prematurely the grand, unexpressed design of himself and Janchi.

'You two are *murderers*,' said Manchi.

Chamon didn't react to this, because he had a brilliant thought: 'If we'd run off with your wife like that judge, I could understand it. Then you'd be perfectly within your rights to have us locked up. Yes, yes. Very good story, Manchi. I'll never forget it.' He looked at the others: 'I mean, Manchi *told* that story so nicely, don't you agree? So dramatically, with that revolver, that naked guy and all. And the horny way that Bubu Fiel here played the judge who'd been caught red-handed.' But he now became very embarrassed because he had assumed the role of the woman caught red-handed, which he would certainly not have done today, and suddenly fell silent.

'You're a *murderer*, Chamon,' said Manchi emphatically.

'Oh, come on,' said Chamon imperturbably. 'It's my partner who's mainly responsible. He puts the heads of your pieces so neatly on the block, that I can't go wrong. I simply *have* to chop their heads off. Sometimes I'm even handed their necks on a plate by your partner here.' He spoke with a tone of mock-sadness in his voice.

'So you're pleading self-defence,' said Manchi, giving him a friendly look.

Chamon burst out laughing, although he found it slightly indiscreet of Manchi to allude so obviously to his brush with the law. After all, that was a very serious matter. Not something to poke fun at just like that at the domino table. But, well, Manchi was *losing* and he had to be prepared to be a little more tolerant than usual. In fact, he was happy to play along, now that he was winning anyway.

'Yes, Your Honour, self-defence. That's it. I'm simply doing my best to defend myself. It's not my fault that in doing so I'm killing off your double pieces in the process.'

'Or would you prefer to plead diminished responsibility?'

Chamon spread his arms wide. The admiration that he usually felt for Manchi, but which had reached an all-time low when Manchi seemed to take the domino setbacks so hard that he opened his shirt and took off his tie, returned in full force, because Manchi didn't seem to care at all, *not at all*, about this terrible defeat. How else could he explain it when the man suddenly started making jokes?

'Shall I tell you something, Manchi?' he said.

'Go ahead. Defend yourself. You have every right as the accused. Can you defend yourself? Do you need a lawyer . . .'

'No, no, let's be serious for a moment, I don't mean that . . .'

'I'm perfectly serious at the moment. You're a murderer, aren't you . . .?'

'All right. I mean that of course you're an implacable judge.'

'What do you mean? Do you mean *hard*, by any chance? Do you mean that I don't know what clemency is? But Chamon, it's your own fault, isn't it, if you're a murderer?'

'Oh, shut up for a minute and let me finish. I mean what with those seven pair of shoes there over your head, and it's soon going to be eight . . . I mean, I admire your courage, you stay so cool under it. The fact that you can even make jokes about it. *That's* what I mean.'

He picked up his pieces again.

'Hm,' said Manchi, 'but I shall think of an appropriate punishment for you.' The reality of the seven pairs of shoes had again hit him directly, and he didn't really know what else to say.

Neither did Chamon. So he simply said, 'Go ahead, Manchi, punish us as much as you like, but *after* the game, please. We'd like to get on with it now. We want to finish it,' he added.

'What do you mean?' said Manchi, looking at him anxiously.

'Nothing.'

'Your Honour,' said Janchi, 'may we finally go on playing?'

'Oh, go on playing and go on dancing. Playing and dancing is all you guys can do. That's why this island's going to the dogs.'

'Take your elbows off the table, for goodness' sake,' said Bubu. He was a little more friendly, because he felt that Manchi's remarks at least slowed down the pace and brought a little distraction to the domino table.

Manchi leant back, taking away his elbows, and said, *'Sentence has already been passed anyway.'*

'You're telling me,' said Bubu, 'but I think you're taking it pretty calmly . . .'

'Your own fault. You should learn to be a bit more responsible. Then you won't be faced with fiascos like this. I've told you often enough!'

'My fault? Do you mean this is all just my fault?'

'Who else's? *Mine?* They're your children, aren't they? You have to look after them, don't you?'

'Well, Manchi,' said Bubu despondently, 'I haven't a clue what you're talking about.' He turned to Janchi. 'You know, Pau, what you said just now, that Nora was perhaps going with Manchi's Solema to give her condolences, doesn't seem right to me. Otherwise they'd have long since come out together again. No, it's not right and I'm wondering what she's up to, that wife of mine . . .' In order to suppress the feeling of absent-minded despondency that he felt returning, he picked up the carafe which Nora had put down beside him, poured a drink and, without saying anything, passed it to Manchi.

'Here, man.'

'I never drink.'

They all looked at him in open amazement.

'Now, now,' said Bubu. *'Never* strikes me as an exaggeration.'

'You've not seen me touch any alcohol today, have you?'

'Come on, Manchi,' said Chamon, 'did we beat the memory out of you or what?'

'Damn,' said Bubu Fiel, suddenly angry. 'What exactly is going on at this domino table today?'

'You two are getting a terrible hammering, that's what it is. That turns everything on its head for you,' said Janchi teasing.

'After this, you'll never have to buy shoes again in your life,' said Chamon.

'Let's get a move on,' said Janchi. 'It's your turn, Bubu.'

'Get a move on? We're losing anyway. And badly, as you yourself say. So why should we get a move on? So where are you going, people? After all, I've got a meeting this evening, not you.'

'It was well meant,' said Janchi, hiding his real intentions. 'We simply want to give you as much chance as possible to draw level before it gets dark.' He looked at the shoes, which scarcely moved on the branch from which they were hanging. 'You want to escape at least once, don't you?'

'That's true, that's true,' said Bubu.

He finally drank the drink he had poured for Manchi himself and, smacking his lips, said, 'Yes, we'll really have to try to bring in some of the seven fat years before it gets dark.'

'Seven years?' echoed Manchi, thinking of the rape of an underage girl, where the man responsible had been sentenced to seven years. He wondered what kind of sentence he would have given in this case. Because no one considered it necessary to respond to his question, he said again, looking at them one by one both timidly and inviting their opinion: 'I mean the sentence, seven years then? Are we all agreed?'

'No,' said Bubu, 'you have to add *fat* to it. I'm still talking about our seven fat years.'

Chamon spoke. 'Seems very over-confident of you to me.

As I just said, even the Bible can't do any more for you. And I'd bear that in mind. I'd bear in mind, for example, that you're probably going to get this pair of shoes as well. Then it'll be eight lean years, instead of seven.'

'Sounds good,' said Janchi. 'Eight lean years. It's true, the eight has got a very thin little waist,' he said, quickly drawing a figure-of-eight in the air.

'Has the prosecutor anything else to say?' Manchi asked Bubu. 'Or does he agree with this.'

'Certainly not. Eight strikes me as really too much. We can't let that happen, can we? Even seven is too much . . . !'

'Well, in this case the counsel for the defence seems to me to have more of the right on his side, Bubu. Let's keep it at eight years.'

'Manchi,' said Bubu in great astonishment, 'you're taking it damn lightly, you know. Eight shoes is a damn lot!'

'I'm sorry, Mr Prosecutor, but nothing more can be done in this case: the sentence is eight years.'

Manchi began to be afraid of the way Chamon slammed down his pieces and asked him not to keep making the pieces jump, but Chamon laughed in his face, saying that slamming down was simply a part of dominoes and that *he* at least was still playing for his pleasure. Manchi began to be afraid of the eyes of the domino pieces, which he found more and more pushy and insolent. And he didn't *understand* them any more. He leant further and further back and played like someone who eats but has little appetite; as it were from a distance, with gestures which would have made a close observer suspect that he was sick of the table at which he was playing. Because of all this, he also began passing with pieces in his hand, which made Bubu particularly short-tempered. A number of times he simply barked at Manchi, which surprised himself most, seeing the respect that he had always had for the man.

But this harshness was welcome to Manchi. It made Bubu Fiel all the more plausible as a prosecutor, which again explained to him why he was sitting playing dominoes here. It's a game among colleagues, he said to himself. Depending on the way the game was going, he saw Janchi Pau one moment as a henchman of Chamon's and the next as a rather annoying defence counsel who kept taking Solema's part, the whore he had condemned to imprisonment for life in the concentration camp near the airport. Now and then he nodded.

Chamon Nicolas, during these strange remarks of Manchi's, which he had taken as rather indiscreet jokes, had worked out who had the double one. He also knew that Janchi had only two pieces left. Janchi played a five, which Bubu covered particularly energetically. On one side there was now a two and on the other a three. Chamon could finish off Manchi's double three but he didn't. He acted as if he hadn't even *seen* this possibility and played two–one on the two that Manchi himself had played. However, as he did so, he said with exaggerated friendliness to Manchi, 'You'll have to choose, you can't get them both at once.'

Manchi did not reply, but did not play immediately either. Bubu said to Chamon, 'You mustn't badger him. Let the man play calmly.'

'You can't call this badgering, Bubu, Manchi's got *both* double pieces, the double one and the double three. I don't know why he's taking so long to think about it. It doesn't matter anyway.' He then looked contemptuously at Fiel and said with taunting slowness, 'And Janchi there has only one piece. Ha. You can *guess* what that is. Turn it over,' he said to his partner, very imperiously for him. 'Turn that piece of yours over for God's sake, then those two here can see what dominoes is. *Double play!*' he exclaimed.

Janchi threw his last piece down on the table. It really was the three–one.

'Why do you think for so damn long, Manchi, when you've got *both* double pieces, eh?' said Bubu.

Manchi did not reply, but picked up the three–one and brought it to his nose. He looked at it carefully and then turned it over a few times and said to Bubu, 'So this is the *corpus delicti*?'

'No nonsense now, Manchi. Why are you thinking for so long when you've . . .'

'The sentence should always be carefully prepared, I would have thought, Mr Prosecutor.'

'Tut, tut,' said Bubu now, 'what do you mean, *prepared*? There was absolutely nothing to prepare. You should simply have got rid of one of your double pieces.'

'Ten–two. Here we go again,' said Chamon.

'Good play,' said Janchi.

'*Excellent* play,' corrected Chamon over-confidently.

'You're right. I admit it,' said Janchi, 'it's a game worthy of me.' He suddenly felt great sympathy for Chamon. The way the man left three open and played one. As if he were clairvoyant. What if Manchi had had the three–one instead of him, though . . .? But Chamon Nicolas seemed to know exactly what he was doing this afternoon.

'Ha! You hang up the shoes for a change, if you would, Janchi,' said Chamon. He added teasingly in the direction of the other two: 'I've done it so often that it's given me a stiff arm.'

Janchi was glad to do it. Then he could finally stretch his legs for a bit.

While Chamon was shuffling for the new game, the double six suddenly turned over with its eyes upwards. This elicited the following comment from Manchi: 'A long time ago, I thought the double six looked like a bride. Now it looks more like a midwife. No, like an octopus: all eyes. The double five is a gorilla or a prosecutor.'

293

'You're saying the strangest things this afternoon,' said Bubu, 'the strangest things.'

'The eyes of the public here are simply driving me mad, Mr Prosecutor.'

'Now, now,' said Chamon, 'no one need go mad here. Ha! Ha! It's just a game of dominoes.'

'Exactly,' said Janchi, 'we're still playing for pleasure.'

'Mad isn't the right word. I just mean they're so pushy, those eyes.'

'Come on, Manchi,' said Chamon, 'you bought them yourself, didn't you? I've always thought they were a bit big too, those eyes, but it was you who ordered them, after all, wasn't it?'

'Oh,' said Manchi, 'none of it matters very much anyway.'

'I think this defeat is getting to you a bit, Manchi, is that right?' said Bubu.

Janchi nodded in agreement and Bubu leant over to hear his partner's answer.

'What defeat, Bubu?'

'This eight–love. These eight lean years. These eight years of *prison*, as you call it. No, it's as though these two judges want to lock us up for life. Can you do anything about it? Haven't you got some cunning device in your book of statutes which can help us to beat them?' He thought and said, 'Can't we appeal, Manchi? It's like a funeral.'

Manchi laughed endearingly.

'Oh Bubu, we *can't* lose because there's nothing to lose. don't forget that this is just a game of dominoes. There are other things in life.'

'Well, I thought you weren't serious enough to start with . . . but no, that's what I like to hear. There are *other* things in life,' he muttered to himself in a dreamy tone.

34

The drivers from the west side of Willemstad harbour, Otrabanda, set off first. Their large, shiny automobiles slid as smoothly as brightly coloured snakes through the narrow streets. The taxis on the Punda side arrived a little later. They had to take the longer route around the Schottegat because the bridge opened to let in a large *Santa* ship. Then came the airport taxis and those from Campo Alegre. So by about five o'clock that afternoon there wasn't a single taxi available on the island. Which meant great inconvenience for all kinds of people, mainly tourists. Including a short, American professor of social psychology and hence perhaps also an operative of the American Central Intelligence Agency. In the little office of Campo Alegre he was busy trying to convince his wife that he was sorry that they'd missed their plane, but that he'd been lost all that time.

'But why didn't you *call*? Then I would have come and got you in a taxi!'

'I simply couldn't find one, darling. I walked my socks off. There really are *no* telephones on this island. Damn! We should never have come here. But I'll be with you in no time. There's a taxi waiting for me.'

'So where are you calling from? And how did you find that taxi suddenly?'

'I'm calling from *somewhere*, darling. I'll be right there. I . . .'

'Screw you! You don't have to *be* anywhere any more. I've called my lawyer to start divorce proceedings against you. The police are hunting for you all over the island. If you'd really got lost then they'd have found you long ago. *Bastard!*' She was furious because she knew who she was dealing with.

'Sweet of you,' said her husband. 'I'll be right there. Really. Don't worry any more, darling.'

But just as he emerged from the office, his taxi drove off.

All the taxi drivers on the island play dominoes. They have to, because outside the tourist season they sometimes have nothing to do for hours. Eventually they even get tired of polishing their constantly gleaming cars.

However, their interest in the thrashing was not directed at the game itself, but much more at the chairmanship of their union, that is, their bread and butter. Wasn't it obvious that they couldn't possibly let themselves be represented for three years by someone who allowed himself to be beaten eight–love or twelve–love (different rumours were circulating)? All this might harm their income, even though Bubu Fiel had shortly before distinguished himself in a different connection.

They gradually took over the road completely. Because they kept beeping their horns at each other to show their solidarity, a festive mood began to prevail everywhere. People came out of their houses, crowded along the roads to look at these beeping cars which sometimes drove past them in whole convoys, like at the wedding of a well-to-do person.

Two television teams set out from Mount Ararat. One rushed straight to Bubu Fiel's house, while the other started filming the procession at various points on the island, with all the traffic problems that it created.

It soon became known that this was not only a sporting event of the first order, but also a happening which, albeit indirectly, might influence the country's economy: among the journalists from the local papers there were correspondents of foreign agencies.

The Wakotans, too, began leaving their houses and they headed in the direction of Bubu Fiel's house.

From the south side of Manchi's house, where one of the three men who sparked off this commotion lived, and where DSW had its headquarters, came the members of this domino association with their chuckling leader at their head.

The people came from beyond the church of Santa Gloria, from the district where Janchi lived.

35

The football match suddenly began losing all its spectators. The players became very impatient because of the excitement of the people who were walking off (without understanding exactly what was going on).

When the linesman also left, they simply couldn't stand it any more.

The young referee tried to continue doing his duty, the more so because it was quite an important amateur competitive match. But when the players left the field *en masse*, he thought it was ridiculous to stay blowing his whistle on his own on the field. After all, he wasn't a bird!

36

With a reverence which can only be compared to that with which she used to go to communion, Nora sat down on one of Solema's fragile, brown upholstered chairs.

Compared with her own house, in which the whitewash was flaking off the walls everywhere, this was really a palace. But she nevertheless felt quite at ease because of the friendliness with which Solema had received her.

Solema, with her hairbrush in her hand, asked Nora to excuse her for a moment: she went back to the bedroom to finish her toilet.

Nora stretched her legs and as she took in Solema's whole house like a child in a museum, her eye fell on the two big suitcases which Solema had put out by the piano. They're going on a trip soon, thought Nora, and then let her eyes wander admiringly through the interior of the house. What a

lot of things, she thought, saying to herself by way of con-
solation that it wasn't impossible that she might one day have
a house like this; perhaps even a big piano like this lady had.
And might also one day go on a trip. She laughed at herself
softly as she did so.

Solema came back with her high Afro hairdo neatly
brushed and put on the television, where they were showing
the Venezuelan horse races, which take place on Sunday
afternoons and on which more is gambled in the Antilles than
in Venezuela itself.

'Why didn't you call out?' she said, sitting down opposite
Nora. 'I saw you coming up the hill from the bathroom and
from the bedroom, standing outside the door here, but when
I'd got dressed and came out, you'd already gone.'

'I thought no one was home,' said Nora, surprised that
Solema was interested in horse-racing.

'Oh.' She didn't dare ask Nora, who was much older than
she was and whom she respected intuitively because of the
large number of children she had, abruptly what she wanted.
Because Nora said nothing, she offered her a cold drink which
after some protestations she accepted.

When the women, each with their drink next to them (on
the side tables on wheels which Solema had brought up) were
sitting opposite each other, Nora felt that she should finally
start explaining why she had come to see Miss Solema. But
saying it was still very difficult for her.

'Do you like horse-racing?' she asked Solema.

'No,' said Solema, who'd only turned on the television to
put Nora at ease, 'I never watch it.'

She felt relieved at this answer. People who were involved
in horse-racing or were keen on the lottery and the numbers
game were constantly short of money. Like her. It would have
surprised and disappointed her if Miss Solema followed
horse-racing.

Pointing to the television picture, Solema said, 'Manchi buys tickets occasionally.'

Nora nodded understandingly. 'So does Bubu Fiel,' she said. 'He spends all his money on those stupid things. *Shon* Manchi doesn't, if you ask me,' she added quickly. Solema smiled, got up and went over to the television.

'You can leave it on as far as I'm concerned,' said Nora.

'I don't understand a thing,' said Solema, turning off the television. Then, 'How's Vera?' She suddenly thought that Nora's visit might be connected with her daughter. She completely forgot her own affairs for a moment, in order to ask Nora at length about the health and circumstances of herself and her large family, ashamed that she hadn't done so earlier.

'They're fine,' said Nora, realizing that she could no longer avoid the reason for her coming.

She drank the rest of the green lemonade that Solema had given her in an oblong glass in one long gulp, and decided, gathering all her courage, to ask for *six* guilders.

'I've come to see you,' she said tilting the empty glass backwards and forwards on the side table in embarrassment, 'about some money.' She scarcely looked at Solema as she said this.

The question did not surprise Solema. But she was disappointed because she'd expected something different, although she couldn't say what.

'How much do you need?' she asked in as friendly a voice as possible.

Nora, who had not expected this accommodating reaction, could have jumped for joy. So it was going to work after all? However, the trace of disappointment on Solema's face hadn't escaped her and, thinking that she would shy away from too large an amount, she said, 'Five guilders.' As she did so, she decided grimly that she would simply have to try to haggle over the price of her son's shoes, or walk around town until she found shoes for fourteen guilders.

'That's not much,' said Solema laughing. 'The way you looked, Nora, I thought you needed much more.'

Solema's friendliness suddenly made her happy and restored all her confidence. She felt childish for not having asked immediately for the six guilders. It would make a strange impression if she did so now.

'Actually,' she said, 'I need six guilders, but if you've got five, that's okay.'

Solema leapt up briskly. She was happy to be able to help Nora with this small amount.

'I'll have a look,' she said. 'Are you sure that it's only six and you really don't need any more?'

'No, miss,' said Nora. 'Six. But I'll pay you back next week; when I get some money from Bubu.'

She felt she should not exaggerate or abuse Solema's kindness. She must also say that she would give the money back. She owed it to her pride. Although Solema would probably not hold it against her if she forgot the following week. She thought Solema, *Miss* Solema, was so good and kind that she couldn't understand why she had married an old man like Manchi, even though he had money.

'That's okay,' said Solema.

She went to the bookcase which took up a whole wall of her sitting-room. She had put her bag down there when she'd come home at midday.

Nora watched her anxiously. She could scarcely believe that her ordeal would be over so soon, and so relatively easily.

Solema picked up her bag and half opened it. 'I haven't got it!' she suddenly said despondently. She opened her bag wide and brought it right up to Nora, who, stretching forward, had a look and then leant back equally despondently. The bag was indeed empty; except for a few women's things.

'But, miss,' said Nora, 'I thought . . .'

Solema closed her bag sadly. 'I had ten guilders this morning,' she said, running her hand nervously through her hair (which spoiled her nice Afro haircut a little) and with such a pathetic look that Nora felt sorry for her, 'but I bought petrol with it. I was going to give you that ten guilders, Nora, but now I remember, I put in a tank full of petrol. It was a little over ten guilders.' She seemed really sad.

Nora said nothing, equally despondent.

'Do you need the money today, dear?' asked Solema, suddenly becoming familiar with Nora in her seriousness.

'Yes,' said Nora. She was on the brink of tears.

'I'm sorry. I'm terribly sorry, but I haven't got it. If you can wait till tomorrow . . . I'll go to the bank tomorrow afternoon after school and you'll have it then.'

Because she realized that she would be gone for good from the house the following day, she said, 'I'll bring it to you myself. You can have much more then if you like.' She spread her arms wide in a gesture of helplessness.

Nora breathed a sigh of relief. She had felt disappointed mainly because she'd thought that Solema, despite the beautiful house she lived in, was as hard up as she was.

'Can't you borrow it from someone else until tomorrow perhaps?'

'Of course I can, miss,' said Nora. 'It's okay. You're much too kind. I won't keep you any longer. I expect you've got your work to do.'

She got up and as she did so looked at the two large suitcases.

'Wait,' said Solema, suddenly, 'wait a minute, Nora, I think I can help you with a little something at least. It's just a trifle, but it may be something at least.' She disappeared into one of the bedrooms of her house and came back quickly, holding a piggy bank with a slot on its back. 'A while ago I put a guilder in this piggy bank of my son's for fun.' Nora nodded furiously and sat down again.

There was a moment's silence broken only by the jingling sound of the guilder which Solema was trying to get out of the piggy bank. In the distance Nora could hear the slamming of the men playing dominoes. She thought they were playing remarkably calmly this afternoon. But really all her attention was here. She looked on tensely while Solema held the pink piggy bank upside-down and tilted it carefully back and forth.

After several attempts, she succeeded: the silver guilder fell out into Solema's hand with a dull thud.

She held it up triumphantly between her thumb and forefinger for a moment and then dropped it into Nora's hand with a laugh.

'Here you are, Nora,' she said. 'So you won't have climbed the hill completely for nothing.'

Nora felt happy that this lady had helped her even if it was only with a little something. Solema wouldn't have been a true child of her people if she hadn't known that the simple people of the island sometimes get a lot of help from less than a guilder.

'That's bread for tomorrow morning,' Nora couldn't help confiding to Solema in her gratitude. 'The rest was to make up the money for a pair of shoes for my son. You know, Ostrik, who's at secondary school. He's good at his studies,' she went on, 'but he's already had to miss a week because I hadn't got any shoes for him. Bubu . . .' she said, but she didn't complete the sentence, because Solema, who had sat down again, was already nodding at her understandingly. 'Well, I didn't want him to miss school again tomorrow and perhaps all week. The shoes cost fifteen guilders, but I've got ten already.'

She lowered her eyes because the memory of the way in

which she'd earned the ten guilders made her feel awkward in these surroundings.

'If only you'd come sooner, Nora. Anyway, you'll have the money from me tomorrow.'

'Thank you, miss. And for the lemonade too. Thank you very much, Miss Solema. I'll really make sure Vera brings them back to you next week. She's still so full of you, you know!'

She had gone to the door and was standing there now, looking at her house down below and also at the houses of Prinsessendorp in the distance.

'You've got a wonderful view here, Miss Solema. Enough to make a person jealous.' When she turned round, Solema was no longer standing behind her. She'd gone back into the room, which Nora thought must be the bedroom, because she could now see a large, beautifully made-up double bed through the open door. Again she thought it was a shame, that such a nice young woman had married Manchi.

'Wait!' she heard Solema calling from the room. 'Wait a minute, Nora. I've got it!'

As Solema took the five-guilder note from the little box in which Manchi insisted she keep it (she almost knew the serial number by heart), she wondered why she hadn't thought about it earlier. It must be connected with the fact that she was in the process of putting Manchi out of her mind completely. In any case, just now, when she'd caught a glimpse of Nora's house over Nora's shoulder she'd thought very vividly of Janchi and of her decision to move in with him for good today. In a last, ecstatic feeling of liberation, she had suddenly remembered those five guilders, with which she would obviously be doing Nora a great favour now. Dear five guilders, she thought, kissing the green note.

Waving the note and laughing she went over to Nora, who looked rather perplexed, afraid give free rein to her joy too

303

soon although she recognized the note that Miss Solema had in her hands as a five-guilder note. Might not the lady make a mistake again?

Perhaps I've been a whore, thought Solema, handing over the note to Nora, but at least it was in a good cause.

Nora accepted it a little timidly. Only when she had it in her hand did she start to laugh. It was real – a real five-guilder note. Her gratitude was so great that she became excited.

'Thank you, miss,' she said, 'thank you very much. I'll make sure Vera . . .'

Solema waved her hand as though it was something awful. 'You keep it, Nora, I don't need it. You can see for yourself that I'd hidden it away so safely that I'd almost forgotten it. Have another lemonade.'

Actually Nora was going to refuse. What she would have most liked to do was to hurry home to put this five guilders with the ten that she already had. She couldn't run the risk of Bubu, through some quirk of fate, discovering the ten guilders under the base of the Sacred Heart. Although he'd never looked there before. She suddenly realized that he would be missing her. Hadn't she said to him that she was going to give someone her condolences for a bereavement? He probably saw her come in here!

But she sat down again anyway. She felt she had the right, here in these wonderful surroundings with kind Miss Solema, to rest a little from all her worries of this Sunday. In fact, of this whole week! She carefully put the five-guilder note, that she still had in her hand, into her black purse. Then she undid her scarf and quickly re-arranged her hair, which she put up in a bun behind. She was glad that she had done as her mother had taught her. As a result, her labours had finally come to a successful conclusion: 'Don't stay at home if you need something. Go out and about and God will help you. If you stay at home praying, God will think you're lazy and abandon you!' Well . . .

This time she had asked Miss Solema for orange, which Solema now put down next to her: it looked wonderfully cool.

As she sipped at it she thought that in her refrigerator she only had a few bottles of water and smiled to herself about the trouble she had making sure her children always kept the bottles topped up.

Solema asked if she should put the television on again. Perhaps the horse-racing was over. But Nora said that there was no need.

'I'll drink your orange, miss, then I'll go home quickly, if you don't mind. You see, I left them to look after themselves. Bubu won't like that very much. You don't mind, do you?'

In fact, she herself thought it was a touch impolite to want to leave with the money so quickly, but she couldn't help it.

Solema nodded understandingly. 'I'd completely forgotten those five guilders,' she said again, explaining her attitude to Nora. 'It's a present from a long time ago,' she added thoughtfully. She felt so liberated now she'd got rid of those damn five guilders in this way that for a moment she felt light in the head.

After that, she was going to tell Nora that she was welcome to call on her whenever she was in difficulties, but did not, because she again thought of her leaving. After that, it would seem like a bad joke. Nor could she tell her that she was going.

Nora repeated her thanks. Then she quickly drank up the rest of her orange and made as if to go. Some people have so much money, she thought, that they don't exactly know where to put it: in the bank, in a piggy bank, or just forgotten somewhere in the bedroom. But be that as it may, the lady was terribly kind.

Again her eye was caught by the two cases. She was going to ask if they really were for a journey, but she restrained herself. It wasn't her business. If that was the case, Bubu would hear about it from Manchi. Manchi would definitely not keep quiet about that, she thought. No, not Manchi. Anyway, she'd only wanted to ask in order to wish the lady a good trip if she really was going somewhere.

She retied her scarf and got up.

'Goodbye, Miss Solema. And . . .' But Solema put a hand on her shoulder to indicate that it was okay and walked with her to the door like that. She was again sorry that she couldn't tell Nora that she was always welcome if she was in difficulties. Not *yet*.

Then they saw the cars! Nora first. 'Miss Solema!' she cried, beside herself and as though Solema were miles away from her. 'Look at all the *cars* outside my house!' She was also immediately struck by the large number of people who were already on the east side of her house and were still pouring in from all directions.

It was indeed an alarming sight: lots and lots of large, shiny, new cars in her yard and on the road in front of her house. They seemed to be parked at least as far as the junction of the Carpata and Tula roads. And more were arriving all the time, parking in front of and between the others. While the two women stood watching, some cars even began looking for a parking place at the beginning of the sandy road past Manchi's house.

'What can it be, Miss Solema? What on earth can it be?'

They both went onto the porch in front of the low wall.

'They're mainly hire cars,' said Solema. 'Most of them have got "Taxi" on their roofs.'

'Yes, miss, now you mention it, I can see that too. What have they all suddenly come to my house for?'

Because of her great excitement, she completely forgot Bubu's involvement with the taxi drivers' union.

'If you wait,' said Solema, 'I'll take you down there. I want to know what's going on at your place too.' She left Nora

306

alone on the porch and went inside. She'd actually been on the point of leaving when Nora arrived and all she had to do was load the two cases into the car. The large number of cars outside Bubu's house alarmed her, because it could scarcely just be out of interest in the game of dominoes. She was now worried that the game would suddenly be interrupted for some reason or other and that Manchi would find her still at home. She began dragging one of the cases which she wanted to put into her car via the back door across the floor. Nora saw what she was doing and quickly came out to give her a hand. She could no longer restrain her curiosity because of her great excitement, and asked if Solema was going on a trip. Solema, who had been waiting for this question, said that her weekly wash was in the cases and that she was taking them to her mother's, who would iron them for her. 'What can be going on down there?' Nora asked again, while they took the case out of the house together and put it in Solema's car.

'The game of dominoes must have attracted special attention.'

'Do you think so?'

'Yes, otherwise we'd have noticed something!' Nora understood what she meant. And she, Solema, thought, Manchi and Janchi! 'Shouting or something,' she said.

'Yes, yes,' said Nora, 'but why would they *hurt* each other? They've been playing dominoes for years, haven't they?' As she said this, she thought anxiously, Chamon and Bubu! As a result, she almost dropped her end of the second case, which they were now carrying outside. Solema noticed her anxiety. 'Come on, Nora. There's *nothing* wrong. You've said yourself that they've been playing dominoes for years!' But she too was suddenly seized by fear that there might have been an eruption between Janchi and Manchi.

She could picture it very well to herself! For some reason

or other, Manchi hadn't been able to restrain himself and had told the story of her and Feliciano and the five guilders, *openly*. Janchi hadn't been able to stand this and . . . She wasn't worried about Janchi, no, but she wanted to be sure.

She got into the car and turned the ignition key. Nora was sitting next to her, trembling with excitement. When she'd started the car and driven as far as the large gate, she suddenly remembered that she had forgotten something. She said to Nora, 'Open the gate for me, I'll be right back.'

She went in through the front door. After some searching, she found a blank sheet of paper and wrote on it:

Manchi. I've left. For good.
Leave me and the children in peace.
Solema

She left the note on the table in the dining area. She put a glass on it, so that it would not blow away. She was then about to hurry off, but had second thoughts and added to what she had written, *I'm with Janchi Pau*. It was more final like that. Becoming slightly over-confident because of the great feeling of freedom that she felt in writing this name, she bent over the paper again and wrote in large capitals:

I THOUGHT I'D TAKE MY FIVE GUILDERS WITH ME!

When she returned to the porch, Nora, who was still holding the big gate open, called out: 'Come on, Miss, let's *go*.' It was only politeness and gratitude to Solema which made her wait for her, otherwise she would have run home along the goat path long ago, the tumult was making her so agitated.

The whole area was now full of cars. And the sandy path in front of Solema's house was already completely blocked by cars which came from both directions and parked everywhere.

Solema reversed onto the road quickly. Nora quickly closed

the gate, and then sat next to her in the passenger seat. There was a car behind them which was already beginning to hoot furiously. She drove as fast as she could, manoeuvring with difficulty onto the Tula road. Next to her, Nora kept repeating, 'But where are all these people coming from?' Suddenly, in annoyance, because she finally remembered the taxi drivers' union, she said, 'Why didn't Bubu tell me anything?'

Solema turned left and shortly afterwards arrived at Nora's house.

On the road there were cars parked, but the yard was mainly full of people. They were congregating at the east of the house where the four men were in the middle of their game; from the road, because of the crowd, they weren't even as visible as usual. Solema found a small spot on the right of the road. People were swarming, bragging and hooting like crazy and now and then there was also cursing. As always when a lot of people are gathered together in Curaçao.

37

As soon as they had got out of the car, Nora began asking people what on earth had happened and why there were so many people here.

'That game of dominoes, ma'am,' said a man who was crossing the road at the same time. 'It must be terrible. It seems they're murdering each other under that tree.'

'What?' asked Solema and Nora together in alarm.

'Well,' said the man, rather surprised that there were still people, even *women*, who didn't know the news yet. 'When I heard the news, and that's over half an hour ago, it was already eight–love or something. By now I expect it's nine–love. And they say . . .'

But Nora wasn't listening any more. She went quickly on with Solema behind her and near the gate of her yard asked someone the question again, who gave her the same answer.

Another man who was standing looking at the throng under the tamarind tree with his arms folded happened to hear. He turned round and whispered something into the ear of the man Nora was talking to.

'What's he saying?' asked Nora suspiciously.

'Well, ma'am, I'd rather not repeat it.'

'What are you saying?' asked Nora directly of the man who'd whispered.

'Well, ma'am,' said the man.

'Come on, tell me,' said Nora in a friendly way.

'Well, the whole thing seems to be the fault of Bubu Fiel himself.'

'Why?'

'They say he spent the whole of last night over there.' The man pointed to the north with an embarrassed movement of his head. It was obvious that he meant Campo Alegre.

'It's not true!' snapped Nora. 'They're lying!'

Without even deigning to look at the man, she followed behind Solema, who had pushed her way through the crowd to a point where she could see something of the players.

Solema at least could make out Manchi, who she thought looked very tired. Then Chamon Nicolas and Bubu Fiel. Because of the triumphant smile on Chamon's face she decided that it must be true what everyone around her was saying; namely that Janchi and Chamon Nicolas were giving Manchi and Bubu the biggest hiding that had ever been given to a team in the history of dominoes.

She studied Manchi's face from the side, and even from a distance thought it looked rather bewildered, but finally turned round because she still couldn't see anything of Janchi. She found Nora in front of her.

'It's nothing. Miss Solema, they're all still alive, I hear.'

310

'But those two are taking a terrible hiding,' said Solema with obvious pleasure. Nora, who didn't care two hoots for dominoes, scarcely noticed this pleasure.

'Yes that's true. But it's nothing terrible as we thought.'

'Yes,' said Solema, 'thank God. I'll be off,' she added, again thinking of the possibility that this game could suddenly be called off. At any rate, Manchi looked as though he couldn't go on for much longer.

Nora walked along with her, through the continuous stream of people still arriving, to the gate. In fact, she thought it was her duty to invite Solema for a cool drink in her house, but she did not, because she also thought of the bottles of water in her refrigerator. Which were now perhaps empty. 'You must come and visit us, Miss Solema,' she said instead. 'When it's less busy.'

'Yes, I'll certainly do that.'

Nora waited until Solema had crossed the road and got back in her Fiat. 'Have a good trip,' she called out, because in her excitement she forgot that Solema had said that she had washing in her two cases.

Perhaps she didn't really believe that.

'Thanks, Nora,' said Solema, setting the car carefully in motion and beginning to drive off, waving with one hand.

'Thanks,' said Nora, waving with her black purse which contained the six guilders that she had been given by Solema.

38

Just after Solema had crossed the junction of the Tula and Carpata roads, she turned right down a narrow sandy path, lined by so many *palu di lechis* that they hid her almost completely with their long, swaying stalks. This made for difficult driving, but by using this road she could get very close to Janchi's house. The road through the woods had the additional advantage that her car would not easily be seen by passers-by, although that scarcely mattered to her now.

Ten yards or so from Janchi's grey-coloured house, she stopped, because the vegetation was so dense here that she couldn't get any further in the car. She took out one of the big cases and dragged it, as well as she could, up to the porch of the house. The *palu di lechis* hampered her in a friendly way. As well as she could, she hoisted one case onto the porch and then went to fetch the second. Then she took the large number of household items that she'd brought with her out of the boot. As she did so, she picked some of the pale white and lilac flowers of the *palu di lechis* and stuck them behind her ears. 'In revenge,' she said, laughing to herself without knowing exactly what she meant by that.

Then she tried the front door of Janchi's house and found it locked. She sat down on one of her cases to think over what she had to do. Her attention was caught by the trunk of the *wabi* tree which Janchi was making into a table for her and again she told herself that it would be very good if he were to make more of those tables. But this one's for me, she thought happily. Or rather, she corrected herself playfully, for *us*!

But she wanted to get *in*. It seemed to her that she was leaving something unfinished or unbegun until she entered this house, set her cases down somewhere and began to put the chaotic mess in which Janchi lived into some kind of order. Apart from that, the sun looked as though it was about to set, and she began to feel slightly frightened in these overgrown surroundings.

So she again felt the door, but it remained locked. The almost ironic thought occurred to her that she'd left the doors and windows of her own house wide open. And perhaps the television on as well. But she shrugged her shoulders about that. From now on, that house on the hill on the other side of Santa Gloria was only Manchi's house. She left her cases

312

on the porch and began walking around the house. She examined the windows at the back, which didn't yet have any hinges and were kept in their frames by cross planks inside and out. They were strong planks, which Janchi had also fixed to the bare walls of the house with sturdy nails. She looked at one of those windows, which in her opinion was exactly above Janchi's bed: she had a plan for getting in.

She looked around the house until she found a large stone. On the porch she found a strong piece of wood. Using both the stone and the wood, she began hammering the cross-planks of the window. She thought she was being stupid for not simply waiting on the porch until Janchi came, but she continued. Because she wasn't making much progress and the planks stayed where they were without budging, she had an impulse to go to her parents, tell them about her decision and see her children, whom she would leave there for the time being. She suddenly realized that she had taken a great risk by writing in the note that she was at Janchi's. What was she to do if Manchi came looking for her here when Janchi had not yet arrived? She thought of his revolver and cursed herself because Nora and she had been in such a hurry that she hadn't thought to take it with her. But she went on working and tugging. She was now frightened not just for herself but also for Janchi. And yet she had only one thought: to get into this unfinished house. She finally succeeded in smashing the planks where they had been nailed into the walls. She said girlishly to herself, 'If at first you don't succeed . . .'

She bravely smashed the other end too.

As she grabbed one half of the window to pull it away, the other suddenly came loose. It fell on her knee and shin bone.

It hurt a lot, but she quickly knocked away the cross-planks on the inside and climbed in.

39

When Solema drove off, Nora felt ill at ease in the large crowd surrounding her house. She became more and more agitated because she hadn't had many people at her house for ages and never such a huge crowd. In fact, she wanted to go straight to Bubu to tell him she was back and ask him why it was that the game of dominoes had suddenly attracted such a huge crowd. He must be missing me now at any rate, she thought, walking quickly into her house to put the money somewhere safe first. He liked parties; he liked people around him; on dreary afternoons when there was little to do, he liked suddenly bringing a number of drivers home with him, pouring a drink for them in the shadow of the tamarind tree, eating some goats' meat with them, getting out the set of dominoes. But *she* had to be there. For a long time she had secretly begun to suspect that he did all this to show her off. And the way that she'd quickly provide the people, however many of them there were, with good food and drink. He seemed to live on those moments when people said as they left, 'We had a wonderful time at yours, Bubu. Nora is a great hostess.' And to think that afterwards she and the children sometimes had scarcely enough to eat.

But *she* always enjoyed all this too.

In her bedroom, she lifted up the statue of the Sacred Heart and took out the ten-guilder note from underneath it. She took the five guilders out of her purse and folded both notes up very small and then put them together under the statue. She kept the last guilder in her purse.

'Thank you,' she said to the statue, crossing herself in front of it. Then she went out by the back door. She wasn't thinking of Diego Manuel any more, though she could still vaguely feel his rough treatment all over her back.

With some difficulty she managed to get to where the

domino players were. She saw Bubu, who was resting his left hand with the pieces in it on the table and stroking his chin with his right hand.

The domino players were completely hemmed in by the crowd. A row of black shoes, which were all hanging on one branch of the tamarind tree, sometimes knocked festively against the heads of some of the audience.

There was a continuous hubbub everywhere. Those who were close to the table kept passing on the moves to those who were right behind them and couldn't see anything: five–two, two–three, pass. Double three, pass, etc.

When she'd finally got to a position between Chamon Nicolas and Bubu, she thought the men looked very tired. Except for Janchi Pau, who kept looking doggedly at the table.

She laid her hand cautiously on Bubu's shoulders. She no longer paid any attention to Chamon. He was completely superfluous now!

'Why are there so many people here?'

He looked at her and his eyes lit up boyishly.

'We're losing,' he said, as though that were an explanation in itself. She leant slightly against him, perhaps to make it extra clear to Chamon that he could get lost from now on.

Bubu took a piece to play and pushed her aside with his elbow for a moment to give himself room. 'We're taking a terrible beating,' he said again, but less cheerfully.

'Why does that matter?' she said. 'You two are sure to win another time. You play every Sunday, don't you?'

'Yes, but this is *terrible*. See for yourself.' He pointed to the shoes hanging in the tree with a nod of his head.

Nora counted them at her leisure: eight pairs.

'Whose are all those shoes?' she asked.

'*Ours*,' he said raising his voice unnecessarily, so that the onlookers who at that moment were concentrating on Chamon's move suddenly focused on him in suspense: was

315

Bubu going to do something? Was Bubu getting angry? Some of them at any rate turned round and just to be sure passed on the fact that Bubu had raised his voice.

'What did he say?'

'I don't know.'

And someone else passed it on, until for those who were furthest away the message really did become that Bubu was very angry and had torn Chamon off a strip.

Nora understood: she thought about what people were whispering and felt they were right, although she didn't openly admit it. She even felt like saying to him, 'It's your own damn fault. If you hadn't been in the whores' camp all night, you'd have been able to play dominoes better today.' But she couldn't bring herself to say this.

'Terrible,' she said feigning as much sympathy with his loss as she could.

He put his arm round her waist and pulled her towards him. He felt stronger like that, not so abandoned. 'And you left us in the lurch,' he said jokingly. 'We're losing because you abandoned us. Nora!'

'Not true,' she said. 'I filled a carafe and put it ready for you here on the bench. Surely you saw it?'

'Where is it now?' asked Bubu teasingly.

Indeed, she had to look for a moment before she found the tray with the carafe and glasses on it, under the wooden bench next to the empty suitcase. The men who had climbed onto the bench to be able to follow the game over the heads of the others had put them underneath it. Nora picked them up. Oddly enough, there was still some rum in the carafe.

'Shall I fill it up again and go round?' she asked, suddenly hitting on an idea.

'Of course!' said Bubu aloud. 'Go on and fill it up and take it round. I expect people will want a drink. I'm really pleased you're there.'

'Right,' said Nora, setting off towards the front of the house with the tray, carafe and glasses and smiling happily; clearing a path for herself through the crowd with the tray. She was recognized by more and more people, because more Wakotans had now arrived. They greeted Nora, who was known throughout the area as a brave and hospitable woman, in a friendly way. But with the extra, understanding friendliness that people have for a popular woman whose husband has just died.

She hadn't hit on the idea of taking the glasses round for no good reason. The hubbub and the throng, the great interest of people in general, reminded her of the time when Bubu was chairman of DSW. It was the happiest period she'd had with him. And often with a throng around her house like now at this time of day. Yes, in those days eight tables were out in her small living-room all afternoon, *eight*. After the final result, the men came outside and the girls from both clubs joined them in their smart uniforms.

The memory made Nora turn round before she went inside and look at her ancient and rusty flagpole. The men and women gathered round this flagpole. The flag of the club which had won was hoisted aloft and songs were sung.

She could still remember the club song of DSW almost word for word. The crowds of people there had been then! No one cared about the score any more at that point. The band had arrived by that time. The tables and chairs had to be taken out of the house, and as soon as they'd done that the two clubs, who'd had been competing with each other all day long, DSW and the other, became one: to dance and party together in her little house, into which everyone seemed to be able to fit. And she, Nora, what else did she do as hostess but go round and make sure that people had enough to eat and drink?

Taking the glasses round. Heavens, how sorry she was now

that because of her rage and and worry that afternoon she had dropped several glasses, when she could use every one she had now. She went quickly into the house and a little later emerged from the back door with her tray. She only had fourteen glasses on it, because she couldn't find any more in her best cabinet. She began serving drinks. With that happy smile of hers which the people in Wakota appreciated so much. When the men saw her coming, they even avoided mentioning Bubu Fiel's name. And she, who realized that all they were talking about was the drubbing her husband was getting, laughed to herself, because she thought that the drubbing was very good for him. Hopefully it would keep him away from Campo Alegre. In her heart she was also grateful to Janchi and she felt warm towards him because, as everyone was saying, he was mainly responsible for this drubbing.

But the game of dominoes wasn't her affair. What was important was that people would also spread the word that they'd had a good time at Bubu Fiel's. Even those who didn't get a drink would have to tell people how they'd seen Nora going round with the glasses of rum. With rum for everybody!

40

The radio reporter from the Antillean programme V (the Antilles have a large number of commercial broadcasting stations and a great lack of political freedom in the media), who had been the first reporter to arrive at Bubu Fiel's house, announced that the ninth set had finished: Janchi Pau had just won the tenth game.

The people closest to the table leapt around exuberantly. They spread the news in all directions.

The reporter, who was light-skinned without being white and wore a red baseball cap and also a tie, conveyed the excitement by his voice in the usual showy (or professional) way. As he did so, he gave the name of the players to his listeners for the umpteenth time.

He said a few times that Bubu Fiel was soon to be a famous trade union leader. He waxed lyrical about Manchi's house, when someone whispered to him about the situation here in Wakota: 'A fantastic house,' he cried, 'with a very unique gallery and fantastic arches.' He also told the listeners that he'd only seen such houses in Spain and Italy, when he'd been on holiday six years before. 'Yes,' he told them, 'six years ago I went away for six months with the whole family. We're going again soon. But,' he also told them, 'this time I'm *not* going to Europe, because I already know it like the back of my hand. Except for Iceland,' he said.

Then he finally returned to the game of dominoes and shouted: 'Yes, ladies and gentlemen, another pair of shoes has been added for a *ten*–love set! They say,' he added with overflowing enthusiasm, 'they say, that it almost, almost, *almost* was *eleven–love*, like the shoes in the third set, which were not only *eleven–love*, ladies and gentlemen, *eleven*, but one in which Janchi Pau won a double play *four times* in succession.' *In succession* may not have been true, but it sounded better! 'A record in the history of Curaçaoan, Antillean, *world* dominoes. *A world record. A world record*,' he cried exuberantly. 'Here, to the east of Bubu Fiel's house this afternoon, a world record has been established!'

He suddenly stopped, because the two men from the television team who were just arriving were friends of his and he had to wave at them. He thought that the arrival of the television people was big news and soon afterwards reported this.

The two television men began filming, but the bright light which one of them pointed towards the players upset Manchi. At a certain moment he suddenly got up and said, 'Take that light away!' Because the television man carried on regardless, he repeated, putting his pieces on the table: 'Get rid of that light, or I'll clear the court.'

The television man, who didn't understand but didn't want to have any effect on the course of this massacre, focused his camera on, among other things, the nine pairs of shoes which were dangling calmly from the tamarind tree.

'I'm Nora,' she said, shoving the tray under his nose, 'Bubu Fiel's wife. Would you like a drink?'

'The wife of the *loser*?'

'Yes,' she said coquettishly. 'Even losers have wives, you know! Come on, have a drink,' she added hospitably.

'Listeners,' cried the reporter, beside himself with excitement and astonishment: 'Right in front of us is the wife of Bubu Fiel, one of the losers of this fabulous afternoon. An attractive lady of about forty, I estimate. And she's even offering us a drink.'

At that moment he saw the sign from the television people, who'd heard his commentary, quickly took the glass off Nora's tray and raised it high, in order to please the cameraman who now filmed himself and Nora. The lighting man crept up to them (keeping his lamp focused on them as well as he could) in order to bring the television microphone towards them too. Then it became a matter for radio and television, with the radio reporter appearing as the main character. With the aplomb of a star introducing a film, pressing Nora to him, he said, 'This is certainly proof of the much-vaunted Antillean hospitality and it makes us feel the sporting atmosphere in which this game of dominoes is taking place, a sport to which up to now we paid little attention. And yet it's a *fascinating* sport: they say that the Dutch only succeeded in capturing the impregnable fortress of El Moro on Puerto Rico because the Spaniards who were guarding the fort were completely absorbed in a dominoes tournament on that day. On one of my holidays,' he added, 'I saw for myself one of the domino pieces with which they played: authentic! It's wood, ladies and gentlemen, and it is a five–three. Yes *five–three*, ladies and gentlemen. A remarkable piece, although it's made of wood.' He laughed down the microphone.

He didn't down his drink in one, as the men playing dominoes did, and Nora stayed waiting next to him with the tray.

'Is the idea for *everyone* to have a drink?' he asked with a glance at the crowd.

'Yes, everyone,' said Nora proudly, standing on tip-toe in order to be able to speak into the microphone, which he held far too high for her. 'Everyone,' she repeated subsequently for the television microphone. And then the radio reporter dropped the microphone a little, and she said, looking straight into the television camera, 'It's my custom to do everything to please the people who come to see us. That's the right way, isn't it?' she said, looking at the radio reporter reproachfully. Again to the camera: 'You know, people from Bandabou are hospitable, more hospitable than people in the town. And that's where I come from.'

The newspaper people, who arrived just at that moment, paid little attention to the domino players in the first instance, because they thought that Nora was holding a press conference, with free drinks into the bargain! The people near Nora dived for the tray with the drinks on it, but as soon as the television camera had pointed elsewhere and Nora had gone back to refill the glasses from the gallon bottle, they returned disappointed to the domino table. The alert radio reporter again beat them to it with his microphone. He reminded his listeners that Bubu was almost certain to be elected chairman of the taxi drivers' union and asked Bubu what he planned to do when he had won. '*The election*,' he quickly added himself, 'not the game of dominoes, because you've already *lost* that.'

'Anything can still happen,' said Bubu stubbornly.

'Well . . . Still?'

'Yes, dominoes is a crazy game.'

'Right. But I really would like to talk to you about the taxi drivers' union for a moment, which you've actually given a boost without being on the board. What are you going to do when you've won?'

Bubu Fiel thought to himself: Ah, the pestering has begun! Anyway, he didn't have the slightest idea what he was going to do when he became chairman of the union. Of course, he could say: 'To promote and maintain order, decency and discipline among the drivers,' which would have won him the support of every member of the NVP. But the contempt of Janchi here . . . 'All kinds of things,' he said slowly, in order to win time to think. Besides, he knew that he made a big impression with his voice if he spoke calmly. It was his calm way of speaking, his *placidity*, which had attracted her to him, she had said to him yesterday evening.

They had reached the second game of the tenth set. Everyone thought that this would be the last set, although there were no fixed agreements about the number that were played. The people automatically took into account the number of available ladies' shoes which were still under the wooden bench: one pair. And also they took account of dusk, which was about to fall and which would make playing impossible.

Bubu Fiel calmly pushed the radio reporter's microphone aside, and took time to consider his move.

'What do you mean, "all kinds of things", Mr Fiel?' asked the reporter, holding the microphone up in front of him again.

'A revolution in prices!' said Bubu, remembering scraps of the conversation at the beginning of the game of dominoes, scraps of arguments of Janchi Pau's which he felt would be of more use than the slogans of the late Doctor, however much he had admired him. 'Yes, prices are too *high* and so have to come *down*.'

'The price of taxis?' asked the reporter, who himself felt that taxi fares were too high, higher at any rate than many countries where he had been on holiday.

'No!' said Bubu emphatically, 'the prices of *groceries and building materials*.' He was going to say more but his words were buried under the applause of the taxi chauffeurs who were standing in the vicinity. It became an endless round of clapping because those who stood at the back began applauding again as soon as they heard Bubu's words being passed on. 'Speak louder! Speak louder!' numerous taxi drivers began shouting. They thought it was too important a matter to hear second-hand.

'We want to hear too!'

'Do you mean that the *government* is doing nothing?' asked the reporter, who as a journalist automatically disliked the ruling party, the DP, because this party, which seemed to be more or less permanently in power, did not allow any political discussion at all on radio or television.

'Yes,' said Bubu Fiel as loudly as possible, 'that's what I mean: the government does nothing to combat imports. The government does nothing for exports. The government does nothing!' There was a thunderous round of applause. Bubu, remembering that he was a taxi driver, suddenly said: 'The government doesn't lift a finger to help us taxi drivers in our battle against the capitalist travel agencies and hotels who collect their own guests in large coaches. Not even free!' he shouted with a laugh: 'The guests pay. These owners of travel agencies, hotels and banks are operating as taxis. These people are corrupt!'

He drew himself up to his full height. The reporter put the microphone close to his mouth, but he pushed it aside because he thought it more important to say what he had to say here to the people, most of whom were taxi drivers after all, than to people at home with whom he didn't have much to do.

'*The government is corrupt!*' he cried, turning his face to the south because that was where he thought most people were standing. Then he sat down again.

The people were applauding thunderously. 'Long live Bubu Fiel! Long live Fiel! Long live Bubu!' they went on shouting. They'd got completely into the atmosphere of the political meeting and in Bubu's own words they had recognized the words of a true leader. They were glad they had come to Wakota. They'd vote for him shortly. Such words!

'Ask Janchi here,' said Bubu into the reporter's microphone when he was sitting down again. He nodded and looked at Janchi, who nodded to him encouragingly. Then he went on cheerfully, 'We are playing a friendly game here, not for money or anything else, but for our *pleasure*. In this atmosphere, we discuss the politics of our country and this afternoon we reached certain conclusions. One of them is that the government does nothing for us!' When there was again applause he said, '*I*, at least, have reached this understanding.' (He waited for a moment to remember Janchi's precise words.) 'The government sells us out to foreigners, who daily force prices up and take over the country. Ask my opponent and friend, Pau here; he should know because he goes fishing. Ask him how many of our beaches are in the hands of foreigners, isn't that right, Janchi?'

'Yes,' said Janchi, who realized that Bubu Fiel was in the process of building up a new image with his improvisational talent (that of a politician and hence also of a trade union leader), now he had lost the old one (that of a good dominoes player). But he couldn't care less, because anyway they were his own arguments. And *Solema's*. And hence *true* arguments.

In a torrent of words Bubu went on (and the taxi drivers went on clapping) by repeating more or less everything that Janchi had said that afternoon and that had stuck in his mind despite his daydreaming. At any rate he had a triumph with the taxi drivers, because of course among the numerous radio listeners at home there were many who disagreed with all this and with him, and found everything that he said simply *dangerous*.

'*A revolution*,' concluded Bubu. 'A revolution which means that taxi drivers don't have to buy a new vehicle every year.'

Although the taxi drivers present did not applaud as enthusiastically, these were perhaps his most deeply serious words. He thought of Nora, who kept saying that he changed cars too often.

The reporter was satisfied and turned to interview Chamon Nicolas, who used the opportunity to say how unhappy he really felt, because since his 'accident' he had not been admitted to any domino club. He told the whole story and concluded by remarking that it was *unjust* that he'd been in prison for a year.

The reporter said consolingly, 'But they certainly won't do that any more. Now it's more or less certain that you and your partner are among the best domino players of all time. How would a self-respecting domino club be able to refuse a player like Chamon Nicolas in future?' he asked into the microphone.

'But it's not necessary any more,' said Chamon perfectly happy with the reporter's words. 'I think that I shall shortly be going back to the Windward Islands.'

'A pity,' said the reporter sincerely. 'We'll be losing a good player.'

'I shall *have to*.'

'Why, you're an Antillean, aren't you?'

'Yes, but there are other reasons.'

'What reasons?'

'Well . . .'

'Personal reasons?'

'Yes,' said Chamon with relief. 'Personal reasons.'

He cursed the fact that Nora had made a slip of the tongue, because that meant that now, at this time of all times, he would have to leave this island. Preferably before Bubu Fiel found out that he really did have houses.

'Safe journey then, when you leave,' said the reporter, and turning to Janchi, said, 'And here we have, as everyone here is convinced, the star of this game of dominoes: the thirty-five-year-old Janchi Pau. Do you also have plans for the future,' he asked, 'like your partner here?'

His question surprised Janchi, who'd been sitting preparing himself for the moment when the reporter would hold the microphone in front of him, thinking that he would mainly ask him questions about the game. So he had no time to decide what he was going to reveal about his plans.

'Yes.'

'For example?'

'Finish my house.'

'Really? So you're building a *house*? Like that of Manchi Sanantonio here?'

'No, smaller. Much smaller.'

'Oh. And afterwards? Have you plans for afterwards?'

He almost said, *Then I shall have Solema come to live with me*.

'Then I'm going to start up a furniture factory.' He announced this plan which had just crystallized in him, because he thought: *Then I'll immediately have free advertising!*

'A *furniture factory*?' cried the reporter in amazement.

'Yes,' said Janchi, 'that's what I intend to do.'

'Well.'

'I'm going to make mainly *wabi* wood tables. I hope to sell

326

them mainly to the tourists, who are crazy about them. Maybe I can also export them.'

'Do you have a name for your factory yet?' the reporter was clearly impressed.

'Yes: *Solema. The Solema Furniture Factory!*'

'Right. And are you going to do it by yourself?' asked the reporter.

'No, I shall use as many people as want to help me. I shall make it into a kind of co-operative venture.'

'Oh,' said the reporter. And turning to Bubu off-mike, he said, 'You could do that with your taxi drivers, make a co-operative.' And again to Janchi, 'Are you getting support from the government?'

'No,' said Janchi. 'They never help anyone. Why would they help *me*? We shall have to do it by ourselves.'

'Excellent!' said the reporter. 'And where is the factory located?'

'Good Hope.'

'Excellent! Excellent! The Solema Furniture Factory, Good Hope. Listeners, don't you think that's a marvellous combination of names? Remember it: *The Solema Furniture Factory!* I can guarantee that it'll be good furniture, because the owner, or' – he looked approvingly at Janchi – 'the *brains behind it* is already an excellent *shoemaker*. Ha! Ha!'

The onlookers laughed along with this joke.

'And now,' said the reporter, turning to Manchi, 'we're going to talk to the owner of the most beautiful house in Wakota: Manchi Sanantonio. What is your profession, Mr Sanantonio? We're very interested . . .'

'Judge,' said Manchi.

The reporter quickly moved the microphone back to his own mouth.

'What? Do I understand you correctly? You are a *judge*, you say?'

'Yes,' said Manchi, emphatically.

Bubu Fiel, who now felt half-way to being chairman of the taxi drivers' union, was suddenly frightened about his image. Just imagine if Manchi publicized the kind of stories they told each other here to everyone on this island through the microphone. He sat up in his chair, grabbed the reporter's hand with the microphone in it firmly and pulled it away from Manchi.

'What's this?' asked the reporter in alarm.

'It's a funny joke of ours here at the table, it doesn't have to be on the radio. Manchi is a bailiff by profession.'

'Oh,' said the reporter speaking cheerfully off-mike. 'But that will be nice . . .'

'I don't think so,' said Janchi, 'it should stay here at this table.'

'Right,' said Chamon, also frightened that Manchi would call him a murderer or something into the microphone.

'You'd better leave Manchi alone,' said Bubu worried. 'He's very tired. And we've still got to play.'

Chamon said insinuatingly, 'We're *all* tired. But that's not the point.' Then he pushed the double six into the middle of the table to begin the third game of the tenth set. The score was already two–love to him and Janchi.

The reporter nodded understandingly and told his listeners that he was taking leave of them for the moment to return with the final score.

Janchi pushed his pieces away. 'Shall we stop?' he said to Bubu, 'if you're so tired . . .'

There was a murmur of disappointment through the crowd around the table.

'I don't mind,' said Bubu Fiel. 'After all, it's a friendly game. Anyway, I don't feel that well today, and besides that, I've got a meeting in a little while, haven't I?'

'Hm,' muttered Janchi. 'So I suggest . . .'

If Chamon Nicolas had held his tongue, Manchi might really have given up and, who knows, perhaps even saved his life.

But Chamon said, '*Everyone* gets tired in a game of dominoes, especially when he loses.' He was now completely convinced that the idea of giving them ten pairs of shoes stemmed mainly from *him*, and that he had to see what he had started through to the end. And he also had a good hand at that moment.

'Well,' said Bubu Fiel hesitating. 'Well . . .' On the one hand, he thought Chamon was being hard and impudent and he also generally disliked him because of his cockiness, which had increased as he won. On the other hand, it went against the grain with him to break the golden rule of dominoes: play on to the end! Otherwise he'd have damn well given up himself long ago. 'What do you think, Manchi?'

Manchi, who had picked up all his pieces, sat looking at them as though he were sleepily reading a book. The hubbub of the crowd annoyed him and gave him a feeling of oppression. He thought vaguely: I have the power to empty this courtroom! But he said, '*We must go on!*'

The rest of the tenth set turned into a noisy affair. There was no restraining the crowd any more. Bubu, who, although he was on the losing side, had been given a new authority by those militant words into the radio reporter's microphone, tried to use this to obtain silence, but it was no good. All the spectators wanted to see the last set. They wanted to see Janchi Pau and Chamon Nicolas because they were winning, and to see how Manchi Sanantonio and Bubu Fiel lost. A few of them forced their way forward and took photographs.

After the third game, it seemed as though things would take a turn. Chamon Nicolas and Janchi Pau lost two games in succession. Both times because Chamon, due to the excitement created by all this interest, which he simply couldn't control any more, made two howlers. Someone in the crowd, who thought it was impossible that one pair of domino players could beat another *ten–love*, began to believe that this time Bubu and Manchi were going to get out of prison. Others went so far as to assume (despite Manchi's obvious tiredness) that this time he and Bubu would be presenting the shoes.

Meanwhile, Janchi was getting angry. He wanted to stop just now because he felt that Manchi had been punished enough, but he didn't want to go on playing to lighten this punishment because of stupid mistakes by his partner. He began to play for himself. He eliminated not only Manchi and Bubu, but also Chamon. He succeeded in winning three games in succession, two of them by blocking the game, slamming the dominoes down hard on the table. The score was six–two and Chamon finally controlled himself a little and won a double play that Janchi had prepared. The crowd was buzzing. Manchi and Bubu Fiel won one more game, because Bubu now blocked the game and had only the double blank left. A little later, the score was ten–three, as everyone could have anticipated. The reporter announced the score through his microphone as if it were the main prize in a lottery. No one felt it necessary to hang up the last pair of shoes.

41

No one *thought* of it! They crowded round the table to talk to the players, especially the winners. They especially wanted to talk to Janchi Pau and ask him how he'd done it, but he had other plans. He got up immediately, shook hands briefly with Chamon, and said that he was in a terrible hurry. A crowd of people accompanied him as far as the gate. He freed himself from them brusquely and crossed the Tula road. He took a different, less accessible path than that past the cemetery and quickly disappeared from view. Manchi left the domino table at the same time. He couldn't stand it a moment longer. He was also able to leave without being noticed because, as is usually the case with losers, no one was interested in him. He took the goat path over the hill between Bubu Fiel's house and his, without the case in which he had brought the shoes that afternoon. That was left behind, forgotten, under the wooden bench against the house.

The radio reporter continued describing the domino fiasco and record until he had shouted himself hoarse. Then he sat down on the bench next to Bubu Fiel to try to persuade him in a whisper to set up a co-operative of taxi drivers such as already existed on the other islands, and as Janchi Pau had said he was going to do with his furniture factory. The taxi drivers crowded round them. So Chamon Nicolas was the only one who was completely at the disposal of the spectators, who wanted to go on having a post-mortem about the game of dominoes itself. Endlessly he repeated the climaxes of the game, the moments of suspense, the *changás*; that special moment that he remembered best of all and would remember all his life, because Janchi had refused, had *twice* refused, to play his double four, which was then hanging by a thread between life and death, and how he, Janchi Pau, had thereby won a double play.

PART III

Dusk

1

The small, yellow *anglos* closed.

The sky, which had for a moment hesitated between grey and black, now quickly became black. In the sky above Wakota, those pristine, curious stars, twinkling brightly, appeared.

As Janchi climbed the church hill, the bells of Santa Gloria began tolling for mass. Strange, he thought, that I talked about a *furniture* factory, when I want to start making *tables*. But a table factory sounds so stupid. Who's ever heard of a table factory? Anyway, he could make furniture too. Tables, chairs and cupboards. Lots of things, and all with local labour. That was for certain. That was the revolution as he saw it, now he was less tense than before. Building something great with a large number of men. *Producing*, because people had never produced anything on this island. Not natives. They'd been dumped here by the Dutch, as Solema said, and abandoned like orphans, who could do little for themselves. But that was finally going to change. *He* in any case would do his part. It was ironic perhaps, he thought, that if ever the Solema Furniture Factory became a flourishing business, he would need more than anything on this island, *wabis*. Yes, this thick, thorny tree, with its twisted, gnarled trunk and its branches full of sharp thorns which were sometimes four inches long, which some people said was cursed because Christ's crown of thorns had been made from it. This despised tree, which is found everywhere on the island, and is second only to the cactus in numbers, would therefore be the starting point of his business. Dear *wabi*! He smiled to himself and thought that because of his furniture factory, the *wabi* would in future grow in esteem. And he thought that he really ought to start planting them; here, for example, all across this extensive area of Good Hope, the land which had in fact always suggested more maize and beans to him. But *alla*. He would have to *plant* them here in any case. He wouldn't work as Solema had told him the Dutch had done in the past: they felled all the Brazil wood that they needed, and which was found in abundance on the island when they arrived here in the seventeenth century, without it occurring to them that they could also plant young trees, so that afterwards there would be Brazil wood for them and for everyone else! Always. But no, they'd quickly deforested the whole, beautiful island and in so doing had driven the rain away, perhaps for good, then went on to complain that it was so 'arid' and 'dry'. They're apes, those Dutch, he thought. Barbarians. Underdeveloped. Savages.

But he was going to plant the wood that he needed: *wabi*. And the wood that he *might* need: *kalebas, wapanas, kibrahachas*. Hell, what a lot of types of tree, what a lot of trees they had here, which grew in abundance, despite the dryness, despite the drought. Which wasn't so bad, come to that.

Didn't everyone talk about Israel and its drought? And didn't they started foresting Israel with the slogan: Every Jew a Tree. Every Jew on Curaçao a tree for Israel! Why didn't they have the idea of each planting a tree here? Then there'd be about five hundred trees on this island. There were at least that many Jews on this island. That many *rich* Jews, moreover. And how many trees could three hundred thousand plant and care for together? He again thought of the radio reporter's question, whether the government would support him with his furniture factory. No, he had said, but why not? Surely he had a right to help, if he wanted to make something of this country? Of everyone! He thought to himself that if he didn't get the help that he was entitled to, he'd do something else. Then he would make a revolution! A revolution for power, a revolution like that in Cuba! Perhaps it wouldn't be necessary: it might be that his factory would do so well that they could even make something of cactuses; so that even the cactuses which were now to be found in abundance on the island would one day somehow become more scarce.

He suddenly interrupted his reflections when he saw light shining out of his house through the *palu di lechis* and other undergrowth.

2

As she did with songs that she liked singing – lots of blues – and with pieces that she liked to play, she had lain for a while on the narrow bed in his house thinking of him.

She had taken off her shoes to make herself more comfortable and had felt so at home, she'd taken off her dress too. No one was going to come here anyway. She'd lain back down on the bed to think of him. All she'd done was enjoy the fact that she had moved in with him for good, so sure of herself.

She had climbed in through the window, after which she had opened the door from the inside. She'd lugged her cases inside and had actually been able to clear up a little. At a certain moment, she felt so tired from all her efforts that she decided to lie down and rest for a little before she continued. The wind and the silence around Janchi's house then made her drop off before she noticed it.

When the church bells rang for evening mass, she woke up. She quickly put the light on, because the darkness in the unfinished house was frightening. She felt a little gloomy, because she had wanted to do much more in the house to surprise him. She had even intended to cook. But it was too late now; she had at most time to brush her hair before he arrived.

3

He ran more than walked the last stretch towards his house, convinced that it was her. But he didn't understand how that was possible, because he was assuming that she could only come after mass.

But hadn't she already surprised him this morning by appearing unexpectedly? Perhaps she'd given up playing the organ in the church of Wakota for good. He didn't mind that much. But if it was her, and it couldn't be anyone else, how had she got into the house? He was still wondering a little later when he saw her car close to the house. He quickly mounted the porch and put his ear against the door. He took out his key, but did not put it into the lock because at that moment he remembered that just now at the domino table he'd made a great error: *he'd said that he was going to call his furniture factory Solema*. Why hadn't anyone reacted?

Why hadn't *Manchi* said anything? After all, Solema was his wife's name! He himself hadn't thought of it because since this morning there had only been one Solema for him – *his* Solema – but he must be careful! As he placed his key in the lock with his left hand, he put his right hand into his pocket to take out his stiletto. But it wasn't necessary, because he recognized her voice, 'Don't look for your key, the door's open.'

She'd heard him climbing onto the porch and thought, when he didn't come in, that he was looking for his key. He opened the door and found her right in front of him:

'I'm here to stay,' she said, pointing to her half-dressed state with an unnecessary nod of her head.

'And what about your children?' he said, taking her in his arms.

'With my parents. For now.'

He was tired from the game and from thinking about the

other things. He was so tired that he could scarcely react to the great surprise she had given him by being there, and by saying that she was staying for good, as he had asked her to that morning.

He walked on, pulling her along by the hand, and stretched out on the bed without saying any more. She helped him with his tie, shirt and shoes, and caressed him with her delicate hands. This revived him a little and he began to tell her how happy he was that she was there.

Then he told her about the game and that he had given Manchi back all the shoes which he had stolen from her. Finally he told her that he was planning to set up a furniture factory that was going to bear her name and that he had announced the plan on the radio.

After that, they became so absorbed in their plans that the screams which announced the disaster near Bubu Fiel's house did not get through to them. Perhaps the distance between Bubu's and Janchi's house was too great.

Two policemen, who parked their car behind Solema's and made their way to Janchi's unfinished house with their flashlights playing over the already sleeping *palu di lechis* like great glow-worms, brought them the news a little later.

4

From a distance Nora had caught a few of Bubu Fiel's enthusiastic words to the radio reporter, and she continued to hear them (through the crowd around her that kept repeating them) as she went back to the kitchen to refill the empty rum glasses.

People's reactions to what he said made her happy and gave her hope. It made her believe that the qualities she had always suspected Bubu possessed had come to the surface. And this time perhaps for good. The radio, the television, all

339

this interest couldn't be purely and simply in *dominoes*!

So maybe the chairmanship of the taxi drivers' union, which up to now she had seen as worthless, meant more than she thought? She'd give him a scolding later, for not telling her exactly how important that chairmanship was. She was convinced that in that case she would have prepared better. Perhaps she could even have offered the people here something to *eat*, a bowl of soup or something, and if not all, then at least *some* of them, like the gentlemen from the radio and the television.

She put the television on in the front room. She wouldn't be able to watch it because she had to look after her guests. But it would be fun, she thought, to be able to see Bubu Fiel here indoors, while he was sitting talking to the east of the house. And herself as well, of course. She thought of the miracle of technology that made all those things possible. Then she refilled her rum glasses and went round again. All her children now came home one by one. Two of the girls and two of the boys left again immediately for mass, because there was no money to go anywhere else. Ostrik and her daughters Vera and Selina, aged thirteen and seven, stayed at home.

After she'd been round a second time with her glasses of rum, she decided to organize the serving of her guests differently, otherwise it would take ages before she reached everyone. So, to save time while she was filling glasses, she got Ostrik to take the little dining-table outside. She had the girls cover it with a white tablecloth and then fetched the carafe, the gallon bottle, the tray and the drinks and put everything on the table by the back door. She stood behind the table and began shouting that those who hadn't had a drink yet could come and get one.

The news circulated quickly, and a large portion of those present hastened to where Nora was pouring out her hospitality. Including the large group of journalists who hadn't yet had a drink.

Despite the large throng which suddenly descended on her, Nora did quite well: her gallon bottle of rum was still largely full when she started taking it round. And the very fact that there was so much rum left (apart from her special feeling for hospitality, of course) may have been behind the idea of going round with glasses. In any case she would have got quite a long way with her rum, if everyone had kept to one drink! But they didn't, or only a few did. And she was too busy to pay particular attention.

5

Her new round of fourteen drinks was gone in a flash. In order to be able to serve the men more quickly, she stopped going inside to wash more glasses: she got Vera and Selina to bring out a small bowl of water with a cloth to give the glasses a wipe before she filled them again, because she liked things to be spick and span when she had guests. Now it didn't matter so much that she had so few glasses, because the girls immediately rinsed out each glass. It went well and efficiently and while she was working she even had time to respond to the numerous compliments which the men paid her, personally and particularly on her hospitality.

But they kept on coming, while her rum was running out. Most of them, particularly the journalists present, weren't satisfied with one drink. Because the drink was free anyway and they'd come quite long distances, they took a second glass and a third. A few of them even decided to get properly drunk. Eventually she held the bottle up to estimate how many drinks she could get out of it. She got into a panic because it was at most two more rounds of fourteen.

What was about to happen to her at that moment would be

341

a disgrace which in her eyes was greater than the ten–love defeat Bubu had suffered. That was just *dominoes*. But this was *serious*. This was very serious, because the radio reporter (who perhaps had already gone, thank God, because she'd lost sight of him) needed only to notice that there was no more drink left and tell his audience, and the whole island would know that Nora, the hospitable wife of Bubu Fiel, had run out of drink! To say nothing of the people from the television!

To be able to imagine Nora's panic, one should remember that Mary, the mother of Christ, panicked when the drink ran out at a party given by a *friend* of hers and not even a party at her own house. (People in the tropics, the Old Testament or 'primitive' *poor* people all seem paradoxically to have a similar belief in something to which everything else is subordinate, namely *hospitality*.) Apart from which, Nora did not have a son who was a professional miracle worker. (At least, her son had not got that far yet.)

She herself had invited the men to the table for a drink, and was she now supposed to tell them that the rum was running out? She thought of the bar-cum-restaurant at the junction of the Tula and Carpata roads where Chamon Nicolas had played a few sets of dominoes that afternoon before arriving at Bubu Fiel's. Next to that bar-restaurant was a shop run by a Portuguese that called itself a fruiterer's and was supposed to be closed on Sundays and at six o'clock, but where you could get all kinds of things, any day of the week and at any time of day; from bars of chocolate to plimsolls, contrary to all the laws of the island.

She said to Ostrik, who was standing next to her helping to dry the rum glasses, 'Go to the big bedroom. Under the statue of the Sacred Heart of Jesus there, in the hollow under that statue, you'll find fifteen guilders. Take it and buy a gallon bottle of rum from the Portuguese.'

342

She spoke into his ear, quickly and in a whisper, because this was no concern of the men waiting for their drinks in front of her. But Ostrik was so astonished by the fact that the fifteen guilders were there that he stood looking at his mother open-mouthed and did not move.

'Off you go!' she said, louder and more like an order. She had scarcely enough left for one round.

'Rum?' he whispered in reply. 'Rum?' That was his second cause for astonishment, that she wanted to buy rum with that vital money.

'But you can't do that, Mummy! When I need . . .'

'Go this instant! Can't you see, child, that the rum's running out? You'll get your shoes. Don't you worry. Surely you don't want us to lose face in front of all these people?' She no longer spoke in a whisper but in a natural tone as though all she were doing was nothing more than persuade her son to go quickly and get a bottle of rum that they had in the refrigerator.

Because he still didn't move, she added in a maternal tone, 'The papers, the radio, television . . . everyone's here, son. Surely you understand that we've got to keep up appearances. Off you go now.'

When he still didn't go after her explanation, she got angry; also because she noticed a muttering among the men waiting for their drinks, which she thought must be about her difficulties with the rum. About the rum running out!

'There's enough for everyone,' she shouted quickly, with her nicest and sweetest smile, but to Ostrik she said, in a whisper as sharp as a knife, 'Go, I'm telling you! I'm your mother! When I tell you to do something, then you damn well *do* it.'

He looked at her with an uncomprehending stare, in which she saw that he seemed to be wondering whether she'd gone mad. But he finally turned sadly and went.

That look of his made her hesitate for a moment!

She stopped pouring and watched him go. He's right, she

thought. His shoes are important too. So she bent down to her daughter Vera and again said in a whisper, 'Go to Chamon Nicolas there to the east of the house, and tell him he must come and listen to what I have to say for a moment over there behind the bath shed. Tell him it's *urgent*. But,' she added very emphatically, *'don't let your father hear.'*

6

Little Vera's problem was that Chamon was standing at the corner of the house in the middle of a group of men basking in the glory of the game that had just ended. The men were so absorbed in the conversation, that they did not immediately make way for her. With lots of pushing and shoving she managed to get through and disappeared into the group. But all this was noticed by Bubu Fiel as he was saying goodbye to the radio reporter, who had explained to him at length how he should set up the taxi drivers' co-operative.

However, his suspicions were only really aroused when Chamon, immediately after Vera walked to the back of the house, also detached himself from the group.

He saw Chamon looking in his direction and acted as if he had not noticed anything. Chamon went to the bath shed. He, Bubu, then walked to the corner of the house and among the people in the backyard saw Nora, also going towards the shed. He saw how she slipped away on the west side and a little later saw Chamon do the same – in a way which would not have awakened any suspicion in someone not paying special attention.

He went to the bath shed too, carefully opened the door, went in and, once inside, carefully fastened it again. Then he sat down on the toilet bowl.

At the table outside the back door of the house Selina and Vera continued to pour drinks for the men, who were jostling

344

each other like children in order to get the last one. The bottle was on the point of running out, but Nora had said to her daughters that if the rum ran out before she (or Ostrik) returned, they should say that their mother would be right back with a new bottle.

7

To begin with, Bubu Fiel could not hear anything they were saying to each other because they were speaking softly and he, sitting on the toilet, was too far away from them. However, afterwards their voices became louder. He also went to the west side of the shed, where the bags of cement were standing, and, leaning against the bags, he could hear most of what they were saying:

'No, Nora. I won't do it. It's over between us.'

'Why not? I'm telling you I'm in a jam! I can't tell the people here that the drink has run out, can I? You'll get it back when you come for the game next week.'

'But that's just the point. I don't intend ever coming back here! It's your fault if you want to know. *You* told Bubu that I've got houses.'

'Yes, I did, but not deliberately.'

'It makes it just as difficult: I told Bubu Fiel that it's not true, that you were lying. When he finds out shortly . . . and he *will* find out, then he'll know all about you and me.'

Bubu was no longer listening, because what mattered to him was not so much the content of the conversation as the fact that they were having secret conversations. He sat down on the toilet again. He told himself that he mustn't do anything stupid, that it was *stupid* to do anything stupid. And so he decided to think things over first.

'I'm going back to Saba,' said Chamon to Nora meanwhile.

'I'll send the money to you there, Chamon.'

345

'Listen, Nora. We've got to put an end to this. And you know that there'll be no end to it, if I give you money again, because then I'll want something back in return and you'll come to me to give me it. And if you come to me to go to bed with me, you'll borrow money from me again that you'll never repay. Or you'll come back and go to bed with me *again*. And I'll lend you money again. And so on. I went to bed with you,' he added emphatically, 'because I'd lent you money that I simply didn't get back! If that hadn't happened, I'd never have gone with you, because after all you're the wife of the man that I play dominoes with every Sunday afternoon. It's not *nice*, Nora, what I'm doing.'

But Nora kept on insisting.

'Give me the money, Chamon. I promise you that this will be the last time. The *very last* time. If you're not concerned about the money, then surely you can *lend* it to me? I'm good to you when we go to bed, aren't I, Chamon? Or isn't that so? Aren't I *good* to you, Chamon? Why are you being so mean to me now? Why don't you help me?'

But Chamon had grown hard. This afternoon he'd pushed himself to the limit and it had made him realize what a person is capable of, if he pushes himself to the limit. If he imposes his will. He wasn't going to melt now.

Because the conversation between the two of them lasted so long, while Bubu Fiel hadn't yet decided what to do, he started eavesdropping again. He still couldn't really believe it. But then he began feeling like a caged tiger. A tiger that the keepers have forgotten to feed, before going on holiday.

'You might as well know, *dear* Chamon,' said Nora. 'I'm fibbing to you. I need the money for something else.' She told him how she'd been trying to find the five guilders for the best part of the afternoon. How she'd tried to make contact with him. 'But now I understand why I wasn't able to,' she said. 'You didn't want me to.'

Finally she told him, without indicating the source, that she had got the money. 'But I just had to send Ostrik to buy rum from the Portuguese.'

'Rum?' said Chamon in disbelief. '*Rum?*' He spoke the word as if he were a teetotaller. Then he said, 'No. No.'

Nora began to cry.

8

As he listened to her sobs outside the shed, Bubu Fiel, despite his rage, told himself that it might after all be best to act as if he'd heard nothing. He told himself this because he completely understood why she had acted as she had. Just as *he* had so often been to bed with women to whom he gave a lift because they had no money for the bus, while the sun beat down mercilessly, his own wife had been to bed with a man out of need. And he could also understand Chamon's having deceived him. That was something male, that was part of life, in which anything could happen.

But there were two things that infuriated him about Chamon: that Chamon was abandoning her and that the man was responsible for his and Manchi's crushing defeat at the domino table. He sat down on the toilet again and buried his face in his hands, partly because the stench, which always hung in the bath shed – the excrement there beneath him had nowhere to flow to and the lid was still missing – eventually became unbearable. They had lost, he told himself, because he hadn't been able to concentrate on the game since that first incident between Nora and Chamon at the domino table, when she'd almost pushed Chamon off his chair! And the way in which she'd walked around the backyard, humming to attract Chamon's attention; and Chamon's taunting laugh and the even more humiliating way in which Chamon kept raising his hand when Bubu had lost. Chamon had made him lose . . . ! Doubly so. Besides, it wasn't *honest* of the guy to ditch Nora now, precisely when she needed him, to terminate an existing contract unilaterally, as it were. It was treacherous!

Something else that made him furious with Chamon was the fact that in all probability he would be elected chairman of the taxi drivers' union that evening. Something that he'd fought against all week, because he saw only ruin in it, for himself, for his way of life, for his *finances*. And it was due to his defeat at this domino table that, by making use of Janchi Pau's words and the chance the reporter had offered him (and to save face!), he had been able to improvise an acceptable leader's statement. Yes, despite his ten–love defeat, he would be elected this evening. Well now, if he hadn't lost, then it wouldn't have been necessary to save face; to save face so well that he now had the responsibility for the whole movement resting on his shoulders. He was caught in a trap, he thought, and Chamon had forced him into it!

Poor Chamon. It was true that he was in the process of terminating a contract unilaterally, which is possibly one of the most treacherous human acts, but what else could he do? Because he didn't know how Nora would behave after his refusal, he decided to let her have her say, even if she tore him to shreds. That is just what Nora did. She became convinced that Chamon wouldn't give her the money. More than that: that he was breaking off with her unilaterally, which she found much worse, because this humiliated her too. It meant that Chamon thought he could simply send her packing now he'd found another woman. Because that was the only thing that made sense to her from all he had said: that he had another woman and so didn't need her!

'Did you think,' she said to him, slowly and emphatically, and now terminating the contract from her side too, and in such a way that Chamon Nicolas began to doubt whether his newly won resolve could withstand *her* hardness, 'that I came

348

to you for my pleasure? Do you think that if I wanted to go to bed with a man, I'd have chosen an ugly Windward Islander like you, who apart from that has got a front tooth missing? Did you think that one prick isn't enough for me? And that *that* was why I needed to have your prick, your insignificant *little* prick as well? That I'm a whore? No, Chamon. Oh, no, Chamon! I only need one prick. And no one else's but Bubu Fiel's! Do you know that in all the years that I've been going to bed with you, I didn't come once? *Not once*! Do you know I didn't once enjoy myself with you? Do you know that I've never had any pleasure with anyone else but Bubu Fiel in my life? Do you hear? Can you hear me properly? You can't hold a *candle* to him as a man, do you hear? And I wouldn't swap him for any other man for a million guilders, do you hear! And certainly not for *you*! I thought we understood each other. But you're a filthy, *dirty* slob,' she said, concentrating all her contempt and hatred in those words. Then she went on, almost meditatively, 'You're a cheating Windward Islander. You're a bastard. *Bai den conjo di bo mama!*'

Chamon reckoned that at least half of what she said was a lie. She had said more than once that she liked his calm ways and had suggested more than once that she had some feelings for him, that it was really not *just* for money. She had never even suggested that she didn't find him man enough, and he'd never noticed this in himself either.

She was just being spiteful. He knew and understood. But it still hurt him to hear her say all those rotten things about him, though a moment before she'd called him *dear* Chamon. Apart from that, he was frightened that if he simply let her go, hurt as she was, she would create a scandal. Then the confrontation with Fiel, which was exactly what he wanted to avoid, would come anyway. Here and now. So he decided to appease her and grabbed her hand. He knew it was pointless trying to calm her with words, and so produced two ten-guilder notes: from the rent that he'd collected that morning.

'Nora,' he said, 'it's okay, don't go on like that. Here's the money.'

But it was too late. The matter had already been brought into the political arena, as it were. Nora now had to defend not only *her* pride, but also that of her island. After all, she was a Curaçaoan, but he was nothing but a *stinking Windward Islander*, who'd come to try his luck on her island. Who now thought he was somebody, because he had some money. A few ten-guilder notes. Well, she would teach him a lesson he could take to his damn island of Saba.

'You can shove that money,' she said, speaking even more slowly than just now and with the hint of a laugh in her voice, 'up your *arse*!'

Actually she wanted to shout it out loud, so that everyone could hear. Because it gave her such indescribable pleasure to be able to say it and show him that when it came down to it, *she* didn't need any money, and wasn't for sale, and couldn't be kept quiet with it. It gave her a feeling of freedom. Just imagine, he'd had the money all along, but had refused to give it to her. All along! Just to hear her beg!

Chamon would not let go of her and kept trying to get her to take the money, which she kept pushing away. When he tried to stuff it down the front of her dress, she was angry and deeply insulted and said, 'I told you, Chamon, that you could shove that money up your *arse*. If you don't let me go, I'll call Bubu. Then he'll kick that dirty money up your arse for me.'

Chamon let her go and she started walking back from behind the bath shed into the backyard. He remained behind in panic, because he thought that she was going to cause a scandal anyway. But he was wrong. She was giving up. She intended simply to go to the people who were waiting for their drink by the back door and tell them that the rum had run out. And apart from that, when Ostrik brought the new bottle, she was going to send him back to get a refund: for his shoes. She couldn't have it all ways. I've got to start doing things differently in general, she realized. There must be other ways to get what one needs, without going to bed, begging or stealing for it. There must be something that stops one from suddenly having to spend money one has scraped together with so much effort for a particular thing, on something else . . .

Besides, lots of people had already had a drink. She might be able to survive the shame of the rum running out.

So by the time she got to the table she wasn't thinking of Chamon Nicolas at all.

9

Bubu Fiel was! Perhaps one thing loomed largest in the hate he now felt for Chamon, perched on the basin of his toilet with his face in his hands: the fact that Chamon had made him lose. Though the pain of what he saw as Chamon's needless humiliation of Nora was also very great. At any rate, he felt that he could no longer leave this bath shed furtively and act as if he'd heard nothing and suspected nothing. He thought Chamon was a spiteful bastard and a rotten opportunist. A contract breaker. A faithless person.

What Bubu finally did might perhaps have been prevented by a more efficient management of the police apparatus on the Antilles. Since the crowd that had thronged around his house was several hundred strong, a number of policemen could easily have posted themselves there. At least to keep an eye on the traffic, which was experiencing enough problems through this game of dominoes, as later emerged from the television crew's film. But also because we know how volatile men are when under stress. All the more so because it's common knowledge that as soon as the completely harmless young people of Curaçao are gathered together in large numbers anywhere on the island (as, for example, in Gomez Square in the heart of Willemstad, where these young people were in the habit of congregating every Saturday afternoon until an American built a big rock club and lured them all away), the police start flapping round the shoulders of these boys and girls like nervous birds . . .

Anyway, the presence there of one or more policeman might perhaps have made Bubu decide to settle matters with Chamon in a less violent way than he now did; through legal actions against him for breach of contract, adultery and perhaps even compensation for his loss of face. As it was, he came out of the bath shed with the heavy end of the jack from 200H in his hand. At that moment Chamon rounded the corner of the bath shed and the backyard and was putting the money that Nora had finally refused back in his pocket. He heard Bubu Fiel say 'Here, you,' and ducked. The massive triangular part of the jack missed him, but the long handle hit him and it felt as if the steel had shattered his shoulder. But what frightened him most was the sucking sound with which he heard the whole, monstrous object coming and then partly missing him and hitting the right corner of the bath shed with a bang, after which it fell to the ground with a dull thud.

10

His first thought was to make a run for it. But he didn't do so for numerous reasons. He was injured and felt too taken aback to make a quick escape. Apart from that, the only route he would be able to take ran along the west side of the bath shed. But he wasn't familiar with that. He could easily stumble into the trenches of the foundations for Bubu's house. No, he couldn't risk the darkness there. For that matter, it was pointless running away, because Bubu would find him anywhere on this island anyway. He would get his car and pursue him if he had to.

Apart from that, he thought it would be terrible, after the triumph of that afternoon, after his words on the radio, *after being on television*, to run away. Janchi Pau would never do anything like that!

For a brief moment, he felt the hopeless need for the protection of a policeman.

True, he took a few steps backwards, *but he didn't run away*, he simply took a few steps backwards to give Bubu Fiel a chance not to continue a confrontation which he, Chamon Nicolas, didn't want at all. But he already had his knife in his right hand, which Bubu, who didn't for a moment consider the possibility that he would defend himself, had not realized. The thing was that he forgot that Chamon had won that afternoon. Apart from that, it was already dark.

The people by the drinks table turned round and started shouting, 'Don't kill him, Bubu! Don't kill him!' But they were careful to stay well clear. Bubu Fiel said nothing. Not a word crossed his lips as he picked up the jack again, almost at the feet of Chamon, who could easily have stabbed him to death right then. But Chamon did not; instead he took another step backwards. This time Bubu Fiel did not throw the jack. Like someone who wants to smash the try-your-strength machine with one blow, he raised it in both hands to smash Chamon Nicolas into the ground for good.

Almost effortlessly, Chamon Nicolas drove his knife into the left side of his chest.

They both fell to the ground and Chamon Nicolas was injured on the knee by the falling jack. But Bubu Fiel died instantly. The knife had penetrated deep into his heart. Those present sighed, screamed and shouted. Mostly, there was great amazement at the sudden violence that had taken them all by surprise.

When she saw Chamon getting up, Nora knew that Bubu must be dead. 'You're dead, Bubu Fiel!' she screamed, sitting on the ground next to him. Her words sounded like a terrible reproach to him. Only then did it dawn on her (as many people had previously felt when the news circulated that afternoon) that this afternoon they were murdering Bubu to the east of his own house! 'You're dead,' she repeated angrily, 'you're dead!'

Still, she had enough presence of mind to send someone for a doctor.

Bubu's two daughters had followed their mother, but fled into the house when they heard Nora's words. Nora did not cry. She just kept repeating, 'Bubu Fiel, you're dead!' As it were, to picture the consequences of his death. (But it still sounded just as fruitless as the reproach which she so often made: 'Bubu Fiel, you're *drunk*!') Another of those consequences was that she would feel terrible grief, because she loved him, in her way, although it might be better to say *his* way. But she didn't feel it, now. Now she felt the new, possible consequence of his death for her, namely, that in future she would need money not only for herself but also for the children for the bus into town!

11

The people didn't pay much attention to Chamon, except to shy away from him. They all thronged around the body of Bubu Fiel and Nora. But he kept repeating to those he could get close enough to, 'I couldn't help it. I couldn't help it. He was going to *kill* me.'

He was speaking his mother tongue. Did he, in this *well* of

354

truth (was it he, or the popular dead man who had used the metaphor during the game?) suddenly not find Papiamento 'serious' enough? He walked across the backyard to the domino table, holding on to his shoulder with his right hand. He was about to sit down on one of the domino chairs, but did not because he suddenly blamed all the misery in which he now found himself on the game of dominoes. He walked on, and at the gate of the front yard Ostrik bumped into him, as he came tearing up, clutching the bottle of rum to him like a baby. The bottle fell out of Ostrik's hand and broke. The pungent smell of rum enveloped them.

'I couldn't help it,' said Chamon in a daze. 'I really couldn't help it.' Ostrik said nothing because he was too crestfallen to speak. Chamon took the two ten-guilder notes which Nora had just refused out of his pocket and gave them to him. 'Buy a new one,' he said. Ostrik said, 'Thank you,' looked at the money and then put it happily in his pocket. He had the feeling that everything was turning out for the best. After all, he hadn't bought a *gallon* bottle of rum as his mother had said, because he simply couldn't bring himself to obey her completely and as far as school was concerned, to dig his own grave. He had been only one-third obedient – that is, he had bought, for seven guilders fifty, a third-of-a-gallon bottle. It was not a good price, but at least he got to keep seven guilders fifty. If a third of a gallon was enough, then with the rest he might still be able to buy a pair of white plimsolls, which would tide him over for a while. The problem of the shoes would return, but by then he would at least have been at school for a week.

That was what he had thought. And he thought she would scold him because he hadn't obeyed her completely ... but he'd also thought that she might be pleased, when she saw how he'd found a solution to their dilemma.

Now Chamon simply gave him the twenty guilders, he was

in two minds. He could go back and do the errand, as his mother wanted him to. But no. Then he wouldn't have enough left for even the cheapest shoes. So he decided to go back and buy a *two-thirds*-of-a-gallon bottle.

As he was about to leave the yard again, the trailing gait with which Chamon was walking down the Tula road and the way he kept clinging on to his shoulder, made him decide to have a look at the backyard first. Something was wrong!

It was lucky he did so, seeing how ironic it would have been otherwise.

12

Chamon walked down the Tula road as far as the junction with the Carpata road. He went into the bar-restaurant owned by the Chinese, where he'd played dominoes that morning.

From there, he rang the police.

13

He didn't find it odd that Solema was not at home, because he assumed quite naturally that she'd gone to evening mass. But he did find it odd that she'd left everything open: door, windows, everything. He decided to give her a stern talking-to about that later.

He took off his tie and shirt, because he intended to have a shower immediately, but felt it was wiser to inspect the house first to check that nothing had been stolen.

Then he found Solema's note on the dining-table, where she'd left it for him.

When he'd read it, he put it back in the same place; with the glass on top of it. He decided to act as if he hadn't seen it. But the capital letters kept dancing in front of his eyes:

'Well, that's not true at any rate,' he said to himself, sitting down on his sofa with his legs crossed, 'I can prove that those five guilders aren't hers. I can prove it with the book of statutes in my hand. Ha! Ha!' Yes, by telling the whole story from A to Z to the court. How he'd found them in that field. How he'd pointed his revolver at that judge and had made him check his pockets, to pay for the unlawful use that he'd made of his personal property. Yes, that naked judge, in that cold field. It was *his* five guilders and so if he wanted he could bring a charge of *theft* against her. Whether she stayed or went wasn't that important, because she was a whore, nothing more. What mattered were his rights; and he knew what they were and could assert them if he wanted to. But *phew!*

He went into the bedroom anyway to check if she'd actually taken the money, because he didn't really believe it. In fact, at first he didn't really believe what was in the note. But when he discovered that it was really true, he became afraid. He thought her a hard she-devil for paying no heed to the scheme he had devised. It hadn't made her feel like a whore, his crafty trick with those five guilders, when she committed adultery again, because committing adultery was a habit with her, because she had a whore's nature. 'Bah,' he said. 'Bah.' But his fear of her became even greater, and he began to think the beginning of her affair with Janchi must date back a long way. Years, he thought, even before my marriage perhaps. Yes, why else would she have married him? Why would a European-educated woman like her marry him, if it wasn't to be closer to her lover here in Wakota? It made him feel weak inside. And that was of course why she had stood her ground when he insisted that she stopped playing the organ of the church up there.

357

He looked to see if she'd taken the revolver with her too perhaps, so that Janchi . . . but no, it was still there. Why hadn't she taken it with her? He picked it up and went back to the living-room. He had to sit down because his head started spinning: so the three children that he'd educated and brought up in his beautiful house weren't his either! Of course not! At any rate, he had no way of knowing if they were already seeing each other before his marriage. And yet, why had she committed adultery with that other judge if she was already going out with this guy? He'd caught her in the act, hadn't he . . .?

He ran his left hand across his face and wondered how he could ever leave his house again, without being *seen* in Wakota or on this island in general.

And yet, he'd caught her in the act, hadn't he? He was walking there by the ditch one evening with the bare willow trees and saw a car standing in the field. He thought he recognized the car and walked towards it. And there . . . But then it couldn't be right, that she was going with Janchi before then!

It was a liberating thought and because his eye fell at that moment on the television, he had an impulse to put the thing on and simply watch the news as he did every evening; as though nothing were wrong, as he had said just now at the domino table, when he told Bubu Fiel in his summing-up that there was nothing to lose. Because there were quite simply lots of other things in life apart from a little game of dominoes. Yes, being a judge, having a weekend cottage! As he stood in front of the set, the thought of the television crew that had been filming just now quickly made him abandon this idea. Something was going on! They shone that bright light straight in his face. No, he didn't want to see himself sitting there again with that bright light in his face. The thought that all Wakota was in the process of doing that, or had already done so, almost made him put a bullet through the television set in anger. But he simply said, 'Tut, tut,' and sat down again. He tried to think of his weekend cottage, but the fear of the sea, which he'd been able to dismiss from his mind while playing dominoes, because of the need to arm himself against defeat, now returned in full force with this new defeat. He had the feeling that he was drowning, even just thinking about the sea. He also hit upon the crazy idea that Solema could easily give him a push there on the rocky coast. That was how devilish she had become in his eyes.

He had the feeling that he was drowning in shame anyway, that he was going under. Threatened from two sides, on that side ten–love and on this side the appalling deceit of Solema's. *Double play*. Damn, damn. Damn, damn. They were hemming him in on all sides. He couldn't make a move without their winning. Or they caught up with him! Oh, perhaps it was a good thing that she'd gone, because he was at least delivered from such a cunning she-devil.

But who would believe him if he said that? Who would believe him if in a little while he took the line, 'Oh, I threw her out myself, because, you know, those women that have been to university always have airs and graces. A normal man simply can't live with them.' Had *Janchi* been to university, then?

He still felt like a judge, and yet also like a nonentity because of these two defeats, which were so dreadful that they even robbed him of the desire to shower, made him afraid of water. What terrible things awaited him in the shower?

No, he wouldn't be able to dismiss them as awkward mishaps. For example, he would not be able to say about that game of dominoes, 'Well, a few slip-ups, that's all.' *Ten*–love was too big a margin for that. Nor would he be able to say about this thing with Solema, 'That wife of mine was feeling a bit lonely because recently my work was taking up all my attention. And in those cases women always look for diversion. You know what women are like! They need attention! And an intelligent man must be able to understand this kind of adultery. Adultery like this doesn't really mean a thing, does it?' No, he couldn't say anything like that, because this wasn't a relatively superficial matter like a fling, which a judge certainly doesn't need to get excited about. No: she was leaving him. She was going to *live* with that man. She didn't even consider it necessary to go on deceiving him. She did it openly! You see, that was the difficulty. She was leaving this house, with everything that a woman like her could wish for; with a husband like him who had a job as judge at the court . . . she was leaving a man like that in the lurch for a gadabout, a womanizer, a knife-thrower like Janchi Pau. No, something like that couldn't be explained, because something like that couldn't even be *understood*.

In his eyes she remained a whore. A cheap whore at that, because she had a strange predilection for shabby surroundings. Back then with that judge, in the cold field in Holland; simply on that wet grass, covered in cows' piss and hard sugarbeets . . . 'Well, now she's also crawling off into an unfinished pigsty . . .'

He went to the kitchen and poured himself a whisky and soda. He waddled around with it a little through his house and then sat down at the piano. He put the revolver, which was still in his hand, on top of it, opened the lid and again ran his fingers over the keys as though he were playing, but without pressing them, because he didn't want to risk making the wrong sounds, like that morning.

From now on the main thing will be, he said to himself, to live as inconspicuously as possible.

The thought of his shower occurred to him again, but he finally dismissed the idea. For that, he would have to un-

360

dress further, and on the contrary he felt the need to *dress*, cover himself, hide.

He put his sweaty shirt back on, because he felt undressed. Naked. He took courage from the thought that thinking about nakedness, and his fear of it, was simply the result of the smutty talk which went around the domino table about it, but the feeling remained and the need to hide actually increased. So he shut the door and windows of his house tightly. As he was doing this, and saw the many lights of Prinsessendorp in the distance, he said to himself that it was the right decision.

It was all right like that. In the dark and shut off from everyone. Here in this house, nothing could happen to him. But as soon as he went outside, he would have to face Janchi. The ten–love would be set against his house all over this island. And that wouldn't be enough. With Solema on Janchi's side, that was too little. People would soon start attributing the fact that Solema had left him to his defeat by Janchi. And would Janchi come to be called *Shon* Janchi? And what about him? A nothing, a prick, a piece of rubbish.

'Domino friend,' he said aloud, thinking of Janchi. 'Colleague,' he added in a mutter. '*Colleague!*'

Then he poured himself a second whisky, but as he was about to start on it, he suddenly remembered what he'd said at the domino table: 'I never drink.'

That was nonsense, of course. He liked a drink. But he must just be sure now that he didn't resort to alcohol. That he didn't become an *alcoholic*. He aimed at the piano and said, acting dramatically, as he had when he told the story of Solema and Feliciano in veiled terms: 'You, colleague Pau, are now of course starting to tremble and shake, now I'm pointing this weapon at you. You think of course, that you'll soon have had it . . .' He interrupted himself in irritation. Pau, of course, had known about everything. He'd been sitting laughing

361

himself to death, and that's why he refused to play a part in the dramatization of the story and had taken the *woman's* side . . . Because why else would he have taken the side of the totally strange Dutch woman whom he didn't know? Well, well.

But re-experiencing his moment of glory gave him such pleasure that he went on in the same style.

'But I'm not a murderer, I'm a judge. I know that I must not kill you, and I won't because in doing so I'd only be lowering myself to your level, you see. What's more,' he added, 'it remains an undeniable fact that even if I shoot you, I've been raising your kids for years . . .'

He said to himself that the only thing he could now do that had any point to it was to concentrate on playing this piano.

Solema had left with the children. And they would stay away. From now on, he was alone in this big house with this large, beautiful piece of furniture. He couldn't go out, because the fact was that from now on he must try to hide his whole life as far as he could. And he didn't even dare to take a shower, although that was a fear which perhaps might fade with the passage of time.

The only sensible thing to do, in this large, beautiful house of his, where for the time being he had everything in hand, was to stay sitting on this piano stool and keep trying to learn to play the piano, until he was able to. It must be possible, because he had all the time in the world! And one day, in the very distant future when he was able to do it, then perhaps he would be able to open the doors and windows again and allow the sounds of the piano to waft all over Wakota: *Manchi Sanantonio is playing the piano*! He decided he might as well try 'Au clair de la lune' and, without thinking, pressed the first key, because he felt that note was always bound to be the right one. He kept pressing down on it, saying to himself that before he tried to find the second one, he'd have to let that whole game of dominoes at Bubu Fiel's ebb away out of his body. And Solema. Yes, that *double* pain. In fact, he kept pressing down so long and so hard that he started sweating. Then he suddenly drew breath and it was as though he had begun a new life. He looked so cheerful. Then he pressed the second key, which he also kept depressed for a long time. He was obviously convinced that it was the right one, and was about to proceed to the third note. But the siren of the police car, driving up the hill fast, confused him. It seemed to disrupt his concentration on the music, which was at that moment very intense, leaving him mainly with a sense of his failure.

He pressed the revolver to his head and fired.

His head fell so heavily onto the keyboard that the two policemen drew their revolvers, alarmed at the reverberating sound which met them from the locked house.

The young officers, a young Dutchman and a young Antillean, only dared enter the house when reinforcements had arrived from town.

Aftermatch

1

The psychiatrist and the social worker charged with drawing up the psychiatric and probation reports for Chamon's trial fell in love. What a love! The man was married, had lots of children, but they committed the maximum possible breach of contract and ran off together; to Europe, the psychiatrist being a Dutchman and the social worker an Antillean. In fact this is typical of the misleading nature of the training of social workers, who generally choose their life partners from the highest echelons of society.

His grand passion, which on the one hand led him to abdicate all personal responsibility, also led him, however, to feel a new responsibility in his professional field.

At any rate he wrote to the judge who had been assigned Chamon's case a letter from Ghana, where he later went with his wife, in which he claimed among other things 'that the precondition for a good psychiatric report in this case is a great knowledge of and skill at the game of dominoes, which I do not possess, because I have always been at most a mediocre piano and bridge player and a quite useful *chess* player, while in my opinion dominoes is a unique game, because the pieces have only figures on them in contrast to cards and chessmen, for example, which also incorporate (beautiful) images. I have some experience of games of chance and the dramas that can occur when someone loses, but dominoes is a different type of game, because of its completely unmaterialistic character.'

In his letter there is also a virulent attack on psychology and psychiatry itself. 'I must tell you honestly,' he writes somewhere, 'that with our present state of knowledge, in a case like this, we are completely lost. We don't have sufficient pure data on the so-called primitive peoples, i.e. blacks, Indians, Eskimos, etc., because instead of observing them as they are, we've always tried to impose our ways on them. In any case, we judge their way of being on the basis of *our* understanding. As a result, our science is geographically bound. At best. But usually *racist*! Our psychological sciences at least. Because of course to a certain extent I agree with you when you say that an appendix remains an appendix everywhere on earth. What I mean is: Freud, Jung and Adler, and even Merleau Ponty, to name just a few, are only of use to me in Europe. And then perhaps only in the large towns, like Vienna, Berlin and Paris.

'And what do we know when all is said and done about the psychology of poverty? Yes, we know far too little about ordinary, poor people. Our science, despite the pedantry of our professors, is in a pretty bad state. It is restricted geographically and racially! (Unfortunately we are still a long way from the cosmopolitan attitude that the writers of our scientific literature so often pride themselves on.) And it is also to a large extent *class-bound*. That's why, to be honest, I am particularly happy to be rid of a case like this. At least at this moment. *Really*. Au revoir!'

However, while the police report was of course no use to him at all, the judge insisted that he had a good overall picture of the game of dominoes at Bubu Fiel's. Anyway, when other psychiatrists, after their colleague's rabid attack became known, showed their distaste for this case (at first they wanted to organize a *conference* about the letter), people appealed to me because of a certain celebrity which I enjoyed at that moment as a freelance court reporter. I was commissioned specially by the judge to inquire whether there were (possibly hidden) elements which might explain in more detail the violent actions of three of the four players after such an 'ordinary' game.

I accepted on one condition: my fee was to be deposited in advance with a notary. Because it's been my experience many times in the Antilles and elsewhere, that there are a great many people who think writers not only can but should live on air.

For example, the director of the Antillean Brewery NV – 'There's nothing down in writing,' he said coolly – refused to pay me a sum of four hundred Antillean guilders (which, as I no longer need to convince anyone, can mean the difference between life and death!) for a brochure that I wrote for him about the beer-making process. And yet the beginning alone is worth that amount, I think. It's the old monastic rhyme:

In heaven there's no beer
That's why we drink it here.

'The man is very ungrateful,' Wakotans will therefore probably comment when they read this.

That's reward enough for me.

2

Because of the disappearance of the above-mentioned psychiatrist, Chamon's trial was greatly delayed. In addition, his defence counsel, I think from laziness, pleaded self-defence, although I advised him to try temporarily diminished responsibility or some such thing. Because I'm sure that the four men were subject to such a high level of stress that afternoon that they couldn't really be considered responsible for anything. It was simply an appalling match!

He, Chamon's counsel, however, maintained that he would in that case have to explain to the judge how the tension of the game had such a *positive* effect on Janchi. Which for me is as clear as crystal. But he didn't dare to adopt my line of reasoning on this point. And after all it was *his* job to defend

Chamon, while I also assumed that he distrusted me a little as an official observer paid by the government. It may have been for a different reason, however, because Chamon, who this time is paying for his defence himself, will of course not be able to afford very much. (His chambers has already investigated Chamon's assets, so they say, in connection with the role they played in the manslaughter!)

Poor Chamon. His island of Saba is imposingly beautiful. But it may be a long time before he sees that island again, longer indeed than if his counsel had followed my advice. In that case he might even have got off completely! And besides, I feel sorry for him, because to judge by an open letter in the paper from an ex-prisoner, the prison system on the Antilles is still completely Dutch, or American – medieval in its barbarity. It seems that the Old Testament with its 'an eye for an eye and a tooth for a tooth' still prevails here against all reason.

3

Janchi Pau is bringing some hope to the Antilles.

Besides his own CMS, that is, *Co-operative Furniture Factory Solema*, he has also helped to set up other co-operatives. That of the taxi drivers, for example, who after the sudden death of 200H kept racing round the island like orphans, completely at the mercy of the large touring coaches.

Solema wants to go even further. In a short interview I recently had with her, she said to me, 'First more co-operatives! Then we'll unite all the co-operatives into a political party. A party,' she said, 'on co-operative socialist principles.'

As part of her plans, she has even gone to Guyana for a while, where people are striving for a similar political system. 'In my view,' she says, 'of the existing ideologies, it is the one which suits our people (who like their personal freedom, but do not think, or rather *feel*, as individualistically as most white peoples). For that matter, we find democracy and the co-operative pattern of organization in Africa and in the past among slaves.' She concluded with a meaningful wink: 'So it's something of our own!' I hope that her endeavours are successful.

One positive point to start with is that the substantial sum she got from the sale of Manchi's house (Janchi would not accept one cent of it!) easily covers the start-up costs of her movement.

If it all works, she may be the first female prime minister in America. I mean, in North, Central and South America.

For the latter two areas particularly, this would be very significant, because women still have a very hard time of it here.

As men do too, for that matter. Although they generally play a lot of dominoes.